FORMATIVE WRITINGS, 1929–1941

■ *Formative Writings*

1929—1941 SIMONE WEIL

EDITED AND TRANSLATED BY

DOROTHY TUCK MC FARLAND AND

WILHELMINA VAN NESS

THE UNIVERSITY OF MASSACHUSETTS PRESS

AMHERST, 1987

Library of Congress Cataloging-in-Publication Data

Weil, Simone, 1909–1943.
   Formative writings, 1929–1941.

   Contents: Science and perception in Descartes—
The situation in Germany—Factory journal—[etc.]
   1. Philosophy. 2. Descartes, René, 1596–1650.
3. Germany—Politics and Government—1918–1933.
4. Weil, Simone. 5. Factories—France. 6. Pacifism.
I. McFarland, Dorothy Tuck, 1938–   . II. Van Ness,
Wilhelmina, 1933–   . III. Title.
B2430.W472E55   1986   194   86–6976
ISBN 0-87023-539-7 (alk. paper)

FOR GERRY
sine qua non

Contents

Acknowledgments

This project could not have been done without the generous assistance of Sylvie Weil and the helpful cooperation of Dr. André Weil. We are also indebted to Fr. Richard Downs, C.S.C., Irving Groupp, and Leone Stein for having read sections of the manuscript and providing valuable suggestions, to Dr. Eric Weitzner for help in translating passages having to do with mathematical questions, and to Gerald W. McFarland for his sustained material and moral support. The project was also supported in part by a grant from the French Ministry of Culture, for which we would like to express our appreciation. Finally, we are grateful to the magazine *Cahiers du Sud* for generously allowing us to translate the essay "La Philosophie."

DOROTHY TUCK MC FARLAND
WILHELMINA VAN NESS

Preface

This volume is intended to help fill a gap in the still unfinished process of translating into English what might be called the first generation of published editions of Simone Weil's writings. This generation comprises the French editions of her writings, grouped loosely under a diversity of headings and published between 1947 and 1966. Most of this material has been translated into English, but a remnant of major formative texts, as well as a scattering of essays and fragments that reflect difficult, unfamiliar, and neglected aspects of Weil as a thinker and a person, has not, and it is impossible to validly assess her thought and person without some direct knowledge of this part of her *oeuvre*.

Formative Writings, 1929–1941 is a collection of texts from this remnant. The equivalent of approximately one more volume of short texts remains to be translated. The texts selected for this volume were written between 1929 and 1941, a crucial and transitional period, one of an anguishing rite of passage for Weil, Europe, and the world. In chronological order, the texts are "Science and Perception in Descartes" (1929–30), a formidable dissertation Weil wrote as a twenty-one-year-old philosophy student at the Ecole Normale Supérieure; "The Situation in Germany" (1932–33), a ten-article extravaganza of dissident Left journalism on the subject of Hitler's rise to power and Comintern politics; "Factory Journal" (1934–35), Weil's unedited, almost daily record of the "year" she spent as an unskilled factory worker; "War and Peace" (1933–40), a selection of essays and fragments reflecting aspects of her pacifist thought culled from the "War and Peace" and "Spain" sections of *Ecrits historiques et politiques;* and "Philosophy" (1941), a light essay that accurately reflects some of the breadth of her mature thought on Eastern and Western art, mysticism, science, and philosophy.

The selections are primary sources for a great deal of what has been said about Weil's thought and psychology over the years. Most have been summarized or presented in digest form by Weil's biographers. "Science and Perception in Descartes," which does not lend itself to any convenient form of packaging, has been largely neglected. "The Situation in Germany," when it is read in its entirety, leaves no doubt about the quality and extent of Weil's participation in French Leftist and Comintern politics. It provides information about Weil that simply cannot be had from any other source, information that has not been conveyed by references to, or summaries of, its content. Similarly, in writing about her factory experience, both Weil and her commentators used her "Factory Journal" selectively. The elapsed time and detail of her experience and the emphases that can be seen in the original are invaluable for evaluating what she and her commentators later made of it. The texts in "War and Peace" are primary sources of the immensely complicated pacifist position that Weil endeavored to sustain during much of the thirties. They episodically trace its development and not incidentally illustrate the Leftist component in it. One of the most anguishing and controversial texts Weil ever wrote—"A European War over Czechoslovakia?"—is included, a text that must be considered in any assessment of Weil and her thought. "Philosophy," published originally in *Cahiers du Sud*, slipped through the cracks of the translation process at least in part because it never found its way into any of the French collections of Weil's works. It is included here as a means of bringing this collection full circle—back to Weil's original love of philosophy and concern with science. The essay also illustrates a fact of Weil's life and *oeuvre* that needs to be more widely recognized: that throughout her life she consciously chose and followed a dual vocation of philosopher and teacher. In "Philosophy" she returns to an academic milieu in which she is completely at home, and in which she operates very much in the role of a teacher—in this case of her peers.

Most of the texts in this collection are more obviously tied to the special milieus—the academic world, the dissident Left and trade-unionist circles—in which they were written than often seems to be the case with Weil's writings. The diversity of "voices" and even "roles" that she to some extent assumes in all of them, however, points to another fact about Weil that is not widely recognized: she is always in some degree composing in a specialized language and/or consciously engaging in an experiment in *popularisation*, by which she meant "teaching" in its purest, broadest sense—the art of transposing and transmitting truths intact to whomever was being taught. In "Science and Perception in Descartes," "A Reply to One of Alain's Questions" (one of the essays in "War and Peace"), and "Philosophy" she is using variants of her academic voice. "Science and

Perception" is written in a florid, baroque prose style that Weil cultivated as a student to carry the youthful forms of her highly unorthodox thinking into mainstream French philosophy. "Reply" was addressed as much to her former teacher Alain as to the academic circles in which she and he circulated and in which his "questions" were being discussed. "Philosophy" was written for the edification and education of amateur philosophy lovers in Marseilles. In "The Situation in Germany" and many of the pre-Munich texts in "War and Peace," Weil translated her concerns directly into the language and in some cases the jargon of the Leftist circles she was addressing. At the opposite pole, Weil compiled her "Factory Journal"—a casual text, sometimes telegraphic to the point of being incomprehensible—for her own private use, and perhaps wrote a few of the sad, general post-Munich texts in "War and Peace" to and for herself.

Readers should also be warned that Weil's style, generally formal and elegant and over a half-century old, adheres to conventions that are now regarded as hopelessly sexist. In her writings "mankind," "man," and "men" stand, as they cannot legitimately do now, for all humanity. We have left most of her usages intact, since it would be untrue to her fundamental style, and sometimes to her content, to use less gender-loaded language. She was, incidentally, and for reasons wholly consistent with the general tenor of her thought, not a feminist. Her loyalties were always to all humanity. She refused on principle to parse the human race into sexual or other divisions, or to extend priorities or privileges to any part except, as a compensation for injustice, the oppressed. By them she meant the suffering underclass of any time and place, those who are always most in need of having a balance redressed.

A further note on Weil's terminology that may be initially puzzling to readers: In "The Situation in Germany" we have kept her usage of the term "Hitlerite," rather than supplying the more customary term "Nazi." Weil rarely used "Nazi" in her writings. In this text she refers to Hitler's followers either as National Socialists or as Hitlerites. Here, as in Weil's later writings, her usage of "Hitlerite" is a constant reminder that she viewed Hitler as the embodiment of a force that exercised a fatal attraction for those in every class who felt themselves powerless. Today the term "Nazi" on a page powerfully blocks the kind of knowledge of the early mechanism of Hitler's appeal that the term "Hitlerite" usefully retains.

In addition to tying up tag-ends from the first-generation publishing process, the publication of Weil's *Formative Writings, 1929–1941* also belongs to the new era of publishing and studying Weil that began in the 1970s with the publication in France of the revised and expanded edition of her three-volume *Cahiers* (1970, 1972, 1974) and the appearance of Simone Pétrement's probably definitive biography, *La Vie de Simone Weil*, which was published in 1973 and has been widely translated. In America and England during the same decade, Conor Cruise O'Brien's article "The Anti-Politics of Simone Weil"[1] and Peter Winch's introduction to *Lectures on Philosophy* (1978) appreciably raised the level of scholarly discussion of Weil and her thought. In the 1980s *Simone Weil: Interpretations of a Life* (a selection of essays by Staughton Lynd, J. D. Cameron, and others, edited by George Abbot White), three monographs on Weil by John Hellman (1982), Dorothy Tuck McFarland (1983), and John M. Dunaway (1984), and Jean Bethke Elshtain's article "The Vexation of Weil"[2] have continued the generally more accurate and high level of discussion of Weil and her works that began in the 1970s.

Most significant of all for the long run, Weil's entire *oeuvre*, published and unpublished, has finally been brought together; a complete microfilm of it was made by the Bibliothèque Nationale in Paris in the late 1970s, and a team of scholars in France is now preparing a new edition of Weil's complete writings that will include a good deal of unpublished material. Since errors, misrepresentations, and severe damage to the nature and integrity of her thought have resulted from the scattering and compartmentalization of her writings that occurred during the first-generation publishing and translating process, this complete edition will greatly facilitate the orderly and intelligent study of her life and work.

WILHELMINA VAN NESS

1 *New York Review of Books*, May 12, 1977, pp. 23–28.
2 *Telos*, no. 58 (Winter 1983–84): 195–203.

FORMATIVE WRITINGS, 1929–1941

Introduction

Simone Weil experienced the uprootedness of the twentieth century early and continuously. She was born in Paris in 1909, the second child of assimilated French-Jewish parents. She was five years old when the First World War broke out, eight at the time of the Russian Revolution, and an adolescent during the immediate postwar years of economic and political chaos. An extraordinarily gifted child (although her self-confidence during childhood and adolescence was severely undermined by the mathematical accomplishments of her brother, André, who was three years her senior and who became one of the twentieth century's most eminent mathematicians in the field of number theory), she blossomed into a brilliant student and received a spectacular training in philosophy, language, French literature, and mathematics in the lycées she attended during the 1920s. She was admitted in 1928 to the Ecole Normale Supérieure, the apex of the French educational system, and passed her *agrégation,* the state examination that qualified her to teach in the upper lycées and universities, in 1931. She began her professional life in the midst of the economic chaos and despair of the Depression, at an optimum time to observe Hitler's rise to power and the early stages of Europe's inexorable progress toward the Second World War. Until 1937 (when her deteriorating health precluded it), she taught philosophy in a series of provincial girls' lycées and put all her extracurricular time and energy at the service of Leftist, revolutionary, and working-class causes. During this period she conscientiously exposed herself to three experiences that eventually led her to despair of finding social solutions for the *malheur,* entropy, and uprootedness that she perceived to be proliferating and worsening throughout the decade: she visited Germany in the summer of 1932 and personally witnessed the "situation" there, the German Communist party's impotence in preventing Hitler's coming to power and in bringing about the long-heralded Communist revolution in Germany; she spent most of 1935 working as an unskilled laborer in three factories in the Paris region; and she served briefly as a combatant in the Spanish civil war in 1936. From 1933 to 1938 she wrote extensively for the Left and sporadically but consistently in support of a pacifism that strove to find ways to oppose Hitler without provoking a European war. She also passed through the early critical stages of the psychological shift toward a preeminently religious orientation that reached its full development after the outbreak of the Second World War. She made the shift privately, without any essential break in either her nature or her thought.

Her lifelong concern with finding equilibriums is reflected during this period in the both great and small ways current events influenced her psychology and thought. Before Munich she was concerned with balancing one set of priorities and injustices, and the specter of European war outweighed every other consideration. After Munich she threw all her weight on the obviously lighter side of the scale: the injustice done to the Czechs and to those Germans who did not wish to fall under a Hitlerite hegemony and suffer an outright form of colonialization on the ancient Roman and modern western European models. After Munich, also, she placed equal emphasis on the details of mounting a practical resistance to Hitler and the transcendent rationale for it.

When France fell in 1940, she lived as a refugee in the south of France with her parents until May 1942, and then traveled with them by way of North Africa to New York City. In Marseilles and New York City she filled notebooks with the vast collection of annotated metaphor culled from Western and non-Western religious, scientific, and folkloric traditions, which is the primary source material of her mature religious thought and writings. In November 1942, she made the dangerous wartime Atlantic crossing to England to work for the Free French in London. She died on August 24, 1943, of exhaustion, tuberculosis, and self-inflicted malnutrition in a sanatorium in Ashford-on-Kent outside London. Her death came in the midst of the uprootedness and *malheur* of the Second World War, but at a stage when it had become clear that Hitler and the Axis powers would be defeated in the foreseeable future. She died before the full dimensions of the Nazi genocide of European Jewry became publicly known. She also did not live to see the onset of the atomic age and the virtually unlimited prospects for uprootedness and *malheur* that were unleashed with it.

Weil became known primarily as a religious writer in the period immediately following the war as the result of a publishing process that tended to popularize the religious writings of her last three years in a partial form and in isolation from her prior life and thought as a Leftist political activist. More significant still, the process never made clear Weil's lifelong vocation of philosopher/teacher or connected her to the training that prepared her for it. At least in part because of the way she was first published and translated, her thought was initially, and often still is, characterized as contradictory and fragmentary. Gradually, more complete editions of her religious writings were brought out and most of her prior writings were published in individual collections under the headings of history, politics, science, and working-class concerns. These editions, although sometimes unwieldy, presented Weil's thought in a more coherent and orderly way than did some of the editions in English that gathered selections from a variety of French collections. But the result of the entire process has been that the *other* Weils, the political activist and the philosopher/teacher, never caught up in the public mind with the religious Weil, or were satisfactorily integrated into the public perception of either her person or her thought. The texts in *Formative Writings, 1929–1941* were written by the two still largely neglected *other* Weils. They were assembled and translated to introduce these Weils to readers who have not met them and to demonstrate some of the continuity that underlies all Weil's thought and that makes the thought, as well as the person, of a piece.

The content of Weil's life and the subject of her thought is the total crisis—social and spiritual—that came to a head in the West and on a global scale in the modern period, a period of transition, upheaval, and convulsion that lasted, loosely speaking, from the late nineteenth century through the first fifty years of the twentieth. By birth and training Weil was remarkably positioned to hold the long view that she took of this crisis. She was an assimilated French Jew of genius, a precarious product of the Emancipation in France. At the same time she was the lifelong recipient of parental affection and support that may have instilled a long-term confidence in the ultimate possibility that pain can be alleviated and contradictions reconciled. She received an exceptional education in preeminently nineteenth-century French academic and cultural traditions which trained her always to discern and direct her attention to the long view. She saw the twentieth century as the culmination of the three hundred years of accelerated development that had taken place in the West since the Renaissance, and concluded that three centuries of revolutionary change in science and mathematics, in manufacturing and communications technology, and in forms of art and literature had not only brought about an expansion of political liberties, economic well-being, and cultural opportunities for human beings on a global scale, but had also brought about unprecedented forms of social and economic injustice and a broad spectrum of wrenching discontinuities of an essentially spiritual nature. One of the most important differences between her and other major figures of her generation is that although she, like so many of them, penetrated to the special existentialist perception of discontinuity and void that separates twentieth-century perceptions from those of preceding centuries, she retained a sense of continuity with the past. She never made the modern break in one of its most familiar forms, that of cutting loose from the nineteenth century: she never broke with the education she received that tied her to pre-twentieth-century forms of thought. Her training allowed her to perceive the world in terms of a handful of beautiful pre-twentieth-century mechanistic and mathematical analogies, which enabled her to keep fixed in her mind both of the polarities of any contradiction; e.g., she could in the midst of the conditions of extreme discontinuity in the twentieth century retain the knowledge and remembrance of continuity. Her trained intelligence matured into a mechanism for ordering and ranking her thought as a "simultaneous composition on several planes."[1]

Her essential thought worked in her person and writings very much in the way the action of water is described in the *I Ching* trigram "The Abysmal." In the text of the trigram, water flows on, merely filling all the places to which it flows, shrinking from nothing, from no danger or plunge, and with no alteration of its nature. Weil's thought flowed through and into all her acts and writings. In its broad outlines, it was—irrespective of the use to which she put it, or the philosophical, political, or religious language that she used to express it—oriented toward the good. Within this broad frame, she incessantly, even obsessively, engaged in a wholesale philosophical and metaphysical cleaning up of Western religious, scientific, and political thinking and metaphor, always with the practical goal of alleviating oppression and human suffering. To her analyses and critiques of the two great "isms" that bore most comprehensively on her concerns and to which she was profoundly attracted at specific periods in her life—

---

1 This is one of the variants of the expression "composition on several planes," which Weil uses repeatedly in her notebooks. It is both a sign of, and an essential criterion for recognizing, anything real or true. Weil attaches it to God, human life, and art.

Marxism and Catholicism—she brought the same high and rigorous standards of philosophical coherence and consistency.

"Science and Perception in Descartes," the first and most difficult text in this collection, is an ingenious and elaborate student effort to effect just such an immense cleaning up of modern science and thought about the nature of the world in general in relation to Cartesian doctrine, which Weil admired and was attracted to in somewhat the same way she later responded to Marxism and Catholicism. In her thesis she brought all her training to bear on an effort to connect the doctrine and person of a man she admired—Descartes—with a deep personal conviction that she had reached during an adolescent crisis occasioned by her brother's accomplishments: the conviction that no one, regardless of inferior mental faculties or lack of visible accomplishments, was precluded from access to "the realm of truth reserved for genius." She wrote her thesis both to confirm that conviction and to authenticate a doctrine of her own devising founded jointly on it and on Descartes. The coup that she attempted to bring off in her thesis was a proof of her conviction that ordinary perception and work are of the same nature and value as scientific and other forms of specialized and elitist knowledge.

The French text of "Science and Perception in Descartes" has lain for years in the collection *Sur la science* and has been regarded primarily as a writing on science. A decompartmentalization of the text and a provisional effort to reconnect it to aspects of the philosophical training Weil received are, for French and English-language readers alike, probably overdue and necessary. American readers of Weil's writings have been made increasingly aware that she was trained as a philosopher, but do not, for the most part, realize that she can probably be said to have essentially remained one, or that much of what has been sometimes regarded as idiosyncratic in her thought has antecedents in and carries forward aspects of the exacting training she received in the Alain/Lagneau branch of the nineteenth-century voluntarist, *spiritueliste* line of French philosophy. This line, as Weil's teacher Alain received it from his teacher Jules Lagneau (1851–94), stemmed directly from Descartes, but had been extensively modified by the philosophical and psychological revision of it made by Maine de Biran (1766–1824), who is sometimes regarded as the French Kant. (In the late nineteenth century and the mid-twentieth century the line branched out into the considerably more familiar forms of *Bergsonisme* and Sartrean existentialism.) Biran's doctrine of effort virtually transformed the Cartesian "I" into a power and the famous *cogito* into *I think, therefore I can*.[2] Weil particularly picked up on an activism derived from Biran's modifications of Cartesianism that Lagneau emphasized, and she carried this aspect of Lagneau's thought over into her own thought on work. (She was also probably heavily influenced by the published class notes of Lagneau's course on perception.)

Any future valid assessment of Weil will depend on our knowing much more about the relationship of her thought to the philosophical training she received and to its antecedents. At present, however, it should be recognized that Weil never put this training behind her, that it informed her vocation as a teacher of philosophy and everything she wrote and did, and that traditional, if now unknown or unfamiliar, antecedents exist for much of the key content of her thought.

In this connection, her references to her training, which she made in the notebooks she compiled in the last years of her life in Marseilles and New York, should someday also be noted and evaluated. In her notebooks she occasionally drew correspondences between aspects of her training and Greek cosmology, and also between the Alain/Lagneau line of teaching on perception and non-Western (Hindu, Tibetan, and Zen) mystical mechanisms and practices. Entries such as those in which she casually paired Maine de Biran and Heraclitus, tentatively identified Biran's "effort" with the "breath of the mouth" in the Upanishads, and observed that the "continued creation" of Descartes was exactly the same thing as the "manifestation" of the Hindus[3] suggest that it may someday be possible for others to go further and establish a broad spectrum of correspondences that will reintegrate into global thought parts of such seemingly separate and specifically Western doctrines as Cartesianism, without denigrating their Western forms or origin.

A final biographical note that is relevant both to "Science and Perception in Descartes" and to understanding all of Weil and her thought is her lifelong affinity for the baroque and the seventeenth century. As children, she and her brother seem to have steeped themselves in seventeenth-century French culture. Simone Pétrement reports that the pair had a period when they spent hours competitively reciting long passages of Racine and Corneille to each other.[4] Weil's early admiration and en-

2 See René Lacrose, *Maine de Biran* (Paris: Presses universitaires de France, 1970), p. 105.
3 *The Notebooks of Simone Weil*, 2 vols. (London: Routledge and Kegan Paul, 1956), 1:328, 43, 307.
4 Simone Pétrement, *Simone Weil: A Life* (New York: Pantheon, 1976), p. 14.

thusiasm for Descartes and the incredibly colored and complicated prose that she wrote during her student years reflect a continuing baroque streak in her psychology. Her mature attraction for the environment of seventeenth-century Venice and the music of Monteverdi, and ultimately her susceptibility to Catholicism,[5] can be better understood in terms of it.

The precise and difficult lines of thought followed by Weil in "Science and Perception in Descartes" will be outlined in a short individual introduction that precedes the text. There are large issues raised by the text that have not been resolved in the years since Weil wrote her thesis. Some more humane match of human beings, on the one hand, and technology, specialized thought, and systems of pedagogy on the other is as lacking and necessary now as it was then. The Descartes she reinvestigated with the aim of discovering an alternative foundation for the modern world is still almost exclusively read and regarded as the foundation of everything that is most oppressive and limiting in modern science and culture. The young Weil has been jeered at and condescended to for having had the impertinence to challenge the accepted interpretation of Descartes, but "Science and Perception in Descartes" may be the most significant neglected text in her published writings. It argues that Descartes could become a different sort of resource for modern culture if more attention were paid to the contradictions in his doctrine. It contains the germ of an important revision of the way Cartesianism is widely regarded today, and it perhaps suggests the ways by which an exact reading of Descartes might someday show how his fundamental doctrine of perception corresponds to non-Western theories and practices, if only it were transposed in an appropriate manner.

"The Situation in Germany," the second text in this collection, was written in 1932–33 during the peak period of Weil's involvement in French Left and Comintern politics. Although generally recognized and appreciated today, this involvement is still sometimes thought of as abortive, preparatory to her mature person and thought, or as a source of colorful or comical anecdotes. Weil's involvement was, of course, true to her form, that of a dissident who never joined the Communist party (although she may have briefly considered it). She was, however, a fairly major Leftist celebrity; one of her colleagues of the Left at the time, Boris Souvarine, called her "the only brain the revolutionary movement has produced in years," and another, Marcel Martinet, compared her to Rosa Luxemburg.[6]

---

5 Weil did not, as is sometimes thought, convert to Catholicism.
6 Pétrement, *Simone Weil: A Life*, p. 176.

Her period of Leftist activity was, moreover, as deliberate, consistent, and integrated a stage of her evolution as anything she ever did. The First World War and the Russian Revolution were formative events in her childhood and she came of age psychologically, philosophically, and politically during the postwar period. At the Lycée Fénelon, which she attended between 1919 and 1924, she is reported to have said to her classmates, "I'm a Bolshevik."[7] She seems to have loved workers, perhaps from childhood. During adolescence, she clearly identified them—and with them—as the oppressed, and determined upon a lifelong political and philosophical vocation to defend them in every way possible. Her "Science and Perception in Descartes" was a massive opening salvo on their behalf on the philosophical front. On her graduation from the Ecole Normale Supérieure in 1931, she also graduated, with no perceptible break in her stride, from being a highly visible and colorful student activist to being a professional revolutionary. Her careers as a teacher of philosophy and as a political activist coincided and dovetailed. The published class notes[8] of one of her students show that she taught, in addition to a wonderfully clear basic philosophy course, the outline of parts of the massive and remarkable theoretical essay she was writing at the time, "Reflections on the Causes of Liberty and Social Oppression." The outline of a lecture that she delivered to a workers' study group in St. Etienne in 1934 on the history of materialism shows that she gave a remarkably clear summary of the same first-class material that informed her own thought.

"The Situation in Germany" is a considerably more specialized "socialist" work than most readers of Weil's writings are probably accustomed to. It is a journalistic piece, a review and analysis of the Weimar Republic's final year (1932–33), of the events during that year that led to Hitler's appointment as chancellor of Germany, and of the "situation" that Trotsky had been discussing since 1930 and that was on the mind and lips of everyone Weil knew and sympathized with: the prospects for, and fate of, Communist revolution in Germany. The subject by itself is fascinating, and a detailed comparison of Trotsky's and Weil's thought on it would be well worth doing. The separate introduction that precedes the text in this collection offers a preliminary comparison, locates the text in the complex evolution of Weil's thought on revolution and society, and

7 Ibid., p. 18.
8 Simone Weil, *Lectures on Philosophy* (Cambridge: Cambridge University Press, 1978).

suggests its relationship to the psychological revolution that took place within her at this time and that was to lead to her mature religious thought. The effect on Weil of the victory of Hitlerism in Germany is not usually recognized as a factor that influenced her development. It is, however, the last nail that events drove into the coffin of her and her generation's revolutionary hopes. For her, and for some in her generation, Hitler's victory compounded with Stalinist statism to deliver the knock-out blow to revolution in general as an option. In her great theoretical essay of 1934, "Reflections on the Causes of Liberty and Social Oppression," she formally buried these hopes, and marked the close of the strictly political stage of her own development. After 1933, Weil withdrew from revolutionary activity and limited herself to efforts to help German Communist refugees (she did, however, go to Spain in 1936 and fight briefly in the Spanish civil war). After 1934, the term "oppression" recedes from Weil's vocabulary and is largely replaced by "suffering," a transformation due in part to the fact that her thought had overflowed its revolutionary banks into deeper and broader channels, and also to the inescapable residual effect on her of her 1934–35 factory experience.

"The Situation in Germany" is an example of Weil's lifelong habit of teaching in the languages of specific milieus, in this case that of the Socialist/Communist Left. It is one of many examples of her adapting what she had to say to the variety of milieus—academic, political, and religious—in which she functioned and through which she passed during her life. The marvelous religious essays that she wrote for Père Perrin (collected in *Waiting for God*) were intended for use in a Catholic school where he taught and are similar experiments in *popularisation*—transposing and teaching aspects of the original and broader thought that she was working out in her notebooks at the time.

Weil compiled the "Factory Journal," the third major text in this collection, for her own use. It is the unadorned, unedited record of the "year" she spent working as an unskilled laborer in three factories in the Paris region. It should be noted that she had described and decried the conditions of modern production in the abstract in her 1934 "Reflections" essay prior to her sustained personal experience of them. Her later (1941) essay "Factory Work" (in *The Simone Weil Reader*) is a concise remembrance and marshaling of her observations and offers some of the conclusions that she drew from the experience. Further observations and conclusions are scattered in letters and essays. A reference to a particularly frustrating situation involving a shortage of boxes for finished pieces turns up in her *Notebooks* and hints at the indelible, scarring impression it made on her.[9]

The complete text of Weil's "Factory Journal" is a conscientious, realistic, and unromanticized record of the jobs she was given, the machines she worked on, and tallies of her hours and wages, interspersed with anecdotes about her foremen and worker-comrades. The account is a far more gender-loaded one than Weil's own later commentaries and allusions to it—and third-person accounts of it—have tended to convey. Weil and most of her comrades were unskilled women workers under the supervision of a variety of male foremen. This journal is the only extended first-person account in Weil's published writings, and the only place where she can be glimpsed (however fleetingly) relating informally to people around her. A more detailed account of Weil's rationale for the project and appraisal of some of what has been said about it in the past can be found in the separate introduction that precedes the text.

The electrician/mechanic who reviewed the technical vocabulary of our text, and who had himself worked in similar American factories in the 1940s, validated Weil's account of factory conditions and the feasibility of some of her recommendations for changes. He had reservations about what he termed "her ideal of total review, that all workers must be of equal (high) skill levels," on the grounds that shops must retool for every large job. He regarded her foremen as generally compassionate and observed that "they put up with her errors and tried to teach her, rather than simply firing her," that "she taxed their patience, but they cared enough not to want her to starve." He noticed that she became a better worker. He wholeheartedly confirmed her conclusion that the main fact is not the suffering, but the humiliation, and added: "Humiliation has driven more men (and women) to violence than suffering; mere suffering only tests one's strength." He thought her closing list of psychological and other observations "true and accurate" and "very sensible."

A closing note on the subject of humiliation. If Weil's "Factory Journal" can be said to have a subject, it is humiliation and the obverse of humiliation: self-respect. The emphasis Weil placed on self-respect in much of her writing has sometimes been trivialized and regarded as a sign of undue scrupulousness about her own personal dignity. A case can certainly be

9 *Notebooks*, 1:76.

made, however, that humiliation on an epidemic scale was probably at the root of much of the violence of Europe's two twentieth-century wars, and that it was the primary vehicle for inflicting suffering during the Holocaust. When Weil, toward the end of her "year" of being a factory worker, climbed on a bus one Thursday morning on the way home from the dentist and experienced a sudden realization that she, a slave, rode the bus by favor and not by right, that it would be completely natural if someone brutally ordered her off and told her that such comfortable forms of transportation were not for her, that she had to go on foot, she can be said to have had a premonition of the kind of intermediate forms of humiliation Jews in Nazi-occupied countries would be subject to only a few years later, and to have penetrated, however momentarily, to the core of the humiliation of segregation suffered at the time by American blacks, and to that of apartheid suffered by South African blacks today.

The section "War and Peace" contains a new translation of "Reflections on War," a classic antiwar essay Weil wrote for the Left in 1933; "A European War over Czechoslovakia?", the most comprehensive of three texts advocating the appeasement of Hitler written by Weil in 1938; and a patchwork of thirteen short essays and fragments that furnish sample defenses of her pacifist position, document the crucial stages through which she passed, and reflect the private transformations she underwent between 1933 and 1940. The texts selectively, but accurately, reflect the complete evolution that took place quietly within Weil during the period and that culminated in an orientation that both contained her social thought and transcended it. The short essay that precedes the section includes a narrative summary of this evolution.

Most American readers who know of "Reflections on War," the first selection in the section, have met the essay in the form in which it was published in Dwight Macdonald's magazine, *Politics*. The *Politics* text was itself a revised version of a 1938 translation that had appeared in the *International Review*. Macdonald and *Politics* were largely responsible for introducing Weil's writings to American readers through this text and through the subsequent publication of "The *Iliad*, or the Poem of Force" (probably Weil's best-known work) and "Words on War" (retitled "The Power of Words" in Richard Rees's more recent translation in *Selected Essays*).

"Reflections on War" fits snugly into Weil's pattern of cleaning up a doctrine for which she has great sympathy and about which she has many reservations. In this case the doctrine is Marxist, and she is trying to straighten out it and her friends on an important point: the equivocations of the Left on the subject of war, which the Left tended to support then, as it does now, when the war is being waged for revolutionary purposes. Weil's purpose in writing it was to try to insinuate a more consistent and comprehensive pacifism into Leftist thought and discourse. Like most of the Left in her generation and ours, Weil was antiwar, anticolonialist, and antinationalist. She was not, however, as "The Situation in Germany" shows, anti*struggle,* in the Communist use of the term, or, in the context of most of the "War and Peace" texts, pacifist in the sense that she would never fight. She coupled a moral opposition to war in all its forms with the anarchist's instinctive distrust of institutions, while more often than not actively seeking alternative ways of resistance.

In "Reflections on War" she argued that even in the context of supporting a revolution war is not justified, that it strengthens bureaucracy and the state, and is therefore the "tomb" of every revolution that decides or is forced to resort to it. The argument is made in terms of the French and Russian revolutions: in both, any hopes for the development of nonoppressive or democratic systems were dashed in the counterrevolutionary wars that both revolutions were forced to fight and that necessarily led to a strengthening of their bureaucracies and oppressive state apparatuses. The argument could be read today with profit by people of good will on both the Left and the Right who genuinely desire that nonoppressive change be given a chance in the Third World, in Rightist and Leftist societies alike. In Weil's airtight argument, *any* (in 1985, read Iranian or Nicaraguan) revolution that is forced into war, counterrevolutionary, defensive, or offensive, is ipso facto a lost cause. In Leftist circles today (in the now obviously unsuccessful aftermaths of so many revolutions) it has become something of a truism to say that revolution doesn't work. Weil's argument in this essay, and in the variant of a part of it that follows in this collection, was a crucial building block in the comprehensive argument that she was at the time preparing to expound in "Reflections On the Causes of Liberty and Social Oppression," her final theoretical word on the whole subject: that the Marxist analysis of oppression was inadequate; that revolution didn't work because the forms taken by oppression were endemic and fixed conditions of human existence; and that the only hope for the future lay in alleviating oppressive conditions in limited ways, but to the fullest extent possible.

The essays and fragments that follow in "War and Peace" furnish a generous sampling of the political and psychological threads Weil strove to weave together into a consistent and moral pacifism that would also effectively oppose Hitler. "A Few More Words on the Boycott" (1933 or 1934) shows her concern that working-class support of any anti-Hitler measures be tactically and morally consistent with working-class interests. It underscores the Leftist component in her pacifist position. "Reply to One of Alain's Questions" (1936) is addressed to her academic peers. It is an interlocking puzzle of definitions and arguments in which she alludes briefly to the advocacy of peace "by itself," but chiefly dissects the expressions "peace with dignity" and "peace with honor." By carefully defining "dignity," "self-respect," and "honor" in terms of their relation to coercion, risk, and humiliation, Weil shows that honor cannot be involved if an individual's actions are not freely taken, and that peril alone rids one of dishonor. Since combatants in a war are under constraint and noncombatants run no risks, she concludes that war cannot be a means of defending honor, and that no peace is dishonorable. She reinforces a brief exposition on the subject of humiliation with a cascade of examples taken from her experience as a factory worker and from hearsay accounts of army life. The insight into humiliation that Weil gained during her year as a worker is not limited to conditions of the working class, but informs her pacifism as well (and still later, profoundly influences her mature religious thought).

The two fragments on Spain written in 1936 are indications of what she might have published at the time had she had the heart to write a comprehensive piece on the subject. Her health and the internal contradictions of Spain totally demoralized and paralyzed her. In "Do We Have to Grease Our Combat Boots?" (1936), the only piece on Spain she published at the time, the issue is much the same one of self-respect and national honor that is the subject of her "Reply to One of Alain's Questions," but in this later essay she raises it in the context of the Leftist romanticism of the period that saw fighting in Spain as a way of proving one's courage. Against the dangers of internationalizing a civil war, neither proof of personal courage nor considerations of national prestige and honor à la Poincaré carried any weight with her. In "The Policy of Neutrality and Mutual Assistance" (1936), her working-class sympathies, anti-Stalinism, and dogged instinct for moral consistency and decency in the aftermath of the French Socialist government's policy of nonintervention in the Spanish conflict combine to make her determined not to go to war for the USSR or for "any central European state." The shadow of Czechoslovakia has begun to fall across her pages. In "Broadening the Policy of Nonintervention" (1936), Weil demands that the Blum government be consistent and refuse to risk war over Alsace-Lorraine, the French colonies (enter anticolonialism, which will become one of the major and most profound concerns of her mature thought), or Czechoslovakia, on the ground that it did not run that risk for Spain.

"A European War over Czechoslovakia?" (1938) and a prior letter to Gaston Bergery, the editor of the pacifist journal La Flèche, are two of the darkest and most controversial compositions Weil ever wrote. Her pre-Munich article envisions and rationalizes a worst-case scenario in which German hegemony over Czechoslovakia—with its probable consequences of loss of rights for Communists and Jews—is traded for European peace. Her indifference to the fate of the disenfranchised is the article's most shocking and indigestible feature. That she meant it is shown by her suggesting, in her letter to Bergery, that France make the same hypothetical concession:

> No doubt the German superiority of strength would impose certain discriminations in France, especially against the Communists and against the Jews. In my eyes, and probably in the eyes of the majority of French people, this would hardly matter in itself. One can easily conceive that the essential might remain intact, and that those who still care about the public good in our country might be enabled, at last, to take a little effective action in housing and schools, and the problem of reconciling the demands of industrial production with the dignity of the workers, and to undertake a massive popularization of the marvels of art and science and thought, and other appropriate tasks of peace.[10]

On the surface, Weil's willingness to sacrifice both groups is incomprehensible; Communists were her comrades and Jews were fleeing Nazi persecution in Germany. Conor Cruise O'Brien offered a formulation in "The Anti-Politics of Simone Weil" that partially accounts for it; Weil, he wrote, characteristically proposed to sacrifice two groups to which she belonged—her "little platoon" in life, in Edmund Burke's phrase—and she fully intended to be sacrificed with them.[11] The root of her indifference

10 Simone Weil, Seventy Letters (London: Oxford University Press, 1965), p. 99.
11 New York Review of Books, March 3, 1977, p. 26.

goes deeper, however. The two texts display the Jewish antisemitism that was an altogether involuntary reflex of her psychology. It absolutely prevented her from recognizing that Jewish culture and life were as valuable a milieu as the many other milieus that concerned her so movingly and beautifully in her late writing—and that they had value for both French and Czech national life. Weil later (in the Vichy era) castigated herself for having committed a "criminal error" by not having seen the treasonous potential of her pacifism and pacifist associates of the 1930s. At the least it must be recognized that she perpetrated something perilously close to another "criminal error" by virtually ignoring and apparently distancing herself from Jewish suffering during the period. That she was willing to avoid a European war at any price does not exonerate her from failing to even notice that in the loss of Jewish rights, a price would be paid. Weil's lifelong reluctance to belong to or uphold a *part* of anything, and something like a fastidiousness—an innate scorn for grossness and stupidity— also prevented her from paying Hitler's virulence and his antisemitic ideology the attention they deserved. This universalism and fastidiousness are two constant Weilian instincts that, although they repeatedly turn out to be unsuited for and irrelevant to short-term uses by her or anyone else, are almost invariably validated in the careful detail of her long-term views.

One interesting postscript to Weil's Munich thought that bears on this lifelong resistance to partisan loyalties of any sort and to any kind of partial thought is a little-noted side effect of the way in which a contributory stream of her preoccupation with colonialism flowed into and merged with her mainstream thought. From Munich on, Weil perceived that the enormity of Hitler's crime in the eyes of Europeans was that he did to white European nations what they were accustomed to doing to nonwhite and non-European peoples: he treated them like colonies. In a 1943 article on the French colonial problem written for the Free French in London, Weil pointed out that the Czechs had been the first to notice this when they protested the Bohemian protectorate in these terms: "No European people has ever been subjected to such a regime."[12] There is almost always a sense in which the holism and accuracy of Weil's long views cancel out the apparent mistakes she makes in the short term.

After Munich, the tenor and tone of the texts in this collection seem to shift abruptly. In "Reflections on Bouché's Lecture" (1938), Weil is

---

12 Simone Weil, *Selected Essays 1934–1943* (London: Oxford University Press, 1962), p. 199.

evincing a distinctly activist and pragmatic interest in a form of nonstatist defense—very like the guerrilla warfare of the later Resistance in Nazi-occupied France. A careful reading of her comments will show that she is being highly selective about the form of defense that she advocates. She begins with a glancing allusion to what is still not a familiar or even moderately acceptable idea: that of a nation resisting a threat nonviolently. She developed this idea in *The Need for Roots* in London in 1943, projecting the following picture of how France might have implemented a policy of passive resistance during the Second World War:

> If [Gandhi's method] had been applied in France, the French would not have used any armed force to resist the invader; but they would never have been prepared to do anything of any kind which might assist the army of occupation; they would have done everything possible to hinder it; and they would have persisted indefinitely, inflexibly in that attitude. It is clear that in so doing, far greater numbers would have perished, and in far more frightful circumstances. This would have been an imitation of Christ's passion, realized on a national scale.[13]

"The Distress of Our Time" (1938) is in a world apart from the earlier texts in this collection that Weil wrote in highly specific contexts and for specialized readers. It is a short literary essay, or perhaps the introductory paragraphs to some long general essay that she never wrote, a frozen moment and a nonspecific sign that she and events had reached a crucial point of no return. The fragments that follow are snapshots of the prewar public mind in France. When war comes, Weil's priorities are those of "holding out" and of defending "positive" milieus, not simply those in which there is an absence of tyranny. France's colonial policy is on her conscience. The anguishing postwar period of France's colonial divestiture and the Vietnam War lie ahead.

Weil wrote "Philosophy" (1941) while she and her parents were living in Marseilles as refugees from the debacle of France's June 1940 defeat and the Nazi occupation. Like so many others during the period, she was in transit and marking time. Weil, however, was marking time in her own private and inimitable way: she was assiduously filling "notebook after notebook with thoughts hastily set down, in no order or sequence"—on Western science, mathematics, and philosophy, on Christian and non-

13 Simone Weil, *The Need for Roots* (New York: Harper Colophon Books, 1971), p. 160.

Christian religion, on global folklore, and on art and literature. To the existentialist philosopher Jean Wahl in late 1942 she wrote the following digest of her researches and the conclusion she drew from them:

> I believe that one identical thought is to be found—expressed very precisely and with only very slight differences of modality—in the ancient mythologies; in the philosophies of Pherekydes, Thales, Anaximander, Heraclitus, Pythagoras, Plato, and the Greek stoics; in Greek poetry of the great age; in universal folklore; in the Upanishads and the Bhagavad-Gita; in the Chinese Taoist writings and in certain currents of Buddhism; in what remains of the sacred writings of Egypt; in the dogmas of the Christian faith and in the writings of the greatest Christian mystics, especially St. John of the Cross; and in certain heresies, especially the Cathar and Manichaean tradition. I believe that this thought is the truth, and that it requires today a modern and Western form of expression. That is to say, it requires to be expressed through the only approximately good thing we can call our own, namely science.[14]

"Philosophy" appeared in *Cahiers du Sud* (which had several months earlier published "The *Iliad,* or the Poem of Force") signed with the anagram "Emile Novis" that Weil used to circumvent Vichy's laws pertaining to Jewish authors. "Philosophy" is essentially Weil's "review" of three lectures she attended whose subjects touched the surface of her own investigations. She offers her observations and comments as helpful and friendly addenda, and gives her readers the benefit of some of her research. Weil's "voice" in "Philosophy" is her academic one. She is addressing friends and colleagues. She is congenial and supportive, being as cheerful as it is possible to be in the circumstances—in her little corner of the "sorrow and the pity" of France, Europe, and the world during this period. Contemporary readers may be struck by Weil's appreciative exposition of Hippocrates' "holistic" approach to medicine in the second lecture. Because she is so often regarded as a Western and Christian thinker, the even-handedness of her consideration of the correspondences between Western and Eastern art and mysticism may surprise readers. The East-West balances found in "Philosophy" accurately reflect the religious and cultural balances that are found in her mature thought.

"Philosophy" is an accurate reflection-in-miniature of the ways Weil used Western philosophy in her later thinking both to reach out to non-

14 Weil, *Seventy Letters,* p. 159.

Western, nonwhite, and non-Christian cultures and religions and to reconnect the cut-out parts of Western culture and religion to the global traditions and continuities from which she thought (as do many people today) they have become separated. The article accurately reflects the flowing, spreading nature of her thinking and her habit of never, while broadening and deepening her thought, discarding any prior stage of it (in this case her philosophical training). "Philosophy" provides a glimpse of Weil's tendency to be always turning and returning on her central self, a little like a planet orbiting in a solar system.

A phenomenal amount of work remains to be done on all Weil's writings, on their content as well as on the linkages and continuities that underlie them. Because both her thought and her psychology were concrete responses to concrete conditions, it may be necessary to wait until a view of them can be had from a perspective of real elapsed time—perhaps from some point in the next century. Penetrating to the full wisdom and beauty of her writings may, moreover, always be extremely difficult, because something like her own intelligence and genius is needed to understand and assess them.

■ *Science and Perception in Descartes*

Introduction

Simone Weil received a superlative training in philosophy in the French lycées and at the Ecole Normale Supérieure, the *grande école* from which come the teachers of the upper lycées and universities, as well as a high percentage of France's cultural, political, and intellectual leaders. In many respects, however, her pre-Ecole years as a student of the famous philosophy teacher Alain[1] at the Lycée Henri IV from 1926 to 1928 were even more important to the development of her thinking. Alain's influence is strongly evident in "Science and Perception in Descartes," even though that work was a dissertation written for the *diplome d'études supérieures* at the Ecole Normale and was (at least nominally) done under the supervision of an Ecole professor, the philosopher Léon Brunschvicg. Weil, however, apparently consulted Brunschvicg little if at all, for she produced an "independent" piece of work that he did not like and to which he gave the lowest possible passing grade.

According to Weil's biographer Jacques Cabaud, the dissertation contains Alain's "entire teaching on Descartes." Its subject is nothing less than a reexamination of the relationship between Descartes and modern science in an attempt to find grounds for a view of science very different from the kind that has actually developed from Cartesian thought. We know René Descartes (1596–1650) best as the dualist and mechanist whose philosophical, mathematical, and mechanical investigations constitute the foundation of much of the modern worldview. The Descartes taught by Alain, however, is a much more fleshed-out, human, multidimensional figure, a Descartes filtered through the revisions and additions of François Pierre Maine de Biran (1766–1824), Alain's own teacher Jules Lagneau (1851–94), and, of course, Alain's own highly idiosyncratic temperament. Alain emphasized aspects of Descartes that are largely unfamiliar to us. We do not tend, for instance, to think of Descartes the psychologist, whose *Traité des passions de l'âme* so much impressed Alain, or the Descartes

1 Emile Chartier (1868–1951).

who took an interest in the work of ordinary people, in tools, and in common trades. Also, most of us lack the kind of exact knowledge of Cartesian mathematical thought that enabled Weil to grandly but accurately make the name of Descartes synonymous with "the double revolution through which physics became an application of mathematics and geometry became algebra." Most unfamiliar of all is the Descartes who most interested Weil. He is a Descartes whose whole thought could perhaps have been understood in a different way, a way that might have led to an altogether different sort of modern science and modern world. In Descartes's affirmation of the scientific value of ordinary perception—he saw perception as a function of the understanding, i.e., as an activity that involves making judgments and coming to conclusions—Weil glimpsed both the possibility of a radically new understanding of what science should be and the possibility of introducing into the core of Western philosophical and scientific thought an understanding of work as a way of knowing the world. In the process of working out these possibilities in the dissertation, she builds a philosophical foundation for ideas that throughout her life were to have a central place in her thinking, e.g., that manual work, properly understood, is a source of moral and intellectual value; that it is of the same value as science as a way of knowing the world; that there is no justification in the nature of science itself for the development of an abstract, purely algebraic science that has no relation to the world of common-sense perception; and that, therefore, there is no justification for the existence of a scientific elite that supposedly has access to knowledge an ordinary person cannot attain. All these are formidable and real issues that have lost nothing of their urgency over the intervening years.

Many aspects of Alain's teaching dovetailed with questions that had urgently presented themselves to Weil in early adolescence, in particular the question of whether only people of genius had "access to the realm of truth." In Descartes, especially as he was taught by Alain, she found a superb mind—a genius—who affirmed the ability of all human beings to discover truth, if only they use their minds correctly. Descartes, then, in his way, confirmed her own earlier conviction (arrived at after experiencing nearly suicidal despair) that "any human being . . . can penetrate to the kingdom of truth reserved for genius, if only he longs for truth and perpetually concentrates all his attention upon its attainment."[2] This core

2 Simone Weil, *Waiting for God* (New York: Harper Colophon Books, 1973), p. 64.

conviction that truth is accessible to all may be the single most unifying factor underlying Weil's psychology.

The dissertation as a whole is divided into an introduction, Part 1 (a historical examination of the problem raised in the introduction), Part 2 (a personal investigation of the problem, analogous to Descartes's *Meditations*), and a conclusion.

Weil begins the introduction with a lofty and abbreviated summary of humanity's quest for indubitable knowledge. Human beings have always sought it, felt that their own "ordinary" thought could not provide it, and made priests and kings of those whom they mistakenly believed had access to it. Thales' discovery of geometry demonstrated that certain knowledge is indeed possible; Weil, however, asks whether that discovery merely replaced the tyranny of priests ruling through the "tricks" of religion with the legitimate authority of scientists who "really have access to the intelligible world," or whether, "by teaching us that the realm of pure thought is the sensible world itself," Thales' discovery made indubitable knowledge available to everyone. In other words, is science necessarily abstract, self-referential, unrelated to the world of common-sense perception, an elite realm that only the initiated may enter? Greek science, Weil finds, does not give a clear answer to the question, and modern science, when looked at in a few particulars, is full of contradictions. Weil suggests that these contradictions are a sign that the separation of scientific thinking from ordinary thinking has come about as a result of the "prejudices" of scientists and does not flow from the nature of science itself. To determine whether or not this is the case, she proposes to return to the origin of modern science—to Descartes—and seek out the principles on which it was founded.

In Part 1 of the dissertation Weil approaches the problem historically. First she cites the ways in which the development of modern science does seem to be in accord with certain aspects of Cartesian thought; for instance, Descartes does indeed reject the evidence of the senses as deceptive, and can be said to have transferred the knowledge of nature from the senses to reason. She presents textual evidence in Descartes that supports the argument that "from its very origin modern science has been, albeit in a less developed form, what it is now." Then, however, she sets the stage for an alternative view, pointing out that a careful reading of Descartes would "bring one up against a multitude of passages that are apparently hard to reconcile" with the outline of Cartesian thought she has just sketched. In this second selection of texts, she shows that real science, according to Descartes, consists in using one's reason properly, and that therefore any person, with proper application, can know all that is within the scope of the mind. Science for Descartes, she argues, does not consist in a body of knowledge—"results"—but in the use of a method. She cites passages showing that he did not confine himself to abstract questions that "are of no use except to exercise the mind"; in fact, he gave up such questions in order to have more time to "pursue another kind of geometry, which proposes for questions the explanation of natural phenomena." While she acknowledges that Descartes is an extreme idealist in one sense, she argues that he is also an extreme realist. His geometry, though abstract, always "grasps something," some real object existing in the world. And although he defines the world as "extension" (a purely abstract idea), she points out that he does not recognize "extension separated from an extended substance." Similarly, she shows that Cartesian science is considerably more concrete than is generally thought; his physics uses familiar comparisons drawn from nature, and in his solutions to problems of physics he uses perceptible objects as models, so that, as he says, "I could submit my reasoning to the examination of the senses, as I always try to do." He finds the human mind—i.e., reason or understanding—at work in the most ordinary kinds of thinking, and recognizes that perception is an act of the understanding and is of the same nature as science. And although he distinguishes imagination from mind and locates it in the body, he does not reject it; rather, he recognizes it as a useful and even necessary tool in knowing the world.

Having cited these contradictory views to be found in Descartes, Weil finds that the historical approach she has followed does not give her the wherewithal to reconcile them, and also leaves unanswered the question of how Descartes's research in physics could lead (as he claims it did) to the acquisition of self-knowledge. She notes, moreover, the impossibility of fully understanding Descartes "from the outside" and "piecemeal," and proposes to undertake a personal rather than historical investigation of the problem in order to try to reconcile these contradictions (an approach called in the Sorbonne *philosophie dogmatique*); she will "become a Cartesian" and pursue a series of reflections on her own in order to discover in herself both the process by which indubitable knowledge is arrived at and what that knowledge can consist of. This meditation forms the second part of the thesis.

Weil's meditation is far from a simple imitation of the Cartesian original. Descartes began his *Meditations* by doubting everything that came to him through the senses in order to determine what could be known with certainty by the mind alone. Weil begins her reflections in a prolonged languor in which consciousness is stripped of everything except its most essential elements, the living being's awareness of self and the world. This state of inchoate awareness consists of feelings of pleasure and pain that are constantly changing and never purely one or the other. These primordial, indefinable feelings are the medium through which the world appears to consciousness, and at the same time it is the world that gives rise to these feelings. However, Weil finds that they cannot give her any certain knowledge about herself, the nature of the world, or even any proof that the world exists independently of her. Even abstract ideas, such as mathematical propositions, which do not in themselves give rise to feelings of pleasure and pain, are mediated through appearances, and although something seems to determine that mathematical ideas can appear to her in some ways but not in others (she can conceive of two pairs of oranges making four oranges, but not five), this phenomenon seems to be something arbitrary and inexplicable arising from her own unknown nature. What happens in the world of mathematics, just as in the sensible world, seems to be the result only of chance. Consciousness alone does not give her any knowledge of the nature or the real existence of what she is conscious of.

Continued reflection, however, leads Weil to see that there is a power in thought, for her thoughts are capable of deceiving her and creating an illusion of a world that seems formidably real. She herself can take command of this power, rather than being simply subject to it, when she doubts whatever presents itself to her mind. In doubting she is carrying out truly autonomous action; the exercise of this power causes her to exist as an active being and moves her from the level of consciousness on which knowledge is not possible to a level on which clear and indisputable truths emerge: "as soon as I reject an idea, even if it should be the idea that I am, at once I am." What she finds to be the cornerstone of the edifice of indubitable knowledge is thus slightly different from the Cartesian formula "I think, therefore I am." For Weil what is crucial is the ability to take command of the power inherent in thought: *Je puis, donc je suis* (I have power, therefore I am).

She then establishes what can be known by means of pure understanding; basically, she concludes, all she can know is herself and the extent of her power (the two are identical, for she is defined by what she can do). For her to know herself is thus to know to what degree she is master of her thoughts and to what degree her thoughts are subject to the world. This, she affirms, is the only knowledge there is. The world's existence is proved, she reflects, by the fact that her power over her own thoughts is extremely limited. Since power, as she understands it, is infinite by nature, this limitation demonstrates that something other than she must exist, something that causes thoughts to arise in her independently or in spite of her own will, something that has power over her through those thoughts. As long as she responds to this other existence with feelings of pleasure and pain, she can know nothing about it. Knowledge of it is dependent on her being able to act on it, to "grasp" it, to have power over it in some way. But the kind of thinking by which she proved her own existence does not help her to grasp the world.

To learn about the world she finds she must now consult the imagination, that "ambiguous being that is a composite of myself and the world acting on one another," even though earlier she had turned away from the imagination in order to determine what could be known by the understanding alone. She finds, initially, that the imagination seems to have two aspects. When it is not controlled by the mind it creates fantastic images out of sense impressions and causes her to be passive, impotent, "delivered over to the world." It mediates a world that can be a cause of joy or sadness to her, but not an object of knowledge. When it is controlled by the mind, however, the imagination mediates ideas in which the world plays a part, but which "do not represent the encroachment of the world on me, since they are made present to me only by an act of my own attention." Such ideas—e.g., the idea of number, or the sequence of numbers, or any kind of orderly series—create a "passageway" for the mind into the world, a clear space in the world in which the mind can be free and act. Moreover, the idea of sequence, since it can be added to infinitely, makes infinite action in the world—that is, action that nothing limits—theoretically possible to her.

Armed with these ideas, she approaches the world. She starts with straight-line motion, the simplest of all the clear ideas. Motion in a straight line, she asserts, constitutes the basic grasp the world allows her, the basic way the mind can act on the world. By combining straight-line motions she arrives at a series of geometrical forms—the oblique line, the circle, the ellipse—that corresponds in its increasing complexity to the series of numbers. Generalizing from this, she postulates that the world is constituted by an infinitely complex combination of straight-line movements, and that this combination is at least theoretically reducible to a movement comparable to the simple straight-line movement she has at her disposal. She recognizes, however, that this physics of movement is not, strictly speaking, true, because it attributes to the world lines and directions, which are properties of the mind. Nevertheless, when she separates from movement what belongs to the mind and what belongs to the world, she arrives at knowledge of what the world is: "the world, in itself, is only extended substance." This is, however, only hypothetical knowledge as long as her uncontrolled imagination persists in transforming her sensations into signs of an animistic world. Geometry and physics alone, which employ one part of the imagination, still leave the other part free. But work, she affirms, unites the two imaginations—work and perception,[3] because both of them involve the directed activity of the body and therefore of the whole imagination (Weil, like Descartes, identifies the body with the imagination). Work and perception, she argues, are the key elements in knowledge of the world. Perception actively controls the imagination and turns sensations into "signs of distances, sizes, shapes, that is, signs of work I may do." Work itself, even more important, enables her to grasp the world as it is in itself, as "naked extension, stripped of all admixture of mind, all trappings of imagination." Work is thus the most direct possible contact of the mind with the world.

In the final pages of Part 2 Weil returns, at long last, to the question raised in the introduction concerning the true nature of science. The basic components of science, she contends, are work and perception; science is nothing more than a collective effort of perception enabling mankind to "grasp" (i.e., determine the actual magnitude and movements of) objects like the sun and the stars whose size and distance cannot be accurately perceived by one person alone. The real purpose of science is virtually indistinguishable from the purpose of work; it is "to render the human mind master . . . of the part of the imagination that perception leaves free, and then to give it possession of the world." Science, she concludes, can add only one thing to what is already known by the person who knows the world through what she calls self-conscious work: it can add the knowledge that such work contains "everything there is to know," and that "there is nothing else."

3 In her analysis of the important role of bodily movement in perception Weil is drawing on the teaching of Jules Lagneau.

■ Science and Perception in Descartes

᾿Αεὶ ὁ θεὸς γεωμετρεῖ.[1]

Introduction

Humanity began, as every man begins, with no knowledge except consciousness of self and perception of the world. That was all man needed (as it is all that primitive peoples, or, in our civilized world, uneducated laborers, still need) to find his way in nature and human society to the extent that was necessary for survival. Why desire more? It seems that humanity should never have left that state of blissful ignorance, or, to cite Rousseau, have become so corrupted as to begin to meditate.[2] But the fact is that, as far as we can know, humanity never, strictly speaking, had to leave that state, for it never confined itself to it. The reason that the search for truth has been and still can be of some interest is that man's original state is not ignorance, but error. That is why men have never been content to be limited to the immediate interpretation of sensations, and have always intuited that there was a higher, more certain knowledge that is the privilege of a few initiates. Men believed that errant thought, given over to sense impressions and passions, was not real thought. They believed that they would find the higher kind of thought in certain men who seemed godlike to them, and they made them their priests and kings. But as they had no idea what this higher way of thinking might be (since, indeed, they could not have conceived it unless they had possessed it), they deified in their priests, under the name of religion, the most fantastic beliefs. Thus the accurate intuition that there was a more certain and higher kind of knowledge than that depending on the senses led them to humble themselves, submit to authority, and acknowledge as their superiors men whose only

---

1 "God geometrizes eternally" (attributed to Plato in Plutarch's *Symposiacs* bk. 8, question 2).

2 Jean-Jacques Rousseau (1712–78), Swiss-born French philosopher. In the *Discourse on the Origin and Foundation of Inequality among Mankind* (1755) Rousseau wrote: "I dare almost affirm that a state of reflection is a state against nature, and that the man who meditates is a degenerate animal." See *The Social Contract and Discourse on the Origin and Foundation of Inequality among Mankind* (New York: Pocket Books, 1971), p. 183.

advantage over them was to have replaced thought that was uncertain in its direction with thought that had no direction at all.

The advent of the geometer Thales[3] was history's greatest moment, a moment that is repeated in an individual's life, for Thales is reborn for each new generation of students. Until the time of Thales, humanity had proceeded only by trial and error and guesswork; from the moment that Thales discovered geometry—after, according to Hugo,[4] he had remained immobile for four years—humanity knew. This revolution, the first and only revolution, overthrew the authority of the priests. But how did it do so? What did it bring us in its place? Did it give us that other world, that realm of authentic thought which men have always glimpsed through the veil of so many crazy superstitions? Did it replace tyrannical priests who ruled by means of the tricks of religion with true priests who exercise a legitimate authority because they really have access to the intelligible world? Must we submit blindly to these thinkers who see for us, as we used to submit blindly to priests who were themselves blind, if lack of talent or leisure prevents us from entering their ranks? Or, on the contrary, did this revolution replace inequality with equality by teaching us that the realm of pure thought is the sensible world itself, that this quasi-divine knowledge that religions sensed is only a chimera, or rather, that it is nothing but ordinary thought? Nothing is harder to know, and at the same time nothing is more important for every man to know. For it is a matter of nothing less than knowing whether I ought to make the conduct of my life subject to the authority of scientific thinkers, or solely to the light of my own reason; or rather, since I alone can decide that, it is a matter of knowing whether science will bring me liberty or legitimate chains.

If we look at the miracle of geometry in its origins, it provides no easy answer to this question. Legend has it that Thales discovered the fundamental theorem of mathematics when, in order to measure the pyramids, he compared the ratio of their height to their shadow with the ratio of a man's height to his shadow. Science here would seem to be merely a more careful kind of perception. But that is not how the Greeks thought of it.

3 Thales of Miletus (c. 624–547 B.C.), Greek mathematician and astronomer. Several theorems in elementary geometry are attributed to him.

4 Victor Hugo (1802–85), French poet, novelist, and dramatist. Alain used this legend of Thales' protracted immobility as an illustration of the important part played by attentive, noninterfering observation in the genesis of great discoveries. See *Elements de philosophie* (Paris: Editions Gallimard, 1941), p. 99.

Plato put it well when he said that, although the geometer makes use of figures, these figures are not the object of geometry, but only the occasion for reasoning about the ideal straight line, the ideal triangle, the ideal circle. As if drunk on geometry, the philosophers of the Platonic school reduced—which that universe of ideas to which they had been miraculously granted access did not—the whole of what is perceived to a fabric of appearances, and forbade the search for wisdom to anyone who was not a geometer. Greek science, therefore, leaves us uncertain. In any case, it is better to consult modern science, for if we leave aside a fairly rudimentary astronomy, it is modern science that, by means of physics, was destined to bring Thales' discovery into the area where it vies with perception—in other words, into contact with the sensible world.

Here there is no uncertainty at all; it is truly another realm of thought that modern science brings us. Thales himself, if he were to return to life to see how far men have carried his reflections, would feel like a son of the soil compared to our scientists. If he were to look at an astronomy book, he would find almost no mention of stars in it. The last things to be discussed in a book on capillarity or heat would be capillaries and fluids, a definition of heat, or the means of its propagation. Those who want to provide a mechanical model of physical phenomena, as the first astronomers did, by representing the course of the stars by machines, are now scorned. In the absence of things or mechanical models that imitate them, Thales would expect to find geometrical figures in our books on nature; again he would be disappointed. He would think his discovery forgotten; he would not see that it still dominates, in the form of algebra. Science, which in the time of the Greeks was the science of numbers, geometrical figures, and machines, now seems to be solely the science of pure relationships. Ordinary thinking, which it seems Thales at least utilized, even if he did not confine himself to it, is now clearly scorned. Common-sense notions such as three-dimensional space and the postulates of Euclidean geometry have been discarded. Certain theories do not hesitate to speak about curved space, or to put a measurable speed next to an infinite one. Speculative theories about the nature of matter are given free rein, in the attempt to interpret this or that result of our physics without the slightest concern for what matter may mean to ordinary men who touch it with their hands. In short, as much as possible, scientists exclude everything having to do with intuition; they no longer admit anything into science except the most abstract form of reasoning, expressed in a suitable language by means of algebraic signs. But since reasoning in common people is closely tied to intuition, an abyss separates the scientist from the uneducated person. Scientists have thus indeed become the successors of the priests of the old theocracies, with this difference, that a dominion gained by usurpation has been replaced by a legitimate authority.

Without rebelling against this authority, one may still examine it. Some astonishing contradictions are immediately evident. For example, let us look at the consequences of the absolute dominion that is exercised over science by the most abstract forms of mathematics. As we observed, science has been so purged of everything having to do with intuition that it is no longer concerned with anything except combinations of pure relationships. But these relationships must have a content, and where is that to be found except in experience? Indeed, physics does nothing but express, by means of suitable signs, the relationships that exist between the givens of experience. In other words, physics may be thought of as consisting essentially of a mathematical expression of facts. Instead of being the queen of science, mathematics is now no more than a language; the result of its absolute sovereignty is that it has been reduced to a servile role. That is why Poincaré could say, for example, that Euclidean and non-Euclidean geometries are only different systems of measurement.[5] In *Science and Hypothesis* he says, "What, then, are we to think of the question: Is Euclidean geometry true? It has no meaning. We might as well ask if the metric system is true, and if the old weights and measures are false; if Cartesian coordinates are true and polar coordinates are false. One geometry cannot be more true than another; it can only be more *convenient*."[6]

Thus, according to the testimony of the greatest mathematician of our century, mathematics is only a convenient language. In one form or another, it always plays the same role that we see it play in the elementary laws of physics, which are represented by curves. Experiments supply the points that, on paper, represent actual measurements. The mathematician only furnishes the simplest curve that includes all these points, so that the various experiments can be grouped under a single law. This was also

5 Henri Poincaré (1854–1912), French mathematician. At the turn of the century Poincaré was widely regarded as the greatest living mathematician. A prolific writer and lecturer, he wrote a number of books for the general reader on the meaning and implications of science and mathematics. His conception of the role of convenience in science is considered his greatest contribution to the philosophy of science.

6 See Henri Poincaré, *Science and Hypothesis* (New York: Charles Scribner's Sons, 1907), p. 50. Emphasis added by Simone Weil.

recognized by Poincaré. In *The Value of Science* he says, "All laws are deduced from experiment; but to enunciate them, a special language is needed. . . . Mathematics furnishes the physicist with the only language he can speak."[7] According to Poincaré, the role of mathematical analysis is limited to this function, and to that of indicating to the physicist analogies between phenomena through the similarity of the formulas that express them. If one believes those who are competent in the field, scientists have reached the point where they translate the results of experiments into differential equations that they are incapable of relating to energy, force, space, or any other strictly physical notion. And so this science that arrogantly scorned intuition is reduced to expressing the results of experience in the most general language possible.

Another contradiction has to do with the relation between science and its applications. Modern scientists, considering (as seems proper for them to do) knowledge to be the noblest goal they can set for themselves, refuse to do research with a view to industrial applications, and loudly declare, with Poincaré, that if there can be no Science for its own sake, there can be no Science.[8] But this does not seem to square with the previous idea that the question of whether such and such a scientific theory is true is meaningless, since a theory is only more or less convenient. Furthermore, the distance that seemed to exist between the scientist and the uneducated person is thus reduced to a difference in degree, since science is found to be not more true, but only more convenient, than perception.

Are these contradictions only apparently insoluble? Or are they a sign that scientists, in separating scientific thinking from ordinary thinking as they have done, are governed by their own prejudices rather than by the nature of science? The best way to decide this question is to consider science at its origin and seek out the principles according to which it was established; but for the reasons given above, we must go back, not to Thales, but to the double revolution through which physics became an application of mathematics and geometry became algebra: in other words, to Descartes.

7 See Poincaré, *The Value of Science* (New York: Science Press, 1907), p. 76.
8 Ibid.

Part One

If we are unsure whether or not science, at its very beginning, substituted an intelligible world for the sensible world, this uncertainty should not take long to dispel. For if we open the *Meditations,* we read at once: "All that I have accepted until now as being the most true and the most certain, I have learned from the senses, or by means of the senses; but I have sometimes found that the senses were deceptive, and it is prudent never to entirely trust those who have once deceived us."[1] Accordingly, when Descartes wants to seek the truth, he shuts his eyes and plugs his ears; he even expunges all images of corporeal things from his mind, or, since that is hardly possible, he at least refutes them as vain and false. It is true that this concerns metaphysical, not mathematical, research, but we know that Descartes considered his metaphysical doctrine to be the foundation of all his thought. Thus the first step taken by Descartes as he thinks is to set aside sensations. True, that procedure is only a form of his hyperbolic doubt, and one could think that this distrust of the senses is only provisional, in accord with the comparison that Descartes uses to explain what he means by doubt in his *Response to the Seventh Set of Objections:* "If by chance he [the Jesuit Père Bourdin, whose criticisms of the *Meditations* Descartes was answering] had a basket of fruit, and he feared that some pieces of the fruit might be spoiled, and he wanted to remove the bad ones lest they spoil the rest, how would he go about it? Would he not first completely remove all the fruit from the basket? And then, examining the pieces carefully one by one, would he not take back only those that he saw were not spoiled, and replace them in the basket, leaving the others behind?" (7:481).[2] Actually, belief in the evidence of the senses is not among the ideas that Descartes, after having thrown them out, takes up again as sound. On the contrary, the aim of Cartesian physics is to replace the

1 All quotations from Descartes in the text have been translated by the editors from the original French and Latin. Simone Weil quotes from *Oeuvres de Descartes, publiées par Ch. Adam et P. Tannery,* 12 vols. (Paris, 1897–1910). The above passage is found in 9:14. Page references to subsequent citations will be given in parenthesis in the text. For the reader who wishes to find the place where the passage occurs in an English translation, a footnote will give page references wherever such a translation is available. The above passage is found in *Discourse on Method and the Meditations* (New York: Penguin Books, 1968), p. 96.

2 See *The Philosophical Works of Descartes,* trans. Elizabeth S. Haldane and G. R. T. Ross (New York: Dover Publications, Inc., 1955), 2:282.

things that we sense with things that we can understand only, to the extent of supposing that a simple vortex is the source of solar rays. The sun itself is deprived of its light by the mind. And in fact here is the way *The World,* also entitled *Treatise on Light,* begins: "Since I intend to discuss Light in these pages, the first thing I want to tell you is that there can be a difference between the impression we have of it—that is, the idea of it that is formed in our imagination with the help of our eyes—and what is in the objects that gives rise to this impression in us, that is, what is in a flame or in the sun that is called by the name of light" (11:3).[3] He demonstrates this with an example drawn directly from experience:

> Of all our senses, touch is the one that we consider to be the least deceptive and the most certain; so that if I prove to you that even touch makes us conceive quite a few ideas that do not at all resemble the objects that give rise to them, I do not think you should find it strange if I say that sight can do the same. . . . A cavalryman returns from a battle; during the heat of the fray he could have been wounded without noticing it; but now that he begins to relax, he feels some pain, and he thinks he is wounded. A surgeon is sent for; the cavalryman is examined, and at length it appears that what he felt was nothing but a buckle or a strap which, having become twisted under his armor, was pressing against him and causing him discomfort. If his sense of touch, in making him feel the strap, had imprinted its image on his mind, he would not have needed a surgeon to tell him what he was feeling. (11:5–6)[4]

Refusing, accordingly, to trust the senses, Descartes puts his trust in reason alone, and we know that his system of the world is the triumph of what is called the a priori method. He applied this method with a boldness that was, according to a famous saying, both unprecedented and inimitable, for he goes as far as to deduce the existence of the heavens, the earth, and the elements. "The order that I adhered to in this," he writes in the *Discourse on Method,* "has been as follows":

> First, I tried to find in general the Principles or First Causes of everything that exists or can exist in the world, without considering to this end anything except God alone who created it, or deriving them from anything other than certain seeds of truth that are naturally in our souls. After that I examined

3 See *Descartes: Selections*, ed. Ralph M. Eaton (New York: Charles Scribner's Sons, 1927), p. 312.
4 See ibid., pp. 313–14.

what were the first and most ordinary effects that could be deduced from these causes; and it seems to me that in that way I found Heavens, Stars, an Earth and even, on the earth, water, air, fire, minerals, and other such things that are the commonest and simplest of all. (6:63–64)[5]

He carries out this plan in the *Principles* with this almost insolent remark, which is also found in the *Correspondence:* "The proofs of all this are so certain that, even if experience might seem to show us the contrary, we would nevertheless be obliged to put more faith in our reason than in our senses" (9:93). To which one may compare this passage from a letter to Mersenne:[6] "I set no store by the Sieur Petit and his words,[7] and it seems to me that there is no more reason to listen to him when he promises to refute my theory of refractions by experiment than if he were trying, with some faulty square, to show that the sum of the three angles of a triangle are not equal to the sum of two right angles" (2:497).

So Cartesian physics is geometrical. But Cartesian geometry, in its turn, is far removed from that classical geometry that Comte so appropriately called "special" because it is connected to particular forms.[8] Since we are considering Descartes historically, it may be useful at this point to consider what form his ideas took among the philosophers who are more or less his disciples. Now, with reference to the *Geometry* of 1637, Malebranche[9] and Spinoza[10] both distinguished (albeit differently) intelligible extension from the kind of extension that is thrown over things like a cloak and that speaks only to the imagination. Although Descartes did not explicitly go

5 See *Discourse on Method and the Meditations*, p. 80.

6 Marin Mersenne (1588–1648), priest, philosopher, theologian. He maintained a large correspondence with the major thinkers of his time, introducing them and their ideas to one another. Descartes was his great friend and his principal correspondent, and it was through Mersenne that the *Discourse on Method*, the *Essays*, and the *Meditations* were first published.

7 Pierre Petit (1598–1677). A provincial commissioner of the artillery, Petit conducted various experiments in physics in his spare time. He was especially interested in the refraction of light. He wrote objections to Part 4 of the *Discourse* and to the *Optics* and the *Meteors*.

8 Auguste Comte (1798–1857), French philosopher and founder of positivism. In the *System of Positive Polity* Comte refers to "the development of general Geometry out of the special Geometry which alone was known to the ancients." See *System of Positive Polity*, 4 vols. (London: Longmans, Green, and Co., 1875), 1:389.

9 Nicholas Malebranche (1638–1715), French philosopher and theologian. He spent many years studying Cartesian philosophy and is regarded as the connecting link between Descartes and Spinoza.

10 Benedict Spinoza (1632–77), Dutch philosopher.

that far, it is he whom we must credit with this forceful idea. Not that he didn't seem to imply it in places, as in the famous passage about the piece of wax in which he strips extension of its trappings of colors, odors, and sounds, and even more in the following lines addressed to Morus,[11] where extension already seems to be conceived in the way Spinoza will later conceive it; true, it is not yet conceived as indivisible, but it is conceived independently of its parts:

> Tangibility and impenetrability in a material body are like the capacity for laughter in man, a property of the fourth kind according to the common laws of logic; but this is not a true and essential specific difference, which I contend consists in extension; therefore, as man is not defined as an animal capable of laughter, but as a rational animal, so a material body is not defined by its impenetrability, but by its extension. And this is confirmed by the fact that, while tangibility and impenetrability have reference to parts and presuppose the concept of division or limit, we can conceive a continuous body of indeterminate or indefinite size, in which nothing except extension need be considered. (5:269)

Nevertheless, it was in the *Geometry* of 1637—which constituted a real revolution for mathematics—that this idea of pure extension, of extension in itself, to use Platonic language, especially burst forth. True, the ancient geometers were not reasoning about the triangle or the circle that they had before their eyes, but about the triangle or the circle in general; still, they remained as though glued to the triangle or the circle. Since their demonstrations depended on intuition, they always preserved something that was specific to the kind of figure that they were studying. Although Archimedes had measured the area enclosed by a segment of a parabola, this wonderful discovery was still of no help at all in similar investigations concerning, for example, the ellipse, for it was the particular properties of the parabola that made this measurement possible, through a construction impracticable or useless for any other figure. Descartes was the first to understand that the sole object of science is the quantities to be measured, or rather the ratios that determine this measurement—ratios that, in geometry, are found only as it were hidden in figures, in the same way that, for example, ratios can be hidden in movements. After this brilliant in-

11 Henry More (1614–87), English philosopher and theologian, one of the leaders of the Cambridge Platonists. He disagreed with Descartes's conception of extension.

sight, geometers from Descartes onward ceased to condemn themselves, as the Greek geometers had done, to making a mathematical expression of whatever degree correspond only to a form of extension having a corresponding number of dimensions—lines for simple quantities, surfaces for the products of two factors, and volumes for the products of three. As a matter of fact,

> all these are used in the same way, if they are considered only with regard to dimension, as must be done here and in the mathematical disciplines. . . . Consideration of this matter throws a great light on geometry, because almost all men mistakenly think that there are three kinds of quantity in geometry: the line, the surface, and the body. For it has already been said that the line and the surface are not conceived as truly distinct from the body, or from one another; in fact, if they are considered simply as abstractions of the understanding, they are no more different kinds of quantity than "animal" and "living being" are different kinds of substance in man. (10:448–49)[12]

In this way mathematics was set free from the superstition whereby each figure has, as it were, its own quantity. From that time onward, figures were no more than givens that posited ratios of quantity; all that was left was to apply arithmetical signs to ratios of this new sort. But Vieta,[13] when he invented algebra, had already applied signs to all possible ratios. Even curves were defined by the law—that is, by the formula—that brought them, as they were traced out, nearer to or further from an arbitrarily chosen straight line. In short, from 1637 on, the essence of the circle, as Spinoza would later say, was no longer circular. It was as if all figures were dissolved; only the straight line still existed, and geometers, following Descartes's example, stopped considering "any other theorems than those that state that the sides of similar triangles are proportional, and that in right triangles, the square of the base is equal to the sum of the squares of the sides. . . . For . . . if one draws other lines and uses other theorems . . . one does not see so clearly what one is doing unless one has the proof of the theorem vividly in mind, and in that case one almost always finds that the theorem rests on the consideration of a few triangles that are either right

---

12 See René Descartes, *Philosophical Essays*, trans. Laurence J. Lafleur (Indianapolis: Bobbs-Merrill, 1978), p. 219.

13 François Vieta (1540–1603), French mathematician. He is said to be the founder of modern algebra.

triangles or similar triangles, and thus one comes back again to what I was saying" (4:38–39).[14]

Furthermore, it is clear that the daring and later almost universally imitated step taken by Fourier[15] in his famous studies on heat—he left out the intermediary of mechanics in order to apply analysis directly to physics—only repeated the *Geometry* of 1637 on another subject. Or rather, the *Geometry* was only one of the applications of the general principle, applied today in all studies that allow it, that ratios between quantities are the sole object of the scientist. One can even think that Descartes would have anticipated modern science by using analysis in physics as well as in geometry, if he had possessed a sufficiently elaborate instrument. One need not be surprised that the inventor of this bold view had, as we observed, only scorn for what Spinoza would call "knowledge of the first kind."[16] No more than Spinoza does he believe that one can be wise without being a philosopher, and on this subject no one has expressed himself in stronger terms. In the preface to the *Principles* he says, "To live without philosophizing is exactly like keeping one's eyes shut without ever trying to open them. . . . And, in sum, this study is more necessary for regulating our morals and guiding us in this life than the use of our eyes is for directing our steps" (9:3–4).[17] Ultimately, one will not be surprised that the Descartes who resolutely discards ideas "that are formed in the imagination with the help of our eyes" and who sets mathematics free from the yoke of intuition has, like Spinoza, reduced the imagination to something consisting only of the movements of the human body. This is shown in a text from the *Rules for the Direction of the Mind:* "One must conceive . . . the imagination to be a real part of the body." And further on: "from this one can understand how all the movements of the lower animals can come about, although they are not considered to have any knowledge of objects, but only a purely corporeal kind of imagination" (10:414–15).[18]

Thus science has been cleansed of the mud of its origin, so to speak,

14 Descartes to Princess Elizabeth, November 1643.

15 Jean Baptiste Fourier (1768–1830), French mathematician. His *Analytical Theory of Heat* (1822) is his most famous work.

16 According to Spinoza, knowledge of the first kind is "opinion or imagination," that is, "all ideas that are inadequate and confused." See *The Ethics* prop. 40, n. 2, and prop. 41 (New York: Dover Publications, 1955), pp. 113–14.

17 See *Discourse on Method and the Meditations*, pp. 174–75.

18 See *Philosophical Essays*, pp. 190–91.

which Thales and his successors had not entirely washed away. It is what Plato had had a presentiment of: an assemblage of ideas. And this provides the opportunity to look at another aspect of Cartesian thought with the help of another of Descartes's disciples: Leibnitz.[19] For even though Leibnitz wanted to construct the whole edifice not only of human knowledge, but even of divine knowledge (which in his system is the same thing as the world), out of ideas, once again it is Descartes who must be regarded as the inspiration of this doctrine. True, in the *Meditations* all Descartes did was observe the existence in his mind of ideas that, he said, cannot be considered to be pure nothing, and were not invented by him, but have true and immutable natures of their own. But in the *Rules*—of which Leibnitz possessed a copy—Descartes goes much further in his doctrine of simple ideas, defining them thus: "I call 'absolute' whatever contains in itself the pure and simple essence with which we are concerned; as, for example, everything that is considered as independent, as a cause, as simple, universal, one, equal, similar, straight, or other things of this sort; and I call it the simplest and the easiest, so that we may use it for the solution of problems" (10:381).[20] And how should we use it? This we see further on: "It must be noted [second] that there are only a few pure and simple essences that we can behold at first sight and in themselves, independently of any others, either in experience itself or by means of the light innate in us; and we say that careful attention must be paid to them, for they are the ones that we call the simplest in each series. All the others, moreover, cannot be perceived unless they are deduced from them, either immediately and proximately or through two, three, or several different stages" (10: 383).[21] And further on there is this even more significant passage: "We conclude, third, that all human knowledge consists in this: that we see clearly how these simple essences come together in the composition of other things" (10:427).[22] Simply by pushing this idea to its furthest consequences we again encounter Leibnitz. For if, in being built, these transparent edifices of simple ideas increasingly approach the complication of existing things, must we not think that the gulf that nonetheless separates our reasoning from the world is due to our limited mind, rather than to the nature of ideas? Hence one can imagine that, for an infinite understanding,

19 Gottfried Wilhelm Leibnitz (1646–1716), German philosopher.
20 See *Philosophical Essays*, p. 164.
21 See ibid., p. 166.
22 See ibid., p. 200.

it is necessarily true that Caesar crossed the Rubicon,[23] exactly as it is true for us that two and two are four. If this is not necessarily true for us, it is because infinite analysis is needed to know an event, properly speaking. "Although it is easy," Leibnitz says, "to determine that the number of feet in the diameter is not contained in the notion of the sphere in general, it is not so easy to determine whether the journey that I plan to make is contained in my notion, otherwise it would be as easy for us to be prophets as to be geometers."[24]

The idea that we can form of Descartes as the founder of modern science thus seems complete. Classical geometry was still as it were glued to the earth; he set it loose, and was like a second Thales in relation to Thales. He transferred the knowledge of nature from the realm of the senses to the realm of reason. He thus rid our thought of imagination, and modern scientists, who have applied mathematical analysis directly to all the objects that can be studied in that way, are his true successors. Poincaré, in substituting analytic proofs for intuitive proofs concerning addition and multiplication, showed the true Cartesian spirit. Those who, following Leibnitz, hope to build, so to speak, the universe out of ideas, or who at least think that the universe in God (or, to put it another way, in itself) is built in precisely that way, also proceed from Descartes. Even the above-noted contradiction between making convenience the rule of science and having contempt for its applications is found in Descartes. For if on the one hand in his youth, when he thought that the sciences were useful only for the mechanical arts, he was of the opinion that such solid foundations had not been used for very lofty purposes, on the other hand he does not seem to require any more than Poincaré that scientific theories be true, but only that they be convenient. For example, he often compares his theories to the astronomers' ideas about the equator and the ecliptic, ideas that, although false, became the foundation of astronomy. Indeed, he wants order, the essence of Cartesian science, not to conform slavishly to the nature of things, but to apply "even to things that do not follow one another naturally."

In short, from its very origin modern science has been, albeit in a less-developed form, what it is now. The question we were asking earlier has been answered; one must accept science as it is, or give it up. There would be nothing to do but let the matter rest here, and there would be no further

23 See Leibnitz, *Discourse on Metaphysics*, in *Philosophical Writings*, ed. G. H. R. Parkinson (London: J. M. Dent and Sons, 1973), p. 24.
24 See Leibnitz, *Correspondence with Arnauld*, in ibid., p. 59.

questions to ask, if a somewhat careful reading of Descartes were not enough to bring one up against a multitude of passages that are apparently hard to reconcile with the outline of Cartesian philosophy sketched above. Let us therefore review some of these passages, which we will arrange in as much order as possible, saving our comments for later.

First of all, it is not true that Descartes, while devoting himself to the sciences, disdains their applications. Not only were the last years of his life completely dedicated to medical science (which he regarded as the only suitable means of making the majority of men wiser, as well as healthier), but, much more, it was only with a view to their applications that he took the trouble to communicate his speculations to the public. For, he says, as long as the only satisfactory results he had obtained had to do with the speculative sciences or morality, he did not feel obliged to publish them. "But," he continues,

> as soon as I had acquired some general notions about physics, and when, beginning to test them on various particular problems, I observed how far they can lead and how they differ from the principles that have been utilized until now, I believed that I could not keep them hidden without sinning greatly against the law that obliges us to procure, insofar as we can, the common good of all men. For these general notions about physics showed me that it is possible to arrive at knowledge that is very useful in life, and that in place of the speculative philosophy that is taught in the schools, we can find a practical philosophy, by means of which, knowing the power and the actions of fire, water, air, the stars, the heavens, and all the other bodies that surround us as clearly as we know the various trades of our craftsmen, we could, in the same way, put these things to all the uses to which they are appropriate, and thus render ourselves as it were masters and possessors of nature. (6:61)[25]

In these lines—which have just about the same ring as those equally forceful ones later written by Proudhon,[26] in which he will go as far as to say that it is through applications alone that scientific speculations "deserve the noble name of works"—science seems to be regarded not as the means of satisfying our curiosity about nature, but as a method for taking possession of it. This does not mean that Cartesian science does not also serve a purpose that may be regarded as more exalted, but this purpose would be

25 See *Discourse on Method and the Meditations*, p. 78.
26 Pierre Joseph Proudhon (1809–65), French philosophical anarchist.

the last one to cross our minds today, for it consists in laying the foundation of morality. Descartes explicitly writes this to Chanut[27] on the subject of the *Principles:* "It may be said that these are only unimportant truths about some matters of Physics that seem to have nothing in common with what a Queen should know. But . . . these truths of Physics are part of the foundations of the highest and most perfect morality" (5:290–91). And Descartes cannot be suspected of understanding this connection in the way Comte did later, for there is no trace of sociology in Descartes's work.

What did Descartes mean by this? It's hard to be sure. But, having been thus forewarned, we will be less surprised when we observe that, if Descartes, like Poincaré, expects science to conform to the mind rather than to things, for Descartes it is not at all a matter of thinking conveniently but of thinking well, that is, by directing one's thought properly. That is why, and not because it is not general or fruitful enough, he cannot content himself with classical geometry, where he had first hoped to find the means to satisfy his desire for knowledge. "But in neither [arithmetic or geometry] did I then happen to come upon writers who fully satisfied me. Indeed, I read in them many things about numbers that I proved by my own calculations to be true; there were even many things about figures that in some way they showed right to my eyes, and they drew conclusions from certain consequences. But they did not seem to make it sufficiently clear to the mind why these things are so, and how they were discovered" (10:375).[28] And if he tries to rediscover the Greek geometers' method of analysis, he makes it clear in his *Responses to the Second Set of Objections* wherein lies the advantage of such analysis. "Analysis shows the real way a thing was methodically discovered, and shows how effects depend on causes; so that, if the reader is willing to follow it, and to cast his eyes carefully over everything contained in it, he will understand the thing demonstrated as perfectly, and will make it as much his own, as if he himself had discovered it" (9:121).[29] This is the opposite of the way science is taught: "Synthesis, on the contrary, works in a completely different way, as it were by investigating causes through their effects (although the proof that it contains is often also a proof of effects through causes). Indeed, synthesis clearly demon-

27 Hector-Pierre Chanut (1601–62), French diplomat and ambassador to Sweden, and a great friend of Descartes. While at the Swedish court he spoke of Descartes's philosophy to Queen Christina and subsequently transmitted her invitation to Descartes to visit Stockholm and explain his *Meditations* and *Principles* to her.

28 See *Philosophical Essays*, p. 159.

29 See *Philosophical Works of Descartes*, 1:48.

strates what is contained in its conclusions, and makes use of a long series of definitions, questions, axioms, theorems, and problems, so that if any conclusions are denied, it shows how they are contained in what has gone before, and it extracts the consent of the reader, however obstinate and opinionated he may be. But it does not, as analysis does, give entire satisfaction to the minds of those who want to learn, because it does not teach the method by which the thing was discovered" (9:122).[30] Thus Descartes does not consider results to be of the slightest importance for the person who wants to learn. One can solve a problem without that being science: "We, who seek a clear and distinct knowledge of things, make all these distinctions, but not the practitioners of arithmetic, who are satisfied if they find the sought-for sum, without even noticing how it is derived from what is given, although it is in that alone that science properly consists" (10:458).[31] To know that one cannot know is, in fact, science: "He will demonstrate that what he seeks exceeds the comprehension of the human mind, and therefore he will not on that account judge himself to be more ignorant, because this is no less knowledge than the knowledge of anything else" (10:400).[32] Science is nothing but order, and Cartesian method—the *Rules* repeats it constantly—concerns nothing but order. There are problems only because often we are given the most compound elements of a series, while the simplest remain unknown; the mind must then proceed in its own way by going over these elements, known or unknown, according to their order in the series. "Thus, when we want to solve some problem, we must first consider it as already solved, and give names to all the lines, the unknown ones as well as the others, that seem necessary to construct it. Then, without considering that there is any difference between the known lines and the unknown ones, we must go through the problem in the order that shows most naturally how the lines mutually depend on one another" (6:372).[33] Thus interpreted, mathematics becomes truly interesting, whereas, in Descartes's eyes, if one kept to the classical method of explanation it held no interest whatever. And he was not surprised, he says in the *Rules*, if indeed clever people scorned mathematics as childish and useless, or as too complicated. "For, in truth,

---

30 See ibid., 1:49.

31 See *Philosophical Essays*, p. 227.

32 See ibid., p. 179.

33 See *Discourse on Method, Optics, Geometry, and Meteorology*, trans. Paul J. Olscamp (New York: Bobbs-Merrill Co., 1965), p. 179.

nothing is more useless than to be so occupied with empty numbers and imaginary figures that we seem to be willing to find pleasure in knowledge of such trifles . . ." (10:375).[34] Thus this new mathematics is worth the trouble it takes to pursue it, not because it provides us with knowledge about numbers or imaginary figures that Descartes calls trifling and is, he says, only the pastime of practitioners of arithmetic or idle geometers, but because it is as it were the outer covering of real science, which alone is worth pursuing. This idea also stands out in the *Rules:*

> Nevertheless, whoever will have considered my thought carefully will easily understand that I am not thinking here of ordinary Mathematics, but am expounding another science, of which [these illustrations] are the outer covering rather than the parts. This science ought to contain the first rudiments of human reason and have only to be developed to bring forth truths from any subject whatever. And to speak freely, I am convinced that it is preferable to all other knowledge handed down to us in the human tradition, since it is the source of that knowledge. (10:374)[35]

Since real science consists only in directing one's reason well, there is no inequality either among the sciences or among minds. One science or part of a science cannot be more difficult than any other. "Indeed, it must be noted that those who truly know recognize the truth with equal ease whether they have derived it from a simple matter or from an obscure one; for they grasp each truth by a similar, unified, and distinct act, as soon as they come to it. The whole difference is in the route taken, which certainly is bound to be longer if it leads to a truth further removed from the first and most absolute principles" (10:401).[36] Therefore no man must give up approaching any part of human knowledge because he thinks it is beyond his reach, or because he thinks he could not make serious progress in a science unless he specialized in it:

> For, since all the sciences are nothing other than human wisdom, which always remains one and the same, however different the objects to which it is applied, and is no more changed by these objects than the light of the sun by the variety of things it illuminates, it is not necessary for minds to be confined by any limits; for the knowledge of one truth does not keep us from the

34 See *Philosophical Essays*, p. 159.
35 See ibid., pp. 158–59.
36 See ibid., p. 180.

discovery of another, as the practice of one skill does, but rather helps us. (10:360)[37]

What is more, where the sciences are concerned one must take into consideration that "they are all so mutually connected that it is by far easier to learn all of them together than one in isolation from the others" (10:361).[38] Thus any man, however mediocre his intelligence and his talents may be, can, if he applies himself, know everything that is within man's reach; every man, "as soon as he has distinguished, concerning each object, the kinds of knowledge that only stock or embellish the memory from those that make someone truly said to be more learned, a distinction it is easy to make, . . . will certainly perceive that his ignorance about anything is not due to lack of intelligence or skill, and that there is absolutely nothing that another man can know that he is not capable of knowing also, provided only that he apply his mind to it in the appropriate way" (10:396).[39]

Viewed in this way, mathematics rules Cartesian physics, but not as it rules ours; it does not play the role of language, but rather constitutes knowledge of the world. To say that Cartesian physics is purely geometrical, although Descartes says that himself, is putting it weakly; the truth is that in Descartes, geometry is itself a physics; which is almost word for word what he actually writes to Mersenne: "I have decided to give up only abstract geometry, that is, the pursuit of questions that are of no use except to exercise the mind. I am doing this in order to have more leisure to pursue another kind of geometry, which proposes for questions the explanation of natural phenomena." Descartes's explanations of reflection and refraction, among others, carry out this plan with an audacity that is unparalleled even today, and that scandalized Fermat.[40] The demonstration in *The World* of the law by which every movement conserves its direction is no less astonishing:

> God conserves each thing by one continuous activity, and, consequently, he does not conserve it as it may have been some time previously, but precisely as it is at the very instant that he conserves it. Now, of all movements, the straight

37 See ibid., p. 147.
38 See ibid., p. 148.
39 See *Philosophical Essays*, p. 176.
40 Pierre de Fermat (1601–65), French mathematician. He disputed the law of refraction Descartes arrived at in the *Optics*.

line is the only one that is entirely simple and whose whole nature can be comprehended in an instant. For, to conceive the straight line, it suffices to think that a body is in motion in order to move in a certain direction, which is found to be the case in every one of the instants that can be determined during the time that it is in motion. Whereas, to conceive circular movement, or any other possible movement, it is necessary to consider at least two of its instants, or rather two of its parts, and the relation between them. (11:44–45)[41]

There is no exemplar, to use a Scholastic term, for such daring idealism.[42] Yet a hundred other passages from Descartes would show that no one has taken realism so far. Descartes wants to know the world as it is in itself, and he writes as much to Morus: "But I hardly need tell you, if it is called a *perceptible substance,* then it is defined by its relation to our senses, which explains only a certain property of it, not its entire essence, which, since it could exist even if no men existed, certainly does not depend on our senses" (5:268).[43] That, after having said this, Descartes chose to define the world by the concept of extension, that is, by an idea, has always been a cause for astonishment. But for him this idealism and this realism, both pushed to their extreme limits, are not only reconcilable but correlative; though he does not explain this, at least he states it quite explicitly in the following passage from the *Letter Concerning Gassendi:*

Several excellent minds, they say, think they clearly see that mathematical extension, which I posit as the principle of my physics, is nothing other than my thought, and that mathematical extension does not have, and cannot have, any existence outside of my mind, since it is only an abstraction I make from a material body; and hence, that the whole of my physics can be only imaginary and make-believe, like all pure mathematics; and that, in the real physics of the things that God has created, there must be real matter, solid and not imaginary. Here is the major objection, and the summary of the whole doctrine of the excellent minds referred to here. All the things that we can understand and conceive are, by their account, mere chimeras and fictions of our mind, which can have no existence at all; from this it follows that there is nothing that one must acknowledge as true, except that which one can in no

---

41 See *Descartes: Selections*, p. 328.

42 An exemplar, in Scholastic philosophy, is the Divine Idea or model according to which a thing is created.

43 See *Philosophical Letters*, trans. Anthony Kenny (Oxford: Clarendon Press, 1970), p. 237.

way understand, conceive, or imagine; that is, one must entirely close the door
to reason, and be satisfied with being a monkey or a parrot, and no longer
a man, in order to deserve to be put on a level with these excellent minds. For,
if the things that one can conceive must be deemed false for the sole reason
that one can conceive them, what remains except that one must accept as true
only those things that one does not conceive, and must compose one's
doctrine of them, imitating others without knowing why one imitates them,
as monkeys do, and uttering only statements whose meaning one does not
understand, as parrots do? (9:212)

We meet with this opposition everywhere. If this geometry, so ethereal
that it seems to disdain figures, proves to be substantial enough to constitute a physics, it is because it is never isolated from the imagination. "The
study of mathematics," writes Descartes to Princess Elizabeth, "chiefly
exercises the imagination" (3:692). Similarly, he writes in a passage from
the *Rules:* "Henceforth we will do nothing without the aid of the imagination" (10:443).[44] It is in the imagination, he says again in the *Rules* (10:
416)[45] that the idea of everything that can be related to the body must be
found. Since the mind engaged in geometry makes use of the imagination,
it does not handle empty ideas. It grasps something. Consequently, in the
name of the imagination Descartes rejects such propositions as: extension,
or a figure, is not a body; a number is not the thing numbered; the surface is
the boundary of a solid, the line the boundary of a surface, the point the
limit of a line; unity is not a quantity, etc. All these propositions, he says,
have absolutely nothing to do with the imagination, even if they should be
true (10:445).[46] When it is a question of number, he wants us to imagine
an object that can be measured by means of several units; he wants us to
imagine that the point that the geometers use to form a line is only something possessing extension, exclusive of every other determining factor.
For Descartes is not satisfied with forcefully admonishing those learned
men who employ distinctions so subtle that they dissipate the light of nature and find something obscure even in things that peasants know; he is
not satisfied to warn them that as far as he is concerned he does not recognize extension separated from an extended substance, or any philosophic
entities of this sort, "which really do not fall within the scope of the

44 See *Philosophical Essays*, p. 215.
45 See ibid., p. 192.
46 See ibid., p. 216.

imagination" (10:442).[47] He finds the same idea even in classical geometry, which is thus convicted of contradictions. "What geometer does not obscure the clarity of his subject with contradictory principles, as long as he thinks that lines have no width and surfaces no depth, and then forms some of these from the others, without noticing that the line, from whose flowing movement he conceives that a surface is generated, is a real body; and that, moreover, the line that lacks width is nothing but a mode of a body" (10:446).[48]

Thus Cartesian science is far more packed with matter than is ordinarily thought. It does not disdain geometrical figures, since Descartes explicitly says that "the ideas of all things can be fashioned" from them alone (10:450).[49] It is so bound to the imagination, so joined to the human body, so close to the most common labors, that one may be initiated into it by studying the easiest and simplest crafts; especially those that are the most subject to order, like that of weavers, embroiderers, or lacemakers. In regard to the part of Cartesian science that is properly called physical, we know quite well (through the countless examples found in *The World*, the *Principles*, and the *Meteors*) that it avails itself of the most familiar comparisons, drawn sometimes from aspects of nature closest to us, such as eddies in rivers, but especially from trades and tools, the slingshot, the pressing of grapes. We might think that these comparisons are only methods of popularization; on the contrary, they are the very substance of Cartesian physics, as Descartes makes a point of explaining to Morin:[50] "And in order to explain their rotation I was obliged to use these perceptible balls, rather than some imperceptible bits of subtle matter, so that I could submit my reasoning to the examination of the senses, as I always try to do" (2:366). And, more significant still:

> It is true that the comparisons customarily used in the School, whereby intellectual things are explained by corporeal things, substances by accidents, or at any rate one quality by a quality of another kind, teach very little; but in the comparisons that I use I compare only movements to other movements, or figures to other figures, etc. In other words, I compare only things that are not perceptible to our senses because of their small size to other things that are

47 See ibid., p. 214.
48 See ibid., pp. 217–18.
49 See ibid., p. 220.
50 Jean-Baptiste Morin (1583–1656), French mathematician and astronomer.

perceptible and that in other respects do not differ from them more than a large circle differs from a small circle. And I maintain that, used in this way, comparisons are the most appropriate means of setting forth the truth about physical questions that the human mind can possess; so much so that, when something is asserted about nature that cannot be explained by any such comparison, I think I know demonstratively that it is false. (2:367–68)

The same opposition is found where simple ideas are concerned. The doctrine of simple ideas is possibly connected to the foregoing ideas, although Leibnitz developed it quite differently. The fact remains that in Descartes simple ideas are far from constituting the world as they do in Leibnitz. One cannot explain the simple ideas, which are understood from the start and in themselves, without obscuring them, for if one wants to explain them, either one explains something else under their name, or the explanation makes no sense. True, Descartes says all that. He even adds that these simple essences "never contain anything false" (10:420).[51] But far from their making up the fabric of the world, they do not even belong to the world per se; they exist in relation to our minds. Thus often "some things, from a certain point of view, are more absolute than others; but considered in another way, they are more relative"; and Descartes adds, "we are examining here the series of things to be known, and not the nature of each one of them" (10:382–83).[52] Therefore the totality of the clear ideas is very far from constituting divine understanding. On the contrary, according to a doctrine that has always seemed obscure, but to which Descartes attached great importance, the eternal verities derive their being solely from the decree of God, just as the essences in Plato are created and nourished by the Sun of the Good. For, writes Descartes to Mersenne, "In God will and knowledge are one" (1:149). And in a letter written some days earlier: "Indeed, to say that these Verities are independent of God is the same as to speak of him as a Jupiter or a Saturn and make him subject to the Styx and the Fates. Do not fear, I beg you, to affirm and publish everywhere that it is God who has established these laws in nature, just as a king establishes laws in his kingdom." Far from reality being idealized to the point that it is made up only of ideas, it is ideas that here seem to be restored to reality. This is made all the more clear as Descartes continues: "They are all innate in our minds, just as a king would imprint his laws in

51 See *Philosophical Essays*, p. 195.
52 See ibid., p. 165.

the hearts of all his subjects, if he actually had the power to do so" (1:145). Thus, that two quantities equal to a third are equal to each other would not be a law of the mind but a law of the world. Here again it appears that geometry is a physics; and, related to that idea, although it is difficult to understand how, it appears that there is no infinite understanding, since God is only will, and understanding is thus limited by its very nature.

In short, not only does Descartes regard every mind, as soon as it makes a serious effort to think properly, as equal to the greatest genius, but he finds the human mind even in the most ordinary thinking. There is, in his eyes, a common wisdom—a wisdom that is to the mind what the eyes are to the body—much closer to authentic philosophy than is the kind of thinking that study produces, "since we see very often that those who have never worked hard at the study of letters judge things close at hand much more soundly and clearly than those who have been in constant attendance at the schools" (10:371).[53] Thus Descartes's great precept for attaining wisdom is not to study excessively. Perception itself, which has been considered by so many philosophers, beginning with Spinoza, as the lowest form of knowledge, is of the same nature as science, as we see in the famous passage about the piece of wax. "What is this piece of wax that cannot be understood except by the understanding or the mind? It is certainly the same that I see, touch, imagine. . . . Although it might have seemed so earlier, my perception is not, and never has been, an act of vision, or touch, or imagination, but is solely an inspection of the mind. . . . and thus I understand, solely by the power of judgment that resides in my mind, what I believed I saw with my eyes" (9:24–25).[54] Descartes explains this in the *Optics* by the comparison with the blind man who directly perceives the objects at the end of his stick, not the sensations that the pressure of the stick makes on his hand. This leads Descartes to construct a theory of sensations as signs, using the example of drawings in which we see not marks on paper but men and towns (6:113). And it is noteworthy that he uses almost the same terms he will later use, in the *Responses to the Fifth Set of Objections,* to explain that the lines drawn on the paper, far from giving us the idea of the triangle, are only signs of the real triangle (7:382). And so Descartes finds in perception a "natural geometry" and "an operation of thought that, although it is only a simple act of imagination, nevertheless contains a form of reasoning similar to that used by sur-

53 See ibid., p. 157.
54 See *Discourse on Method and the Meditations,* pp. 109–10.

veyors when, by standing in two different spots, they measure inaccessible places" (6:138).

Thus, although from a distance Descartes seemed to offer a coherent system befitting the founder of modern science, on looking into it more closely we no longer find anything but contradictions. And, what is more serious, these contradictions all seem to proceed from one initial contradiction. For it is not apparent what interest science could have for this founder of modern science, this man who had taken for his motto the maxim from the temple at Delphi thus put into verse by Seneca:

> Illi mors gravis incubat
> Qui notus nimis omnibus
> Ignotus moritur sibi.[55]

How could the man who had thus adopted the Socratic motto "know thyself" devote his life to the kind of research into physics that Socrates scoffed at? The obscurity is only deepened by the passage in which Descartes asserts that he mainly used his God-given reason to know God and know himself, adding that he "would not have been able to discover the foundations of his Physics if he had not sought them in this way" (1:144). Yet is it any wonder that we find in Descartes nothing but obscurities, difficulties, and contradictions? He himself warned his readers that they would find nothing else if they tried only to learn his view on such and such a subject, looking at it from the outside and in a piecemeal fashion. Cartesian thought is not something that one can comment on from the outside; every commentator must become, at least for a time, a Cartesian. But how does one become a Cartesian? To be a Cartesian is to doubt everything, and then to examine everything in order, without believing in anything except one's own thought insofar as it is clear and distinct, and without trusting the authority of anyone, even Descartes, in the least.

Let us therefore have no hesitation about imitating the Cartesian stratagem in commenting on Descartes. Just as Descartes, in order to form accurate ideas about the world in which we live, imagined another world that would begin with a sort of chaos and in which everything would be ruled by figure and movement, so let us imagine another Descartes, a Descartes brought back to life. This new Descartes would have at first neither genius, nor knowledge of mathematics and physics, nor force of

---

55 Death lies heavily on that man who, too well known by everyone, dies unknown to himself.

style; he would have in common with him only the fact of being a human being and of having resolved to believe only in himself. According to Cartesian doctrine, that is enough. If Descartes was not mistaken, such contemplation of one's own thought, starting from absolute doubt, ought, if it is freely conducted, to basically coincide with Cartesian doctrine, despite all differences and even all apparent contradictions. So let us listen to this fictitious thinker.

Part Two

We are living beings; our thinking is accompanied by pleasure or pain. I am in the world; that is, I feel that I am subject to some external thing that I feel is more or less subject to me in return. Depending on whether I feel this external thing submitting to me, or myself being subject to it, I feel pleasure or pain. All the things that I call objects—the sky, the clouds, the wind, stones, the sun—are primarily sources of pleasure insofar as they make my own existence manifest to me; they are sources of pain insofar as my existence finds its limit in them. Thus pleasure and pain are mixed with one another, as the poets have said; my pleasure cannot be so great that it may not be spoiled by the desire for an even greater pleasure:

> medio de fonte leporum
> Surgit amari aliquid quod in ipsis floribus angat.[1]

Conversely, pain is never tasted without some pleasurable sensation; for to breathe, run, see, hear, even to hurt myself is more than anything else to taste the pleasure that is, as it were, the tang of my very existence. For me the presence of the world is above all this mixed feeling. What the swimmer calls water is for him above all a feeling made up of the pleasure that comes from swimming and the pain induced by fatigue. Depending on whether, as he swims, he wants to go on swimming or to rest, the water will be more pleasurable or more painful, more friendly or more unfriendly, but, because the feeling is mixed, always treacherous. And, as in a mixture of indistinct noises I suddenly hear a few words pronounced by a

---

1 "Amid the fountain of delights something bitter springs up that torments us even among the flowers" (Lucretius *De Rerum Naturae* 4. 1133–34).

familiar voice, or on awakening perceive strange animal or human shapes in a rumpled piece of clothing, so in this indeterminate feeling does the swimmer perceive the water under his body and in front of his arms, or the runner perceive the ground under his feet, the air in front of his knees, on his face, and in his lungs. In my dreams, when I move toward joy or toward sadness, I summon up landscapes that are either luminous or dim; when I walk or run, my strength manifests itself to me in the form of clean and bracing air and springy ground, or my weariness makes itself known to me in the form of air that is oppressive and ground that is slippery. This feeling with its shadings of pleasure and pain, which is the only thing I can experience, is thus the fabric of the world. It is all that I can say about the world. If the swimmer thinks that the ambiguous feeling that makes the water present to him is the effect, or mark, or image of a coolness, a transparency, a resistance that is not constituted by that very feeling, he is saying more than he knows. So I can say nothing about the world. I cannot say, "This thorn hurts my finger," or even, "I have hurt my finger," or even, "I feel pain." As soon as I give a name to what I feel, I am saying, as Protagoras observed, more than I can know.

These things that are so intimately present to me are so only through the presence of this feeling that is inseparable from my very existence, which is revealed to me solely through them. But I would be too hasty if I concluded that outside of this feeling I can affirm nothing; for it seems that abstract truths, which are independent of it, are not undermined by my uncertainty about things. Arithmetical propositions are devoid of pleasure and pain; they are easily forgotten; but, if only I examine them, I find the prohibitions they contain irresistible. My thirst, which I feel just now through the medium of the oranges in front of me, cannot, even if I am dreaming, manifest itself in two pairs of oranges that add up to five oranges. My existence manifests itself to me through the medium of appearances, but it can appear to me only in certain ways; there are ways of appearing that do not define anything that can appear to me. Why will I not go out of my way if someone wants to show me a square that is twice the size of another square in regard to both the surface and the side? Because if, as I draw, I double the side of a square, I cannot prevent a quadruple square from appearing to me. A square that is twice the size of another in regard to both the surface and the side would be a square that I could neither reproduce, sketch, nor describe. It would not be a square with an unintelligible form, it would not even be a form.

The world is not transparent to me. Appearances are impenetrable insofar as they make present to me the feeling that creates out of them the density, the bittersweet savor of my own existence. For this savor is mine, but it is not something I have created. If nothing in me were alien to me, my thinking would be uncontaminated by pleasure and pain. But, insofar as this impenetrable thing is clear and defined for me, insofar as it manifests itself to me, it takes its form from me. Say that, half dreaming, I feel myself bathing in water "softer than sleep," as the poet says, and then, awakening, I feel that I am in my bed; the water and the bed are only particular forms of the indeterminate softness that makes them present to me. Why is it that I can grasp that two pairs of oranges make four oranges, and not that two pairs of oranges make five oranges? That's the way I am. I see no way of learning why I am like this, since I recognize that my thinking cannot give me information about anything except myself. No improvement in my thinking can teach me. (Not that improvement is forbidden to me.) Certain properties of a figure or of a combination of quantities cannot become evident to me without forms or additional quantities; the sum of the three angles of a triangle can be present in my mind solely by means of parallel lines and their accompanying properties, like the genie that appeared to Aladdin only by means of the marvelous lamp. But on the other hand, to make me see that a space cannot be enclosed by less than three straight lines, nothing is needed but the corresponding forms. Why? It is chance. What I call the world of ideas is no less chaos than the world of sensations. Ideas impose their ways of being on me, take hold of me, escape me. If, moreover, instead of utilizing forms so as to elicit their properties, I approach them in another way, e.g., by measuring them, nothing assures me that I will find the same properties; thus the renowned geometer Gauss[2] did not think it was pointless to measure the sum of the three angles of a triangle. If geometry, measurement, and action are in agreement, it is by chance. Everything is given over to Descartes's "evil genius," which is nothing but chance. Chance, not necessity. In other words, nothing that transpires in my consciousness has any reality other than the consciousness that I have of it; the only knowledge I can have is to be conscious of what I am conscious of. To know a dream is to dream it; to know a pain is to suffer it; to know a pleasure is to enjoy it. Everything is on the same level. It is useless for me to go from what is called the sensible plane to what

---

2 Karl Friedrich Gauss (1777–1855), German mathematician, one of the greatest mathematical geniuses of all time.

is called the intelligible plane; I know a property of a triangle when that property leaps to my eyes—or, more exactly, to my imagination—after I have made the appropriate constructions. If mathematical ideas give me a feeling of clarity and obviousness that sensations do not provide, it does not follow that this feeling exists independently of my consciousness of it. No thought, no action has more value for me than any other. Nothing makes any difference as long as I am bound by chance. Not that perhaps a scale of values, about which I know nothing, might not be applied to my thoughts; but even that is chance. Chance is clothed, disguised, in blue, in gray, in light, in hardness and softness, cold and heat, in the straight line and in the curve, in triangles, in circles, in numbers; chance is anything and everything. I am never conscious of anything except the trappings of chance; and this very thought, insofar as I am conscious of it, is chance. There is nothing else.

Is there nothing else? No, if nothing reveals itself to me as existing except insofar as I am conscious of it. Insofar as I am conscious of myself, I am anything whatever; what my consciousness reveals to me is not me but my consciousness of myself, just as it does not reveal things to me, but the consciousness that I have of things. I never know what it is that I am conscious of; I know only that I am conscious of it. But here is something that I do know: I am conscious; I think. And how do I know this? It is not an idea, a feeling among the ideas and feelings that occur in my mind. I feel that the sky is blue, that I am sad, that I am enjoying myself, that I move; I experience the feeling, but I know nothing about it. I think what I think; there is nothing else to know.

Nothing? Yes, there is something. What, then? Everything that I feel is illusion, for everything that presents itself to me without my receiving from it contact with real existence is trifling with me. And not only pleasure, pain, sensation, but consequently this being that I call me as well, which enjoys itself, suffers, and feels. All that is illusion. What does this mean? That all these things seem illusory? No; on the contrary, it means that these things create illusion, and consequently seem certain. I can hardly admit that this table, this paper, this pen, this feeling of well-being, and I myself are only things that I think—things that I think and that make a show of existing. I think them; they need me in order to be thoughts. But how? For I do not think what I want. And the things that I think delude me by their own power. So what do they borrow from me? Belief. It is I who think these things that produce illusion, and whether I think of them as certainties or as illusions, the spell that they cast over me remains intact. The power that I exercise over my own belief is not an illusion; it is through this power that I know that I think. Might what I take for my thought not be the thought of an Evil Genius? That could be so in regard to the things that I think, but not for the fact that I think them. And through this power of thinking—which so far is revealed to me only by the power of doubting—I know that I am. I have power, therefore I am [*Je puis, donc je suis*]. And in this flash of thought several things whose nature I did not previously know are revealed to me: doubt, thought, power, existence, and knowledge itself. Nevertheless, that is not a reasoned argument; I can resist this knowledge. Or rather, I can disregard it; I cannot reject it. For as soon as I reject any thought as illusory, in so doing I am thinking something that I do not derive from the thing that presents itself to my thought; for the only thing I can derive from my illusory thoughts is the illusion—that is, the belief— that they are true. To the extent that I receive an idea, I do not know if I accept it or if it merely presents itself; as soon as I reject an idea, even if it should be the idea that I am, at once I am. My own existence as I feel it is an illusion; but my existence as I know it is not a feeling but my creation. To exist, to think, to know are only aspects of a single reality: to be able to do something. I know what I do, and what I do is think and exist; for from the moment that I do something, I cause myself to exist. I am a thing that thinks. Will it be said that, without knowing it, I exist and perhaps do something else, apart from thinking? What does that mean? What would a power that I do not exercise consist of? Certainly an unknown god could make use of me without my knowing it with the intention of producing results about which I know nothing; but I do not produce those results. And as for knowing my own being, what I am is defined by what I can do. So there is one thing I can know: myself. And I cannot know anything else. To know is to know what I can do; and I know to the degree that I substitute "to act" and "to be acted upon" for "to enjoy," "to suffer," "to feel," and "to imagine." In this way I transform illusion into certainty and chance into necessity.

But this opposition between "to act" and "to be acted upon" is premature; for I know only one power, that of doubting—a power whose exercise nothing can obstruct. It is not that most (or, more accurately, all) of the objects and ideas I have decided to doubt have not seemed to grant me some power over them. At this very moment, it is I who move my pen over the paper. I make everything that I see disappear, reappear, or move by closing or reopening my eyes or turning my head. I can move most of the objects I touch from one place to another. I can walk, jump, run. But do I know that these eyes, this body, these objects exist? A power exercised over illusions can only be illusory. The belief these illusions inspire in me is something real, and therefore the power I exert over my belief is real; once again, I exist only through doubt. If later I come to be aware of having another power, it will certainly belong to me; but only the power of doubting defines me, for it alone is immediately known. However, don't I have the same power over some of the things I think as I have over my belief? Can't I create or destroy at least some of my own thoughts? Often I make up what I am thinking about, and I call this daydreaming; it would seem then that I have complete power over myself, that I play the role of Evil Genius in regard to myself. But this is not so. First of all, I never deceive myself. Even though I would like to, I can never arouse in myself the same belief in the existence of things in my daydreams as that inspired in me by what I call real things. Thus I recognize that my power over my belief is only a negative one; I can doubt, but I cannot believe. Then who produces these daydreams? Nothing assures me that it is I. If I have the feeling that I produce them, it is because even when they are painful they do not present themselves to me except to the extent that I accept them; but I can always say, of the fantastic series they form, what the events of his life inspired Figaro to say: "Why these things and not others?"[3] I can reject them, but if I do create them, it is by a power (quite different from the power of doubting) that does not give me certain proof that it exists.

Perhaps the things that I dream are as external to me as the things that I think I hear, see, or touch. Perhaps also what in the highest sense of the word I call "things" come from me as much as daydreams. Although it may be strange to say so, this supposition, if it were true, would make the power I think I have over things an illusory power; unexpected sensations or intentional ones, falling or running, all would be mine in the same way. It *is* true that events take me by surprise, even when they are desired; in what I perceive, even when it is pleasant, there is always something I have not desired, something that takes hold of me and imposes itself on me like an alien thing. This is what makes me almost invincibly convinced that, if my daydreams exist only for me, on the other hand this paper, this table,

3 Pierre-Augustin Caron de Beaumarchais, *The Marriage of Figaro*, Act 5: "Oh! Fantastic series of events! Why should they happen to me? Why these things and not others?"

the heavens, the earth, Paris, all exist independently of me. But this conviction is not a proof. I have never believed that my anger exists independently of me, and yet don't I get angry suddenly, often even when I want to remain calm? Do I have any reason to think that the blue of the sky, the white or gray clouds, the touch of the paper on my hand, or the warmth of the sun are more distinct from me than my anger, my worry, or my joy? And just as a feeling of anger is followed by a calm that I can think I have achieved, so light and colors are followed by a sensation of darkness that I think I produce, at the same time that my eyelids make contact, when I close my eyes. But it is easy to see that my irritation comes from me in the same way as the subsequent cooling of my anger, my fear in the same way as my boldness, my sadness in the same way as my joy. Similarly the darkness that I thought I produced and the feeling of my eyelids making contact are related to me in the same way that earlier the light and my open eyes were. Certainly, if the light tires me, darkness comes at once when I want it; and likewise legs, even aching ones, move immediately at the least desire to run. But the running that I want is one thing, the running that I feel is another. Nor did I want the darkness that accompanies the closing of my eyes to be strewn with spots. In a word, to want to feel is one thing, to feel is another. On the other hand, to want to refrain from making reckless judgments about all these things is to refrain from making reckless judgments. As long as it is a matter only of my thinking, and not of the things I think, the will is effective in itself, and its effect is simply what has been willed. Here willing and acting are one. And so, if joy and sadness, darkness and light belong to me in the same way, my thinking of these things belongs to me much more; it *is* me. What causes me to exist is not that I move but that I think of moving. What I call my power to move is only a relation between my desires and the sensations that seem after a fashion to be the response to my desires; thus my desire for a piece of fruit may have as its response the sensation of a piece of fruit in my mouth, or only the sensation of my outstretched arm. But I exercise no power in desiring, even if the response to my every desire were to be pleasure. And so the desire for darkness that makes me close my eyes in the presence of a blinding light is no more me than is the sensation of pain in my eyes. Neither alien to me nor an essential part of my being, desires, passions, sensations, and daydreams cannot be used as proof of any existence at all, not even—except insofar as I think them—of my own.

I can say the same about arithmetic, reasoning, or ideas. Thoughts such as these present themselves to me neither as daydreams, desires, nor perceived things; I find them only if I search for them, and then, since I have no power to change them, they are like an incorruptible treasure hidden in me. It is equally true that I learn nothing from thoughts of this sort except that I, who think them, exist. Thus what is true of the knowledge that I exist is true of all knowledge. I must give up the idea of learning by examining my thoughts. The things that I think cannot prove anything to me. I who think—I am the only proof. I am the only proof of my own existence, but also, if I can ever know anything other than myself, the only proof of the existence of that other thing. The only proof necessary. It was enough for me to set aside the supposition that anything exists to know at once that I exist; now I set aside the supposition that other things exist. I suppose that I alone exist. But who am I? A thing that exercises this power that I call thinking. Except through the free—in other words, real—exercise of this power, the being that I call me is nothing. So, in order to know myself, I must know the extent of this power. But what does that mean? This power no more allows of degrees than existence itself, which I have recognized is identical to it. I have power [je puis], as I exist, absolutely. A power such as I would attribute to a king, which is a relation between one thing and another (for example, between the king's words and the actions of his subjects) can be measured. But my power is not this shadow of power; it resides entirely in me, since it is that property of myself, which is me, whereby, for me, to decide and to act are the same thing.

All real power is infinite. If nothing but me exists, nothing exists except this absolute power. I depend on nothing but my will, I do not exist except insofar as I create myself, I am God. I am God, so, in regard to the things I make judgments about, I must exercise positively the same sovereign power that I exercised over myself negatively when I forbade myself to judge; that is, dreams, desires, emotions, sensations, arguments, ideas, or calculations must be only acts of my will. Have I ever attributed a greater power to God? But it's not so. I am not God. Although this power that I possess is by nature infinite, it has some limitations that I must recognize. My sovereignty over myself, which is absolute as long as I want only to suspend my thought, disappears as soon as it is a matter of giving myself something to think about. Freedom is the only power that I possess absolutely. Therefore, something other than myself exists. Since no power is limited by itself, it is enough for me to know that my power is not absolute to know that my existence is not the only existence. What is this other existence? It is defined by this imprint stamped on me, which deprives me of sovereignty although it leaves me freedom. But this freedom must be won. It would be absurd to imagine, on the one hand, my freedom as being inviolate, and on the other hand the things that I think as being similar (as a famous saying has it) to silent tableaux; for as soon as my thoughts are something other than acts of my will, I am bound by them. My belief is indeed bound, as the difficulty of doubting makes me only too aware, but more simply I—that is, my will—am bound by the things that I think.

Everything that appears in one way or another to my imagination—dreams, objects, or forms—is made present to me, as I have acknowledged, by a feeling in which pleasure and pain are mixed, that is, by the fact that I accept and reject this feeling at the same time. It is through this combined repulsion and acceptance, which seem to me to constitute the imagination, that my thoughts bind me; I am free only to the extent that I can disengage myself. To put it another way, however much the other existence has power over me through the intermediary of my thoughts, so much, through the same intermediary, do I have power over it. Consequently, although I cannot create a single one of my thoughts, all of them—from dreams, desires, and passions to reasoned arguments—are, to the extent that they are subject to me, signs of myself; to the extent that they are not subject to me, signs of the other existence. To know is to read this double meaning in any thought; it is to make the obstacle appear in a thought, while recognizing in that thought my own power. Not a phantom of power like the supernatural power that I sometimes believe I possess in my dreams, but the same power that causes me to exist, which I know is mine since I know that as soon as I think, I exist. Moreover I can say that all the thoughts that I call "clear" and "distinct" are true; that is, all the thoughts whose model is "I think, therefore I am." To the extent that I affirm thoughts of this kind, I am infallible; God himself guarantees me this infallibility. All my other thoughts were nothing but shadows; only the idea of God was able to prove an existence. So only the idea of God was the idea of a true, and consequently real, power; true power could not be imaginary. If the All Powerful could be a fiction of my mind, I myself could be a fiction, for I exist only to the degree that I participate in the All Powerful. Thus God himself guarantees me that, as soon as I think properly, I think the truth. I have no ground for supposing that this guarantee is false, that this other existence to which I believe I am subject is only an illusion imposed by God. True, if I come up against the limit of my power, all I will know, strictly speaking, is how God prevents me from being God; but that is all there is to know, since that knowledge is knowledge of the world.

And now I am able to know, and by the very means I had dimly foreseen, that is, by reading in the feeling of my own existence, in its coloring of pleasure and pain, its clothing of appearances and illusions, only the obstacle submitted to and overcome. To know in this way is to know myself, to know under what condition I am master of myself; this is the only knowledge that matters to me, and, furthermore, it is the only knowledge there is. It is my responsibility to acquire this knowledge, for I cannot receive it except from myself, and I am capable of giving it to myself. The authority of others can persuade me, the reasons of others convince me, the example of others guide me; but I can learn only from myself. Even God teaches me nothing; he only gives me a guarantee. So I have no one at all to help me, and have as working materials only some confused daydreams, some very clear ideas, some sensations as obscure as they are imperious—and none of these things, as I have experienced only too acutely, constitutes knowledge. I will no longer make the mistake of wanting to consider these things in themselves, for I never believed I grasped them without immediately realizing that I had hold of nothing. I now want only to try to find out what power I have over myself. Perhaps this is a never-ending undertaking, especially as it does not consist in my becoming aware little by little of a power that I might be exercising unbeknownst to myself—an idea that, only a short time ago, seemed plausible to me, but now seems just as absurd as the idea of any uncertainty about my own existence. I now know that to learn to know my own power is simply to learn to exercise it. Thus I recognize that becoming learned and attaining self-mastery are the same thing, although these two undertakings used to seem entirely distinct to me, and the first, moreover, seemed very much less important than the second. So it is possible that this twofold process of learning may never come to an end, that there will always be some power for me to acquire; perhaps too I will immediately come up against the limit of my power. But from now on I know that knowing depends only on myself; I will come to know nothing by chance.

But then what must I do to learn more than I know at present? For, up to now, I expected to learn only through studying what others had discovered before me; I regarded myself as an empty book in which nothing but a few axioms were written, but a book in which a page was filled by each day spent in study. It did not occur to me that one could receive fresh knowledge except from the outside, either by being taught it or by coming upon it by chance. Thus, although I did not give up hope of perhaps one day being able to make some new contribution to the wealth of acquired knowledge, I did not plan in advance how I would go about it; I simply intended to bring together, compare, and combine in every way I could think of the various kinds of knowledge acquired through study, and then, in the mass of probabilities, problems, and uncertainties generated by mixing them all together, I expected to have enough good luck to pick up some true ideas. How, indeed, could one embark on the search for truths as yet unsuspected except in a random fashion?

I knew, however, of one sure method of using the knowledge I possessed to prove the legitimacy of an assertion: it is what is called logic. But I observed that this method was only a simple form of analysis, absolutely sure because it was absolutely fruitless; I could use it to extract from the totality of my knowledge the knowledge that I might need, but it was powerless to make me acquire anything new. I was aware of only two ways of coming to know something new: the first is merely the chance encounters that are part of experience. Most of the scientific knowledge that study had brought me consisted of the answers that a few stubborn men who had asked all sorts of questions about the stars, the seas, the movements of bodies, light, heat, and all the transformations of inert or living bodies had had the good luck to obtain. I found the other means of learning in the almost miraculous power of geometers; they draw a triangle, recall some of its properties, draw as if at random or by inspiration other lines whose properties they also state, and that is enough for a hitherto unknown property of the triangle to be suddenly called forth, as if by magic. But, though the proofs forced me to accept this new property, strictly speaking I understood nothing about it. If perhaps I thought I might one day be able to add something to the totality of mathematical knowledge, I did not expect to invent proofs instead of being subject to them. I merely supposed that when I combined figures, properties, and formulas—with a little help from a certain instinctive skill—a new property would sometimes miraculously appear by itself, chance playing the role of an instruction manual for me. If I had been convinced then that neither study, nor experience, nor the elements of chance in mathematics can provide anything else but the illusion of knowing, I would have given up the idea of knowing anything once and for all.

But is it permissible to resign myself like this, now that I have put knowledge in my possession by defining it as knowledge of myself, of my power over myself, of the conditions of this power? It would be cowardice at this point to give up trying to satisfy myself about everything. This is not to say that I have my heart set on answering every question that could be put to me; I used to believe, with regard to any problem whatever, that to know was to solve the problem; now I realize that it means to know how the problem concerns me. To actually answer a question, or to know under what condition it is in my power to answer it, or to know that it is insoluble for me—these are three ways of knowing, and for the same reason they constitute knowledge. I will not derive this knowledge, which is without gaps, from any source other than myself. I will neither try to find some method nor depend on chance with an eye to bringing forth some entirely new truth; a truth of that sort is only a chimera, in my view, and the only method available to me is analysis. That is, what I know now—that I think, that I exist, that I depend on God, that I am subject to the world (knowledge that I have had to carefully develop even though it is intuitive and one with the act of knowing)—contains everything that I have to know; I must find in it the means to satisfy myself on any subject whatever.

Does it follow that, thanks to this knowledge, I can either solve every problem or recognize it as insoluble? For instance, I shall ask myself what this piece of paper is on which I am writing. Is it something other than the impressions of color or touch that I think I receive from it? Or is this question beyond my scope? But I find that I am ignorant on both counts. Before I try to resolve this contradiction, I want to examine more carefully what I already know about the nature of the world with regard to me. The knowledge of myself that is given me by the sole fact that I think, would, if I were God, be the totality of knowledge; but I remain impenetrable to myself insofar as I do not create myself by the act of thinking, that is, to the extent that I am subject to the imprint of a world. As I have recognized, the world presses on me with all the weight of aversion, desire, and belief, leaving me no other power than that of refusal. And what can I refuse? For instance, just now I am enjoying a breath of purer and fresher air,[4] I desire to be in the countryside, take a walk, and feel the spring breeze; at the same time an

---

4 Weil is composing the dissertation in her seventh-floor room in her family's apartment overlooking a vista of Paris that includes the Pantheon, to which she will refer later. Apparently a fresh breeze has just blown through the open window, causing her to respond with a wish to take a walk in the countryside.

overriding conviction makes me believe in the existence of this overcast sky and this noisy city; and, in the midst of all this, I feel a vague anxiety in regard to some absent friends. Does my will have any power over my enjoyment, my desire, my belief, or my anxiety if I want to get rid of them or change them? Not the slightest. All I can do is refuse my assent to what I believe or desire. The only thing I have that is really mine is my judgment. I do not have sovereign power over my thoughts; I am only their arbiter. Does this mean that I possess only the ineffectual freedom of approving or disapproving of myself? If this is so, I can hope for no other virtue than the one that, according to the poet,[5] allowed Medea to "see the best course and approve it," while pursuing the worst; nor can I hope for any other knowledge than the intuitive knowledge of my existence and my dependence on some unknown thing, and the consciousness of my passions. But this phantom of freedom could not even be called freedom; I know that I am free only to the extent that I am actually master of myself. And in truth even if, when I feel overwhelmed by desire for vengeance, I am free only not to consent to what the poet calls this anger "sweet as honey,"[6] still the exercise of my freedom is not something unimportant. However narrow its scope, my power is effective, my refusal is an act. The only thing I possess is my judgment, but the exercise of my judgment changes something. It is not possible to shape the desires and beliefs by which the world takes hold of me; so at least my judgment encroaches on the world itself. The almost insurmountable difficulty that a free judgment costs me proves this. The world weighs on my free will in such a way as to make me, if I do not resist, the plaything of my impulses; in return, the exercise of my free judgment cannot leave the world untouched. As a result, however much the contents of my passions have a hold on me, to that extent they also allow me a grasp; and thus the world, although it does not depend on me, ceases to be something that exercises an inexplicable mastery over me. Rather, as I had foreseen, it is the obstacle. The world is the obstacle; this means that the act of doubting (which causes me to exist, and to experience the weight of the other existence at the same time that I exert all my power to resist it) does indeed imply all knowledge for me, but it does not give me the means to solve the most insignificant problem having to do with anything outside my power.

5 Ovid *Metamorphoses* 7. 20.
6 Homer *Iliad* 18. 109.

Earlier I imagined there were only two ways of learning: selecting from acquired knowledge, and unexpectedly encountering knowledge unconnected with my thought; but the world, which does not depend on me in any way and which at the same time I can change, must allow knowledge the same kind of grasp as it allows action. To the extent that I can change the world (and to the extent that, consequently, knowing the world is only a way of knowing myself), I know by means of analysis; to the extent that the world does not depend on me, I have no way of satisfying myself about questions concerning the world, such as what this piece of paper is. Therefore I must invent a kind of analysis unknown to logicians, an analysis that is the source of an orderly progression. But isn't that absurd? What could such a progression be based on? It must be based on the world. (Indeed, as far as I am concerned, the necessity of learning only little by little is evidence that a world exists.) Or, more exactly, this progression must be based on the charter that binds the world and me, namely that, since the only thing I possess is my freedom, I exercise only an indirect power.

What is the nature of this power? How is it that, without its having any effect except on myself (and that only a negative one), I act on the world at the same time? That is difficult to know, for I can neither deduce, explain, nor verify the grasp that I have on the world; I can only make use of it. But what constitutes using it? Must I make up my mind to act blindly? But to act blindly is not to act, it is to suffer. And to possess a power that I do not control would be to exercise no power at all. So I need a way of taking control of my own action. Where shall I look for it? In my thought; in any case there is nothing, at least with regard to me, that is not thought. Or at least I can learn about what is not my thought from my thinking alone. My thinking proved my own existence; my thinking proved the existence of the world. My thinking must also prove that I act on the world. As sense impressions are instrumental in my being subject to the world, I must find another kind of thought to serve as a tool for changing it. It is by means of thoughts of this sort that I will define the passageway that the world allows me. What are these thoughts? The "I think, therefore I am" is of no use to me here; I find myself in a new realm, confronting a new kind of knowledge. Up to this point, to know meant to make a thought clear. When I said "I think, therefore I am," I knew that I existed; I knew it immediately, in a perfect and complete way that satisfied me so entirely that I do not conceive divine thought to be any different; for, by one and the same act, I thought, existed, and knew, so that in me, as in God, knowing and willing were one. At the very moment that I conceived my existence, it made itself clear to me in such a way that I cannot even think that there might be reason to know more; for I exist because I think, I think because I will to do so, and the will is its own reason for being. But the knowledge by which I grasp something other than myself is entirely different; there is no longer any question of asking for something to be made clear. The grasp that the world offers me does not depend on me, and whatever that grasp might be, there is no reason for me to think that it must be what it is. To a high degree it gives me—or will give me, when I know what it is—the occasion to ask Figaro's eternal question, "Why these things and not others?" and to give myself the only answer that this question allows: "That's the way it is." I must accept the relationship that exists between my action and things, and likewise I must accept as knowledge the thoughts that determine this relationship; from now on, knowing is far from being the same as willing. Thus, when it is a matter of the world, it is useless to ask myself questions. What, then, ought I to question? The world? My actions must be guided by it, but, although the world holds fast to my thought and never lets it go, it would be difficult for the world to guide or enlighten me, for guiding and enlightening are acts of the mind.

Since the world cannot teach me and I have to instruct myself, I will go and ask oracles about things; I will not consult mute things, nor myself who am ignorant, but I will go to this third, ambiguous being that is a composite of myself and the world acting on each other. This seems to have been what the Greeks did at Delphi; they questioned this point of intersection between matter and a mind in the person of a woman whom they probably thought they had reduced to being nothing more than that. Since I wish to believe only in myself, I will consult this bond of action and reaction between the world and my thought in myself alone. I will name this bond the imagination, as opposed to the understanding, the name of the "I" who thinks, and the sensibility, my name insofar as I am acted upon. Henceforth the imagination alone will be my teacher—the imagination that is the sole cause of all my uncertainties and errors. For the understanding cannot deceive me, inasmuch as by itself it teaches me nothing except *I think, therefore I am;* and sense impressions cannot deceive me since it is always true that I feel what I feel. If I were only understanding and sensibility, I would know that I see a flash of lightning or hear thunder almost in the same way I know that the words I see in silent film titles are uttered by the voice of a man or a woman. My impressions and my thoughts would not be all blended together, and, outside of the certainty that I exist, I would have neither opinions, beliefs, prejudices, nor passions; my wisdom would be negative, but perfect. I would be always like a spectator at a badly staged play in which the storm, riot, or battle is represented in a ludicrous way. But this supposition is absurd, so contrary is it to reality, for the only way sense impressions reach my mind is by causing a disturbance in it, and, far from being an understanding to which senses have been added like telephone operators to a staff headquarters, I am first and foremost nothing but imagination. From the fact that thunder crashes it follows, not that I become aware of a sound, but that my thinking is disturbed at its source; my will is no longer my own, since in grasping the world it is delivered over to it and, losing in effectiveness everything that it loses in autonomy, it becomes fear, anxiety, aversion, desire, hope. In default of a thunderclap, a faint whisper is enough to establish this mutual hold of the world and myself on one another—a hold that is indissoluble except by my death. The world and my mind are so thoroughly intermingled that, if I think that I conceive one of the two separately, I attribute to it what belongs to the other; thus, confused thoughts fill my whole soul. The slightest disturbance of the senses hurls me into the world, but, as I am not given the direct grasp on the world that I am groping for, my will, far from being active, lapses into passion. I then attribute more or less influence to this will of mine depending on whether it is more or less thwarted; I regard my existence as constituted by this imaginary power that comes only from the world and, in return, I endow the world with passions. In this hand-to-hand struggle the world is always the winner, but then the world always deceives me. I must leave the world if I want to get a foothold in it. I must not make a frontal attack and try to throw my arms around it, but use cunning, search for a hold and grasp it obliquely.

Earlier I was able to disengage myself from the chaos that results from the intermingling of the world and myself. By doubting I momentarily rendered my mind blind and deaf to assaults from the outside, and I silenced the tumult of the imagination that prevented me from recognizing in myself not a being who eats, walks, stops, loves, and hates but a being who thinks, and I finally came to know that I exist. At this point I know everything that I can know by means of pure understanding. Now I no longer have to suspend the imagination; rather, I must give it free rein so that I may learn from it. It is in this knot of action and reaction that attaches me to the world that I must discover what is my portion and what it is that resists me. In this regard the impulse that, at the slightest creaking sound, sends me forth to re-create the world misleads me every time; for the impressions that follow it and through which it is satisfied or thwarted— or rather satisfied and thwarted at the same time—are fortuitous. Therefore I must not study the imagination as action, that is, in relation to its effects, but only as thought. The world is not outside my thought; it is above all what is not me in me. I must not try to go out of myself in order to define the obstacle.

Thus I am going to put questions to the imagination. Not in order to make it speak, for it speaks enough by itself; I hear nothing else in me; I was able to silence it only momentarily in order to listen to pure mind. But I must learn to listen to it, to distinguish when it is speaking the truth. This I can do, for it is only a matter of distinguishing, in thoughts in which the imagination plays a role, those in which it is uncontrolled (or rather, in which it leads me) from those in which the mind holds the reins. For the imagination by its nature has two aspects. It shows me either the presence of an external world that I cannot comprehend, or my grasp on that world. But the imagination cannot give me information about the world; if I rely on the imagination, the world will never be anything except a cause of sadness or joy, that is (since I always think of a cause as being of the same nature as its effect), a will foreign to mine, formidable, well or ill disposed; it will never be the obstacle. For there is no obstacle except for someone who acts, and there is no possibility of action for the mind dominated by the imagination. The imagination represents, or rather constitutes, the grasp that I have on the world, the correspondence that exists, through the union of the soul and the world, between a thought of mine and a change outside me. But this correspondence does not amount to an act; I am merely able to utilize it in order to act.

It is according to this dual nature of the imagination that I am going to examine everything in me that has to do with imagination. So I am summoning back the multitude of thoughts whose presence I forced myself to forget: the city, clouds, noises, trees, forms, colors, odors, emotions, passions, desires. All of these thoughts have a meaning for me again; the question is to know what that meaning is. The imagination seems uncontrolled in all thoughts that bear the mark of passion, that sometimes impose themselves on me as forcibly as sense impressions, that then change, as I change, and escape me. Thus at times something at a bend in the road frightens me; what is it? Not a sense impression; impressions have no more access to my thought than do the strange designs formed by the letters when I am reading. What frightens me is the idea, formed by the imagination out of what I see, of a hostile and powerful will that threatens me. A few moments later my imagination forms another idea: that of some harmless being, a tree. Sometimes, afterward, I can play with my fear, evoke it again if I want, but then it either escapes me altogether or it seizes me in spite of myself. In all the things that surround me and that I would like to believe are independent of me I observe similar games of the imagination. In every way the ideas that I have of these things clearly show the presence of the world in me and not my grasp on the world, for they are formed in me at least partly in spite of myself. I am subject to them, so they bring me nothing but ignorance.

But let us continue. Are there no other thoughts in which the imagination plays a part? Yes, there are many others. When I count these same things that allow the imagination to dominate me, I come across an idea of another kind, one that does not impose itself on me, that exists only through an act of my attention, and that I cannot change; it is, like the "I think, therefore I am," transparent and invincible. This idea of number and ideas like it replace the random changes to which other ideas are subject with an orderly progression that originates in themselves. They are primarily useful for kinds of reasoning that, although clear and immutable like them, seem to force me to accept what they present almost in the same way the senses do, and as it were throw truths at me. But sometimes I also find an order among these ideas that lets me form one idea after another in such a way that each is marked by the same clarity that the initial idea had by itself. It is in this way that I think of the number two after the number one, the number three after the number two.

If I try to discover how much trust should be put in the thoughts harbored by the imagination, I find that the clear ideas alone do not represent the encroachment of the world on me, since they are made present to me only by an act of my own attention. Nevertheless, the imagination plays a considerable part in them, for they are not, like the idea of "I think, therefore I am," entirely transparent. Why is seven a prime number? Why not nine? I don't know. That's how it is. These ideas are not self-explanatory. I must take them as they are. Consequently, they proceed from something external to me, in other words, from the world; and since the imagination is the only intermediary between the world and me, they proceed from the imagination. But the imagination does not form clear ideas insofar as it makes thought subject to the world; on the contrary, it forms them insofar as, guided by the mind, it opens a passageway into the world for the mind. So this is the way the mind arms itself against chance. There would be no room for chance if my thoughts left everything outside of me untouched, or (what in this connection comes to the same thing) if they left an exact imprint of themselves in things. But the clear ideas leave on the world a mark that bears no resemblance to them. I, however, constantly try to find such a resemblance, and to a greater or lesser degree think I have found it. This is the origin of superstitions, passions, and every kind of folly, in all of which thought is handed over to chance. But the nature of the mind is to eliminate chance. That is its task; it is the only thing left for it to do. It is a negative task, for in posing the "I think, therefore I am," the mind gave all it could of a positive nature. But here the mind finds what it can use against chance; for its passions will give way to a will that, despite the condition to which the world reduces it, will imprint itself directly in things, provided that what it wills is only the kind of change that it is capable of bringing about, and that constitutes its mastery over the world. So from now on clear ideas, offspring of the docile imagination, will be my only support.

It is true that this support seems very fragile, for these ideas are obviously insufficient. It cannot be otherwise; if the grasp on the world to which they correspond were not insufficient, it would constitute direct domination; I would not be subject to the world, and my mind would remain pure, without conflict. On the contrary, the world limits this sovereign power over itself that is the mark of the mind. It reduces the mind to being capable of only partially changing the external existence by which it feels held. But the action of the mind is the very essence of the mind; and if the world can thus reduce the mind to being merely a finite thing, the world is the stronger, and the mind perishes. But in itself this partial action is not action, it does not define me, it is at the disposal of infinite thought. Although the mind is reduced to exercising a wretchedly ineffective grasp, it becomes itself again by its power of infinitely compounding this finite action. Through this power the mind escapes the domination of the world and becomes the equal of the world. In this way the very insufficiency of the clear ideas is evidence of their value for me. A clear idea does not constitute knowledge; I demonstrate that I know only when I add a clear idea to itself and conceive that such addition is endless. Thus I add one to one. What I know in this way is not the world; a series is only a model or a plan of action for me. But this model is the model of real action, that is, action that nothing limits, that is infinite by right and makes me in a way equal to God. Thus, at least to the extent that the world is subject to my action, order gives me the power to hold the world as a whole before my eyes, to examine it, and to be assured that it in no way surpasses my thought.

If I now examine what constitutes the grasp that the world allows me and that the clear ideas will help me to define, I find that it consists simply of what I call straight motion. I will not try to explain what motion is, since, except for my own thought (from which it does not proceed), nothing is more clearly self-evident. Thus the world, this unknown source of the thoughts produced in me by the senses and the imagination together, is defined as something on which I act through the intermediary of straight motion. This idea of straight motion, understood in a way consistent with the infinite power whereby I add one action to another, is simply the idea of the straight line. Hence the world is once again defined as that which receives the straight line. And now (since in my hand-to-hand struggle with the world I decided to conceive of it as a wrestler, so to speak, like me, but one with countless heads) I am going to combine one straight motion with another, one straight line with another. For instance, I will imagine that I am pulling an object by a string and that this object is at the same time drawn in another direction or held back by an edge; it will only be able to move at an angle in relation to the direction in which I am pulling it. This gives us the definition of the oblique line, which is to geometry what the number two is to the series of numbers. If I now suppose that the object I am moving is no longer pulled in some direction or other but is connected to a fixed point, I define the circle; if I suppose it is connected to two fixed points, I define the ellipse. This is a rough outline, and for the present I cannot take the series further. But at least I understand from the very outset that, if I consider the series from a slightly different point of view, the relationship of one straight line to another that is parallel to it plays the role of the number one. The relationship between two straight lines that intersect is next in the order of complexity; the distance between the straight lines is no longer constant, but changes like the series of numbers; now is the time to state Thales' famous theorem on which analytic geometry is based.[7] All other lines are defined in the same way, in relation to the straight line, by

---

7 Parallel lines cut proportionate segments on other lines.

their distance at each point from the straight line. This is how the sequence of numbers—in other words, arithmetic—is applied to geometry. Actually, it is not appropriate to apply arithmetic itself to geometry; rather, we must use an arithmetic carried to the second power that has the same relation to the second type of series (which is said to be appropriate for gaining knowledge of the world) that simple arithmetic has to the first type of series, which defines my action. This other kind of arithmetic, which is called algebra, is formed by substituting multiplication for addition as the generative principle of the series.

This is the sort of structure of ideas that I must build before I turn my mind toward the world. I have thus the means to replace the ideas that the deceptive imagination makes me read in sensations. I will now suppose that this house, which seems to me to be a mysterious and treacherous being, is merely the object of my action, the resistance my action meets with. I can conceive of such resistance only as being similar to the action that I apply to it, that is, not as thought, will, or passion, but as movement. And in order to represent what I am in relation to the world, I will suppose that, in opposition to the single movement that I control, the world offers an infinitely complex movement that is to motion in a straight line what the number the mathematicians call infinity is to the number one, the movements that correspond to the oblique line, the circle, and the ellipse being like the numbers two, three, and four. But the only way I can clearly conceive of this infinitely compounded movement is to conceive of an indefinite number of impulses in a straight line that are combined, and to conceive of each of them separately, on the model of the motion that I have at my disposal. I will suppose there is an indefinite quantity of simple motions in the world, and I will define each of them, like my own, by a straight line. That is, insofar as the direction of the straight line is changed in the world, I will suppose that it is distorted, twisted out of shape by its countless sisters. I will also define this motion as uniform; in short, I will suppose that the initial impulse is reproduced endlessly, always in the same form. In this way the part played by the world is reduced to that which distorts, halts, accelerates, or retards a straight and uniform motion. I can then reduce this part again by considering it afresh as a straight and uniform motion. In this way I can analyze the world endlessly. It is not that I hope to achieve a result; it is the nature of my condition that I can never exhaust the world. I will never succeed in bringing the world back to straight motion. But at least I have learned that there is no limit to my analysis, that it is always valid, that I can always find that the world is made up of one movement, then another, then another. In this way I enter into a relation with the world—not, it is true, as one man does with another, but as a man does with a multitude. In the same way that a movement in the world is the response to one kind of thought in me (which I call will), so I assume that the thoughts that I call sense impressions are my response to this multitude of movements. But this multitude no longer frightens me, now that I create it by adding one unit to another. I see clearly that the direction my thought gives it must immediately become unrecognizable because of all the movements that are combined in it; but I also see that that direction is combined in its turn with movements that I am subject to, and in this way I conceive that it may be possible for me to direct them. I begin to envisage how one can learn to tack about on this sea.

Is this physics accurate? I can't swear that it is. For its basic assumption is that all the changes in my impressions are the result of movements in the world, straight-line movements. But the very idea of motion proceeds from the imagination, and although it is clearer than all the other ideas the imagination plays a part in, it is no less ambiguous; for the idea of motion, like the imagination itself, has some of the characteristics of both me and the world. Thus a straight line is both one and divisible; unity is the sign of me in it. When I connect the idea of a movement with an act of will, I can say in two senses that the movement is continuous. In the act of will—in the project that is intended—the movement is one from start to finish. On the other hand, no sooner is the movement accomplished than I think of it as dissolved and, far from being one, it constantly begins over again. Thus, through movement, my will is as it were dispersed in time. But that is what constitutes the part of the world in me. It is this dual nature of my action that is found as it were mirrored in every kind of order, for instance in the sequence of numbers. Therefore I can say that the world as a whole is potentially contained between the numbers one and two. "One" and "two"—these may be regarded as forming a pair of pincers with which to grasp the world. But if my thought, insofar as it is joined to the world, is thereby as it were cut up into pieces, constantly outside of itself, it is because the world is that which is endlessly exterior to itself.[8] What

8 That is, matter is characterized by divisibility, the mind by unity. Weil's way of expressing this comes from Alain, according to whom material things are "always separated and formed of parts exterior to one another." See Alain, *Elements de philosophie*, p. 48.

gives unity to movement—direction—comes from the mind; if I try to discover what remains of movement apart from direction, I find it is juxtaposition, and juxtaposition belongs to the world. In the world everything is set apart from everything, everything is unrelated to everything, everything is neutral with respect to everything. If there is a reason why in my thought, insofar as it is joined to the world, nothing is immediate, it is because in the world everything is immediate.[9] In short, what comes from me in movement is the fact that it is directed; what does not come from me is that it is extended; and what constitutes the world is extension. And one cannot say that the world is defined in this way only insofar as it is an obstacle for me, and consequently only in relation to me. If the world is an obstacle for me, it is so to the degree that it is joined to my thought; to that degree thought must conform itself to the world, must follow the proper nature of the world, which has no relation to the mind. What acts as an obstacle to me in the world is the world itself. The world is what it is, and it does not make thought its model when it unites with it; this is why it is an obstacle to thought. Thus I can say that the world, in itself, is simply extended substance. In attributing lines and directed movements to the world, the ideas of geometry and physics not only go beyond what I can know; they are not even true. Does this mean that they do not teach me anything? Strictly speaking, they cannot be said to teach me anything, since I know everything there is to know when I know that the world is extension. Still, they do teach me—not insofar as I am understanding, but insofar as I am also imagination. They help me to suppose that, in those impressions in which I originally read thoughts that are alien to me, hidden thoughts, the true text is extension.

Is this the ultimate form of wisdom? Can I never do more than suppose extension? That would be a very partial, barren kind of wisdom, lacking any positive content, stemming purely from mistrust. For as long as the wild imagination makes me think that I see the most fantastic things in sensations and makes me conjure up a god in every thought, it is useless for me to try to counter this eloquent madness with the simple supposition that what is actually signified by sensations is extension. The faculty of

9 Weil is punning on two possible philosophical meanings of the word "immediate." Sometimes things are called "immediate" because they are so connected that they need no mediation. Sometimes, less frequently, they are called "immediate" because they are so separate that no mediation is possible. The word is used in the first sense in the first clause, and in the second sense in the second.

reason would then be set aside and, being separated from the imagination, could not prevent it from being given free rein. I am always a dual being, on the one hand a passive being who is subject to the world, and on the other an active being who has a grasp on it; geometry and physics help me to conceive how these two beings can be united, but they do not unite them. Can I not attain perfect wisdom, wisdom in action, that would reunite the two parts of myself? I certainly cannot unite them directly, since the presence of the world in my thoughts is precisely what this powerlessness consists of. But I can unite them indirectly, since this and nothing else is what action consists of. Not the appearance of action through which the uncontrolled imagination makes me blindly turn the world upside down by means of my anarchic desires, but real action, indirect action, action conforming to geometry, or, to give it its true name, work.

It is through work that reason grasps the world itself and masters the uncontrolled imagination. This would not be possible if I knew the world by pure understanding. But the uncontrolled imagination that I want to shape in accordance with reason is none other than the docile imagination, which teaches me geometry, or rather is the instrument I use in doing geometry; there is only one kind of imagination. The simple imagination and the one with complex heads are the same thing, the mutual grasp of the world and myself; it is seen as one or the other depending on whether it submits chiefly to the world or chiefly to me. Only through the intermediary of the world, through the intermediary of work, do I reunite them; for if through work I do not unite the two parts of myself, the one that undergoes and the one that acts, I at least can cause the changes I undergo to be produced by me, so that what I am subject to is my own action. This was impossible as long as I could only desire, since the response to the desire for any kind of happiness is only a movement in the world, a movement that is entirely unrelated to happiness. But if I bring my will to bear only on the idea of a direction, a motion conforming to that act of will immediately follows it; my will leaves its living imprint in the world. But that is not enough; it is necessary to find intermediaries that connect the straight-line motion I alone can produce to this complex change that I want to be conveyed to my senses. I must use cunning, I must impede myself by using obstacles that steer me where I want to go. The first of these obstacles is the imagination itself, this tie, this knot between the world and me, this point of intersection between the simple movement that I have at my command and the infinitely complex movement that represents the world for my understanding. The point of intersection of these two kinds of movement is a thing that receives the movement; it is an extended thing, a body. I call it my body, and, in the highest sense of the word, the body. In it, and in the world to the extent that I take hold of it by work, the two kinds of imagination are reunited.

They are completely joined in my thought; in fact (as I now recognize) they have been joined ever since the first thoughts I can remember having formulated. For when I reviewed my thoughts I was wrong to see in some of them only imagination guided by the understanding—the kind of imagination that determines geometry—and in others only passive sensibility and the kind of imagination that is deceptive. In this latter class I ranked, with passions and dreams, the thoughts of all the things present around me: this room, this table, these trees, my body itself. Now I recognize that the two kinds of imagination, which are found separately in the emotions and in geometry, are united in the things I perceive. Perception is geometry taking as it were possession of the passions themselves, by means of work. It is impossible for me to directly experience my own action, since this is the condition that the world imposes on me. But, at least, instead of taking impressions as signs of fantastic beings, I can take them merely as intermediaries for grasping my own work, or rather the object of my work: the obstacle, extension. This is what perception consists of, as can be seen by the famous example of the blind man's stick. The blind man does not feel the different pressures of the stick on his hand; he touches things directly with his stick, as if it were sensible and formed part of his body. Right now I feel the paper at the end of my pen—even more so if I close my eyes. The pressure of the penholder on my hand—the only thing, it seems, I should feel—I must pay attention to in order to notice, just as I need to pay attention to see glazes of red or yellow pigment on the canvas that portrays the Gioconda, instead of seeing the skin of a woman. What sensations present to the mind is never themselves but an idea that corresponds to the disturbance they cause in it. When I respond with work, rather than with feelings of joy or sadness, to the assaults of the world that I call sensations, they provide the mind with nothing but an object for work. Thus the blind man, far from purely and simply being subject to sensations of contact, as we are apt to think, uses his stick as a hand and touches, not perceptible matter, but the obstacle. And conversely, for each of us the blind man's stick is simply his own body. The human body is like a pincer for the mind to grasp and handle the world. But—to take things in their proper order—I am not naturally the master of my body. I must take possession of it. To each of my thoughts are joined various movements of my body; thus, when I am afraid, my body runs. But I determine only a few of these movements; all that I can do is impart a straight-line motion to certain parts of my body. But although I do not determine more complicated movements, my body does. It deflects, according to its own structure, the direction that I give it. I must learn to use this deflection, to turn the obstacle to account in order to make up for my lack of power. Thus I do not know how to impart a circular movement, but I have the remedy for that, since I am hindered in the very act of moving my arm in a straight line by the attachment of my arm to my shoulder. In addition, since the body's extension puts several straight movements at my command, I can combine them; but first I separate them and, just as I do in a problem, I break the difficulty down into several parts in order to consider each element of it separately; in the same way I learn to move only the limb that I want to move, and not the whole body, by a thought. Then, by a kind of geometry in action, I combine these movements according to an order leading from the simple to the complex. It is not the number three that teaches me about the number three, nor the circle that teaches me about the circle, but the number one and the straight line. In the same way, if I am afraid, my body knows how to run; but if I want to know how to run, I learn not by running but by training myself in the separate motions of raising my knees and lengthening my stride, exercises that no more resemble running than the straight line resembles the circle. This intermediary between geometry and work is gymnastics. I learn to use my senses in a similar way, for all my senses are kinds of touch. More accurately, I see only by acting and touching; thus, as Descartes's famous analysis shows, I seize each object with my two eyes, as if with two sticks. As soon as I have taken possession of my body in this way I no longer only conceive, as geometry allowed me to do, that one can tack about in this sea of the world; I do tack about in it. Not only do I have a grasp on the world, but my thought is, as it were, a component part of the world, just as the world, in another way, is part of my thought. From now on I have a share in the universe; I am in the world.

That, however, does not satisfy me. The body is not what is needed for work. For work consists, as has been said, of this: if I am to feel what I want, I must employ movements that are in themselves indifferent to what I want. But if these movements are in themselves unrelated to what I want to feel, they are not unrelated to what I do feel; pleasure or pain is attached to each of them, and I must take this into consideration. Thus I cannot put my hand under a heavy stone in order to lift it. In addition, it is true that the structure of my body sometimes helps me, as in running or throwing, but at other times it hinders me; it is an obstacle that sometimes leads me whither I want, sometimes not, and I cannot throw it away and replace it by another. Thus I need other human bodies, so to speak, human bodies that have no feeling, that I can use anywhere, that are at my disposal, that I can take up, put aside, and take up again, bodies in short that perfectly correspond to the indirect nature of work. I am in possession of these simpler human bodies that, out of the blend of sensibility and work, retain only the characteristics that make them suitable for work; they are tools. Thus the movement conceived by the mind is not only cast in the unchangeable mold of this first tool that is attached to me (my body); it is also cast in the form of tools properly so called, whose structure I can change as I like. Moreover, although they extend my reach, these tools play the same role in regard to me as the body itself. They are obstacles fashioned in such a way as to transform the impetus I give into more complex movements. The attachment of my arm to my body lets me make a circle; this transformation of straight motion is perfect for the peasant when he has put a scythe at the end of his arm. The wheel and the winch let me make circles wherever I want, while those that I make with my arm always have my shoulder as a center. The knife grinder gets the circular movement of his wheel by raising and lowering his foot perpendicularly to the ground, that is, through a straight motion. The lever, on the other hand, transforms one vertical movement into another. One could try in this way to rank tools in a series according to a geometrical order. Moreover, these tools themselves, like the body, allow me only the simplest movements; the power they provide me with differs only in degree from the power furnished by the body. Therefore, if I want to further extend my domain, I have only one means of doing so, which is to combine simple tools. In this way human action increasingly approaches the infinite complexity of the world, without ever attaining it. Man creates machines with the wheel and the lever, just as he constructs any given point of a conic section with compass and ruler. It is in this way that industry is an extension of work.

It is in this way that I can distinguish several ways of knowing the world. I grasp it through work. The pen that I am moving over the paper serves as an intermediary between me and the world. Since the sensations it gives me are of no interest to me in themselves, I relate them only to my action and to the paper that receives it. In the same way, I hide the Pantheon by my shutter with a movement of my head, then, with a reverse movement, uncover it, and in this way grasp that the shutter is between my eyes and the Pantheon. Again, it is in this way that I relate the sensations that I get from my two eyes to one Pantheon, whose relief, distance, or size I determine by changing this double contact of my eyes through my own movement. For, although this kind of exploration is made at a distance, puts in motion only my own body, and is not intended to change anything, it is, if not work, at least preparation for work. It turns sensations into signs of distances, sizes, shapes; in other words, signs of work I may do. Conversely, actual work is related to knowledge insofar as it explores the world, not insofar as it changes something in it. I sense, or rather I perceive, the stone at the end of the lever, as I perceive the Pantheon at the end, so to speak, of my gaze, at the point where my two lines of sight meet. Likewise, to the degree that I can act upon the world through my body and the simplest tools, to that degree I grasp extension itself in my sensations. I am no longer content with drawing geometrical figures; I am practicing geometry. The ambiguity that exists in theoretical geometry, which is related to both the mind and the world, now disappears; in the actual practice of geometric action, in work, the direction that I impart and the obstacle that I encounter are clearly separated; the mind's object is no longer order, it is that element in order that belongs to the world alone; I grasp unmediated order. Unmediated order is naked extension. This extension, which I perceive as it were directly, stripped of all admixture of mind, all trappings of imagination—this extension grasped intuitively is space.

Extension, however, is more than space, for space escapes my perception to the extent that it escapes the grasp of my body and the tools I have at my disposal. I make the Pantheon glide across the sky with only a movement of my head; I cover the parts of it that I want with my hand, change its relief by my movements, determine at what distance from me my two lines of sight, fixed on it like two sticks that grasp it, converge, and in this way I perceive space; but I do not touch it. All I do is imagine its consistency. For insofar as I have no grasp on an object I imagine one; but here the imagination, insofar as it is not controlled by the memory of earlier work and exploration, is free and consequently deceptive. For example, the Pantheon is indeed at the vertex of a triangle determined by the distance between my eyes, which I know, and the direction of each of my two lines of sight, which I also know; but no such triangle exists for the sun. If

I wanted to grasp objects with two sticks that I could make longer or shorter at will, I would separate the sticks to take hold of distant objects; but since I cannot separate my eyes, this pair of pincers that constitutes my sight is unable to get a hold on the sun. And so I do not perceive the distance of the sun from me; all I ever do is imagine the distance—for example, two hundred paces. The sun can be grasped, not by two eyes of the same man, but by two men; if they stand far enough apart from one another, and if they know the distance between them and the direction in which they are looking, they can determine the distance of the sun just as I perceive that of the Pantheon. But if I were to participate in this measurement, my way of perceiving would be unchanged, for this act that grasps the sun is collective; it is not something I can do by myself. I know that the sun is 93 million miles away, but I no more perceive it as being 93 million miles away than one of my eyes, if it could think, could perceive how far away the Pantheon is. One can say that two observers who measure the distance of the sun are like two eyes of humanity, that humanity alone perceives the space separating the earth from the sun; just as one can say that in industry it is humanity that works. To take another example: if, at night, a wheel is set spinning in front of me, illuminated only by a light that flashes intermittently, I will see only successive positions of the wheel, but I will still perceive its movement; in the same way, one can say that through observations, records, and archives humanity perceives the return of comets.

That is what science is. The connection that I, as a perceiving being, have to establish between my sensations and my actions science must first undo, for in the realm of science such a connection can only be imaginary, and consequently deceptive. In perception, however, I cannot separate the connection made by the imagination from the real connections that constitute space. Science does not regard the observer as a perceiving being but, as far as possible, it reduces him to something similar to a simple sense organ. Every possible deception on the part of the imagination is done away with, owing to the fact that the observer is strictly reduced to the grasp that he actually has on the observed phenomena; this grasp, however small it may be, always exists, for insofar as the world allows us no grasp it escapes our senses entirely. Thus the grasp that we have on the sky consists precisely in hiding certain parts of it by interposed objects; and so for the astronomer the starry sky is merely some bright spots in the quadrants determined by the cross hairs on his telescope. That is what observation is. As tools form parts of machines, so each observer (insofar as, by his extremely simple grasp, he seizes complicated phenomena that are beyond him) is as it were a part of science. On the other hand, as the simplest geometry is as it were contained in my body, there are other manufactured bodies, such as telescopes, that are completely free of sensibility and at the same time contain a higher form of geometry; these are instruments. In this way, in situations in which men do not grasp space, science helps them to infer extension. For science uses geometrical figures to imitate the perfect connection between what is observed and extension that work establishes. To this end science imagines, so to speak, that beneath observed phenomena there are combinations of simple tools, such as those from which machines are made. Science does not claim that these mechanical models of things duplicate the world; that would be meaningless. But at least they let us place phenomena that we do not understand in a series with those that we do, ranking them in a geometrical order that proceeds from the simple to the complex. Thus all the mechanical models of a phenomenon, provided that they put it in the same place in the series, are equivalent. Or rather they are more than equivalent, they are one, just as the ellipse a gardener draws by means of a cord tied to two stakes is the same as the section of a cone; and the uniformity of all these mechanical models is determined by what expresses the degree of complexity they have in common, that is, by an algebraic formula. Perhaps Maxwell's[10] famous statement that, when one has obtained one mechanical model of a phenomenon, one can find an infinite number of them, can be interpreted in this way. Also one can understand in this way how analysis can be directly applied to physics. But in applying analysis to physics there is a risk that what legitimates it may be forgotten; it is only in geometry and mechanics that algebra has significance. If the purpose of science were to add real knowledge to the understanding, perhaps a purely algebraic science would be worth more than, or at least as much as, the sciences of geometry and mechanics. But this is not the case; the understanding cannot gain anything from science; we know all there is to know when we know that the world is extended. The purpose of science is entirely different; it is first of all to render the human mind master, as far as possible, of the part of the imagination that perception leaves free, and

10 James Clerk Maxwell (1831–79), Scottish physicist. In *The Treatise on Electricity and Magnetism* (1873) Maxwell wrote, "The problem of determining the mechanism required to establish a given species of connection between the motions of the parts of a system always admits of an infinite number of solutions."

then to give it possession of the world; and perhaps, when these two purposes are considered closely, they amount to the same thing. That is true even for astronomy, provided that one understands what is meant by possession. Those industrial discoveries that have come about by chance or as a result of blind technique and that allow us to turn the world upside down through changes we do not understand do indeed give us the illusion of having a sort of tyrannical power. But that power is something external to us; these innovations do not make the world any more ours than it was before. On the other hand, just as I grasp the Pantheon by my gaze, so astronomy, although it does not give us any real power over the sky, nevertheless brings it into our domain; so much so that the pilot dares to use the stars—which the power of all humanity together could not divert from their courses by a hairsbreadth—as his instruments.

In the end, the only wisdom consists in knowing that there is a world, that is, matter that work alone can change, and that, with the exception of the mind, there is nothing else. But to take one step is enough to make the universe appear. Between one step and another I touch the world directly. Between the numbers one and two I have only a presentiment of the world; for that matter, to count is merely to understand that one can walk, walk in a way that leaves one where one is. The wisdom that I have laboriously sought is contained in the simplest perception. Then is the order I thought I had to follow meaningless, since I, since everyone, even the least meditative person, without having doubted everything, without having concluded from his thinking that his own existence is the only certain thing, without having thought about God, or searched for reasons to believe in the existence of external reality, or reflected on the nature of movement, geometry, or extension, possesses the wisdom that I thought I attained only after all these preliminaries? Not so. In a flash, the mind that tears itself away from what it feels retrenches itself in itself and acts; the pilot who holds the tiller in a storm, the peasant who swings his scythe, knows himself and knows the world in the way meant by the statement "I think, therefore I am" and the ideas that follow from it. Workers know everything; however, when their work is done, they do not know that they had all wisdom in their possession. And so outside of effective action, when the body, in which past perceptions are inscribed, is relieved from the necessity of exploration, human thought is given over to the passions, to the kind of imagination that conjures up gods, to more or less reasonable-sounding arguments received from others. That is why mankind needs science, provided that instead of imposing its proofs it is taught in the way that Descartes called analytic, that is, in such a way that each student, following the same order he would follow if he were methodically making discoveries himself, may be said less to receive instruction than to teach himself. Science so conceived, by reducing the heavens, the earth, all things, and even the imagination (under the name "human body") to a system of machines, will add only one thing to the knowledge that is implicit in self-conscious work, namely, it will add the knowledge that that knowledge contains all there is to know, and that there is nothing else.

Conclusion

Now that we have come to the end of this somewhat daring series of reflections, it appears that it departs from Cartesian doctrine to the point of sometimes seeming to contradict it. Still, it would be surprising if a sketch of this sort, however tentative and inadequate it might be, did not, by the mere fact that it imitates the development of Cartesian thought without actually following it, illuminate it to some extent. Perhaps, in fact, it will allow us to envisage how the apparent contradictions and other difficulties pointed out earlier in Descartes can be resolved. We can understand why in Descartes's *The World* motion is said to be a simpler notion than figure, how this idea is connected with the idea of analytic geometry, how consequently it is through becoming as concrete as possible that geometry apparently became extremely abstract, and how by the same act of the mind Descartes identified geometry with algebra on the one hand and physics on the other. Unfortunately, Descartes purposely made the explanation of his geometrical discovery obscure, but at least his *Geometry* shows that his principal intention was to set up a series of geometrical lines comparable to a series of equations. Descartes, however, could do nothing more than sketch this series in two different ways; Lagrange[1] constructed it later in his immortal works. On the other hand, we can see how it is the same innovation that reduced physics to geometry and based physics on comparisons with phenomena familiar to us from everyday experience and the commonest kinds of work. We can also see—and this is something that

1 Joseph Louis Lagrange (1736–1813), Italian-born French mathematician.

astonished his contemporaries—how, although he continued to imagine various kinds of movements, Descartes thought that as far as possible he ought to admit only simple motions in order to restrict to the utmost the part of the mind that physics was forced to seem to attribute to the world. And finally, we can see why, after having based his entire physics on movement, he seemingly ruined it by positing movement as purely relative. It also appears that there is no contradiction involved in reducing the imagination to the human body, and in making it the only instrument of knowledge for everything concerning the world. We see that simple ideas can be ascribed to the mind and at the same time considered as laws of the world, if it is true that simple ideas are expressions of neither the world nor the mind but of the passageway that the world allows the mind; we also see why it can be said that simple ideas are created by God, since the role of God in relation to me is to warrant, in some manner, the union of the soul and the body.

The great correlations that form the core of the doctrine become apparent; there is no longer any contradiction between freedom and necessity, idealism and realism. To no longer be brought up short by this last opposition it is enough to observe that the whole mind acts when thought is applied to an object. That is why Descartes goes as far as to say, in direct contradiction to the way deduction is defined by philosophy as currently taught, that "it is the nature of our mind to form general propositions from the knowledge of particulars" (9:111). Thus in the *Rules* Descartes is satisfied with those intuitive proofs of the four arithmetical operations that Poincaré later thought must be replaced by analytical reasoning. When the mind is viewed in this way, clear and distinct ideas seem infallible, and science seems uniformly simple, clear, and easy, however far it extends. For science does nothing but establish series in which each idea is as easy to grasp after the preceding one as the first was by itself; in other words, the only order is the one that rules the sequence of numbers and makes it as easy to conceive of a thousand as to conceive of two.

In short, we understand that, according to this same view, when the mind applies itself to the world it may take geometrical figures, algebraic signs, or even sensations as intermediaries, but it is always the same mind, the same world, and the same knowledge; and it is this that Descartes, in all his writings, makes very clear.

It is not that the ideas that have taken form in the course of this rash attempt at reconstruction can claim to be the very ideas of Descartes, or even to resemble them. A rough outline of this sort does not even need to comment on the texts themselves; it is enough if it simply allows us to approach them afresh and more fruitfully. And so it can best be concluded by citing (as Descartes did to justify his *Optics*) the example of the astronomers "who, although their assumptions are almost all false or uncertain, nevertheless . . . do not cease to derive from them a great deal of knowledge that is very true and certain" (6:83).[2]

2 See *Discourse on Method, Optics, Geometry, and Meteorology*, pp. 66–67.

■ *The Situation in Germany*

Introduction

From the very beginning of Simone Weil's professional life, the interest in the worker she had shown in "Science and Perception in Descartes" was translated into action on behalf of the working class. When she was appointed a professor of philosophy at a girls' lycée in the provincial city of Le Puy in 1931, she also became both a political activist and an indefatigable supporter of the revolutionary working-class movement. She was a vocal member of two teachers' unions, one affiliated with the reformist CGT (*Confédération générale du Travail*) and the other with the Communist-dominated CGTU (*Confédération générale du Travail unitaire*). She traveled weekly to the industrial city of St. Etienne, about fifty miles from Le Puy, in order to work with a revolutionary syndicalist group and with the Labor Exchange (the regional trade-union organization) there. She wrote for *L'Ecole émancipée*, the publication of the teachers' trade union affiliated with the CGTU, the revolutionary syndicalist journal *La Révolution prolétarienne*, and *L'Effort*, the newspaper of the construction-workers' trade union of Lyon. In less than a year her tireless activity, her dedication, and her penetrating and critical intelligence had made her something of a minor celebrity within the French Left.

Weil was a revolutionary, and she passionately hoped that, out of the profound economic crisis afflicting Europe that seemed to signal the decay of the capitalist system and the imminence of proletarian revolution, a truly egalitarian worker democracy would emerge. Though not an ideologue in the sense of being a doctrinaire adherent of any system of political belief, she was probably ideologically closest to the revolutionary syndicalists, trade unionists committed to the necessity of revolutionary change who believed that society could be transformed through economic pressure exerted by the trade unions directly. Nevertheless, for Weil it was the revolution that was of primary importance, not the group that one belonged to, and she repeatedly supported efforts to get the different (and often warring) factions of the Left to set aside their ideological differences and work together; without unity, she wrote late in 1931, "the working class will be condemned to disappear as a revolutionary force."

Weil found that Trotsky's January 1932 article "What Next?" brought the critical nature of the situation in Europe in general and Germany in particular into sharp focus, and specifically said so in her July 1932 article "Conditions d'une révolution allemande." In Germany, where the economic crisis was most acute, Trotsky saw bourgeois democracy on the verge of collapse and about to give way to one of two possible alternatives: fascism or proletarian revolution. In other words, because both Trotsky and Weil understood fascism to have as one of its principal aims the destruction of the working-class organizations and the reduction of the proletariat to an amorphous and hence helpless mass, what was imminent was either the complete triumph or the complete destruction of the proletariat. Moreover, as Weil wrote in her response to Trotsky's article, a fascist Germany, "forming a bloc with Italian Fascism and the countries of white terror around the Danube, and giving strength to the fascist currents that are already apparent in various parts of Europe and the United States, would threaten the entire world and even the USSR." Yet despite the seriousness and extremity of the situation, both of the two major parties, the Social Democratic party and the Communist party, remained, she wrote, "criminally inactive." She blamed this inactivity largely on the bureaucracies of both parties, and on the willingness of the members, for different reasons, to blindly follow the bureaucrats. A bureaucracy, she wrote, can do many things (she cited the industrial progress accomplished by the bureaucratic dictatorship in Russia), but "what it cannot do is make a revolution." And it was the Russian state bureaucracy, she contended, that, through its domination of the Comintern, was determining the do-nothing policies of the German Communist party.

Shortly after this essay was published Weil spent a month in Germany to see for herself what the situation there was like. She found it very quiet, disappointingly so; she wrote her parents that she had come at a bad time, that there was no chance of "observing very much." She was deeply moved by the plight of the ordinary members of the German working class, especially the young people. She saw what was happening in Germany not only as an occasion for political analysis or political criticism but as a human tragedy, one that would, in all likelihood, grow worse. Perhaps most significant, what she observed in Germany altered her thinking about the real prospects of international proletarian revolution. The revolutionary syndicalist movement, she concluded, had "no international significance";

the German trade unions, she found, far from being a "force capable of making the revolution," were "organically reformist," basically "associations for mutual welfare." Moreover, what she saw destroyed whatever faith she still had in the Communist party as a party capable of leading a successful proletarian revolution. "In Germany," she wrote, "I lost all the respect that in spite of myself I still felt for the Communist party. The contrast between its revolutionary phrases and its total passivity is much too scandalous. Actually it seems to me as culpable as the Social Democracy. I think that at the present moment all compromise with the party or any reticence in criticizing it is criminal. Trotsky himself seems to me to still retain a kind of timidity toward it that gives him some share of the responsibility for the Third International's crimes in Germany."[1]

After Weil returned to France she wrote, first, a quite compact description and analysis of the German situation entitled "L'Allemagne en attente" that was published in *La Révolution prolétarienne* in October 1932; she then wrote the considerably expanded version that is translated here and that was published in ten installments in *L'Ecole émancipée* between December 4, 1932, and March 5, 1933.

Her first article paints a picture of depression Germany, and implicitly poses the question of why, in this objectively revolutionary situation, in which the economic crisis is affecting every area of the workers' lives, there are "no precursory signs of the revolution in peoples' actions"? Weil's initial answer is that the working class lacks unity. What, she asks with apparent ingenuousness, can unify it? A truly revolutionary organization. She then asks, does such an organization exist? She proceeds to examine the three main working-class organizations—the trade unions, the Social Democratic party, and the Communist party—in the light of this question. The German trade unions, four million strong and very wealthy, have done too well within the capitalist system and have too much to lose to support revolution, and the Social Democratic party is compromised by its reformist principles and its ties to the Weimar Republic; neither, therefore, can provide organization and leadership for a revolutionary working class. However, there should be nothing, presumably, to prevent the Communist party from carrying out that task. But 84 percent of the Communist party's membership is unemployed; the Party reflects, rather than reme-

---

1 Quoted in Simone Pétrement, *Simone Weil: A Life* (New York: Pantheon, 1976), pp. 133, 136, 137.

dies, the split between the unemployed and the workers in the factories, and thus only replicates in itself the enfeebling lack of unity in the working class as a whole. To be the strong revolutionary organization the working class desperately needs, Weil argues, the Party must win the confidence of the workers in the factories who are either reformist or uncommitted. She sketches the strategy necessary to do this, a strategy based on the formation of a united front "from above," that is, one organized and led by the Communist party and the Social Democratic party working together for specific objectives.

The last four articles of "The Situation in Germany" are a step-by-step indictment of the failure of the Communist party to take any of the actions necessary to unite the working class against either the threat posed by the Hitlerites or the danger that, with or without the Hitlerites, the government will become fascistic. Weil details situation after situation in which the reformist masses were ready to act either against the government or against the Hitlerites, and the Communist party contented itself with appeals to spontaneous action and did nothing to actually organize and direct that action.

But the responsibility for this state of affairs does not lie with the rank and file of the Communist party, Weil contends, despite the myth to that effect within the Party, and despite the fact that the "docile mass" of newcomers that constitutes 80 percent of the Party membership supports the decisions handed down by the bureaucracy. In an attack that gathers increasing momentum in articles 9 and 10, Weil charges both the German party apparatus and the apparatuses of the Comintern and the Russian state with betraying the proletariat. A working-class party's mistakes are treasonous, she argues, when they are the result of organic connections with interests opposed to those of the proletariat, and the German Party apparatus is "organically subordinated to the apparatus of the Russian state," whose interests are "distinct from those of the world proletariat." In a masterful summation that is both reasoned and impassioned Weil lists the ways in which what she calls the Party's "mistakes" were imposed on it by the Moscow-dominated Comintern, and charges that a genuine correction of things within the Party would be "directly opposed to the interests of the Russian state apparatus."

Her last look at the situation, at the end of February 1933, is both clear-sighted and immeasurably sad. She sees the German working class facing an imminent and deadly battle unarmed, the weapons it had forged (i.e., all the working-class organizations) being actually in the hands of those whose interests are not its own. And she reports that the Party, as a party, continues its policy of inaction, despite the increase in anti-Left activities and Hitlerite terror after Hitler became chancellor.

Within a day or two of the writing of Weil's last article on Germany, the Reichstag was set afire. The Communists were blamed and immediately afterward more than four thousand Communist officials and numerous Social Democrats were arrested and sent to concentration camps. The destruction of the working-class movement against which Weil had been so passionately warning had begun.

With the exception of Trotsky's articles,[2] there has been virtually nothing in English on the role played by the German Communist party in the critical months just before Hitler's accession to power, despite the fact that the Communist party was the largest party in Berlin at the end of 1932, and the third largest party in Germany as a whole (after the National Socialists and the Social Democrats). The standard histories see the period almost exclusively in terms of the struggle between the National Socialists and the bourgeois democratic parties, between the democratic ideology of the Weimar Republic and the totalitarian ideology of the Nazis. The fate of the Communist party—and even the fate of the German working class— has not aroused much interest. Weil's articles, however—articles written within the Left and for the Left—provide an account of the destruction of the hopes of the working-class movement in Germany (a destruction aided and abetted by a Russia posing as the leader and champion of the proletariat) that not only fills in a blank space in our knowledge of the political struggle in Germany but is filtered through a mind that was sensitive to the tragic and almost epic quality of the events taking place.

Weil's concern for the actual detail of human suffering in depression Germany, her romantic admiration and empathy for German working-class youth, and the moral idealism of her concept of worker democracy all separate her analysis of the situation in Germany from Trotsky's. Nevertheless, Weil's analysis is based on a knowledge of what Trotsky had to say on the subject, and both she and Trotsky put great stress on the necessity for the German Communist party to immediately form a united front with the Social Democrats. Trotsky's proposal for a united front, however, is a baldly tactical one that looks forward to a quite treacherous future

2 Collected in *The Struggle Against Fascism in Germany*, ed. Ernest Mandel (New York: Pathfinder Press, 1971).

reckoning with Social Democracy after fascism has been defeated. Weil's concern is an immediate one—to save lives, to prevent the massacre that otherwise is imminent—and she takes Social Democracy's understandable distrust of Bolshevik tactics into account in her analysis of the difficulties of bringing a united front into being. In her view, these treacherous tactics must be set aside, and the Party must persuade the Social Democratic workers to come over to it by being both a genuinely revolutionary and a genuinely democratic party. Though Trotsky, too, placed a high priority on open discussion and party democracy, he did so chiefly with the aim of having the views of the Left Opposition aired and adopted.

Weil's analysis was not well received within the Leftist circles for which she was writing, for those circles were committed to the belief that, if revolutionary conditions existed, revolution would necessarily follow. Weil's articles, however, analyze why revolution was not happening, and why, moreover, it would not happen; like Ajax, she was counseling her friends not to let empty hopes lead them astray. This, understandably enough, was not a popular attitude. Her articles—one imagines each installment being eagerly awaited, hastily read, and heatedly discussed—generated a small storm of letters in response, including three lengthy formal replies castigating Weil as a defeatist. But it was typical of Weil's psychology to be hardest on her friends and on what she was most attracted to, to be unwilling to have her friends remain in ignorance of the truth of their situation. Whether or not she was listened to, she went on in the direction in which these articles show that she was beginning to move—to question whether, in general, there were any real prospects of the revolution predicted by Marx (in "Prospects: Are We Heading toward a Proletarian Revolution," published in November 1933), and finally to subject Marxism itself to a trenchant criticism in her masterful essay "Reflections on the Causes of Liberty and Social Oppression" in 1934.

■ The Situation in Germany

One

Everyone who has pinned all his hopes on the victory of the working class, even everyone who cares about preserving the past gains of the liberal bourgeoisie, ought right now to have his eyes on Germany. Germany is the country where the problem of the social system is being posed in a concrete way. For us in France, even for militants, the problem of the social system is a topic of speeches at meetings, newspaper articles, and café discussions. At most, it is a subject of theoretical study. All day long it is forgotten in favor of current business, trivial events, passions, interests. But for the majority of the German people there is no problem in their everyday lives that is more urgent or more acute.

In Germany you see former engineers who manage to eat one cold meal a day by renting chairs in the public gardens; you see elderly men in stiff collars and bowler hats begging at subway exits or singing in cracked voices in the streets. Students are dropping out of school and selling peanuts, matches, or shoelaces on the street; their comrades, luckier thus far, but who for the most part have no chance whatever of finding a job when they finish school, know that any day they can come to that. Peasants are being ruined by low prices and taxes. Factory workers' earnings are both precarious and miserably reduced; every worker expects some time or other to be thrown into the compulsory idleness that is the lot of nearly half the German working class; or, rather, into the exhausting and degrading hectic state that consists in running from one office to another to get one's card stamped and receive relief (*stempeln*). Once a worker is unemployed, the relief payments (which are proportional to the wages he drew before he was dismissed) are reduced again and again until they become almost nothing, as the day on which he stopped having a part in the production process recedes into the past. An unemployed man or woman living with a father or mother, husband or wife who is working receives nothing. An unemployed worker under twenty receives nothing.

Published in *L'Ecole émancipée*, December 4, 1932.

The impossibility of living except at the expense of his family reduces the unemployed worker to a state of total dependence that sours all family relationships. Often this dependence, when it is made intolerable by the reproaches of parents who poorly understand the situation and whom poverty has driven to distraction, forces the young unemployed workers out of the paternal home and drives them to vagabondage, begging, and sometimes to suicide. As for starting one's own family, marrying, having children, most young Germans cannot even contemplate it. Is there anything left that a young unemployed worker can call his own? A little freedom. But even this freedom is threatened by the institution of the *Arbeitsdienst* [labor service], work done under military discipline for soldiers' pay in kinds of concentration camps for young unemployed workers. Although so far this form of labor is still optional, any day now Hitlerite pressure may make it compulsory. There is no area of a worker's or a German petty bourgeois's private life, especially if he is young, where he is not touched or threatened by the economic and political consequences of the crisis. The young, for whom the crisis is the normal state of affairs, the only one they have known, cannot escape it even in their dreams. They are deprived of everything in the present, and they have no future.

In that lies the decisive aspect of the situation, and not in the poverty itself. The decisive aspect lies in this, that on the one hand, rightly or wrongly, in Germany there is less and less belief, especially among the young, in the transitory nature of the crisis; and on the other hand no man, no matter how intelligent or energetic, can have the slightest hope of escaping, through his own resourcefulness, from the general misery created by the crisis. A mild crisis, which forces only the least efficient workmen, clerks, or engineers out of the factories, lets one go on feeling that the fate of each individual largely depends on his own efforts to get himself personally out of trouble. A severe crisis is essentially different. Here, too, "quantity changes into quality." In Germany today almost no one in any profession can depend on his professional worth to find or keep a job. So everyone constantly feels entirely in the power of the regime and its fluctuations; conversely, no one can even imagine what kind of effort he could make to take his own fate in hand again, unless it is one that acts upon the very structure of society. For almost every German, at least in the petty bourgeoisie and the working class, prospects, good or bad, that concern even the most intimate aspects of one's own life are immediately formulated, especially if one is young, as prospects that concern the future of the regime. Thus the amount of a people's energy that ordinarily is almost entirely absorbed by various passions and the defense of private interests is, in present-day Germany, brought to bear on the economic and political relationships that constitute the very framework of society.

The situation in Germany can therefore be called revolutionary. The most conspicuous sign of this is that everyone's thoughts and conversations, including those of eleven-year-old children, turn constantly and naturally, with the earnestness and sincerity characteristic of Germans, to the problem of the social order. But one sees no precursory sign of the revolution in peoples' actions. The wave of strikes that just swept across Germany, instead of inflaming the country, died out one after the other, including that transport workers' strike that had seemed certain to stir up Berlin. Yet the situation that exists now has gone on for a long time. We have to understand that the crisis is posing the problem of a new system of production, not hidden behind other apparently easier problems, as it was for the Russians in 1917, but brutally and directly, and to a nonhomogeneous working class. By depriving the unemployed of every future prospect, the crisis has led almost all of them, especially the young, to feel at one time or another that the transformation of the system of production is the only way out. But too often, as the period of unemployment lengthens, the effect of this same crisis is to deprive them of the strength to try to find a way out. This life of idleness and poverty, which robs skilled workers of their skill and the young of any possibility of learning a trade, which deprives the workers of their dignity as producers, which after two, three, or four years finally leads—and this is what is worse—to a sort of sad tolerance—this life is no preparation for assuming responsibilities in the whole system of production. Thus the crisis constantly brings new ranks of workers to class consciousness, but it also constantly pulls them back again, as the sea brings in and pulls back its waves.

The German proletariat is also weakened by the number of office workers in it, a number that German capitalism increased during the period of prosperity with the same foolish extravagance it displayed in building its factories and modernizing its machinery. For the office workers, who thus make up a considerable part of both the German wage earners and the unemployed, are not much inclined to join ranks with the factory workers and are incapable, by the very nature of their profession, of wanting to take their fate into their own hands. Finally, there is a split between the factory workers and the unemployed. The factory workers can manage, in spite of everything, to live within the system; they have something to lose and they are clinging to it; they too are at the mercy of the eddies of the crisis but, unlike the unemployed, they are not conscious of it all the time. This lack of solidarity deprives the unemployed of any influence over the economy and at the same time it in some measure deprives the factory workers of the confidence needed for any struggle. Thus, even though the crisis forces almost every German worker or petty bourgeois to feel, at one time or another, that all his hopes are being dashed against the very structure of the social system, it does not by itself group the German people around the workers determined to transform that system. Only an organization can remedy such weakness. Is there, among the organizations that group German workers together in such large numbers, one that can in fact remedy it?

This is literally a life-and-death question for a great many German workers. In October 1917 Lenin observed that it is during revolutionary periods that the unconscious masses, as long as they are not being dragged along by the action in the wake of the conscious workers, most avidly consume counterrevolutionary poisons. The Hitlerite movement is another example of this. And despite the electoral defeats, as long as the crisis continues and a revolutionary movement does not triumph, the Hitlerite storm troops (which may have the apparatus of the state behind them any day) constitute a permanent threat of extermination for the best elements of the working class. Even excluding the possibility of a systematic extermination, the crisis itself (assuming that it lasts for some time yet) will destroy generations of German workers, especially the younger generations. Already, among those who have been able to survive three or four years of unemployment, the less resistant ones have been weakened morally and physically by poverty and idleness. They are going to have to get through a winter, which may be severe, without heat or hot meals; and after this winter, possibly still another one. Those who do not die of it will lose their health and strength to it. And the life of the German workers is of vital importance to us as well. For, in the breakdown of the capitalist economy that is threatening to wipe out the gains of the workers in the democratic countries and even in the USSR by a wave of reaction, our greatest hope lies in the German working class, the most mature, the most disciplined, the most educated in the world; and especially in the working-class youth of Germany.

Nothing is more crushing than the life of dependence, idleness, and deprivation that is the lot of the young German workers; at the same time one cannot imagine anyone more courageous, more lucid, or more fraternal than the best of them, despite this life. On the whole, in spite of the poverty, theft and crime have little hold over these young people, and fascist agitation, for its part, has relatively little influence on them. They are not trying to forget; they are not complaining; in this hopeless situation they are resisting every form of despair. In general they are trying—some with more energy than others, and the best wholly achieve it—to build a fully human life within the inhuman situation in which they have been placed. They don't have the money to satisfy their hunger, but many deprive themselves of the necessities of life to obtain what makes life worth living. They find a few pennies in order to remain in the sports organizations that send them, boys and girls alike, cheerful in spite of everything, off in bands to the forests and lakes to enjoy the wholesome, free pleasures of water, air, and sun. They cut down on food to buy books; some form study circles where they read the classics of the revolutionary movement, write, or debate. It is not unusual to find among them minds more cultured than are some of the supposedly educated bourgeois among us. But more striking yet is the degree to which this youth is conscious of itself. In France there are only the young and the old; over there, there is a youth. In these working-class girls with their sunburnt complexions, in these young working men with their feverish eyes and hollow cheeks whom one sees walking the streets of Berlin, one senses at every turn that, underlying the sadness as well as the apparent insouciance, there is a seriousness that is the reverse of despair, a full and unremitting consciousness of the tragic lot that they have been dealt; an unremitting consciousness of the weight with which the regime—this old regime that they have not accepted—is pressing down on them, crushing all their aspirations. The fact that in this period of crisis the regime is depriving them completely of those future prospects that are the natural prerogative of youth makes more acute, by contrast, their awareness that they have a future locked up inside them. And they do have a future locked inside them. If in our disintegrating system there are any men capable of giving us something new, it is this generation of young German workers. Provided, that is, that the fascist gangs, or simply cold and hunger, do not deprive them either of their lives or, at any rate, of their vital energy.

We can scarcely be anything in this drama but spectators. Let us, at least, give it the attention it deserves. To start with, let us take stock of the situation; let us establish the relation of forces.

Two

On the sixth of November, while the big bourgeoisie[1] was massing all its forces behind the von Papen government, 70 percent of the electorate voted for the slogans "Down with the Government of the Barons!"[2] "Down with the Exploiters!" "For Socialism!" But the big bourgeoisie continues to rule Germany. Yet seven-tenths of the population—what a force for socialism! But this seven-tenths is divided among three parties.

THE HITLERITE MOVEMENT

Of these three parties, the National Socialist party is by far the strongest. Even though it lost votes between the thirty-first of July and the sixth of November, on the latter date it still grouped a third of the voters behind it. The fundamental characteristic of the National Socialist movement—one that makes it almost incomprehensible for a Frenchman—is its incoherence; an incredible incoherence, which is only a reflection of the essential incoherence of the German nation in its present situation. First of all, the movement is socially incoherent. Every serious crisis rouses the masses to rebellion at every level of the population except the highest. Among these masses there are some men who are capable of becoming the conscious and responsible architects of a new regime. But there is a far greater number of unconscious and irresponsible men who can only blindly desire the end of the regime that is crushing them. Grouped behind the first, they constitute a revolutionary force; but if one man manages, as Hitler did, to form a separate group of the larger number, they necessarily fall under the control of big capital, in whose service they form armed gangs to support the worst kind of reaction and dictatorship and carry out pogroms. Since the Hitlerite movement is of this nature, it groups those who feel the weight of the regime without being able to look to themselves to transform it: the majority of the intellectuals, the broad masses of the petty bourgeoisie of town and country, almost all the agricultural workers, and finally a good many urban workers, almost all of them unemployed.

Published in *L'Ecole émancipée*, December 18, 1932.

1 *Grande bourgeoisie*. Weil uses the term in the Marxist sense meaning "big capitalists."
2 Of the ten members of von Papen's cabinet (known as the "Cabinet of the Barons"), seven belonged to the nobility.

Among the latter, who are in the storm troops at least in some degree as simple mercenaries, there are many fifteen- to eighteen-year-old adolescents who have scarcely any relationship to the working class, for they met with the economic crisis on leaving school and there has never even been any question of working as far as they are concerned. If one adds some members of the big bourgeoisie (the majority of whom are behind the scenes, although a few belong to the party) and a prince or two, one will have a complete picture of the composition of the Hitlerite movement.

The propaganda is no less incoherent. It attracts romantic young boys with the prospect of heroic struggles and self-sacrifice, and brutes with the implicit promise that some day they will be able to beat people up and kill them right and left. It promises high sales prices to the countryside and a low cost of living to the cities. But the lack of any coherence in Hitlerite policy is most obvious in the National Socialist party's relations with the other parties. The party to which the Hitlerites are essentially related is the German National party, the party of the big bourgeoisie, the party that supports the "barons"; like the "barons," the Hitlerites' basic goal is a struggle to the death with the Communist movement and the crushing of all opposition from the working classes; they claim that they are supporters of private property, the family, and religion, and that they will relentlessly fight against the class struggle. But they are estranged from the parties of the big bourgeoisie by the social composition of the movement, the resultant demagogy, and the personal ambitions of the leaders. On the other hand, surprising as it may seem, there are such striking similarities between the Hitlerite movement and the Communist movement that, after the elections, the Hitlerite press had to devote a long article to denying rumors of negotiations between Hitlerites and Communists with an eye to forming a coalition government. The fact is that from August to November 6, the slogans of both parties were almost identical. The Hitlerites, too, inveigh against exploitation, low salaries, and the poverty of the unemployed. Their main rallying cry is "Down with the System"; they, too, call the transformation of the system revolution; they, too, call the system to come socialism. Although the Hitlerite party refuses to acknowledge the class struggle and often uses storm troops to break strikes, it can just as well (as was quite evident during the Berlin transport strike) publish extremely violent articles supporting a strike, fire off slogans implying the existence of a bitter class struggle, and call all the reformists traitors. And although the Hitlerites accuse the Social Democrats of betraying both

Germany by being internationalists and the proletariat by being reformists, the Hitlerites have one thing in common with them that is of paramount importance, namely, the economic program. For both the National Socialist party and Social Democracy, socialism is nothing but the control of a more or less considerable part of the economy by the state, without a preliminary transformation of the state apparatus and without the reorganization of any effective workers' control; it is, therefore, nothing but state capitalism. This likemindedness is the basis of a tendency in favor of a government that would in some as yet undetermined way be turned into a main wheel of the economy, a government that would be supported both by the Social Democratic trade unions and the National Socialist movement. Leipart,[3] in the trade-union bureaucracy, and Gregor Strasser,[4] in the Hitlerite camp, support this tendency. It also has the support of some young and brilliant economists associated with the review *Die Tat*, who defend it in the interests of finance capital, and its principal representative is said to be von Schleicher himself.[5]

This highly disparate movement seems at first glance to find unity of a sort in nationalist fanaticism, which reaches the level of hysteria in some petty-bourgeois women and which the Hitlerites are trying to use to revive the Union Sacrée[6] of the old days, under the new name "Socialism of the Front." But they are not really succeeding. Nationalist propaganda by itself is not enough. The Hitlerites are bound to profit from the feeling shared by all Germans that their nation is being crushed not only by the oppression of German capitalism, but also by the added weight of the oppression of the victorious nations that is burdening the whole German economy. The Hitlerites try to give out, on the one hand, that the latter burden is by far the more crushing, and on the other that the oppressive nature of German capitalism is due solely to the Jews. The result of this is

3 Theodore Leipart (1867–1947) was the chairman of the workers' division of the General Federation of German Trade Unions.

4 Gregor Strasser (1892–1934) was a National Socialist party organizer and leader of the socialist left wing of the party.

5 General Kurt von Schleicher (1882–1934) became chancellor on December 2, 1932, a few days before Weil's first article on Germany appeared. Von Schleicher was attempting to solve the more than two-year-long governmental crisis resulting from the inability of any one party to gain a majority in Parliament by creating a broad-front government based on support from the National Socialists and the trade unions.

6 National unity resulting from all political groups putting aside their differences and joining together against an external enemy. The term was first used by President of the Republic Raymond Poincaré at the outbreak of the First World War, when he appealed to all the French, Right, Left, and Center, to unite "in the same patriotic faith."

a patriotism quite different from the idiotic adulation of the army that we know as nationalism in France; it is a patriotism based on the feeling that the victorious nations, France in particular, represent the current system, and that Germany stands for all the human values crushed by the regime; in short, it is a patriotism based on the feeling that there is a radical opposition between the terms "German" and "capitalist." One can only admire the powerful influence that the proletariat possesses in Germany at present when one sees that the Hitlerite party, which is controlled by the big bourgeoisie and primarily draws recruits from among the petty bourgeoisie, has to present even patriotism as nothing but a form of the struggle against capital. What is still more wonderful is that, in a situation like this, Hitlerite propaganda has on the whole little hold over the workers, including the Hitlerite workers. The latter, in their frequent and sometimes almost amicable discussions with the Communists, rightly scoff at them for their illusions about a supposed international solidarity that does not exist; but they do not accuse them of betraying the fatherland. Even when they argue with the Communists, the Hitlerite workers generally leave the national question in the background and stay in the area of working-class interests. They accuse the Russian government of making the Russian workers miserable, whereas Hitler would make the German workers happy by giving them each a plot of land and protecting them in a paternalistic way against the excessive demands of the bosses; and they bitterly reproach the German Communists for betraying the revolution when they side with the Social Democrats, those upholders of the regime, against them, the Hitlerite workers, who sincerely believe themselves to be good revolutionaries.

In short, Hitlerite propaganda, although it gives the workers it reaches the most confused ideas and prevents them from attaining true class consciousness, allows them their working-class spirit. A German worker, even a Hitlerite, remains a worker before everything else. And in the Hitlerite movement the young workers, especially, keep intact the feeling that lies at the heart of all German working-class youth, the urgent feeling that there is a future that belongs to them, to which they have a right, from which the social system is mercilessly cutting them off, and for the sake of which they must destroy the system. The petty-bourgeois Hitlerites, for their part, remain petty bourgeois, swinging back and forth between the influence of the big bourgeoisie and the influence (clearly stronger at the moment) of the proletariat. The big bourgeois in the Hitlerite movement remain big bourgeois; the aristocrats remain aristocrats; as for the common brutes who, whatever their social class, are readily attracted to the Hitlerite movement, they remain common brutes. Although Hitler has succeeded in bringing together all classes in his movement, he has by no means succeeded in dissolving class barriers. But the more disparate the composition of Hitler's party becomes, and the more its policies entail essential contradictions, the greater is the need for something to hold these diverse elements together in a single bloc. But what?

What unites the members of the Hitlerite movement is, first of all, the future that it promises them. What future? It is not described, or it is described in several contradictory ways, and therefore it can take on the color of each man's dreams. But what is certain is that it will be a new system, a "third reich," something that will resemble neither the past nor, above all, the present. And what attracts intellectuals, petty bourgeois, office workers, and the unemployed to this undefined future is that they sense a force in the party that is promising it to them. This force is glaringly apparent everywhere—in the parades of uniformed men, in the acts of violence, in the use of airplanes for propaganda. All these weak elements fly toward it like moths to a flame. What they do not know is that if it appears to be so powerful, it is because it is the force not of those who are preparing the way for the future, but of those who rule over the present. The prospect of an unknown future and the feeling of a mysterious force are more than enough to lead disciplined gangs of these desperate men thirsting for a transformation of the social system to massacre those who are preparing for that transformation.

But hasn't this danger been averted? Isn't the Hitlerite movement in rapid decline? And haven't the Hitlerite workers been converted to the practice of the class struggle?

There is no doubt that the Hitlerite movement has lost strength. But this weakening is due less to working-class opposition than to the fighting among the bourgeois factions. In July the Junkers set von Papen's authoritarian government before Hitler instead of Brüning's weak one.[7] In August

---

7 This is not quite right. Brüning resigned as chancellor on May 30, 1932. President Hindenburg then appointed von Papen to rule with a temporary presidential cabinet until new Reichstag elections could be held July 31. When the July elections gave no party a majority, and Hitler refused (on August 13) to accept the position of vice-chancellor, Hindenburg insisted on retaining von Papen and his presidential cabinet. Moreover, although von Papen's government was more authoritarian than Brüning's, Brüning was more consistently opposed to the National Socialists; von Papen favored bringing them into the government where, he thought, he could both control them and benefit from their mass support.

heavy industry, without completely abandoning Hitler, also aligned itself behind von Papen. As soon as Hitler ceased to appear to be the stronger force he lost a good deal of his prestige, which is what explains his setback on the sixth of November. But vis-à-vis the big bourgeoisie, this rapid loss of strength is a means of blackmail, and that is a strength. The big bourgeoisie would like to make use of Hitler without handing the government over to him. But if it were to continue to leave him out of the picture, as it did from August to December, the Hitlerite movement would break up and the big bourgeoisie would find itself isolated, cut off from the masses, facing a growing wave of working-class discontent. Despite its machine guns it would then doubtless be lost, barring a swift return of industrial prosperity, which in Germany is highly improbable. There is little reason to hope for such foolish tactics on the part of the big bourgeoisie, especially since the *Deutsche Allgemeine Zeitung,* the mouthpiece of heavy industry, has constantly warned against this danger since the beginning of November, and called for a consolidation of all the nationalist parties. Von Schleicher is going to try to obtain either the more or less openly declared support of the Hitlerites alone, with a view to a nationalist bloc, or the support of the Hitlerites and the trade unions together, with a view to a "trade-union government." If the Hitlerites, under the influence of the revolutionary feelings of the base and the personal ambitions of the leaders, completely refuse to negotiate, one sees no way out for the big bourgeoisie other than a Hitlerite government; that is, the suppression of the working-class organizations and organized massacre.

As far as the Hitlerites' revolutionary actions are concerned, it would be dangerous to have any illusions about them. They also are a means of blackmailing the big bourgeoisie. Along with the Communists, the Hitlerite party supported the wave of strikes that came in response to von Papen's emergency decrees; it particularly supported the strike of the transport workers that turned Berlin upside down at the beginning of November, a strike in which the whole population took part and that wrung cries of alarm from the *Deutsche Allgemeine Zeitung.* For the National Socialist party the strike was a means both to win working-class votes and to remind the big bourgeoisie that the National Socialist party was indispensable to it, and, to judge by the commentaries in the *Deutsche Allgemeine Zeitung,* it succeeded perfectly. The day after the elections, the strike, against which the trade-union bureaucracy had been fighting for several days, became embarrassing and dangerous for Hitler as well; it was brought to an end immediately, and it ended in defeat. On the very eve of the elections, the Hitlerite press was issuing slogans identical to those of the Communists; the day after, it began a series of sensational articles designed to prove that Hitler alone could wipe out communism in Germany. As for the strikers themselves, as long as the strike is not an infraction of party discipline, the fact that some Hitlerite workers are striking is no guarantee at all that these same workers will not use the same violence a few months hence to put down strikes; all it would take would be for the Hitlerite party, in the meantime, to have had a share in power. And these workers would think that they were continuing to serve their class, just as, with better reason, the Bolshevik workers who put down the anarchist movements after the October Revolution thought they were serving their class. Thus the fact that they have drawn the Hitlerite workers over to their side in a struggle does not constitute a success for the Communists as long as they have not separated the Hitlerite workers from their party. It can even be said that as long as the united front between Communists and Hitlerite workers is not extended to include the Social Democratic workers, it increases Hitler's prestige in the eyes of the working-class masses, as the elections of November 6 showed in Berlin.

There is only one way the conscious workers can defeat the Hitlerite movement; it is, on the one hand, to make the masses understand that a nationalist movement, founded on the union of classes, cannot bring about a new system, and, on the other hand, to make them feel the existence of another force confronting the force of Hitler's movement, that of the proletariat grouped in its own organizations.

But no sooner does one set forth this program than one is astonished that it has not already been carried out and the Hitlerite movement broken up. No nation is more accessible to effective propaganda than the Germans, who read and reflect so extensively. As for the question of strength, four million workers are organized in the German trade unions, and on November 6 there were six million Communist votes.

What does the German working-class movement lack? To understand this, it is necessary to examine both its reformist and revolutionary aspects.

Three ■ German Reformism

"In a revolution," Marx wrote in 1848, "the proletarians have nothing to lose but their chains. And they have a world to win." Reformism is based on the denial of the truth of this formula. German reformism's strength is based on the German working-class movement's being a movement of a proletariat whose experience has long failed to bear out the truth of this formula, a proletariat that for a long time has had something to hold onto inside the regime.

The working-class movement, which from 1792 to 1871 had developed primarily in France, where it took an adventurous, violent, almost always illegal, and moreover anarchistic form, found a sort of homeland in Germany after 1871, but there it took a prudent, methodical, carefully organized, and almost always legal form. The German workers were organized at the beginning of the imperialist period; they took advantage of the new expansion of the capitalist economy to win themselves a more human existence within the framework of the regime. Interrupted by the misery of the war and the postwar period and by the revolutionary impetus that resulted from it, the working-class movement took up where it left off after October 1923, as soon as that revolutionary impetus had been smashed; and from 1924 to 1929 it found excellent soil for growth in a Germany somewhat giddy from economic prosperity. It can be said that the working-class organization in Germany has given its full measure within the limits of capitalist legality. The results should not be disregarded. At present, in spite of more than four years of economic crisis, the General Federation of Labor there has more than four million members; factories that employ only trade-union members are not uncommon; and the key industries, the railroads, and the state enterprises are, because of the proportion of union workers in them, in the hands of the Federation. This formidable organization secured quite high wages for the German workers during the boom. But organizing the workers in the factories is only a part of the German trade unions' efforts to increase the workers' health, happiness, and prosperity. Subscriptions serve to maintain numerous and very substantial relief funds. In addition there are trade-union libraries, trade-union schools where workers selected by the unions can stay at union expense,

Published in *L'Ecole émancipée*, January 8, 1933.

and freethinkers' associations and sports organizations that are organically tied to the unions, all of which allow the workers to devote their leisure time to the cultivation of mind and body. All this is wonderfully organized, and housed in magnificent buildings where one again meets with the same almost mad extravagance as that displayed by the capitalists during the boom. One must recognize that German reformism has done a marvelous job of ordering the lives of the workers as humanely as it is possible to do within the capitalist regime. It has not freed the German workers from their chains, but it has obtained some valuable benefits for them: a little comfort, a little leisure, some cultural opportunities.

But the German trade-union organizations not only have to adapt themselves to the conditions created by the regime; through the force of circumstance, they are bound to the regime by bonds they cannot break. They grew with the regime, and they have assumed, so to speak, its exact shape; they can exist only within the capitalist system and in the shadow of the power that is the protector of the present order, the power of the state. It goes without saying that, for the offices, schools, and libraries that are laid out in such beautiful buildings, an illegal existence is not even conceivable. As for the trade-union funds, their very wealth makes them dependent on the state, the protector of capital.

"The assets of the trade unions," writes the trade-union mouthpiece *Die Arbeit,* "are, for the most part, invested in mortgage bonds. To obtain liquid funds, the unions have to mortgage these bonds to the Reichsbank or sell them on the Stock Exchange. The government can block off these two channels if the unions spend this money not for social welfare but to finance major struggles."

In this way the trade unions are bound to the state apparatus by golden chains; and by these same golden chains, which they themselves have forged, the workers in their turn are bound to the trade-union apparatus and, through it, to the apparatus of the state. For expulsion, a weapon the trade-union apparatus frequently uses against workers who would like to orient it toward the struggle against the state, is a genuine hardship; the expelled worker loses his rights to aid from the relief funds to which he made such heavy contributions. And the organizations that are tied to the trade-union federation necessarily adopt a similar attitude toward the state. The Social Democratic party is a case in point. The pure trade unionists sometimes try to shift responsibility for the political line followed by the German trade unions onto the Social Democratic party, to which all the militants of the trade-union movement belong. But even before the war the German trade unions had a far less combative attitude toward the regime than Social Democracy, and the same is still true today. Far from the Social Democratic party's controlling the trade-union movement, it can be said that the party is more the parliamentary expression of the relations between the trade-union apparatus and the state apparatus; the events of the twentieth and twenty-first of July 1932 furnish an example of this.[1] The very way the German trade unions are structured prohibits them from cutting their ties to the present social system for fear of being crushed. Even should there come a stage of the capitalist economy in which Marx's formula is proved to be true, in which the regime deprives the workers of everything except their chains, it would not be possible for the German trade unions to change the purpose for which they were originally intended and become instruments suitable for overthrowing the regime; any more than a file, in case of need, could change itself into a hammer.

Well, that time seems to have come. Or at any rate it is incontestable that the formula cited above has proved true for the duration of the crisis, and has proved true generally insofar as the capitalist economy is doomed to remain, as most people think it will, in a state of latent crisis. And as the capitalist regime was shaken more severely by the crisis, the German trade unions, far from disengaging themselves from the regime, in fact clung more and more fearfully to the power of the state as the only element of stability.

Several years have already passed since the German trade-union federation openly subordinated its action to the state by agreeing to what the Germans call the "rule of wage rates." According to this rule, every labor contract has the force of law, and every dispute has to be brought before an arbitration board whose decision also has the force of law. If the workers want to strike without the employers' having violated the conditions of the labor contract or the decision by arbitration, the trade unions, bound by the *Friedenspflicht* (literally "duty of peace"), must oppose it, under penalty of losing their legal status. Of course, the trade-union apparatus scrupulously respects the *Friedenspflicht*, not only by cutting off aid to all so-called wildcat strikes—that is, strikes not approved by the union—but even by occasionally expelling union members who participate in them.

---

1 On July 20 Chancellor von Papen deposed the Social Democratic government of Prussia. The Social Democrats and trade-union leaders considered calling for a general strike, but decided against it out of fear that it might lead to civil war.

This law of wage rates—which, it was said, was to protect the workers against arbitrary actions on the part of the employers—has in fact served to shield the factory owners in their attacks on wages. As for the Social Democratic party, one knows how it constantly capitulated under the Brüning government;[2] at the time labor contracts were renewed it allowed Brüning to reduce all wages by emergency decree. The result of this policy was that by the time Brüning lost power the factory workers had slipped, almost without resistance, from a fairly high standard of living to an impoverished state.

Then came von Papen's government and the coup d'etat of July 20 which, by abruptly expelling Social Democracy from the government of Prussia, stripped it of what remained of its political power. Everyone expected vigorous resistance. At the time of the Kapp putsch in 1920[3] German Social Democracy had shown how vigorous it could be. In July 1932 it remained inert. Why? In private conversations, trade-union militants gave the following explanations, thus revealing the real relations between Social Democracy, the trade-union organizations, and the state: "To us, the safety of our organizations is the primary consideration. Political reaction, in itself, does not endanger them in any way. In its present stage of development the capitalist economy needs the trade unions. And we're not afraid of Hitler; if he attempted a putsch, he would be faced with us on one side and the government apparatus on the other."

The conclusion was that the only thing the trade-union organizations have to fear is a struggle between them and the state, a struggle in which they would certainly be crushed.

2 Heinrich Brüning, a member of the Catholic Center party, was chancellor from March 28, 1930, until May 30, 1932. Unable to form a government supported by a majority in Parliament, Brüning was obliged to resort to article 48 of the constitution, which allowed him to govern by decree. In July 1930 the Social Democrats, the Communists, and the National Socialists voted to overrule Brüning's emergency decrees relating to the budget; the Reichstag was dissolved and new elections set for September. The September elections showed an overwhelming increase in National Socialist votes—more than six million, up from 810,000 in the election two years previously, an increase of 700 percent. The National Socialist party had become the second largest party in Germany. Alarmed by this growth, the Social Democratic party decided to "tolerate" the Brüning government as a "lesser evil," and it remained in power nearly two more years.

3 The Kapp putsch was led by General Walther von Luttwitz and Wolfgang Kapp. Its major cause was the Weimar Republic's attempt to reduce the German armed forces, as required by the Versailles Treaty, by disbanding some of the Freikorps formations. Two Freikorps brigades occupied Berlin; the regular army refused to intervene, the government fled to Stuttgart, and Kapp proclaimed himself chancellor. The trade unions, however, called for a general strike, and the putsch collapsed.

The unions were forced out of their passivity, however, when the emergency decrees of the fourth and fifth of October authorized the factory owners, in certain cases, to lower wages below the rate fixed by the labor contract. One after another the factories affected by the decree went on strike. The unions approved these strikes insofar as they were based on the law of wage rates and, consequently, were not contrary to the *Friedenspflicht,* but, again out of respect for the *Friedenspflicht,* the unions openly did all they could to prevent each strike either from being extended to other objectives than the fight against the emergency decree or from going beyond the confines of the factory by joining up with similar movements. They succeeded in this all the more easily as the employers, attracted by the production bonuses that von Papen had just instituted, generally gave in immediately. Some factory owners appealed to the arbitration board, which of course decided in their favor; the union, conforming as always to the *Friedenspflicht,* then broke the strike. Only one strike was difficult to break: the famous movement of the Berlin transport workers, when Communists and Hitlerites together succeeded in bringing streetcars, busses, and subways to a complete halt for a period of several days; but on November 8 the striking transport workers went back to their jobs, having gained nothing.

The ministerial crisis[4] caused by the elections of November 6 marks the beginning of a new stage in the history of the relations between German reformism and the state. Social Democracy announced that it would fight von Papen by every possible means if he returned to power; it let it be understood that its opposition to von Schleicher would be more moderate. When von Schleicher became chancellor, Leipart, a leader of the trade-union bureaucracy, said to the special correspondent from *Excelsior:* "We have nothing to reproach the Chancellor with as regards his political past; the social problem is very much in the forefront of his concerns."[5] In order to appreciate this statement, one needs to know that it was von Schleicher

---

4 The November 6 election gave no party a majority. Von Papen resigned on November 17, expecting to be reappointed by President Hindenburg and to govern by decree until the constitution and the electoral laws could be changed. Von Schleicher, however, charged that the reappointment of von Papen would run the risk of civil war, and Hindenburg asked von Papen to step aside. On December 2 von Schleicher, who expected to be able to form either a national-front government that included the National Socialists or a broad front including the National Socialists and the trade-union leaders, was appointed chancellor.

5 Leipart later flatly denied having said this, but the journalist stands by what he wrote. All that one can affirm on this subject is that the statements reported by *Excelsior* are wholly consistent with Leipart's reputation in Germany. (Note of s w)

who gave the Hitlerite storm troops the right to wear uniforms again and who organized the coup d'etat of July 20. Leipart announced that the unions were ready to grant von Schleicher a truce if he organized work for the unemployed, abolished the emergency decrees by which von Papen had reduced wages and unemployment relief, and gave up the idea of changing the electoral law and the constitution. However, so far neither Social Democracy nor von Schleicher has done anything to bring about a rapprochement; each is standing his ground, the one with its social demands, the other with his declarations of attachment to the traditional economy and the economic measures of von Papen. Perhaps some underground deals are being made. In any case, for both sides it's a waiting game.

In what direction will German reformism move? To a great extent the crisis is making it lose its effectiveness, not only from the point of view of the proletariat but also from that of the capitalists. When the bourgeoisie is in a position to allow the workers some comforts, it can count on the benefits they possess inside the regime to tie them to the regime; when nothing is left to them but their chains, the bourgeoisie cannot count on the memory of the benefits that the workers once enjoyed to keep them pacified. In the first instance, the bourgeoisie is satisfied with corporative organizations under the indirect control of the state; in the second, it may need organizations from the inside of which it can exercise direct constraint over the workers—that is, fascist organizations. For, notwithstanding the oratory of the Communist parties, the German trade unions are not yet fascist. In a fascist union, the factory owners and the workers are organized together, membership is compulsory for the workers, and the government intervenes directly; none of these characteristics is found in the German trade unions. Will the secret complicity of the trade-union apparatus be enough for the German bourgeoisie, or will it have to establish a fascist regime? All that can be said for certain on this subject is that the present equilibrium is unstable. The most unstable equilibrium may last a long time but the slightest shock is enough to destroy it, and in Germany manifestations of despair on the part of the unemployed may produce that shock. But if the German bourgeoisie resorts to fascism, another question arises: will it unleash the Hitlerite gangs, under the command of von Schleicher or of Hitler himself, against the working-class organizations, regardless of whether they are revolutionary or reformist? Or will it turn to the trade-union apparatus itself in order to painlessly transform the unions into fascist organizations?

Would the union workers allow their own organizations to cynically betray their cause in this way? Before asking this question, one must ask how it happens that they have accepted everything they have accepted so far.

Four

The cadres of German Social Democracy are creatures who are as naturally found lodged in the magnificent offices of the reformist organizations as is the nautilus in its chambered shell; they are contented, self-satisfied creatures, brothers of those chambered in the most luxurious offices of government or industry, and they are wholly estranged from the proletariat. Our German comrades call them "bonzes."[1] But the base, despite the presence of some members of the petty bourgeoisie, is essentially working class; and, moreover, it is composed of workers who are fully conscious of belonging, above and beyond all else, to the proletariat.

Some may deny this. Certainly the German workers, finding within the regime a little comfort and the occasional possibility of enjoying the only pleasures that mean anything to them—music, intellectual culture, physical exercise, outdoor life—have become attached to the organizations that provide these benefits and have been diverted from dangerous attempts to destroy the system of production in order to construct another. But one cannot reproach them for that. It is natural that a worker who neither looks to the revolution for adventure nor views it simply as a myth does not embark on the revolutionary path unless he sees no other way out and that course seems feasible to him. The most fully conscious worker is the one who has the clearest idea not only of the main defects of the regime but also of the immense tasks and the crushing responsibilities that a revolution entails. True, for the generation that has now reached maturity, the war made the essentially inhuman character of the regime clear enough, especially in starving and defeated Germany. But the revolutionary movement that followed the war was twice crushed, first through the bloody

Published in *L'Ecole émancipée,* January 15, 1933.

1 "Bonze" is a Japanese word meaning "priest." As used by the European Left it was a derogatory term for members of a parasitic and powerful bureaucracy.

defeat of the Spartacists[2] and then without a fight in the defeat of October 1923. What is surprising in the fact that afterward the German workers again took it easy in this capitalist world that prosperity was once more making habitable? And if some of them succumbed to giddiness during that wave of prosperity that made Ford himself reel, it must be remembered that everyone around them was predicting, with the eloquence that comes from conviction, a period of continuous progress for the capitalist economy and a continuous increase in comfort, cultural opportunities, and newly won political liberties for the workers.

Now the crisis is upon us. Because it is a purely economic phenomenon, the crisis shows the inhuman character of the regime even more clearly than the war did. It is more effective than any propaganda in making the workers (all of whom have been more or less brutally hit by it) understand that they have no place in the system as human beings, but are mere tools, tools that are left to rust when there is nothing to be gained from using them for work. At the same time the regime is losing its trappings of democracy. And now the crisis is in its fourth year and the German proletariat seems powerless and bewildered by the catastrophe, as it was during the early years of the war—powerless, as then, to cut its ties with organizations that served it in happier times but now can only hand it over to the mechanical cruelty of the system.

However, there is no doubt at all that Social Democracy has lost quite a lot of its influence since the beginning of the crisis. In the July 31 elections, it lost 700,000 votes; in the November 6 elections, another 600,000.[3] But the main thing is that even inside the reformist organizations there are signs of disagreements, sometimes of an extraordinarily violent nature,

2 The Spartacist League, founded by Karl Liebknecht and Rosa Luxemburg, was originally a Left, antiwar, revolutionary opposition group within the Social Democratic party. During the soldiers' and workers' revolt of November 1918 that ousted the kaiser, the Spartacists tried to utilize the workers' and soldiers' councils that grew out of the revolt to establish a revolutionary government in Berlin in competition with the new Social Democratic government. This failed, and at the end of December the Spartacists separated from the Independent Socialists and formed the German Communist party. Early in January they called for an end to the Social Democratic government and occupied the Social Democratic party's newspaper building and the Berlin police headquarters. The government responded with military force, and, with the help of the newly created Freikorps, the Spartacist uprising was put down within a few days. Thousands were killed in Berlin alone, including Liebknecht and Luxemburg.

3 Weil has the figures turned around. In July the Social Democratic party lost 618,000 votes; in November, 711,700.

between those who represent the organizations (and, like them, are indissolubly tied to the regime) and the workers who make up the organizations and whom the regime itself repulses. As it is, the Social Democrats only reluctantly agreed to vote for Hindenburg.[4] Social Democracy's passivity on July 20 caused indignation in the entire rank and file, and even in the part of the trade-union apparatus that is in contact with the rank and file. After July 20 debate began in the Social Democratic sections, something hitherto unheard of. The older members supported the leaders; the young demanded action, a united front with the Communists, and a struggle against all the terroristic measures the bureaucracy is trying to impose by raising the specter of civil war. But the young are not changing the attitude of the organizations. And even though the organizations are not keeping up their full numerical strength, they are at least—and this is more important—maintaining their strategic positions. The trade unions continue to rule in the factories, and so far they have succeeded in crushing every movement of any scope to which they are opposed. The reformist bureaucracy continues to control the wheels of the production process. The workers are balking, but the bureaucracy does what it wants.

What does it want? To save its offices. To save the organizations, without asking what purpose they serve. The bonzes are assisted in this task by honest militants who, out of long habit of devotion to the organizations, consider them ends in themselves. But what danger threatens these organizations that capitalism, as one trade-union functionary used to say, doesn't need? Only one: civil war. A working-class insurrection would begin by sweeping them away, and an armed attack by the Hitlerite gangs would crush them. So it is a matter of avoiding acute forms of the class struggle, of preserving peace at any price, that is, at the price of any capitulation whatever. It would probably not frighten the bonzes to accept a fascist regime, especially since the measures of state capitalism that fascism entails could easily seem like "a little bit of socialism" to people for whom socialism is nothing more than state capitalism. On the other hand, the united front does frighten them; like everyone else, they know that Kerensky[5] would have done better to ally himself with Kornilov rather

4 In the presidential elections of 1932 the Social Democratic party urged its members to vote for Hindenburg as a "lesser evil" than Hitler, although it had opposed the monarchist and conservative Hindenburg in the previous presidential election in 1925.

5 Aleksandr Kerensky (1881–1970) became head of the provisional Russian government in July 1917. In September Lavr Kornilov, the commander-in-chief of the Russian army, at-

than Lenin. There is nothing to equal the tone of hatred with which they speak of the Communist party. Moreover, although they repeat their fine words of the old days, they do so without conviction; at times their contradictions prove they are lying and have no illusions. "One cannot arrive at socialism except by passing through democracy," they say. But in August they asserted that the only favorable times for proposing socialist measures are times of acute crisis. Because such times are always periods when democracy is suspended and when Social Democracy has no share in power, this is a confession of impotence. They also say, "The issue is not whether there will be a fascist Germany or a soviet Germany, but a fascist Germany or a Weimar Republic." It is not by such hollow formulas that the bonzes are able to win over the workers. How, then, do they do it?

When the German workers, whom we used to count on to ensure world peace, found themselves face to face with war, they were thrown into disarray not only by nationalist lies but also by the fact that they had only one organization, and that organization was sending them to war. German workers find it infinitely difficult to make up their minds to take any action that is not organized. And so, if they were in the same situation now, one would understand their allowing themselves to be led by the reformist bureaucracy. For reformist tactics are the only sensible tactics to use inside the regime and, consequently, the only sensible ones for anyone who doesn't want or doesn't dare to overthrow the regime. These tactics are, by definition, tactics of choosing the lesser evil. The regime is evil; if it is not overthrown, it must be made as comfortable as possible. When the bourgeoisie is forced by the crisis to tighten its grip, tactics of choosing the lesser evil are necessarily tactics of capitulation. The older workers, who during a crisis continue to think as they did before the crisis, submit to these tactics quite naturally. The young workers cry out that they want to fight; but as they don't dare to initiate the struggle to overthrow the whole system of production, and as they are all aware (though they are careful not to say so) that the struggle has no other objective, they, too, finally agree to capitulate. Once again, all that would be entirely understandable in an unarmed proletariat whose organizations were in the hands of its enemies.

The Hitlerite party is indeed in the hands of big capital, and Social Democracy is in the hands of the German state. But the German proletariat

tempted a coup to establish a conservative military government. The coup was crushed largely by the workers' soviets of the radical Left. In October the Left, led by Lenin, overthrew the Kerensky government.

now has what it didn't have in 1914, a Communist party. Certainly, since the beginning of the crisis, the Communist party has attracted broad masses of the unemployed and some members of the petty bourgeoisie; similarly, the Hitlerite party has attracted broad masses of the ruined petty bourgeoisie and a quite significant number of the unemployed. Having lost everything due to the crisis, these people are naturally ready to try anything, and are flinging themselves at the two parties that promise something new; those who feel solidarity with the working class are moving to the party that proclaims the dictatorship of the proletariat. But the factory workers are not being swept along by this current. Those workers—that is, the ones who play a responsible role in the production process and who, through their daily work, maintain society and can transform it—either remain indifferent or else follow the reformists. There are, of course, exceptions, but they are relatively few in number. And so Social Democracy is little concerned about losing the unemployed and the petty bourgeoisie—which, by the way, it is far from losing completely. Its strategic strength is in the factories, and, whatever the future may bring, up to now this strength has remained almost intact. Social Democracy will be defeated only when the employed workers embark on an action coherent and extensive enough to jeopardize the social system.

That the workers in the factories are resisting Hitlerite demagogy proves that, in spite of the miserable situation to which they have been reduced—their low wages, the lack of job security, the factory shutdowns that shorten their working hours and affect their whole family—they are not giving way to despair. One cannot admire them enough. But how are we to understand their allowing themselves to be crushed by the regime when a Communist party exists that is completely suited, it seems, to be a powerful tool in their hands to destroy and rebuild the system of production? What is it that prevents the working masses who still have jobs in the factories, and particularly those among them who are still young, from having confidence in the Communist party?

Five ■ The Communist Movement

In times of prosperity, the revolutionary movement generally depends mainly on the strongest part of the proletariat, on those highly skilled workers who feel that they are the essential element in production, know that they are indispensable, and are afraid of nothing. A crisis radicalizes the unemployed, but it also allows the bosses to drive the revolutionary workers out of the system of production, and forces those who are still in the factories (who are all, even the most skilled, afraid of losing their jobs) into a submissive attitude. Thereafter, the revolutionary movement relies on the weakest part of the working class. This displacement of the revolutionary movement's axis is the only thing that enables the bourgeoisie to get through a crisis without foundering; and conversely, an uprising of the masses left in the factories is the only thing that can really endanger the bourgeoisie. The existence of a strong revolutionary organization, therefore, is a nearly decisive factor. But for a revolutionary organization to be said to be strong, the phenomenon that reduces the proletariat to impotence in times of crisis must not be reflected in the organization, or reflected in it only to a very slight degree.

The apparent strength of the German Communist party is considerable. The still-living memories of 1919 and 1920, and even those of 1923, give it a radiance and a prestige that we French, whose revolutionary tradition broke off in May 1871, can hardly imagine. In November the Communist party attracted six million voters; its own membership then stood at 330,000. Groups such as the worker relief section, the Red relief section, the association of proletarian freethinkers, and especially the Red sports associations are also numerically strong, influential, and vigorous. However, the most important of these organizations, a military organization intended for street fighting (*Rote Front Kämpferbund*) was banned two years ago and has been unable to carry on an illegal existence. Since then part of its membership has even gone over to the Hitlerite storm troops. As for the Party itself, although it is numerically strong, newcomers are in the majority. Some people say that only one-fifth of its members have been in the Party more than three years. This phenomenon, which is also found in several other sections of the International, and which is evidently due, at

Published in *L'Ecole émancipée*, January 29, 1933.

least in part, to the Party's recruiting methods and its internal regime, is particularly dangerous in a revolutionary period. Finally, and most important, the German Communist party is for all practical purposes a party of the unemployed; by last May, the proportion of the unemployed had already reached 84 percent (cf. *Internationale Syndicale Rouge* no. 19–20, p. 916). As for the trade-union organizations under the control of the Party, their total membership is less than that of the Party itself, and they are about half composed of the unemployed. Thus the German Communist movement offers no remedy for the split that the economic crisis itself produces between the unemployed and the workers in the factories; it reflects that split, and reflects it in an intensified way.

The fact is that the Communist party had failed to become solidly rooted in the factories. The main cause is probably the Party's unionization tactics. Faced with the exclusionary measures that time and time again struck down the revolutionary members of the reformist unions, one could choose between two methods: invite all the politically conscious workers into the Red unions, as our CGTU[1] does, or establish, with the expelled workers alone, Red unions that do not recruit and that try to increase their influence, not their numerical strength. The Belgian "Knights of Labor" chose the latter method; the Borinage[2] strike demonstrated its value, and it seems the most appropriate when only individual expulsions occur. But in Germany no choice was made; Red unions were organized that paralleled the opposition organizations, and the two contradictory slogans "Strengthen the Red Unions" and "Work in the Reformist Unions" were always maintained side by side. As a result, the Red unions have remained skeletal in the face of the four-million-strong reformist unions; but their existence has been enough, on the one hand, to allow the reformists to portray the Communists as enemies of the trade-union organizations in the same way as the Hitlerites are, and on the other hand, to make the Red militants neglect propaganda in the Social Democratic unions. What is more, at one time the slogan "Destroy the Unions" was openly proclaimed. Although this slogan was abandoned, the fear of being ac-

1 *Confédération générale du Travail unitaire*, the Communist-dominated French trade-union association.

2 There had been a miners' strike in the Borinage region of Belgium from July 6 to September 7, 1932. Weil visited the area on September 6, on her way back from Germany, and discussed the strike with a Trotskyite who was one of the leaders of a nonrecruiting Red trade union called the Belgian Knights of Labor.

cused of returning to a slogan denounced by the Brandlerites[3] ("Make the Bonzes Fight") kept the militants paralyzed for a long time. This unprecedented negligence in regard to propaganda in the reformist unions came to an end only quite recently. Then again, both the Red unions and the opposition groups suffer from a stifling regime of bureaucratic dictatorship. As for the task of organizing in the factories, an inconceivable indifference in that regard has been the rule for a long time.

In contrast to Social Democracy and the Hitlerite movement—the one so powerfully entrenched in the factories through its influence over the workers, and the other having, in addition to its working-class followers, the advantage of the secret or overt support of the bosses—the German Communist party has no ties to the production process. It's not surprising that the existence of such a party is not enough, by itself, to turn the oppressed masses toward revolutionary action. Consequently everything depends on the influence that the German Communist party can manage to acquire inside the two other parties; in other words, at the present time the German Communist party must be judged in terms of its relations with the Hitlerite movement on the one hand and with Social Democracy on the other.

How can the German Communist party gain influence within the Hitlerite movement? Every attempt in this direction must keep in mind that, even if the Party were to bring over to its side everything in the Hitlerite movement that is connected to the proletariat, it would not thereby become capable of fulfilling its revolutionary tasks. For one thing, the membership of workers who could allow themselves to be deceived by fascist demagogy would not exactly be of a nature to raise the political level of the Party; for another, apart from members of the big bourgeoisie and the petty bourgeoisie, some office workers and some unemployed workers, the Hitlerite movement contains only a few factory workers, the majority of whom, it is true, are situated at key points of the economy, but they are too few to constitute a significant force by themselves. On the other hand, if the Communist party could win the confidence of the reformist masses in the factories, it would thereby acquire almost invincible strength. And so a partial agreement between Hitlerites and Communists, even if it may facilitate the spread of Communist propaganda among Hitlerite workers, is highly

3 A right-wing opposition group that unconditionally supported the policies of Stalin and the USSR. Its leader, Heinrich Brandler, was expelled from the German Communist party in 1929.

dangerous if it is likely to arouse the mistrust of the Social Democratic workers. Besides, the tactics of partial agreement are not effective tactics in the struggle against Hitler's influence. For the Hitlerite leaders are first of all demagogues and adventurers, and they do not shrink from illegal action when the need arises; thus, in certain determined circumstances, they can, unlike the reformist leaders, not only issue the same slogans as the Communist party but also go at least as far as it in implementing them. Furthermore, it goes without saying that in a strike, for instance, one cannot refuse the support of Hitlerite strikers; but in such a case great care must be taken not to do anything that could give this unity of action a suspect character in the eyes of the Social Democratic workers; and every possible means must be used to try to draw them into the struggle. In short, the only way the Communist party can win over the Hitlerite workers without alienating the Social Democratic workers is to unsparingly denounce both the petty treacheries that the Hitlerite leaders commit every day and the essentially reactionary character of their entire policy. Or rather, there is another still more effective way, which is for the Communist party to become truly strong. But that is what it cannot do without winning the confidence of the reformist workers.

In regard to the reformist workers, propaganda by itself is not of much use. They certainly feel, the young especially, that their leaders are capitulating, but they are not convinced that there might be another alternative. Obviously on this point words alone are not effective. One can convince them only by making them feel through experience, in action, the strength that the organized working class possesses. And to do this, it is they who must be brought to act, for the Communist party is too weak, by itself, to successfully lead an action of any scope. What the Communist party must do, therefore, is organize a united front with limited objectives, and lead the struggle effectively enough to inspire in the workers more confidence than they now have in themselves and in it. True, the reformist leaders are constantly maneuvering to prevent such a united front, and their maneuverings are facilitated by the Communist party's isolation. The latter has only one way of outmaneuvering these schemes, and that is to make concessions. There is one concession it can never make, namely, to relinquish its right of criticism. But it can moderate the tone of its criticisms, and give up a violence that is perhaps legitimate but is really harmful. In order to show that it is not the enemy of the trade-union organizations, despite its disastrous slogans, the Party can suspend recruiting for the tiny Red unions or even ask for the reinstatement of the expelled workers. Above all, it can address all proposals for a united front not only to the base but to every level of the reformist hierarchy. Under certain circumstances such tactics could probably force the reformist leaders to accept a united front; in any case, it would make it much more difficult for them to reject it without discrediting themselves in the minds of the workers who follow them.

Six

The German Communist party's policy has actually been, up to now, exactly the opposite. The only means being used to win over the reformist workers is purely verbal propaganda; revolution is being preached to people who are wondering not if it is desirable but if it is possible. The Party accuses the reformist leaders of treason, but it has no business judging the Social Democrats' policy of capitulation in this way unless it demonstrates that it is itself capable of victoriously leading the proletariat on the opposite path, that of struggle. This can't be demonstrated by words alone, and so far the Party hasn't demonstrated it in any other way. Also, the oft-repeated formulas that refer to Social Democracy as the "main enemy," as "social fascism," etc., only have the effect of cutting the Communist party off from the Social Democratic workers; especially when it goes as far as to apply the term "social fascist" to the tiny Socialist Workers' party, which is made up partly of revolutionary workers and partly of reformist elements, but which is revolted by the Social Democrats' capitulations. In the area of trade unions, the German Communist party stubbornly maintains two contradictory slogans. As for a united front with the trade unions, it refuses to address proposals elsewhere than to the base, and the maneuvers of the reformist leaders are thereby made so much the easier.

With the Hitlerites, on the other hand, the German Communist party has several times formed a sort of united front. In particular, during the Berlin transport strike, it even went as far as to suspend for the National Socialists the famous "right of criticism" that it correctly refused to sacrifice for a united front with the Social Democrats. What is most serious of

Published in *L'Ecole émancipée*, February 5, 1933.

all is that the united front between Hitlerites and Communists sometimes seemed to be directed against Social Democracy, and in some instances actually was. Furthermore, it is understandable that, as a result of Hitlerite demagogy, the National Socialist party and the Communist party might sometimes appear to take nearly identical courses of action in the social struggle, but the German Communist party has gone as far as to follow the Hitlerite movement's lead in the area of nationalist propaganda. It placed great emphasis—and sometimes, especially during elections, primary emphasis—on nationalist demands, on the struggle against the Versailles system, and on the slogan "National Liberation." At the time of the July 31 elections it accused the Social Democrats of treason not only against the working class but against the country (*Landesverräter*). What's more, it published as a propaganda pamphlet, without any commentary, the collection of letters in which the Army officer Scheringer[1] made it clear that he had abandoned National Socialism for communism because communism, which involves prospects of military alliance with Russia, is better suited to serve Germany's national interests; this same Scheringer formed a group based on this idea, which people of the best society have joined and which is officially under the control of the Party. It should be noted that this nationalist orientation bears no relation at all to the feelings of the German Communist workers, for their internationalism is sincere and deep. The only arguments given in favor of this policy are that it gets votes in the elections and that it makes it easier for workers seduced by Hitler's demagogy to cross over to communism. However, it makes the reverse crossover just as easy. And among the Social Democratic workers it provokes only indignation and derision. What is one to think of a revolutionary party whose Central Committee said, in an appeal issued with an eye on the November 6 elections, "The chains of Versailles are getting heavier and heavier on the German workers"? So it's the chains of Versailles that the German proletariat has to break, and not the chains of capitalism? Even if the Central Committee adds that only a socialist Germany can break the chains of Versailles, its formula is nevertheless a valuable aid to the Hitlerite demagogues, who are trying above all to convince the workers that their misery is due to the treaty of Versailles and

---

1 Lieutenant Richard Scheringer, a Reichswehr officer and an avid nationalist, had been arrested in 1930 and sentenced to eighteen months in prison for trying to win over other officers to National Socialism. While in prison he abandoned National Socialism and went over to communism.

not to the fact that the whole system of production is subordinated to the pursuit of capitalist profit. Generally speaking, in times of crisis the bourgeoisie of every country always does its best to turn the discontent of the masses of workers and peasants against foreign countries, thereby avoiding being called into account itself. In Germany the Communist party publicly associated itself with this maneuver, despite Liebknecht's great saying, "The main enemy is in our own country."

In the end, the German Communist party remains isolated and left to its own strength, that is, to its own weakness. Although it continues to recruit, the rate of its progress in that area does not correspond at all to the real conditions of action; there is a monstrous discrepancy between the forces at its disposal and the tasks that it cannot abandon without losing its reason for existing. This discrepancy is all the more striking if one takes into account the appearance of strength given the Party by its electoral successes. The vanguard of the German proletariat is on the whole composed of men who are truly dedicated and courageous, but for the most part they are devoid of experience and political education, and almost all of them have been thrown out of the production process, out of the economic system, condemned to a parasitic existence. Such a party can spread feelings of revolt, not put forward revolution as a task.

The German Communist party does what it can to conceal this state of things from members and nonmembers alike. In regard to its members, it uses dictatorial methods that, by preventing free discussion, also suppress every possibility of real education within the Party. In regard to nonmembers, the Party tries to hide its inaction with endless talk. It is not that the Party remains completely inactive; in spite of everything, it's trying to do something in the factories; it has made some attempts to organize the unemployed; it leads tenants' strikes (which it has not, however, managed to carry beyond the limits of a street or part of a district); it fights Hitlerite terrorists. All of which doesn't amount to very much. The Party makes up for this with verbiage, boasting, and ineffectual slogans. When the Hitlerites want to give the appearance of being a workers' party, their propaganda and that of the Communist party sound almost the same. However, this demagogic attitude on the part of the Communist party only heightens the factory workers' distrust of it. On the other hand, in the organization of meetings, in the ritual words and gestures, Communist propaganda increasingly resembles religious propaganda; it's as if the revolution were on its way to becoming a myth whose purpose, like that of other myths, were simply to make an intolerable situation bearable.

Many comrades will be tempted to believe that this description has been deliberately exaggerated. Nevertheless, they will find at least partial confirmation of it in the Communist press, especially in no. 19–20 of the *Internationale Syndicale Rouge* and in Piatnitsky's[2] speech to the Twelfth Plenum of the Executive Committee of the Communist International. In truth, several facts could be cited that would seem to contradict this description, and in recent weeks, in particular, there seems to have been at least some slight progress. In order that our comrades can judge if, on the whole, this description is accurate, they must have before them as objective an account as possible of the recent history of the German Communist movement.

2 Josef Piatnitsky (1882–1938), an Old Bolshevik, became a member of the Executive Committee of the Communist International in 1921, and was one of the leading figures of the Comintern after 1930.

Seven

At the Twelfth Plenum of the Executive Committee of the Communist International, Piatnitsky said,

> The German Communist party showed that it is capable of shifting and reorganizing its work when necessary. You know, for instance, that the German Communist party leadership decided against participating in the referendum on the dissolution of the Prussian Landtag. Lead articles against participating in the referendum were published in several Party newspapers. But when the Central Committee, together with the Communist International, decided that the Party should take an active part in the referendum, the German comrades mobilized the whole Party in a few days. Except for the Communist party of the U S S R, no party could have done as much.

What Piatnitsky is congratulating the German Communist party for in these terms is something analogous to the sudden reversals that we sometimes see at federal congresses. Remember the most typical of these sudden turnabouts, and imagine the effect it would have produced if it had concerned a question of primary importance for the whole country, and of burning immediacy. That's exactly what happened in Germany a year and

Published in *L'Ecole émancipée*, February 12, 1933.

a half ago, when the Hitlerites organized a referendum against the Social Democratic Landtag of Prussia. The Social Democratic workers laugh even today when they relate how their Communist comrades suddenly began to make propaganda for the referendum, although only the day before they were swearing that their taking part in it was out of the question. The consequences of their participation are still being felt. The Hitlerites initiated the referendum with the avowed purpose of taking over the government of Prussia; thus it was a question of a struggle between the Social Democratic party (which, by its very nature, always tries to establish a certain equilibrium between the proletariat and the bourgeoisie) and the Hitlerite party, whose objective is the complete crushing of the proletariat and the extermination of its vanguard. The German Communist party sided with the Hitlerite party in this struggle, by formal order of the Comintern. That is what is officially known as the "Red referendum." According to *Die Rote Fahne*,[1] this abrupt turnabout was accepted in the Party "without discussion." It was at this time that "national liberation" began to be spoken of, and Scheringer's statements about "war for liberation" and "the dead of the world war who gave their lives for a free Germany" were published in the Party press (*Fanfare*[2] of August 1, 1931). The impression that all this produced on the reformist masses is easy to imagine.

The logical consequences of this orientation unfolded during the remainder of 1931 and the first months of 1932. During this period of the vertical, vertiginous rise of National Socialism the German Communist party directed all its efforts against Social Democracy. Piatnitsky acknowledges this. "After the Eleventh Plenum," he says (that is, beginning in June 1931), "Social Democracy is correctly characterized in the documents of the German Communist party as the main social bulwark of the bourgeoisie, but then they forgot about the fascists." Even at that time a strange strategy had begun to develop in the Party, that of setting "the trap of power" for Hitler. The consequences of this entire policy became apparent in the course of the presidential elections in which Social Democracy succeeded in marshaling all its troops for Hindenburg and practically not a single Social Democratic worker voted for Thaelmann.[3]

In the months that followed, this course was very clearly corrected; but the credit for that goes not to the German Communist party but to the

1 Daily newspaper of the German Communist party.
2 German Communist party journal.
3 Ernst Thaelmann (1886–1944), leader of the German Communist party.

Hitlerite storm troops. The Hitlerites actually began to murder Communists in their homes or in the streets; there was a whole series of bloody skirmishes between Hitlerites and Communists. From that time on the Communist party was forced, despite the resolutions of the Eleventh Plenum, to reverse its position and direct its efforts mainly against fascism. But the Hitlerites rendered an even greater service to the German proletariat when they began to attack Communists and Social Democrats indiscriminately; they thus provoked the spontaneous formation of a united front, and nearly brought into being that "Marxist bloc" which unfortunately existed only in the declarations of their leaders. The Communist party could have organized this spontaneous united front, broadened it, and carried it into the factories. It did nothing of the sort. This is verified by Piatnitsky:

> How was the united front brought about? In the streets. Thanks to the fact that the Nazis did not distinguish between Social Democrats and Communists, but struck down Social Democratic workers, reformists, and those without any party affiliation as well as Communists; thanks to that the united front was formed. It's a perfectly good united front and I have nothing to say against it. It's the united front of the class struggle. But we came to it indirectly, not in the factories, not in the Labor Exchanges, not in the trade unions. And when it was carried into the factories, then, in the majority of cases, it was not thanks to our own work, but because the workers were shocked by the murders and organized strikes on the day of the victims' burial.

In July, however, the united front began to take an organized form. In many places committees of antifascist struggle were created; contrary to the doctrine of a united front "only from below," proposals for a united front were made from organization to organization. What's more, the united front was even carried into the parliaments; in the Landtags of Prussia and Hesse, the Communists gave their votes to a Social Democrat to avoid the election of a Hitlerite. Nevertheless, the Party continued to use the phrase "social fascism," and nationalist demands headed the electoral program. The incoherence of this policy, the mistakes of the preceding months, and the paucity of contact with the masses had as their natural outcome the disaster of the twentieth and twenty-first of July 1932.

The twentieth of July is the day on which von Papen's coup d'état expelled the Social Democrats from the Prussian government. The German Communist party decided to take up the defense of the Prussian government against von Papen—the same Prussian government that it had, a year earlier, attacked in alliance with Hitler. This decision could have rapidly increased the Party's influence on the reformist masses, for the split between the cadres and the base of Social Democracy (a split that made it impossible to muster even the support that the Social Democrats had given Hindenburg's candidacy) became, thanks to Social Democracy's passivity, an accomplished fact on that historic day. If the Communist party had been able to contrast this passivity with its own capacity for action, it would thereby have gained considerable authority.

What did it do? It did absolutely nothing, except, with no preparation, issue a hasty call for a general strike. This call met with no response whatever, even in the very bosom of the Party. "The Party organizations did not respond to the call for the strike," says Piatnitsky, and he adds that this was not at all unexpected. Not one Social Democratic worker—what's more, not one Communist worker—took seriously a call that, issued under such conditions, could only end up discrediting the slogan "general strike." The German Communist party gave the impression on July 20 that it was trifling with such an important slogan, that it was practically using it as an alibi to conceal its inaction. Among the Social Democratic workers, the memory of July 20 arouses both indignation and laughter; indignation when they think of Social Democracy, laughter when they think of the Communist party. As for the Communist militants, the events of that day brought on a very profound depression in their ranks. For the first time they clearly perceived to what degree their party was isolated from the masses, and how completely incapable it was of any kind of effective action.

The electoral success of July 31 gave them the impression that at last they had a breathing space. But this success also prevented the salutary consequences that might have resulted from their depression; namely, a serious examination of the Party's mistakes. What's more, the Central Committee of the Party decided to censure the parliamentary fractions of the Prussian and Hessian Landtags, and to return to the practice of forming the united front "only from below." Or at any rate that's what the Trotskyites said; at the base of the Party nobody knew anything about these decisions. But what is certain is that after July 31 there were no longer any proposals for a united front made from organization to organization; moreover, as the Hitlerite acts of violence became more infrequent and soon stopped, the committees for a united front that had sprung up spontaneously in July rapidly disappeared.

Eight

All during August 1932, the Communist party was practically reduced to illegality. Its press was muzzled; its meetings, sometimes even private ones, were prohibited; its militants were hit with incredibly harsh penalties when there were clashes between them and the Hitlerites, even if no blood was shed; and, of course, its partisans were hounded out of the factories. Isolated as it was, and lacking any experience of illegal action, it could offer no resistance. It feared being reduced to a completely illegal status if it acted. In Berlin, during that whole month of August, one had the painful impression most of the time that the German Communist party did not exist. However, the Party was frantically trying to regain a foothold in the factories, and it was directing its efforts in accordance with the theory that had been in favor in the International for some time: "Fight for everyday demands, even the smallest."[1] Thus the same Communist International that so often wanted to artificially politicize wage disputes was now wanting to drag into the area of wage claims a proletariat quite convinced that the situation left room only for a political struggle. Fortunately for the Party, the emergency decrees of September 5 and 6[2] gave every wage dispute the character of a direct struggle against the power of the state.

These emergency decrees finally precipitated a spontaneous wave of strikes. In many factories the workers—thanks to the three-party united front and especially to the recently instituted production bonuses that made the employers want to avoid conflict—were victorious after one or two days of struggle, or even on the strength of mere threats. The Communist party took credit for everything, strikes and victories, with no further explanation, so that anyone reading its press was tempted to suppose that a miracle had transformed the extreme weakness of the proletariat and the Party into overwhelming strength within the space of a few days. The Party thus failed in its most elementary duty, which is to inform the workers and give them a clear idea of the relation of forces. In addition, the influence of the Red trade-union organizations probably increased

Published in *L'Ecole émancipée*, February 19, 1933.

1 "Partial" or "everyday" demands were ordinary economic demands that were not revolutionary in nature.

2 Evidently a misprint for October 4 and 5. See p. 113.

during this period, but they were unable either to coordinate or to extend the strike movement.

Two weeks after this movement had apparently ended, one week before the elections, a dispute broke out in the Berlin transport system.[3] Fourteen thousand reformist union members out of 21,000 called for a strike, but it fell short of the statutory majority. The Red union led the workers out on strike, despite the reformist bureaucracy and with the support of the Hitlerites. Social Democracy portrayed the Reds and the Hitlerites as being in agreement in wanting to destroy the organizations. It accused them of having purely electoral aims and denounced the strike as a Hitlerite maneuver imprudently supported by the Communists and perhaps intended to pave the way for a putsch. It wanted to make it appear that in trying to break the strike it was not betraying the workers but was struggling against fascism. The Communist party's attitude was the one best suited to give these formulas the appearance of truth. *Die Rote Fahne* enthusiastically recounted how Communists and Hitlerites together demolished a truck belonging to *Vorwaerts,* the Social Democratic newspaper; and it celebrated as a proletarian victory this action in which fascists had taken part. The Communist party did nothing to guard against the danger of an increase of Hitlerite influence on the workers under cover of the strike; during the week the strike lasted, up to and including the day of the elections, it directed all its attacks against Social Democracy and virtually suspended its struggle against fascist ideas. And it certainly seems that the National Socialist party gained worker votes in Berlin at that time, although it was losing them everywhere else. Now, the political aspect of the strike was all the more important in that, since the strikers were transport workers, everything happened in the streets. The Hitlerites threw their storm troops against the strikebreakers and thus got possession of the streets in certain districts. The workers also, it is true, and especially the unemployed, went spontaneously into the streets en masse to aid the pickets; judging by the panic of the bourgeois newspapers and their calls for repression, at that time the proletariat must have shown its strength. The Communist party did nothing to organize this spontaneous solidarity, even though it had enough militants in Berlin to be able to do so; but these militants were almost entirely absorbed with election propaganda. On Sunday, election day, the bureaucracy of the reformist trade

3 The Berlin municipal transport organization had announced that, due to the financial emergency, wages would be reduced.

union redoubled its efforts, and the Hitlerites began to sow disorder among the strikers by spreading false rumors. But the Communist militants had spent all their strength on electoral propaganda and kept nothing in reserve, not dreaming that another more important task awaited them. Berlioz, in *L'Humanité*,[4] recounted how they slept that night, totally exhausted, with clear consciences. The next day *Die Rote Fahne* announced in giant headlines that the strike would continue until victory was won; but layoff notices arrived, demoralizing the strikers who were no longer supported by the masses in the street. The Party indignantly rejected the proposal made by a few oppositionists not to struggle any longer except to get the layoffs rescinded. Nevertheless, that very evening traffic started to move again. And the strikers returned to work the next day, accepting not only the wage cut that had been the reason for the dispute but even the layoff of 2,500 of their comrades, who thus found themselves thrown out of work without even the paltry resource of unemployment relief. And *Die Rote Fahne* dared to report this under the headline "Betrayed, But Not Beaten."

So, in the city that is the citadel of communism in Germany, at the very moment when, having gained nearly 140,000 votes, it was far ahead of any other party in Berlin, the German Communist party had to terminate, by a complete capitulation, a strike unleashed under its sponsorship, a strike of considerable political significance, and one in which the action of the masses was as important a factor as that of the strikers themselves. The very next day after the electoral victory that had given the Communist party the appearance of such great strength the real powerlessness of the Party became as clearly and tragically evident as on the twentieth of July. Furthermore, it goes without saying that the entire official press of the Communist International celebrated the strike as a victory.

But if the strike did not increase the strength of the proletariat, it indirectly, and decisively, increased that of the bourgeoisie. For the Hitlerites, the strike was a means of blackmailing the big bourgeoisie; it was intended to make the big bourgeoisie understand that, for its own safety, it had to prevent, at all costs, the Hitlerite party from losing strength or from even temporarily turning against it. Besides, the only relations that exist between the Hitlerites and the big bourgeoisie consist of permanent and reciprocal blackmail; each would like the other to be subordinate, and

4 Daily newspaper of the French Communist party.

each would be lost without the other's help. But a party can run risks that a class cannot; that's why the maneuver the Hitlerites attempted with the transport strike ultimately led, after von Schleicher's unsuccessful attempt to domesticate the Hitlerite movement, to Hitler's being appointed chancellor.

During the three months that have elapsed in the meantime, the German Communist party did almost nothing. A few days before the strike, a special Party conference expelled Neumann,[5] charging him particularly with having too vigorously criticized the mistakes of the twentieth of July, mistakes the conference admitted. It also reaffirmed the Party's confidence in Thaelmann, who will certainly not criticize those mistakes too vigorously, in that it is he who commits them. It also gave up, it is true, certain nationalist deviations (the substitution of the slogan "People's Revolution" for "Proletarian Revolution") by wrongly casting all the responsibility for them on Neumann; but in reality the nationalist policy continued, scarcely toned down at all. Much greater emphasis was placed on the solidarity of the French and German proletariats in the struggle against Versailles, which seems all to the good, but that was only dust thrown in the eyes of the German proletariat, since the French Communist party is not doing much in this regard apart from giving it flashy headlines in L'Humanité.[6] It is also true that the conference decided to orient trade-union propaganda mainly toward gaining a solid position inside the reformist unions; but one cannot say how far this very belated resolution has

5 Heinz Neumann (1902–1937?), one of the leaders of the German Communist party, was responsible (with the support of Moscow) for the nationalist emphasis in Party propaganda. He was censured (not expelled) by the Twelfth Plenum of the Executive Committee of the Communist International for a variety of errors, and was relieved of his position as candidate member of the politburo of the German Communist party. At the Party conference of October 15, 1932, Thaelmann made a savage attack on Neumann and the conference endorsed the ECCI's censure.

6 We should not hide our responsibility in the German situation from ourselves. The favorite argument of the Hitlerites against the Communists is "a French worker is first of all French, and only after that a worker." It would be our right to immediately organize an extensive campaign, with articles, tracts, pamphlets, or meetings, or all these means, to demonstrate to the German proletariat our active solidarity, to make the French people understand that France, through her aggressive imperialism and her ties to the Versailles system, is directly responsible for the Hitlerite movement, and finally to prepare a fraternal welcome to the German comrades whom fascist terror will soon, perhaps, force to cross the frontier. To remain inactive in this area would be a serious mistake, and should the Communist party not undertake anything serious in this direction, it would only make this obligation more urgent for independent organizations like our federation. (Note of SW)

been carried out. As for the united front, the tactics have stayed the same; even though a renewal of Hitlerite terror in December and January created a strong current of opinion in the masses in favor of a united front, nothing has been tried that would make these fleeting impulses effective by bringing them into the realm of the organization.

Like July 20 and November 7, January 22 was a day that again demonstrated, this time even more tragically, the powerlessness of the Communist party. A week earlier the Hitlerites had announced that they would organize a demonstration on that day in the center of the northern part of Berlin, that is, in the Red section of the city, and in front of the very headquarters of the Communist party (the Karl Liebknecht House). The counterdemonstration announced by the Communist party was prohibited. The Party saw that as nothing but a provocation leading to a ban against it, and it remained inactive before, during, and after the Hitlerite demonstration, apart from making a few appeals in its press and organizing one peaceful counterdemonstration on January 24 at the same place, that is, in the district that it controls. Péri,[7] whose special job in *L'Humanité* is to transform the defeats of the German Communist party into successes, crowed victory, both over a few spontaneous demonstrations that took place on January 22 while the Hitlerite parade was passing by and over the state of passivity from which the Party did not budge, a passivity that was presented as a triumph of "Communist discipline."

Actually, the assessment made by the Party was entirely false. It was not a question of a curtain raiser to the banning of the Communist party; it would have been pointless to stage such a show for that purpose. What was involved was a sort of dress rehearsal for the fascists, intended to test the strength of the Berlin proletariat's resistance, and, when put to the test, that strength was shown to be nil. Certainly the Party was right not to send its militants to a massacre; but the proletariat can fight in other ways. Its strongholds are the factories. Now, there were protests from the factories, but no revolt. And yet, according to the Communist press, which must have told the truth on this point, the reformist masses were stirred by feelings of intense indignation. Despite this indignation, and although it was warned several days in advance, the Party made no proposal whatever for a united front from organization to organization; it confined itself to vague and ineffective appeals for spontaneous action on the part of the workers.

7 Gabriel Péri (1902–41), French Communist politician and journalist.

As such appeals don't constitute action, or even an attempt at action, one is forced to say that on that decisive day the German Communist party purely and simply capitulated. A few days later the long-foreseen and long-dreaded event took place: Hitler was appointed chancellor.

Hitler's appointment, however, has not yet decided the outcome of the struggle. It is an extremely serious matter that the gangs of fascist murderers now have behind them the power of the state, with its coffers and its police and court system. But the bourgeoisie has not yet handed Germany over to fascism; it has kept the Hitlerites out of all the important ministries, notably the Ministry of Defense.[8] Hitler is forced to continue, inside the government, the struggle that he has been waging against the parties of the big bourgeoisie for eight months. But let us not forget that he holds the same trump card thanks to which, despite Hindenburg's reluctance, he obtained the position of chancellor; namely, the fact that the Hitlerite movement is indispensable, and it would run the risk of disintegrating if the purely bourgeois parties kept it out of power or domesticated it.

So it all comes down to a matter of knowing which—the proletariat or the bourgeoisie—will be the first to achieve unity of action within its own ranks. The bourgeoisie is very much further ahead in this area. Certainly, as soon as Hitler came to power, the Communist party and Social Democracy jointly issued appeals for united action, but they were careful to formulate them in the vaguest possible way. On the other hand, there has been, in recent days, a fairly large number of mass demonstrations and even strikes in which the united front was formed spontaneously. But, even now, nothing is being done to organize this united front. One can obviously expect no initiative whatever from Social Democracy in this regard; however, it would be quite difficult for it to refuse clearly defined proposals for a united front made by the Communist party. But the Communist party has not made up its mind to give up the tactic of forming a united front "only from below." If it attends mass demonstrations against fascism organized by Social Democracy, it does not take advantage of this fact to force the Social Democratic leaders to side with it; it does nothing but issue vague appeals addressed only to the workers, as it did recently at the Lustgarten—appeals that leave reformist bonzes and Hitlerite terrorists completely undisturbed.

8 Of the eleven-member cabinet, only two were National Socialists.

As for the Party's future, it is first of all necessary to warn the militants not to have any illusions. No doubt there will be spontaneous movements, strikes, and street fights led by Communists, because those who rally under the Communist flag are usually also those who are the most ardent and resolute. But the Party as such will be entitled to take credit only for those actions that are due to the strength it has as an organization, not to those due to the individual heroism of its members. The heroism of the best elements of the German working class, whether or not they carry Party cards, does not lessen the responsibilities of the Communist party; rather, it increases them.

On the other hand, if the Party does change its political line, one must ask not only if the change is for the better, but also if it is complete and rapid enough. This is no mere matter of a difference of degree; it is one of those situations in which "quantity changes into quality." There is a difference only in degree between Rigoulot[9] and a ninety-pound weakling if one sets a twenty-pound weight in front of them; if they are faced with a 200-pound weight, the difference between them is a difference in kind. If the Party corrects its errors too slowly or too half-heartedly, it would be the same as if it made no corrections at all.

And one can doubt the effectiveness of even a radical change if that change is only a bureaucratic about-face and is not preceded by an honest and free examination of the situation at all levels of the Party. For a bureaucratic about-face would guarantee nothing, and would run the risk of confusing the militants and discrediting the Party still a little more in the eyes of the masses. The decisive question is thus one of internal Party democracy; but democracy is not restored overnight, especially in the semi-illegal state to which the Party is now reduced, and which threatens to become worse from day to day.

Meanwhile, in order to completely settle the question of whether one can retain some faith in the leadership of the German Communist party, it is necessary to examine the Party's internal structure.

9 Charles Rigoulot (1903–62), a French weight lifter, set Olympic records in 1924 and was long considered the strongest man in the world.

Nine

The Communist party—especially in Germany, where organization is held in such high esteem and other revolutionary tendencies are nearly non-existent—attracts the most conscious and determined part of the prole-tariat. What hidden flaw in the organization prevents the dedicated and heroic proletarians grouped in the German Communist party from ef-fectively serving their class? Ordinary Party members sometimes ask themselves this question, and, with touching good faith, answer it them-selves using the established formula, "The base is responsible."

The base, it is true, is rather mixed. Besides young workers who give the impression, because of their maturity, resolve, and courage, of being equal to the task of building a new society, it contains others, driven to commu-nism by desperation or a taste for adventure, who could just as well have gone over to fascism, and who sometimes come from it. Above all, it con-tains a great many newcomers, who are full of good will, but are also very ignorant. By and large, their capacity for making decisions and taking ini-tiative is certainly not very great. On the other hand, there is no doubt that the base strongly supports the Party's political errors. In particular, many Communists let themselves be blinded by the legitimate loathing that Social Democracy inspires in them, especially the older militants who have not forgotten the tragic days when the Social Democratic minister Noske styled himself a bloodhound.[1] Since their bluntness makes all their conver-sations with the Social Democratic workers degenerate into arguments, they are not aware that the latter feel a similar loathing for Noske, and say so loudly in their own party. However, one cannot deny that there exists among the Communists a certain current of sympathy for the Hitlerites, whose obvious energy sometimes contrasts favorably with Social Demo-cratic capitulations, especially during strikes. One often has the impres-sion that Communist and Hitlerite workers are vainly trying to find the point of disagreement in their disputes, and that their fights are a sham. At the height of the Hitlerite terror Hitlerites and Communists could be heard

Published in *L'Ecole émancipée*, February 26, 1933.

[1] Gustave Noske was the Social Democratic minister of the interior at the time of the Spartacist uprising of January 1919. The government felt that the task of suppressing the up-rising should not be given to a general. Noske was suggested for the job, and he accepted, saying, "All right, someone has to be the bloodhound."

nostalgically recalling the time when they struggled, as they put it, "side by side"—that is, the time of the Red referendum; and one could hear a Communist exclaim, "Better to be a Nazi than a Social Democrat." However, statements of this sort did arouse some protests, for there is also a strong current in the Communist party in favor of a united front with Social Democracy. Many Communists clearly realize that they can do nothing without the support of the reformist workers. They liked the policy followed in July; they did not see its inadequacies, and they have not realized that it was given up at the beginning of August. Broadly speaking, especially since July 20, there has been a feeling of uneasiness that has found expression in a renewal of life in the cells; but it is an undefined uneasiness. It took a long time for the young Communists to become aware that the situation is acute and that every moment is of inestimable importance; they did make some progress in this regard in October, if one believes Berlioz's account. Nevertheless, as far as one can tell, their anxiety is still not taking an articulate form.

It is the Party apparatus that prevents it from taking an articulate form by keeping the threat of expulsion for "Trotskyite" or "Brandlerite" deviations hanging over every Communist's head. It is the apparatus that, by suppressing all freedom of expression within the Party and weighing down the militants with insignificant and exhausting tasks, kills off all decisiveness and initiative and prevents any real education of the newcomers by the experienced militants. Moreover, this mass of newcomers, who are as ignorant as they are enthusiastic, is the real support of the internal Party apparatus; without this docile mass how could those complete shifts of orientation, accomplished with no discussion and within a few days—shifts for which Piatnitsky naively congratulates the Party—be brought about? In addition, the policy imposed on the Party by the apparatus has on many occasions encouraged those entirely understandable but highly dangerous feelings of hatred for the Social Democrats and lenient or even sympathetic feelings for the Hitlerites. Generally speaking, it is the apparatus that, by adorning its own policy with all the prestige of the October Revolution, has sowed confusion in the mind of every German Communist, in exactly the same way as priests rob the enthusiastic faithful of their critical faculties by covering up the most flagrant absurdities with the authority of the church.

If the responsibility for the weakness of the German Communist party lies with its leadership, what is the nature of that responsibility? The

Trotskyites have repeatedly said, with reference to this subject, that "the mistakes of the Social Democratic party are acts of treason; those of the Communist party are merely errors." Certainly the Communist International hasn't yet done anything comparable to voting for war credits on August 4, 1914, or to the Social Democrats' massacre of the Spartacists in 1919. But if one sticks to the present period it is difficult to understand what the Trotskyites' formula means. Does it mean that Social Democracy steers the workers away from all revolutionary action, and that even if the Communist party is getting off to a bad start in paving the way for the revolution, it at least involves the workers in looking for a way out on that path? But revolution is not a religion with respect to which a lukewarm believer is worth more than an unbeliever; it is a practical task. One can no more be a revolutionary through words alone than one can be a mason or a blacksmith. Only action that paves the way for a transformation of the regime is revolutionary (though analyses and slogans that prepare for such action, and do not merely preach, can also be considered revolutionary). It would not be safe to assert that the German Communist party as an organization, and independently of the feelings of the base, is more revolutionary in this sense than the Social Democratic party; moreover, in the area of reforms the latter can boast of having rendered services of much greater importance than the Communist party in the past. Or does the Trotskyites' formula mean that the intentions of the Communist bureaucrats are purer than those of the Social Democratic bureaucrats? The question is insoluble, and of no interest besides. In practice, a working-class party's mistakes can be called errors when they are due to an incorrect assessment of the proletariat's interests, and acts of treason when they are due to an organic connection, whether conscious or unconscious, with interests opposed to those of the proletariat.

P.S.   What about the united front?
On February 5 it was rumored that, according to Trotsky, Moscow had given an order to form it.

Nevertheless, toward the middle of the month, the German Communist party responded by bluntly rejecting the Social Democratic party's proposal for a "nonaggression pact." The Social Democrats made it clear that each party would keep its point of view and its independence, but heinous attacks would be brought to an end. This proposal was a very acceptable base for negotiations, and in these negotiations the Communist party (which would naturally have proposed actual unity of action with complete freedom of criticism on both sides) would have found valuable support right at the very base of Social Democracy. The Party deprived itself of that support by refusing even to negotiate.

Ten

The German Communist party, like all the sections of the International, is organically subordinated to the apparatus of the Russian state. Forced by necessity, the Bolsheviks did what Marx saw that all previous revolutionaries except the Communards had done, namely, they perfected the machinery of the state instead of destroying it. As Marx wrote in April 1871, "The destruction of the bureaucratic and military machine is the precondition of every popular revolution on the Continent." After Marx, Lenin pointed out (in *The State and Revolution*) that a state apparatus distinct from the population, made up of a bureaucracy, police force, and permanent army, has interests distinct from the interests of the population, especially from those of the proletariat. We do not have to go into Russian domestic policy here. But, although it was born of a revolution, insofar as it is a permanent apparatus, the state apparatus of the Russian nation has interests distinct from those of the world proletariat; distinct—that is, in part identical, in part opposed. One could, perhaps, consider the famous doctrine of "socialism in one country"[1] as constituting the theoretical expression of this divergence.

How far does this divergence go? To what degree does it explain the political orientation of the Communist International? We don't know. What we do know is that the chief mistakes of the German Communist party, namely, the sectarian struggle against Social Democracy as the "main enemy," the sabotage of the united front, the participation in the so-called Red referendum, and the shameful nationalist demagogy, were all imposed on the Party by the International (cf. esp. no. 21–22 of the *Communist International*). And, speaking of the Communist International, we

Published in *L'Ecole émancipée*, March 5, 1933.

1 In 1924 Stalin announced that the Communist party in Russia would set aside efforts to actively further international proletarian revolution in order to first build socialism in Russia.

must not forget that we are talking about an apparatus with no mandate, since the congress hasn't been convened for five years; an irresponsible apparatus, which is entirely in the hands of the Russian Central Committee. This was quite apparent when the Russian party forced out Zinoviev,[2] who was the head of the International, without consulting the other sections or even giving them any of the particulars. And, as for the nationalist orientation of the German party, we know that it was in perfect agreement with the foreign policy of the USSR, which was at that time especially concerned with preventing France from drawing Germany into an anti-Soviet bloc. In addition, if the conversations between Leipart and von Schleicher make our blood boil, we are also entitled to wonder what Litvinov, during his recent visit to Berlin, could have said to von Schleicher in the course of their private conversation.[3] Finally, in a general way, one observes a continuity and perseverance in the mistakes of the German party which would be quite unlikely if the error were accidental; and the methods the Comintern employs against those who criticize its mistakes are quite similar to the methods a state apparatus uses against those who threaten its interests. Thorez and Semard[4] demonstrated this when, during a discussion concerning Germany, they had the Trotskyites beaten up in the middle of a public meeting.

Possibly all that would not be enough to justify an accusation of treason. But this much is certain: a change in the Party's internal regime—which would be the first condition for a genuine reform—is directly opposed to the interests of the Russian state apparatus. The Russian state apparatus, like every state apparatus in the world, deports, exiles, and directly or indirectly kills those who try to diminish its power; but, as a state born of a revolution, it needs to be able to say it has the approval of the vanguard of the world proletariat. That is why driving out the oppositionists comes

2 Grigori Zinoviev (1883–1936) was the head of the Communist International until 1925, when he was removed by Stalin. The following year he formed a joint opposition with Trotsky, and he and Trotsky were both expelled in 1927.

3 Maxim Litvinov (1876–1951), the Russian commissar of foreign affairs, met with von Schleicher on December 19, 1932. According to E. H. Carr, von Schleicher "complained of the subversive activities of [the German Communist party], and hinted at the possibility of a legal ban. . . . Litvinov . . . responded by declaring that measures taken by the German government against German communists were no concern of the Soviet government, and would not affect Soviet-German relations." See Carr, *Twilight of the Comintern, 1930–1935* (New York: Pantheon, 1982), pp. 80–81.

4 Maurice Thorez (1900–1964) and Pierre Semard (1887–1942) were leaders of the French Communist party.

before every other consideration, not only in the Russian party but in the International. Given the seriousness of the situation in Germany, it can be said that every time the German party apparatus expels a Communist for disagreeing with the Party line, it is betraying the German workers in order to save the bureaucracy of the Russian state.

Only a few tiny opposition groups are fighting against the triple apparatus of the Party, the Comintern, and the Russian state. In addition, the unconditionality of their opposition varies from group to group. Urbahns's "Leninbund"[5] goes as far as to entirely refuse to call the USSR a workers' state; on the other hand the Trotskyites, who are otherwise energetic and courageous, show a perpetual desire to be loyal to the "workers' state" and the "Party of the working class" that often impairs the clarity of their judgment.[6] Brandler, whose partisans are the only oppositionists with any influence in the reformist unions, goes much further still, since he approves of everything that is done in the USSR, including the deportations. A few Brandlerites, grouped around courageous militants like Frölich,[7] finally decided that this attitude was a capitulation, and because they also despaired of getting the Communist party to correct its mistakes, they went over to the little "Socialist Workers' party," to which they were attracted by a genuinely revolutionary youthfulness of spirit. But they found themselves caught in an organization that combines the numerical weakness of a sect with the lack of cohesion of a mass movement—a paralyzing situation for a militant. Furthermore, the struggle that these groups are carrying on is nearly hopeless. How does one, within the Communist party, discredit a leadership that has so many ways of preserving its authority? As for trying to discredit the Party itself in the eyes of the proletariat, no oppositionist group would dare do that for fear of thereby encouraging reformism or fascism. And, at the base, among some young

5 Hugo Urbahns was a leader of the German Communist party in the mid-1920s. Expelled in 1927, he became one of the founders of the Leninbund, a Left opposition group. He became the leader of the Leninbund in 1930.

6 The German Trotskyite group has not been "liquidated," contrary to what *L'Humanité* loudly declared; it simply lost a considerable fraction of its members (a quarter, some say), who not only disowned Trotsky but condemned all the oppositionist groups. A month earlier, the same ones were boasting that they were the best Trotskyites. The departure of elements of this sort is a good thing for the group, but the way in which it was brought about seems to indicate an internal regime that differs little from that of the Party. (Note of SW)

7 Paul Frölich (1884–1953) was one of the founders of the German Communist party. He later became a member of the Brandlerite opposition, and then became a leader of the Socialist Workers' party.

Communist and Social Democratic workers, a movement in favor of a new party is just beginning to take shape.

SO THAT IS the situation of the seven-tenths of the German population who yearn for socialism. Thanks to Hitlerite demagogy, the politically unconscious, the desperate, and those who are ready for any adventure have been recruited as soldiers to fight a civil war in the service of finance capital; the prudent and level-headed workers have been handed over by Social Democracy, tied hand and foot, to the German state apparatus; and the most fervent and resolute proletarians have been kept powerless by the representatives of the Russian state apparatus.

Is it necessary to try to formulate future prospects? The various combinations which the play of conflicts and alliances between classes and fractions of classes can result in, produce a multitude of prospects that cannot be altogether dismissed—even the prospect of a spontaneous proletarian uprising and the emergence of a new commune on the scale of Germany. Weighing the probabilities would be pointless. Besides, the significance of the various elements of the German situation depends entirely on what may happen in the world, especially on the arrival of that "turning point" about which people in Berlin have been talking for more than six months; on the rate at which prosperity will be restored; and on the order in which the different countries will be affected by it. We cannot say anything with real precision about this subject. The weakness of the revolutionary movement is doubtless largely due to our ignorance of economic phenomena—an ignorance, moreover, that is disgraceful for materialists who consider themselves to be in the line of Marx.

At least we clearly perceive the decadence of the regime, a decadence that goes beyond the present crisis. Increasingly, expenditures devoted to economic warfare (of which military warfare can be considered a particular case) outweigh productive expenditures; and in a parallel way, the system is more and more caught up in the machinery of the state—machinery that, in the course of history, has been always perfected and never destroyed. The ideal limit of this process could be defined as absolute fascism, that is, a suffocating grip on all forms of social life by the power of a state that itself serves as an instrument of finance capital. A return to prosperity can seemingly interrupt this process, but the danger will remain the same as long as the capitalist regime continues to break down. Already the general state of crisis of the regime seems to be spreading not only to what remains of genuine bourgeois culture but also to the little that we possess in the way of rough outlines of a new culture; the working-class movement and the proletariat are being affected materially and morally, especially at the present time, by the decadence of the capitalist economy. And it would be wrong to be sure that this decadence may not also manage to stifle what survives of the spirit of the October Revolution in the USSR, perhaps even without military aggression. The attack by the dominant class, forced by the crisis to constantly make its oppressive power more burdensome, is taking place in Germany now; and we cannot measure the importance of the battle that will possibly break out there tomorrow.

On the eve of such a battle, facing the formidable economic and political organizations of capital, the gangs of Hitlerite terrorists, and the machine guns of the Reichswehr, the German working class is alone and bare handed. Or rather, one is tempted to wonder if it would not be even better for it to be bare handed. The instruments that it forged, and that it thinks it holds, are in reality in the hands of others, in the defense of interests that are not its own.

P.S.   Right now signs of dissension are becoming evident in the capitalist camp. Von Papen has just called for a "black-white-red" front including the "bourgeois parties," that is, the parties of the Right, with the exception of the National Socialists. The *Deutsche Allgemeine Zeitung* is turning out propaganda against state intervention in the economy. Social Democracy sees in these internal battles of the bourgeoisie a sign of Hitler's weakness, but nothing is less certain. The tone of the articles in the *Deutsche Allgemeine Zeitung* seems to reflect a sort of panic, as if the big bourgeoisie felt overwhelmed by the Hitlerite movement. And under present conditions it would be unreasonable to count on the idea that the big bourgeoisie will ever categorically turn against Hitler; that would be to clear the way for a proletarian uprising, and the bourgeoisie knows it.

Actually, Hitler's position keeps on getting stronger and Hitlerite terror is on the increase; the police have been given formal orders to systematically attack the parties of the Left, and have been assured that the murders committed by them will always be covered up;[8] the entire Communist

8 When Hitler became chancellor, Hermann Göring was appointed Prussian minister of the interior. He immediately purged the Prussian state service, especially the higher levels of the police force, which he then filled with his own appointments. In mid-February he instructed the police to show no mercy to "organizations hostile to the State" and assured

press has been suppressed; the Party headquarters (the Karl Liebknecht House) has been closed, as has the Karl Marx School, a famous Berlin school offering primary and secondary courses, including special secondary courses for young workers; all the secular schools are expected to be closed by Easter; an auxiliary police force, composed of members of the Hitlerite storm troops and the Steel Helmets,[9] has been created; etc., etc.

Resistance is taking the form of one-day local strikes and mass demonstrations, in the course of which the local organizations usually form a united front. This resistance remains disorganized and widely scattered, as spontaneous movements tend to be, and on the whole it has been, up to now, ineffective. Similarly, the united front has been achieved only locally, partially, and in an equally disorganized way, which shows that the cadres are letting themselves be borne along by a spontaneous mass current in favor of unity of action instead of organizing it. This current is stronger every day; one sign of it is the resolutions regarding joint action (which, it must be added, are as vague as they are passionate) adopted by all the reformist unions' general assemblies that are now taking place.

The Red federations of the metal and building trades and the Berlin Red trade-union organization have made precise proposals for a united front to the corresponding reformist organizations, but of course to no effect. The Red trade-union organizations of Germany, which only "reproduce the party" in their organization and activity (*Internationale Syndicale Rouge*, no. 19–20, p. 914), and which remain inferior to the Party in both numerical strength and influence, are too weak to have any serious chance of bringing about joint action with the corresponding reformist organizations except by going to the extreme limit of concessions, that is, asking to be admitted into the reformist Central. It is difficult to say from a distance whether these tactics, recommended by the Trotskyites, would be the best or not.

In any case, one will not be able to believe that the Communist party genuinely wants to do everything in its power to achieve proletarian unity

---

them that "police officers who make use of fire arms in the execution of their duties will, without regard to the consequences of such use, benefit by my protection; those who, out of a misplaced regard for such consequences, fail in their duty will be punished in accordance with the regulations. . . . Every official must bear in mind that failure to act will be regarded more seriously than an error due to taking action." See Alan Bullock, *Hitler: A Study in Tyranny* (New York: Harper and Row, 1964), p. 261.

9 The Steel Helmets was a First World War veterans' organization that began accepting nonveterans in 1924 and became a right-wing paramilitary group.

of action until the Party itself, as a party, makes proposals that are specific and conciliatory enough to leave the reformist leaders no way out.

But despite the state of mind of the masses and the urgent danger, the Party's Central Committee has been silent ever since the vague appeal it issued the day after Hitler was appointed chancellor. One might think it doesn't exist.

■ *Factory Journal*

Introduction

In 1933–34 Simone Weil became increasingly convinced that there was little likelihood of revolutionary change through political activity; moreover, she began to perceive that the real enemy was not the capitalist economic system per se but the bureaucratic, centralized apparatus of the modern state, whose power was consolidated through war. She clearly foresaw that the European states were on a trajectory toward war—very likely, she thought, toward "another conflagration" involving "the whole of Europe and beyond"—and she feared that the efforts of the Left on behalf of "liberty, the proletariat, etc.," would, in reality, only serve the interests of the Russian state and the Franco-Prussian military alliance and consequently spur war preparations. For this reason, she decided in mid-1934 to "take no further part in any political or social activities, with two exceptions: anticolonialism and the campaign against civil defense exercises." Still, her consuming desire to liberate the oppressed remained. She had been coming more and more to believe "that the liberation (relative) of the workers must be brought about before all else in the workshop."[1] She turned, then, to the workplace itself, the factory.

Having applied for a leave of absence from teaching for the 1934–35 school year, Weil made arrangements with Auguste Detoeuf, the managing director of the company that owned the Alsthom factory (a plant that made electrical equipment for subway cars and streetcars), to be hired as an unskilled worker. She used connections in order to get only this first of the three jobs she held between December 1934 and August 1935, and once employed, she lived as fully as possible the life of an ordinary, anonymous unskilled worker. She rented a room in the neighborhood of the factory and lived on her skimpy earnings, going as far as to insist on paying her parents the price she would have had to pay for a meal when she dined with them, and going hungry when she ran low on money during a month-long period of unemployment. She became a member of what was perhaps

1 Simone Pétrement, *Simone Weil: A Life* (New York: Pantheon, 1976), pp. 211, 212, 227.

the most despised class in the French factory system—the class of unskilled women workers. The jobs that she and the other women did, under the supervision of male foremen of varying degrees of technical ability and human decency, were tedious, extremely repetitive, often dangerous, and physically exhausting. Maladroit and not physically strong, subject to frequent migraine headaches that the noise of the factory made excruciating, Weil found the experience almost unbearable; "I came near to being broken," she wrote of it. Her "Factory Journal," the notebook in which she entered an almost daily record of her eight and a half months as a factory worker, is larded with the actual pointless, mindless detail of this life; it is full of computations of pieces made, rates of speed achieved, attempts (sometimes incorrect) to calculate her hours and meager earnings; it boils over with her frustration with the timekeeping system, with her anxiety at failing to make the rate, and with her impotent rage at the way she was treated. It also conveys a sense of the intense psychological reality of factory life that is largely missing from her later letters and essays on the subject.

Weil had long felt, she wrote early in 1935, that in a factory one should make a hard but joyous contact with "real life."[2] Ideally, a factory would be an environment in which one did the sort of work she described in "Science and Perception in Descartes"—work through which the workers exercised their minds correctly and came to know both the world and their own true natures as thinking *and* active beings. Though obviously she did not expect to find this ideal when she entered the factory, what she found was far worse than anything she had imagined. In order to make the minimum rate and not be fired she had to turn herself into an automaton who neither thought nor felt, who mindlessly and rapidly produced so-and-so many hundreds of pieces per hour. She found the experience not only morally and physically painful but also completely dehumanizing. Everything conspired to turn the worker into nothing more than a beast of burden. To remain conscious—a thinking being—in those circumstances was unbearably painful.

Weil had been aware before she entered the factory that the organization of production was by its very structure oppressive. In her 1934 essay "Reflections on the Causes of Liberty and Social Oppression" she had argued that if the proletarian revolution is to have any meaning, it is the

2 Simone Weil, *Seventy Letters* (London: Oxford University Press, 1965), p. 20.

system of relations in production that must be changed—the system in which one group gives orders and another carries them out—and not simply the capitalist ownership of the means of production. But what had been an intellectual awareness was given a more profound dimension by her actual experience in the factory; what she had not known before—and what marked her, she said, for life—was the experience of being treated as a slave, of being submerged in an environment in which she did not count, was given no respect, was regarded as having no rights at all, and as a result of which she came, finally, to feel that she was not entitled to be treated otherwise. Intellectually, she concluded from this experience that working conditions that constantly humiliate and degrade workers and destroy their sense of having any value will never produce a working class capable of revolution. There were, she observed in the factory, no revolutionary feelings at all among the workers; the idea of resistance, she wrote, "never occurs to anyone." She also saw that economic inequality alone was an inadequate explanation of the problem of oppression; the factory gave her the first glimpse of the fact that, however much economic inequality was a contributing factor, oppression was essentially maintained by the systematic humiliation and the instilling of a sense of inferiority in the oppressed. What she learned in the factory contributed to her later understanding that, as she would write in her 1943 essay "Human Personality," a truly nonoppressive political system would have to start from a real recognition of the respect due every human soul.

Perhaps even more important than the intellectual conclusions she drew from her factory experience were its psychological effects on her. When she attempted to describe it in letters to friends, she found it inexpressible; she became almost inarticulate and could only sum it up in such generalities as "it's inhuman." She obviously tried very hard—in her letters the following year to the manager of the Rosières foundry at Bourges and in her 1942 essay "Factory Work"—to convey the profound and important psychological effects of working conditions upon the worker. To judge from the general response to these writings, she did not succeed; most of those who have commented on her experience have tended to explain her response as completely atypical, due to her temperament, her awkwardness, her oversensitivity, and so on, and to see her description of herself as a slave, as someone permanently marked with the brand of slavery, as a romantic and perhaps slightly hysterical exaggeration. In short, the truth of her experience has tended to be dismissed.

Although what she is trying to say comes across more clearly in her "Factory Journal" than elsewhere, it is, indeed, very hard to hear, because it describes an experience of deep psychological wounding against which one habitually and instinctively protects oneself, an experience that it is impossible to fully appreciate on an intellectual level alone. The psychological suffering Weil underwent in the factory—a suffering that she made every effort to remain conscious of and not to flee from—unquestionably affected her very soul and brought about her real entry into the community of human suffering. From being a dedicated worker on behalf of the oppressed she became one of them and one with them.

The factory experience was a watershed in Weil's life. It was her first profound contact with affliction (a central concept in her later religious writing), especially with the aspect of social degradation that she considered such an important part of the totality of affliction. It led directly to her understanding, later expressed in her moving essay on the *Iliad*, that "the sense of human misery is a pre-condition of justice and love."[3] It was, finally, of major importance in her receptivity to Christianity. Having been brought to a condition in which she considered herself a slave, while traveling in Portugal a month or so after leaving the factory she came upon a group of Portuguese fishermen's wives carrying candles in a religious procession and singing "ancient hymns of a heart-rending sadness." Describing this incident later, she wrote, "the conviction was suddenly borne in upon me that Christianity is pre-eminently the religion of slaves, that slaves cannot help belonging to it, and I among others."[4]

3 *The Iliad, or The Poem of Force* (Wallingford, Penn.: Pendle Hill, 1956), p. 34.
4 *Waiting for God* (New York: Harper Colophon Books, 1973), p. 67.

■ *Factory Journal*

πόλλ᾽ ἀεκαζομένη, κρατερὴ δ᾽ ἐπικείσετ᾽ ἀνάγκη[1]

Not only should man know what he is making, but if possible he should see how it is used—see how nature is changed by him.

Every man's work should be an *object of contemplation* for him.

FIRST WEEK

Started work Tuesday December 4, 1934.

Tuesday. 3 hrs. of work in the course of the day. Beginning of the morning, 1 hr. of *drilling* (Catsous).

End of the morning, 1 hr. at the *stamping press* with Jacquot (that's where I met the warehouse keeper). End of the afternoon: ¾ hr. turning a crank to help make cardboards (with Dubois).

Wednesday morning. Fly-press the whole morning, with some periods of no work. Done without hurrying, consequently without fatigue. Didn't make the rate![2]

From 3 to 4, easy work at the stamping press; .70 per hundred. Still didn't make the rate.

To 4:45: *machine with buttons.*

Thursday morning. Machine with buttons; .56 per hundred (should be .72). 1,160 in the whole morning—very difficult.

Afternoon. Power failure. Waited from 1:15 to 3 o'clock. Left at 3.

Friday. Right-angle pieces, at the stamping press (tool only supposed to accentuate the right angle). 100 *pieces botched* (crushed, because the screw came loose).

From 11 A.M. on, *handwork:* removing cardboards from an assembly that they want done over (fixed magnetic circuits—replace cardboard with small copper plates). Tools: mallet, compressed-air hose, saw blade, flashlight; very tiring for the eyes.

---

1 Much against your will, under pressure of a harsh necessity. *Iliad* 6. 458.

2 Weil uses *coulé* ("didn't cut it" or "blew it"), a variant of *couler le bon* or *bon coulé*—working-class slang meaning that one failed to reach a minimum speed on a given order.

Tour of the tool shop, but no time to see much of it. Bawled out for having gone there.

Saturday. Cardboards.

Didn't make the rate on a single voucher.

Women workers:
  Mme Forestier
  Mimi
  Tolstoy fan (Eugénie)
  My co-worker on the iron bars (Louisette)
  Mimi's sister
  Cat
  Blonde from the munitions factory
  Redhead (Joséphine)
  Divorced woman
  Mother of the burned kid
  Woman who gave me a roll
  Italian woman
  Dubois

Big shots:
  Mouquet
  Chastel
  Warehouse keeper (Pommera)

Set-up men:
  Ilion
  Léon
  Catsous (Michel)
  "*Jacquot*" (has become a worker again)
  Robert
  "*Biol*" (at the back)
  (Or V . . .?)
  ". . . ." (furnace)

Male workers:
  violinist
  conceited blond
  old man with glasses (the one who reads *l'Auto*)
  singer at the furnace

worker in drilling goggles ("we'll see" . . . very nice)
boy with the mallet (drinks—the only one)
his co-worker
my "fiancé"
his brother (?)
young blond Italian
welder
coppersmith

SECOND WEEK

Monday, Tuesday, Wednesday. Personnel manager sent for me at 10 A.M. to say they are setting my hourly base wage at 2 F (actually, it will be 1.80 F). *Removing cardboards.* Violent headache Tuesday, work goes very slowly and badly (Wednesday I managed to do it quickly and well, tapping very vigorously and accurately with the mallet—but terrible eyestrain).

Thursday. From 10 A.M. (or even earlier?) until about 2 P.M., *metal polishing* on the big fly-press. Work had to be done over again, after it was completely done, by order of the foreman, and in a way that was *uncomfortable* and dangerous.

Order to do it over again justified, or bullying? In any case, Mouquet had me do it over in a way that was exhausting and dangerous (I had to duck every time in order to avoid being struck full on the head by the heavy counterweight). Pity and mute indignation of neighbors. Furious with myself (for no reason, since no one had told me I was not hitting hard enough), I had the idiotic feeling that it wasn't worth the effort to pay attention to protecting myself. Still, no accident. Set-up man (Léon) very annoyed, probably with Mouquet, but not explicitly so.

At 11:45, observe. . . .
Afternoon: no work until 4 P.M.
From 4 to 5:45. . . .

Friday. Stamping press—*washers.* The tool formed them and made a hole ((•)). Worked all day. Made the rate, in spite of having to replace a spring—*the spring was broken.* First time that I worked all day on the same machine; great fatigue, although I did not go at top speed. Error in the count, corrected at my request by the woman who came after me (very nice!).

Saturday. 1 hr. drilling holes in brass ferrules placed against a very low stop that I didn't see, which made me botch 6 or 7 (a new woman who had never worked before did the job successfully yesterday, according to Léon, who bawls you out every chance he gets). Didn't make the rate—but no reprimand for the botched pieces, because the count is right.

¾ hr. for cutting small brass bars with Léon.

Easy—no blunders.

Break for cleaning machines.

Made the rate on 1 voucher (for 25.50 F).

A woman who was fired—tubercular—had several times botched hundreds of pieces (but how many times?). Once it was just before she fell very ill, so she was forgiven. This time, 500 pieces. But on the evening shift (2:30 to 10:30 P.M.) when all the lights are out except the portable lamps (which give no light at all). The drama is complicated by the fact that the set-up man (Jacquot) is automatically considered partly responsible. The women I'm with (Cat and others who have stopped working—one of them the Tolstoy fan?) are on Jacquot's side. One of them: "You've got to be more conscientious *when you have to make a living.*"

It seems that the woman had refused to do the order in question (probably for painstaking and badly paid work)—"work that was too hard," someone says. The foreman had said to her, "If this isn't done by tomorrow morning. . . ." It was probably thought she had botched the work on purpose. Not one word of sympathy from the women, even though they know the disgust you feel facing an exhausting job, knowing you will earn 2 F or less and be bawled out for not having made the rate—a disgust that illness must increase tenfold. This lack of sympathy is explained by the fact that if one woman is spared a "bad" job, it is done by another. . . . One woman's comment (Mme Forestier?): "She shouldn't have talked back . . . when you have to make a living, you have no choice . . . (repeated several times). . . . Then she could have gone and told the assistant manager, 'Yes, I was wrong, but even so it's not completely my fault; it's hard to see very well, etc. I won't do it any more, etc.' "

"When you have to make a living": this expression originates partly in the fact that some of the married women aren't working for a living, but to be a little better off. (That woman had a husband, but he was unemployed.) A great deal of inequality among the women workers. . . .

Wage system. Below 3 F per hour you don't make the rate. Vouchers on which you didn't make the rate are adjusted every two weeks in a little committee made up of Mouquet and the timekeeper. . . . (The timekeeper is pitiless. Mouquet probably defends the women a little.) They set arbitrary values on these vouchers—sometimes 4 francs, sometimes 3, sometimes the amount of the hourly base wage (2.40 F for the others). Sometimes they pay only the amount actually made by deducting anything over and above the hourly wage from the bonus. When a woman thinks she is the victim of an injustice, she goes to complain. But it's humiliating, since she has no rights at all and is at the mercy of the good will of the foremen, who decide according to her worth as a worker, and in large measure capriciously.

The time lost between jobs either must be marked on the vouchers (but then you risk not making the rate, especially on small orders) or is deducted from your pay. So you end up with fewer than 96 hours for the two-week period.

It's a form of control; without it you would always be marking down shorter periods of time than you actually spent.

System for estimating hours beforehand.

Story about Mouquet: Mimi's sister goes to find him to complain about the pricing of a voucher; he abruptly orders her back to her work. She goes away grumbling. Ten minutes later he goes to find her, asks "What's the matter?" and takes care of it.

"Not very many dare to fall below the minimum rate."

THIRD WEEK

Jobs:
Monday, 17th, morning. At the small fly-press.
Polishing all morning—tiring—didn't make the rate.

The memory of my adventure at the big fly-press makes me afraid of not hitting hard enough. On the other hand it seems you mustn't hit too hard. And the voucher calls for a speed that seems fantastic to me. . . .

End of the morning: washers from metal bars, with Robert's heavy press.

Afternoon—*stamping press;* pieces very difficult to position, at .56 per hundred (600 from 2:30 to 5:15); ½ hr. to reset the machine, which was out of adjustment because I had left a piece in the tool. Tired and fed up.

Feeling of having been a free being for 24 hours (on Sunday), and of having to readapt to slavery. Disgust at being forced to strain and exhaust myself, with the certainty of being bawled out either for being slow or for botching, for the sake of these 56 centimes. . . . Augmented by the fact that I am having dinner with my parents—Feeling of slavery—

The speed is dizzying. (Especially when in order to throw yourself into it you have to overcome fatigue, headaches, and the feeling of being fed up.)

Mimi beside me—

Mouquet: don't use your fingers. "You don't eat with your fingers. . . ."

Tuesday, 18th. Same pieces—500 from 7 A.M. to 8:45, *all botched.*

From 9 to 5, work in pairs, paid by the hour; iron bars 3 meters long, weighing 30 to 50 kilograms. Very hard, but not nerve-racking. A certain joy in the muscular effort . . . but in the evening, exhaustion. The others look at me with pity, especially Robert.

Wednesday, 19th. No work from 7 A.M. to 11.

11 to 5, *heavy press cutting washers* out of a bar of sheet metal with Robert. Didn't make the rate (2 F per hour; 2.28 F for a thousand washers). Very violent headache, finished the work while weeping almost uninterruptedly. (When I got home, interminable fit of sobbing.) No blunders, however, aside from 3 or 4 botched pieces.

Advice from the warehouse keeper—illuminating. Pedal only with your leg, not with your whole body; push the strip with one hand and hold it in position with the other, instead of pulling and holding with the same hand. Relation of work to athletics.

Robert quite severe when he sees that I botched two pieces.

Thursday, 20th, and Friday, 21st. Stamping rivets at the light press—.62 per hundred—made 2.40 F per hour (more).

(Pleasant warning from the foreman: if you botch them, you'll be fired.) 3,000—earned 18.60 F. Even so, didn't make the rate: 3 F minimum. No blunders, but slowed down by irrational scruples.

Riveting: assembly work. Only difficulty is doing the operations in order. Example: I absentmindedly botched two because I did the riveting before I had assembled everything.

Thursday, payday; 241.60 F.

Saturday, 22nd. Riveting with Ilion. Work pleasant enough—.028 per piece. *Made the rate,* but did it by going at top speed. Constant effort—not without a certain pleasure, because I am succeeding.

Probable wages: 48 hrs. at 1.80 F = 86.25 F. Bonus: for Tuesday, if I worked at 4 F per hr., 17.60 F; for Wednesday 1.20 F; for Thursday and Friday .60 × 15 (approx) = 9 F; for Saturday, 1.20 × 3.5 = 4.20 F. Therefore:

17.60 F + 1.60 F + 9 F + 4.20 F = 32.40 F. That would make 86.25 F + 32.40 F = 118.65 F. Perhaps out of that a deduction corresponding to the job on which I botched 500 pieces.

Actually I had a bonus of 36.75 F (but ¾ hr. was deducted, that's 1.20 F). So 4.35 F more than I had thought. Undoubtedly an adjusted voucher—probably Monday morning's polishing.

Made the rate on one voucher (for 12 F).

FOURTH WEEK

Laid off (week between Christmas and New Year's Day). I caught cold—had some fever (very slight) during the week and some terrible headaches; when the end of the holidays and the time to go back to work came, I still had a cold and was, above all, worn out with fatigue.

Young unemployed workman encountered on Christmas Day. . . .

FIFTH WEEK

Wednesday, 2nd. 7:15 to 8:45 A.M.: *cutting pieces out of a long metal strip,* at the large press with Robert. 677 pieces at .319 per hundred. Put down 1 hr. 10 min. Held up at the beginning by lack of oil. Difficulty cutting the strip. Pulling it. Took out pieces too often. Earned 1.85 F; at the hourly wage they ought to pay me 2.10 F. *Difference of .25 F.*

8:50 to 11:45 A.M.: *holes for connectors* with the little fly-press (name?). Slow in the beginning because I drove the tool in too deeply. Kept the piece in place too long—and looked from the wrong angle. 830 pieces at .84 per hundred. Earned 7 F; didn't make the rate, but by only a little. Actually 2.30 F, put down for 2.80 F.

For the morning: 1 hr. to make up.

1:15 to 2:30: had no work, put down only 1 hr.

2:30 to 4: *stamping press. Cambered pieces* cut out in the morning;

600 at .54 per hundred, so earned 3.24 F. Put down 1 hr. 20 min. (15 min. less and I would have made the rate).

4:30 to 5:15: *furnace.* Very hard work; not only intolerable heat, but the flames come up to lick your hands and arms. You have to control your reflexes or botch . . . (one botched!). There are 500 pieces (the remainder to be done Thursday morning), paid at 4.80 F per hundred. So 24 F for the lot.

I have 8 hours.

In addition to that, in the course of the day I have 3 hrs. 40 min. + 1 hr. 15 min. + 1 hr. 20 min. = 6¼ hrs. 2¾ hrs. to make up. Must keep track of this. Tomorrow I will probably not do more than 3½ or 4 hrs.

Furnace. The first evening, about 5 o'clock, the pain from the extreme heat, exhaustion, and headaches make me completely lose control of my movements. I can't lower the furnace damper. A coppersmith jumps up and lowers it for me. What gratitude you feel at such moments! Also when the kid who lit the furnace for me showed me how to lower the damper with a hook, which made it much easier. On the other hand, when Mouquet suggests I put the pieces on the right so as to pass less often in front of the furnace, my chief reaction is to be annoyed for not having thought of it myself. Every time I burned myself, the welder threw me a sympathetic smile.

Made the rate on 3 vouchers (2 furnace, 1 riveting) for 24.60 F + 9.20 F + 29.40 F = 63.20 F.

Thursday, 3rd. 7 A.M. to 9:15: *furnace.* Clearly less hard than the day before, in spite of a violent headache from the moment I woke up. Have learned not to expose myself so much to the flames, and to run fewer risks of botching. Still, very hard. Terrible racket of mallet blows a few meters away.

Earned 24.60 at the furnace. Put down 6 hrs. Took 3 hrs. (therefore 8.20 F per hr.).

9:15 to 11:15 (or 11:30?): spent the day drilling. *Riveting* fun: putting rivets in stacks of thin metal plates in which holes had been drilled. But inevitably didn't make the rate on the voucher. Put down how much time? Probably 1¼ hrs.—or ½, or ¾? In any case, below my hourly base wage (probably a difference of more than 1 hr.).

11:30–3 o'clock: ate lunch at the Russian restaurant. Riveting fun and easy. 400 pieces at .023 = 9.20 F. Put down 2½ hrs. (at 3.70 F per hr.). On resuming work at 1:15, suffering from a crushing headache, I botched 5 pieces by putting them wrong side up before doing the riveting. Fortunately the young drilling foreman came to take a look. . . .

Done at more than 3 F per hr.

3:15–5:15: *furnace*. Much less arduous than yesterday evening and this morning—made 300 pieces (tempo of 7.35 F per hr.).

Friday, 4th. 7–8:30 A.M.: *cutting pieces out of brass strips* at the large press. Took my time, learning how before I started. Meditated on an exasperating mystery: the last piece cut out of the strip was notched; now, the one that came out notched was the seventh. Simple explanation given by the set-up man (Robert): 6 of them were still left in the die. Put down 1¼ hrs. 578 for .224 per hundred. Earned 1.30 F! *Difference between that and the hourly base wage* = .95 F.

8:45–1:30 (standing): *polishing*. A small order, marked 10 min., then 300 pieces at .023. Earned 6.90 F. Put down 2¾ hrs. (or 2½?). 2.40 F. or 2.70 per hour. Work with the polishing belt, tricky. Did it slowly and, apparently, *badly* (didn't catch on to the knack); nevertheless, pieces not botched. But M——t made me stop, and turn over the remaining 200 pieces to another woman.

Furnace. Totally different place, although right next to our shop. The foremen never go there. Relaxed and brotherly atmosphere, no more servility or pettiness. The smart young man who serves as set-up man. . . . The welder. . . . The young Italian worker with the blond hair . . . my "fiancé" . . . his brother . . . the Italian woman . . . the husky fellow with the mallet. . . .

At last, a happy workshop. Teamwork. Coppersmiths' shop, tools: mainly the mallet. They bend pipe elbows with a little hand machine, then make fine adjustments with the mallet; so knack is indispensable. Numerous calculations, needed for measurements—they assemble boxes, etc. Work by twos or more, most of the time.

Wednesday, went to a meeting of the 15th Socialist and Communist section about Citroën. Confidential. No workers from	*Hours min.*	*Sous*
	1¼	1.85 F
	2½	7.
	1	1.80
	1¼ ± ¼ ?	3.25
	. . . 6	24.60
	1½	(?) 1.

		6½	9.20
		1¼	1.30
		2¾	6.90
5 min.		[¼] 10 min.	?
5 min.		1½ 25 min.	2.45
		1¼	1.30
		7¾	29.40
		¾	2.10

31(½) 20 min.	92.15
(1 hr. ahead, per-	Hrly. wage
haps 1 hr. 25 min.?).	1.80 F in
	30½ hrs. =
	54.60 F;
	bonus: 37.55 F;
	that makes a
	little more than
	3 F per hr.
	(.65 more).

Citroën, apparently.

Not much reaction about it at the factory. 2 women: "Sometimes you're upset, but with good reason." That was all. Warehouse keeper: "That's the way it is. . . ."

In the coppersmiths' shop, one worker had on his table the pamphlet distributed the night before.

1:30–3:05 *(standing): with the set-up man from the back (Biol?). Large pieces.* Position the piece while pushing down; tighten with a movable bar; pedal; loosen the bar; tap a lever to free the piece; pull it out forcibly. . . . 1 F per hundred! Put down 1 hr. 25 min.—244 pieces. Earned 2.44 F. Set-up man rugged and very likable. I had already helped him cut some sheet metal, with great enjoyment. Didn't make the rate, but it was because the timekeeper made a mistake.

Difference between what I earned and the hourly base wage: .25 F.

3:15–4:50 (approximately): *sheet-metal boxes.* Apply oil, place around a shaft, stamp; the tool forms them. Put the solder on the correct side. Exhausted from having spent all day and the day before standing up; movements slow. Great pleasure in thinking that this box had been made by my teammates in the coppersmiths' shop, soldered. . . . During this job, a collection was taken up for a woman who is sick. Gave 1 F. Put down 1¼ hrs. Earned? Made 137 pieces, .92 per hundred—earned approximately 1.30 F. However, the foreman said nothing. *Difference between what I earned and the hourly base wage: .90 F.*

Saturday, 5th. 7–10 A.M.: *furnace.* Hardly difficult at all. No headaches, made 300 pieces at a leisurely pace. Earned 29.40 F for the lot of 600. Put down 7¾ hrs. Worked at a tempo of 4.90 F per hr.

10–11 A.M.: *cardboards* (continuing). Easy. Only one stupid mistake you can make: cram. I did it! Bawling out from Léon. 50 centimes per hundred. Did 425. Earned 2.12 F. Put down ¾ hr. Paid at 10 o'clock; 115 F; amount over the hourly base wage: 36.75 F.

Total of differences between what I made and the hourly wage: .25 F + 1 F + .95 F + .25 F + .90 F = *2.50 F* (it won't bankrupt the factory . . .).

SIXTH WEEK

Monday, 7th. 7–9:30 A.M.: continued the *cardboards*. Did 865 of them from 7 to 8:45 A.M. (1¾ hrs. at 50 centimes per hundred); I ought to have done 1,050 of them. Then went to clip the ones that were too large, which is why Bret put me down for ½ hr. (actual time).

From 9:15 to 9:30 worked on clipping them. Put down ½ hr. on the 1st voucher (so 1¼ hrs. for 680 pieces), that is, for 3.40 F; therefore 2.72 F per hr.; *didn't make the rate*. Put down 1 hr. 10 min. on the second voucher for a few more than 700 pieces; MADE THE RATE. Total time: 1 hr. 10 min. + ½ hr. + ½ hr. = *2 hrs. 10 min.*

9:30–10:20: 1 hr. of *work paid by the hour* (sheared off ends of long precut strips for Bret).

10:20–2:40: *polishing* at the press (with the nice set-up man from the back) the large pieces out of which I had cut little tongues on Friday from 1:30 to 3 (another woman had cambered them in the meantime). .80 per hundred! Did 516 in 2 hrs. 50 min. Put down *2 1/2 hrs.* Earned 4.15 F, that is, officially 1.65 F per hr. Difference between what I made and the hourly base wage for 2½ hrs.: *.37 F.*

2:45 to 5:15: *press to shape into ovals* small pieces that are going to be soldered. .90 per hundred. Very easy. (The timekeeper must be crazy!) Made 1,400 of them; so earned 1,400 × .90 = 14 × 90 = 12.60 F. Actual tempo: 5.05 F! Put down ½ hr. + ¾ hr. + 2¼ hrs. [3 orders] = 3½ hrs.; tempo there is 3.60 F (more to do).

Total hours: 2 hrs. 10 min. + 1 hr. + 2½ hrs. + 3½ hrs. = *9 hrs. 10 min.;* that is, *25 minutes ahead* (that is, 1 hr. 25 min. or 1 hr. 50 min.).

Total earnings: 3.40 F + 4.15 F + 12.60 F = 20.15 F; add to that 1½ hrs. paid by the hour (between 4.50 F and 6 F). (The whole day at 3 F per hr. would be 26.25 F; but for the polishing voucher on which I didn't make the rate they owe me more than on 1.80 F.) Say 25 F in 8¾ hrs. Exactly 2.88 F per hr.

Tuesday, 8th, morning. 7:30–11:15: *1,181 pieces planished at the stamping press.* Accident at 7:15: a piece stuck in the tool jams it. Set-up man (Ilion) composed and patient. Only 25 botched pieces. Not my fault; but from now on I'll be careful with this machine. *2 3/4 hrs.* 5.30 F (.45 per hundred). *Didn't make the rate.* (While it was being repaired, spent 1¼ hrs. turning a crank to cut out cardboards. The woman working with me was raising the crank too soon and accused me of turning too quickly. . . . 515,645. Work paid by the hour.)

11:15–3:40: *large press* with Robert; removing rough edges—easy. C 280–804—put in *2 1/2 hrs.* (just *made the rate;* didn't have the voucher except at the end). Robert, a bit curt earlier, became very nice, patient, and concerned about helping me understand my work. The warehouse keeper must have spoken to him. Robert is decidedly likable. Importance of a set-up man having human qualities.

3:45–5:15 and [incomplete in the original text]

Wednesday, 9th. 7 A.M.–1:30 *cambering on the machine operated by buttons.* The tool was jamming—oil every piece—(by the way, the foreman spoke to me in a nice tone of voice that he rarely uses)—long job—62 per hundred; but the rate probably doesn't mean anything. Did 833— put down *6 hrs.* total. Work not too boring, thanks to the feeling of responsibility (I was studying how to avoid the jamming).

1:30–3:30, *drilled holes at the stamping press* (pieces like the ones I planished the time the foreman made me start over). At first the stop was set wrong. Ilion doesn't worry about it much—takes his time correcting it—sings snatches of songs. I worked slowly because I was being careful to check everything (I was afraid of not placing the pieces correctly against the stop). *Hrs.?* Put down 1¼ hrs.—*didn't make the rate.*

3:45–5:15 *riveting with Léon; steel caps wrapped in paper.* Easy; just pay attention to positioning the washers correctly (countersunk hole on top). Worked at the required tempo, i.e., uninterruptedly. But worked very slowly in the beginning (curb that tendency in the future).

6 vouchers, made the rate on 4 of them. Worked on average at a tempo of 2.88 F.

Uneventful day. Not particularly hard. Feeling of silent fraternity with the rugged set-up man from the back (the only one). Spoke to no one. Nothing very instructive.

I feel much better about the factory after being in the workshop at the back, even though I am no longer there.

A woman drill operator had a clump of hair completely torn out by her machine, despite her hairnet; a large bald patch is visible on her head. It happened at the end of a morning. She came to work in the afternoon just the same, although she was in a lot of pain and was even more afraid.

Very cold this week. Temperature varies greatly according to where you are in the factory; there are some places where I am so chilled at my machine that my work is clearly slowed down. You go from a machine located in front of a hot-air vent, or even a furnace, to a machine exposed to drafts. The cloakrooms aren't heated at all; you freeze for the five minutes it takes you to wash your hands and get dressed. One of us has chronic bronchitis, serious enough that she has to apply cupping-glasses every other day. . . .

Thursday, 10th. (Awakened at 3:30 A.M. by intense earache, had chills, felt feverish. . . .)

7–10:40 A.M.: continued—fast tempo, in spite of feeling ill. An effort, but after a while a mechanical, rather degrading sort of happiness— botched one piece (no bawling out). Toward the end, bureaucratic incident: 10 washers short.

The bureaucratic incident is very funny. I report the shortage of 10 washers to Léon who, displeased (just as if it were my fault), sends me back to the foreman. The latter curtly sends me to Mme Blay, in the glass cubicle. She takes me to the storeroom managed by Bretonnet (who isn't there), doesn't find any washers, concludes from that that there aren't any, returns to the cubicle, telephones the office from which she thinks the order comes; they refer her to Mr. X. She telephones his office, where they tell her that he has gone to Mr. Y.'s office, and they won't go and get him. She hangs up, laughs and fumes (but still good humoredly) for a few minutes, and telephones Mr. Y.'s office, where they give her Mr. X., who says he has nothing to do with that order. Laughing, she tells her tribulations to Mouquet, and concludes that there is nothing for it but to work with the quantity they have. Mouquet calmly approves, adding that they are not equipped to make washers. I go to tell this to the foreman, then to Léon (who bawls me out!). While I am doing my voucher, someone apparently made a fresh search of Bretonnet's storeroom; Léon brings me about fifteen washers (still bawling me out!) and I proceed to do the 10 remaining pieces. Of course, all this bureaucratic rigamarole represents so much time for which I am not paid. . . .

In the meantime—the foreman and Léon have a slight row about finding a machine for me.

10:45 to 11:25, *annealing* at Léon's furnace—25 pieces—had to remain continuously in front of the furnace (small, however) in order to watch. Discomfort from heat tolerable. Put down 35 min.—.036 the piece; worked for .90 F.

11:30 to 5 P.M., *holes in large and heavy baffle plate* (.56 per hundred; price capriciously set). C. 12190, B55—213 pieces—put down 4 hrs.

Drama—a little cowardice on Léon's part ("I don't intend to be responsible for somebody else's mistakes"). He goes with my worst piece to the foreman (his rage—) —The foreman—who contrary to his usual habit is rather kind—comes to look and discovers that the stops are inadequate. He orders them changed. Léon installs a continuous stop at the back. I turn out another defective piece, fooled by the old stop. Léon storms and goes to the foreman. Fortunately, I then make a good one. I continue, trembling. As a last resort, I get the warehouse keeper, who explains it all to me gently and in a luminous fashion (instead of gripping the piece, support it from underneath, and push steadily forward with my thumbs; slide it along the stop to make sure it is there). Mimi, who had come to my assistance earlier, hadn't been able to help me, except to advise me not to worry so much.

Tremendous distance between the warehouse keeper and the set-up men—especially Léon, who is the least competent.

I tell Mimi, showing her the price: "It can't be helped, I just won't make the rate." She answers, "Yes, *since they don't want to pay us for badly made pieces,* there's nothing else to do" (!).

Friday, 11th. 7–8:05 A.M.: same job, made 601 pieces, that's 5.04 F. Put down 1½ hrs. *Made the rate.* Worked at almost 4 F per hr., officially for 3.40 F.

8:15–10:15: *contacts:* drilling small copper bars while you set them against the stop; no difficulty. I ask Ilion what they are for; he answers me with a joke. Robert, on the other hand, always gives me an explanation when I ask him a question, and shows me the plan; but the warehouse keeper had to speak to him. As for Léon, when I look at his orders, he bawls me out. Why? Hierarchy? No. He thinks that I am trying to fix it so that I have the best jobs. In any case, it's not comradeship.

9C 412087, B 2, 600 at .64 per hundred = 3.84 F. Put down 1¾ hrs. Didn't make the rate. At the end, slight tiff with the shearer (I refuse to do some pieces over, which turns out to be unnecessary anyway).

10:45–11:30—*Robert's large press.*

11:45–5:45—*shearing and drilling copper strips* (with Léon). Second drama. —After 250 pieces have been done, Léon notices that the holes aren't centered (I had noticed nothing). Fresh shouting. Mouquet turns up, sees my disconsolate expression and is very kind. As soon as Mouquet shows up, Léon—who doesn't give a damn since he is released from responsibility—will say nothing further. As for me, instead of realizing that the exact placement of the holes apparently doesn't much matter, I stop at every piece to see if it is against the stop and constantly compare it to the model. Léon bawls me out again, but this time with good intentions, evidently not being able to understand that it is possible to be conscientious at the expense of one's pocketbook. I speed up a little, but at 5:45 have done only 1,845 pieces. Paid .45 per hundred; so earned 4.50 F + 3.60 F + 20 centimes = 8.30 F, which is barely 2 F per hr. Would have to make up more than 1½ hrs. There are 10,000 pieces.

Léon is doing me a great favor by giving me this job. It really is a large order. Still, even on the last day, when I was used to the job, and going at top speed because I was anxious to make up for my lost time, I barely made the prescribed 3 F. True, I was slightly ill. But the work is still very badly paid.

Saturday, 12th. —Same job. Go as fast as I can. Find some ways of working: first, put the strips in straight (Léon had adjusted the supports badly). Then slide the strip along the stop with a continuous movement. At first I made 800 pieces in a little more than an hour, then slowed down because of fatigue. *Very* hard. Back-breaking work that reminds me of digging potatoes—right arm constantly extended—pedal slightly stiff. Thank heaven, it's Saturday!

Couldn't catch up. Made 2,600, that's 9 F + 2.70 F = 11.70 F in 4 hrs. Far from catching up, I'm still about 30 centimes (that's 60 pieces) under the prescribed speed. And I gave it all my strength. . . . True, went to sleep too late.

Did in all: 4,400.

Afternoon and Sunday painful: headaches—slept poorly, my one night [worrying . . .].

SEVENTH WEEK

Monday, 14th. —Same job. Go even faster—developed greater continuity in pedaling. Ended up making 10,150, that is, 5,050 in the course of the day, or

$$22.50 \text{ F} + 3.75 \text{ F} = 26.25 \text{ F in } 8\tfrac{3}{4} \text{ hrs.}$$

Barely 3 F per hr. (to hell with the 60 centimes).

I'm exhausted. After all that I'm still not caught up, for I ought to have done the 10,000 pieces (45 F) in 15 hrs., and it took me 16¾.

At 5:45, I shut off my machine in the dejected and hopeless state of mind that accompanies total exhaustion. However, it was enough just bumping into the singing boy from the furnace who has a nice smile—running into the warehouse keeper—overhearing a more cheerful than usual exchange of jokes in the cloakroom—these little displays of brotherly feeling put me in such a joyful frame of mind that for a while I no longer feel the fatigue. But at home, headaches.

Tuesday, 15th. 7–7:30 A.M.: same job—finished (about 200 were left). Put down a total of 17½ hrs. Didn't make the rate, but the last 200 were above 2.50 F.

Wandered about a little, to no purpose.

8 A.M.: *collars* with Biol. Very large press (stamping press)—very heavy pieces (1 kg.?). There are 250 of them to do. Paid 3.50 per hundred. Have to oil each piece and the tool every time. Very hard work; I have to stand, and the pieces are heavy. Not feeling well; earache, headache. . . .

Incident with the belt, Mouquet–Biol.

First incident, in the morning; Biol and Mouquet. The machine's belt was adjusted before I worked on it, but incorrectly, it seems, for it rides over the edge. Mouquet orders it shut off (Biol was at fault to a certain extent; he should have shut it off before), and says to Biol, "The pulley has shifted, that's why the belt rides off." Biol, eyeing the belt thoughtfully, starts a sentence: "No . . ." and Mouquet interrupts him: "What do you mean, No! *I* say Yes! . . ." Biol, without a word of reply, goes to find the guy in charge of repairs. As for me, fierce desire to slap Mouquet for his peremptory manner and his humiliatingly authoritarian tone of voice. (Later I learn that Biol is universally regarded as a sort of half-wit.)

Second incident. In the afternoon, all of a sudden the tool stamps a piece and I can't remove it. A little rod preventing the bar on top of the tool from coming down had slipped out of its hole, and I hadn't noticed it. So the tool had gone too deeply into the piece. Biol speaks to me as if it were my fault.

Tuesday at 1 P.M., leaflets from the unitary syndicate[3] were passed out. Accepted with visible pleasure (which I share) by almost all the men and not a few of the women. The Italian woman smiles. The singing boy. . . . People hold the leaflets in their hands ostentatiously, several reading them as they enter the factory. Idiotic content.

Story overheard: a workman made some bobbins with the hooks a centimeter too short. The foreman (Mouquet) told him, "If they're fucked up, you've had it." But luckily *another* order called for exactly these bobbins, and the worker was kept on. . . .

The effect of exhaustion is to make me forget my real reasons for spending time in the factory, and to make it almost impossible for me to overcome the strongest temptation that this life entails: that of not thinking anymore, which is the one and only way of not suffering from it. It's only on Saturday afternoon and Sunday that a few memories and shreds of ideas return to me, and I remember that I am *also* a thinking being. The terror that takes hold of me when I realize how dependent I am on external circumstances: all that would be needed is for circumstances someday to force me to work at a job without a weekly rest—which after all is always possible—and I would become a beast of burden, docile and resigned (at least for me). Only the feeling of brotherhood, and outrage in the face of injustices inflicted on others, remain intact—but how long would all that last? I am almost ready to conclude that the salvation of a worker's soul depends primarily on his physical constitution. I don't see how those who are not physically strong can avoid falling into some form of despair—drunkenness, or vagabondage, or crime, or debauchery, or simply (and far more often) brutishness—(and religion?).

Revolt is impossible, except for momentary flashes (I mean even as a feeling). First of all, against what? You are alone with your work, you could not revolt except against it—but to work in an irritated state of mind would be to work badly, and therefore to starve. Cf. the tubercular woman fired for having botched an order. We are like horses who hurt themselves as soon as they pull on their bits—and we bow our heads. We even lose consciousness of the situation; we just submit. Any reawakening of thought is then painful.

---

3 *Confédération générale du Travail unitaire*, the Communist-dominated trade-union federation.

Jealousy between workers. The conversation between the tall conceited blond workman and Mimi, who was accused of having hurried so as to be there at the right time for a "good order." Mimi to me: "You aren't jealous. You're wrong not to be." However, she says she isn't—but she may be anyway.

Cf. incident with the redhead Tuesday evening. She claimed a job that Ilion was in the process of giving me, arguing that she had stopped before me (but she had an order started, only it was interrupted; she didn't tell Ilion that until after I had gone away . . .). The job was bad (.56 per hundred, setting pieces against a stop so flat it's almost impossible to see if it's really there). However, I had to force myself to give it to her, since I was between one and three hours behind. But I'm sure that when she saw that the job was no good, she thought that was the reason I gave it up to her.

The same redhead, at the time of the layoffs, didn't much like the idea that single women with kids should be exempted from being laid off.

I don't find anything else to do. Robert refuses me one job because, he says, I would botch half of it. So I just go and chat with the warehouse keeper, quite content in one sense, for I am exhausted.

Tuesday evening of the 7th week (January 15) Baldenweck diagnoses me as having otitis. I go to rue Auguste-Comte[4] on Thursday and remain there the 8th and 9th weeks. The 10th, 11th, and 12th weeks (until Friday) I am at Montana in Switzerland, where I see A.L.'s brother and Fehling. I go back to rue Lecourbe[5] Saturday night (February 23). Return to the factory the 25th. Absent a month and ten days. Had asked for a leave of 15 days beginning the evening of February 1. Took 10 days more: 25 days. As of February 24th, have worked a total of 5 weeks (counting only days actually worked).

Was off 6 weeks.

THIRTEENTH WEEK

(40 hr. week; quitting time 4:30, Saturday off)

Monday, 25th. 7–8:15 A.M. (approx.): time without work, spent with Mimi and Eugénie—Louisette's friend, etc.

After 8:15: *stamping rivets* at the light press. Same work as Thursday

4 The street on which Weil's parents' apartment was located.
5 The street in the factory district where Weil was renting a room.

and Friday of the 3rd week, except that only one side can go against the stop, which makes it necessary to look at each piece, and slow down. I can't go fast. I do a total of 2,625 pieces, that is, almost 400 per hour (allowance made for the fact that I lost 10 min. drawing my pay at 11 A.M.). The first hour I can't work; my hand trembles with nervousness. After that I'm all right, except for the slowness. But I work without tiring. Besides, I don't have the voucher.

If I were no more debilitated and fatigued than this every day, I would not be unhappy at the factory.

Tuesday. Rivets again. I have the voucher: .62 per hundred, like the other time (when, however, either side could go against the stop). I do the remainder at about 500 per hour, that is, 3 F, but don't make up the time lost the day before. At noon, return home gripped by extreme exhaustion; hardly eat anything, can barely drag myself back to the factory. But once I start work again, the fatigue disappears, replaced by a sort of gaiety, and I leave without feeling tired. Finish the screwthreads between 3:30 and 4 (ord. 406367, b. 3). There are 6,011 of them. So I did 3,375 in more than 7 hrs. (even so, that's less than 500 per hr.), that is, 21 F. Total 37.20 F. Put down 13¾ hrs.

From 4 to 4:30: washers, as usual with Jacquot, at a hand press. Necessary to support them with my hand to feed them into the die. Mouquet wants to do a set-up that is easier to use; Jacquot can't do it because there aren't any blocks of exactly the right height, and only makes me lose time. 110 washers.

Wednesday. Finished 8:10. *560 washers* in all, at .468 per hundred; earned 2.60 F! Mimi follows me (I hold her up a little), complaining bitterly about the voucher in a rather tired voice [c. 406246, b. I].

Put down 1½ hrs.

Foil. At first I think I won't be able to do it, but I manage very well. Jacquot, very gentle, had told me to tell him if I couldn't do it. Mistake on the price: 2.80 per hundred, but it means for 100 packets of 6, that is, for the whole order! At least that's what Mimi says. I had never hurried before. Finished at 10 A.M., earned exactly 2.80 F! Put down 2 hrs.— ord. 425512, b. 2.

Conversations when there is no work. Louisette's friend had an abcess in her throat—was out 5 days—came back: "Kids don't ask you if you're sick"; worked two days, out again; came back after the abcess burst. She's always cheerful. She's becoming irritable, she says, can no longer stand her kids tearing around when they play, etc.

Mouquet said to her, "Your hair is as long as your body." She was really mortified. Would have liked to tell him off. "You can't answer back." Mimi's sister does. Once she went to find him to complain about a voucher; he abruptly ordered her back to her job; she went back, but didn't stop complaining. Fifteen minutes later he went to find her and straightened out the voucher. . . . "When the job isn't going right, it's better to speak to him than to a set-up man or to Chastel; and at times like that he's very nice." But angry sometimes; and he's tactless. They quote one of his mortifying remarks (to Mimi's sister): "You've never been hunting?" —Eugénie interrupted her work and comes to tell me excitedly that she saw circus animals at the Porte de Versailles (2 F admission); that she petted the leopard. . . .

Woes of the young unskilled worker: he had 2 years of Latin, 1 year of Greek, 1 of English (he naively brags about it), is an office worker by profession (he is very proud of that), and has been demoted to being an unskilled laborer! "You have to obey these assholes who can't even sign their names!" And you even get bawled out by them. "If that's working-class comradeship! . . ." After that smiles are exchanged when he passes by. He is perhaps 17. Rather pretentious.

Léon isn't there (hurt his arm). Indescribable relief. Jacquot replaces him, relaxed and altogether charming.

Riveting at the large fly-press. Difficult—the pieces don't all go right. One botched piece, which makes Jacquot look solemn. The count is wrong; work with the quantity given! (108 pieces, I think, instead of 125.) Paid .034 per piece, that is, 3.65 F total (1 hr. lost). And I finished at 2:45! Put down 3 hrs. Then spent ¾ hr. when there was no work at Bretonnet's (cutting scrap); finally some *cardboards* that I finished at exactly 4:30, with Jacquot, at a press that can be hand- or foot-operated, as you like. Jacquot nice, as usual (got a packing case for me, etc.). The young unskilled worker comes and bothers me. Price not marked, but didn't make the rate.

Earned these 3 days: 37.20 F + 3.60 F + 2.60 F + 2.80 F + 3.65 F + (admit it!) 2.50 F = 52.35 F!!! That is, 17.43 F per 8-hr. day, that is, an average of 2.20 F per hour! Below the official hourly base wage!

In the late afternoon, working on my cardboards, headaches. But at the same time a feeling of having physical resources. The factory noises, some of them now meaningful (the mallet blows of the coppersmiths, the sledge hammer . . .), simultaneously give me profound moral joy and cause me physical pain. Very curious sensation.

Back at my place, headaches worse, vomiting, don't eat, scarcely sleep; at 4:30 decide to stay home; at 5 A.M., get up. . . . Hot compresses, headache powder. Thursday morning, okay.

Thursday. "*Terminal strips with airgaps.*" Ord. c 421346, b. 1, .56 per hundred. 1,068 pieces, that is, 6 F. Finished at 9:05 (?), put down 2 hrs., *made the rate* (the only one).

"*Baffle with the movable finger*" with Robert—pieces that I think at first will be difficult to position; but then I realize the tool positions them as it comes down, and it goes faster. 510 pieces, .71 per hundred, that's 3.50 F. Finish at 10:45, put down 1½ hrs. [that's 2.30 F per hr.]. Ord. 421329, b. 1.

No work (scrap). Bretonnet puts down ½ hr.

Rail clips at the shearing machine (with Jacquot), (standing, one foot on the pedal, at the press where I made the large 40-kg. bars with Louisette). Ord. 421322, b. 1. .43 per hundred, it says 350 (I learn the next day there were more; I hadn't counted). 1.50 F. Put down 35 min. Finished at 11:45; this morning earned 6 F + 3.50 F + .90 F + 1.50 F = 11.90 F in 4¾ hrs.; that's exactly 2.50 F per hour.

Afternoon: cut out cardboards by the hour with Mimi's sister; I turned the crank. Very pleasant, no jerks like the time before. Put down 1¼ hrs.

At 2:30 put on *Terminal Connectors* by Jacquot (parts for electrical motors, says the warehouse keeper). C. 421337, b. 1—.616 per hundred, piece work.

The difficulty was to put the pieces against the stop so that the 2nd right angle is made. If they weren't flush against the stop, the piece was botched.

Jacquot explains it to me in a nice way. I set to work confidently. I succeed several times. One piece, too wide, doesn't fit into the hollow of the die, and since it isn't held in place, backs up. Chatel,[6] right behind me, tells me (not too roughly) to put them against the stop more carefully. I succeed with a few more, then botch another one. Not only are some pieces too wide, but others are too narrow, and they slip because the stop is rounded-off through use. I show Jacquot; he says to put the wide ones in sideways. I call him over again; he speaks to Chatel, tells me to continue and, if it doesn't work, to tell Chatel. I try again, then go to Chatel, holding a botched piece. He says, "That one's had it. You have to put them against

6 sw drops the "s" from Chastel's name for the rest of the journal.

the stop." I try to explain. He says, not getting up, "Get on with it, and try not to keep on doing things like that." I immediately call the warehouse keeper over, who says, "It doesn't work right, obviously, although *I* could make them all turn out." He tries putting them in with his finger and holding them when the tool comes down . . . and also botches quite a lot of them! He thinks about that for a long time, calls for a guy from the tool shop who tells him that the stop is worn (I had seen that right away!), removes the die, proceeds to file the stop, and resets the machine. I continue the finger method (dangerous!). It works better, but still not well. I go to find him again; he's with Mouquet, who comes to look, gives an order to widen the die a little and set the tool lower so there's no chance of my hand passing under it. It works until 4:30. . . . A little over 100 pieces done, and about 40 botched.

I was paid 66.55 F for these 4 days (4 F withheld for Social Insurance). But the last 2 were paid at the hourly base wage: for me, 14.40 F per day (1.80 F per hour). I made 12.95 F over the base wage for the first 2 days.

28.80 F + 12.95 F = 41.75 F. Where the devil did they get that? There was the period when there was no work (1¼ hrs., that is, 3.25 F?). And what else?

Friday, March 1st. Do my terminal connectors. Finish at 10:30; made 2,131 in all, that is, about 2,030 this morning in 3½ hrs. (that's 580 per hour, at .616 per hundred!). Earned in all 13 F. Explain to Chatel that I lost 2 hrs. the afternoon before; he mutters, "2 hours!" and puts "time lost" on the voucher . . . but not *how much!* I put down 2 hrs. and 3½ hrs.

No work until 11:45.

Argument between Dubois, Eugénie, and the redhead during the period of no work.

Annealing at the small furnace after lunch; it goes all right; that is, I don't lose my presence of mind when I take out the pieces. Hard, because I am continuously in front of the furnace (not like at the big one). Interrupted at 2 o'clock because . . . the pieces are supposed to be laminated cold!!! I put down only my time on the voucher. Put down ¾ hr.

Wait for Robert a good twenty minutes. Another woman, too. . . .

On the advice of the warehouse keeper, went to ask Delouche for permission to stay until 5:15. Granted. The same afternoon went to the tool shop. The foreman didn't see me.

"Handles" at the shearing machine, c. 918452, b. 31. With Robert.

300 to do, at .616 per hundred, that is, 1.85 F for the lot. I didn't think about the price, the required speed, and I took my time doing them, being very careful each time to place the rounded end of the piece right against the stop. Some bars were twisted and were difficult to hold against the stop. Took much too long; finished at 3:25 (but had begun late). Put down 1 hr.

Terminal Connectors. The same kind. Still .616 per hundred—final operation is making them V-shaped. With the button-operated machine with plierlike jaws. Often slowed down by the difficulty of disengaging the piece from the tool; otherwise, easy to put in.

The piece bends slightly while the tool is making it V-shaped. I show it to Jacquot (who had told me, however, that I needn't look at the pieces); he shows it to Chatel; both discuss it solemnly, then Chatel says that it will be planed (but how?) and orders me to continue. I continue at a very comfortable pace, much too slowly. Did only 281 pieces! 1,850 remain to be done in *at most* 3¼ hrs., which means, allowing for losses of time, at a tempo of 600 per hour. Essential!

If I put down 1 hr. Friday for the terminal connectors, I've lost ½ hr. But better, if possible, to lose 1 hour than not make the rate on my voucher. ¼ hour lost (if cleaning counts as ¼ hr.).

But no; actually the rate is .72 (buttons), and in 5 hrs. I made 15.30 F. 4 hrs. left, and to catch up I would have to do 460 an hour. I should have to do only 425 in 1 hr. If on Monday I do only 425 per hour, in order not to fall below the rate I still lose 20 min. Friday.

But no, again; there's ¼ hr. for machine cleaning. So have to count only ¾ hr. Friday, and have to make up only 5 min., negligible. So still have 4¼ hrs. Have to finish by 11:15.

Much less tired than I feared. Even moments of euphoria at my machines, such as I had not had even at Montana (delayed effect!). But still have trouble eating.

FOURTEENTH WEEK

Monday, 4th. Acute headaches Monday when I got up. As ill luck would have it, the turning thing that makes the infernal racket is going all day long right next to me. At noon, can hardly eat. Still, I work fast, and without headache powders.

Terminal Connectors. Don't finish until 11:45, but not my fault; over ½ hr., I'm sure, was lost in the morning (even much more) due to the machine. "With the buttons," says Jacquot, "it never works right." I persuaded him to set up the pedal, though that's more dangerous. It doesn't work any better; I have to call him again. On Mouquet's order, he resets the buttons. Still doesn't work. Little Jacquot loses his patience. . . . At 11:10, starts to disassemble the machine—broken spring. But when he reassembles it, it doesn't work at all. He gets very rattled. . . . The shift foreman, when I hand him my voucher (for I gave up finishing the pieces, since what had been done was more than the count) is sarcastic about J.

Afternoon: no work for ½ hr. Then 2 orders for *terminal strips*, 520 each, at .71 per hundred (c. 421275, b. 4). I lost some time at the beginning extracting the pieces, counting them—also positioning them, for I took some unnecessary precautions—and pedaled inefficiently (not all the way down; stiff pedal). 1st order finished at 3:15. 2nd begun at 3:25 (I lost 5 min. waiting, not having noticed Jacquot had the machine ready), done at a hellish rate, my maximum, finished at exactly 4:30. I made 3.60 F per hour on it. Put down 1 hr. 20 min. for each order. 4½ hrs. + ½ + 2 hrs. 40 min. = 7.40 F. Earned Friday and Monday: 12.30 F + 1.35 F + 1.85 F + 14.40 F + .90 F + 7.80 F = *39.60 F.* Of that, 21.20 F for Monday. Put 1 hr. for Friday and 4½ hrs. for Monday.

Friday, I saw Biol's heavy machine being set up (not ready). The warehouse keeper told me, "Don't take that, it's too hard." I found something else. On Monday I see Eugénie doing that job all day long. Am conscience stricken. If I had *wanted* to be available for it, I probably could have. And I know how hard it is; I did it—or something like it—the last afternoon I had otitis. At 4:30 she is visibly exhausted.

Jacquot and the machine.

The warehouse keeper, the draftsman, and the "universal tool."

The tool shop and its foreman.

What did happen with the machine? (idiot, not to have observed more attentively).—When I pressed the buttons, the tool sometimes came down twice; the shift foreman, seeing that, said, "It shouldn't do that" (that was all!). Later, it did the same thing again, only the 2nd time it stayed down! Jacquot raised it and I continued . . . until the problem began again. He finally had me stop. Ilion, who passed by, told him that the "finger" (the

spring) of the large wheel is broken.
It's true. But it seems there was still
something else wrong. It's clear that
for little Jacquot the machine is a
strange beast. . . .

Tuesday morning. 3 orders similar to those of Monday afternoon.

1) 600 at .56 per hundred, small pieces difficult to take out, put down
1¼ hrs.

2) 550 at .71 per hundred, put down 1 hr. 20 min.

3) 550 at .71 per hundred, put down 1 hr. 20 min.

Very tiring over an extended period of time, for the pedal is very stiff
(cramps). Jacquot charming as usual.

Afterward, came across Biol (which made me long for the heavy pieces
that had made me conscience stricken); he set me up at the "piano," where
I then spent the whole afternoon, except for the period from 2:45 to 3:45
when there was no work. The 2 orders paid .50 per hundred; one was for
630, the other for 315.

For time, put down 2 hrs., then 3¼ hrs.

Total: 1¼ hrs., 1 hr. 20 min., 1 hr. 20 min., 2¾ hrs. = 6 hrs. 40 min.;
I would need 1 hr. 20 min. of time when there was no work; I think I have
1 hr., which would make 20 min. lost.

At 4:30, very tired, so tired that I leave right away. In the evening, acute
headaches.

At the "piano" at first had a great deal of difficulty due to my fear of not
putting the pieces properly against the stop. By the end of the afternoon, it
went a little better. But my fingertips were bleeding.

Wednesday morning. Still piano (630 pieces). Went even better, except
for sore fingers—still, took over 1½ hrs. Put down 1 hr. 20 min. Immediately afterward, Robert had me do a 50-piece order (c. 421146 27)
(Paid?). Nice enough to give me another voucher for an order of 50 of the
same, which he had already done because it was urgent. Difficulties: some
of the pieces don't fit against the stop. He makes me put them aside so he
can do them himself. Slowed down by severe fatigue and headaches, I
spent ½ hr. on the two orders. Afterward, the "piano" again; the same
630, to do again in another way. I try to go quickly and narrowly miss
botching some; for all that, I no longer let my fear of botching hold me
back too much (although Biol told me that I mustn't lose a single piece,

because the count may be short, or exact). I count the pieces again while I'm redoing them. The first time, had found 610. Now come up with 620, give or take a few. The woman who had done them before said she had found 630. The 2nd time I say that the count is right, to have done with it. How do they expect you to keep a decent count at a rate of .50 per hundred? Put down 1 hr. 20 min. Afterward, Robert reprimands me. 2 orders marked 25 minutes each (what?).

Finished all that (including filling out the vouchers) at 11:15. I tell the foreman I finished at 11:05; he fills in a voucher saying I stopped at 11 o'clock, in return for which I didn't claim any time lost this morning. He reprimands me for having filled in all my vouchers at the same time.

Afternoon, no work until 2 o'clock. Then *covers:* 200 at 1.45 per hundred! So I should do the job in less than an hour. But they are heavy, they have to be taken out of a packing case, and you work the pedal 4 times for each one, and there are 2 operations.

First you position them like this: then you turn them over. The 2nd operation is like this:

then you turn them over. So, you do them all set up the 1st way, pedaling twice for each one, then set up the 2nd way, the same thing—so you have to pedal 800 times. But they are not that easy to position. The screws have to go through the holes, etc. I got the voucher only after the 1st operation was finished. I often had the feeling that I wasn't going as fast as I could. Still, I was exhausted. In the late afternoon I felt for the first time really crushed by fatigue, just like before leaving for Montana; the feeling of sliding back into the condition of beast of burden. Stuck it out, however; had a conversation with the warehouse keeper, visited the tool shop.

Thursday. Continued with the same pieces until 8 A.M. Put down 3½ hrs.; the truth (forgot to note down the order). Afterward, c. 421360, b. 230, rail clips at 1.28 F per hundred. Finished at 9:45. Put down 1 hr. 10 min. (was there a ½-hr. interval when there was no work? I no longer know). Worked with Jacquot, at the small hand press. Jacquot's smiles as usual charming.

Afterward, no work until 11 A.M. During the interval, felt the full brunt of fatigue, waited for the job to be given me with a sickish feeling. During

the periods of no work the women get angry at frequently losing their turn
to get a job for orders of 100 pieces (especially Mimi's sister). Jacquot
came, bringing an order for 5,000 pieces; it was my turn. It was for cutting
washers out of metal strips, with uninterrupted pedaling. Price .224 per
hundred (more or less). I very much wanted not to fall below the rate. I set
to work singlemindedly. Jacquot gave me only one bit of advice: don't let it
jam, for fear of breaking the tool. Fatigue and the wish to go fast made me
a little nervous. When I began I didn't insert one strip far enough, which
forced me to start the 1st pedal downstroke over again, and I botched one
piece (one botched piece out of 5,000 isn't much, but if it happened with
every strip, it would be a lot). It happened several times. Finally, on edge,
I inserted the strip again, this time too far; it slid over the stop and instead
of a washer out comes a cone. Instead of calling Jacquot right away, I turn
the strip over but, unaware of the mistake that I've made, I again overshoot
the stop (at least it's very likely that's what happened), and another cone
falls out and, immediately after it, the "grenadier" of the tool (?). The tool
is broken. What upset me most was the curt and harsh tone in which dear
little Jacquot talked to me. It was a rush order; the set-up, which was perhaps difficult, had to be done over, and everyone was on edge because of
similar accidents that had happened on preceding days (and perhaps the
same day?). The shift foreman, of course, bawled me out like the sergeant-
major that he is, but as it were collectively ("it's unfortunate having
women workers who . . ."). Mimi, who sees me looking desolate, comforts me gently. It's 11:45.

Afternoon (acute headaches). No work until 3:30. 500 pieces, cutting
rings out of metal strips again (what rotten luck!), but at the small hand
press. Fear of beginning again makes me horribly nervous. Actually, I
more than once slide the strip a little over the stop on the 1st pedal stroke,
but nothing happens; each time I tremble. . . . Jacquot found his smiles
again (I have to send for him because the machine behaves capriciously—
refuses to start, or works n times in succession for one pedal stroke), but
I haven't the heart to respond to them.

Incident between Joséphine (the redhead) and Chatel. It seems she was
given a very poorly paid job (at the press beside mine, the one with the buttons opposite the foreman's office). She complained. Chatel gave her a
first-class bawling out, saying very vulgar things, it seemed to me (but
I couldn't make out the words very well). She made no reply, bit her lips,
swallowed her humiliation, visibly repressed a desire to cry, and, proba-

bly, an even stronger desire to answer back furiously. 3 or 4 women witnessed the scene in silence, only half keeping back their smiles (Eugénie among them). For if Joséphine hadn't gotten this bad job, one of them would have had it; so they were quite pleased that Joséphine got the bawling out, and say so openly, later, during a period when there is no work—but not in her presence. Conversely, Joséphine would not have minded the bad job being palmed off on someone else.

Conversations during the period without work (I ought to take them all down). On houses in the suburbs (Mimi's sister and Joséphine). When Nénette is there most often there is nothing but jokes and confidences that would make a regiment of Hussars blush. (Cf. the woman whose "friend" is a painter [but she lives alone] and who boasts of sleeping with him 3 times a day, morning, noon, and night; who explains the difference between his "technique" and another's—who gives out she is aided financially by him, and "deprives herself of nothing"; as far as I understood, the time she doesn't spend making love, she spends cooking and eating.)

But there's more to Nénette than that—when she speaks of her kids (the boy is 13, the girl 6)—of their studies—of her son's liking for reading (she speaks of it with respect). The last few days of this week, in which she had no work a lot of the time, she has been serious in a way that is unlike her; she is obviously wondering what she will do to pay for the kids' schooling.[7]

Argument revolving around Mme Forestier. There is talk of taking up a collection for her. Eugénie declares that she will contribute nothing. Joséphine also (but she probably doesn't give too often), and adds that Mme Forestier went through the factory to say hello to everyone (the same day I came back) because of the collection. Nénette and the Italian women, who used to be great friends of hers, won't give anything either. Apparently she has done some injury, not to them, but to several others (?).

The Italian woman is ill. My 2nd week, she had asked for leave and Mouquet refused; but there were only 2 of them, and there was no work. She has 2 kids; her husband is a brickmaker (unskilled work) and earns 2.75 F per hour. So she can't take care of herself. She has a bad liver, and headaches that the din of the factory makes unendurable (I know about that!).

---

7 Met her in the metro when I was at Renault. She told how a week earlier she had been ill, hadn't been able to inform them and no longer dared to return to Alsthom— (what does she have to lose? But . . .). Certainly an impulsive act. . . . A look of pained compassion when I told her I was at Renault. (Note of s w)

Friday. Period of no work. I don't spend the time, as I would have a few weeks earlier under such circumstances, trembling at the idea of blunders I will perhaps make. Proof that I am a little more sure of myself than before.

Ilion calls me (what time?) to notch covers for use on metros. They have a right side and a wrong side. I have a lively fear of absentmindedly doing the wrong one. 149 covers (voucher for 150) at 1.35 F per hundred. I don't really try to go fast, too afraid of botching, for here even one "messed up" piece would matter a lot. One thing to watch out for: the tool failing to penetrate and the notch not coming out. A great deal of time lost in manipulation; there are 3 tool carriages. My count came to 147 covers; the foreman was in a state and made me spend ¼ hr. doing the count again (but this ¼ hr. won't be on the voucher, but considered a part of the period when there was no work), ord. 421211, b. 3. Finished at 9 A.M. No work until 10; tired, apprehensive, I would have liked the time without work to have lasted all day. At 10 A.M. I was called to remove cardboards from magnetic circuits (work that I had done at the end of the 1st week). I saw that there were enough to last until evening. Considerable relief. I used the technique discovered the last day I had done it (many little taps of the mallet) and worked well and quite quickly (more than 30 pieces per hour; on the first days I had done 15, and Mouquet had estimated the value of my work at 1.80 F per hr., since he had told me that in 5 hrs. I had done barely 9 F worth of work). No fear of making blunders, so I was relaxed. Nevertheless (and although I had eaten at noon at a restaurant), toward the middle of the afternoon I felt myself overcome by very great weariness, and welcomed the notice that I was laid off.

FIFTEENTH WEEK

Laid off (from March 8 to March 18). —Headaches Saturday and Sunday—state of almost total prostration until noon Wednesday; in the afternoon, in magnificent spring weather, went to Gibert's bookstore from 3 to 7 P.M. The next day went to Martinet's, bought a textbook on industrial design. Friday afternoon, prostration. Didn't sleep that night (headache); slept until noon. Saturday saw Guihéneuf (at the place where he works) from 2 to 10:30. Sunday uneventful.

SIXTEENTH WEEK

Monday, 18th. Washers out of a strip until 7:50 (?). With Léon, who has returned (my dear little Jacquot is back being a worker again). .336 per hundred. 336 pieces. Still fearful. Made the same blunder twice, which fortunately passed unnoticed; I became aware of it only after it had happened the 2nd time. I turned the strip over after the 1st pedal stroke; the hole that it drilled wasn't in the middle of the strip, because you support it from behind. This resulted in some bent pieces, which I hid, and the tool was probably none the better for it. Very slow work, no concern at all for speed. Put down 40 min.

Planishing the same washers on the small fly-press, which allowed me to dispose of a botched piece that had slipped by me. Ord. 907405, b. 34, .28 per hundred. Finished at 8:30, put down ½ hr. (so lost 20 min. in all), earned .95 F! My hourly base wage. . . . I hadn't really tried for speed.

Planishing shunts at the small fly-press c. 420500. Had done 796 pieces by 2:15. Put down 4¼ hrs. Paid 1.12 F per hundred; earned 8.90 F (barely over 2 F per hr.). Chatel had me hit 4 or 5 times per piece (2 on one end, 2 or 3 on the other). I told him, when I handed him the voucher, that under these conditions I hadn't been able to make the rate. He answered in the rudest manner, "Not make it at 1.12 F!" That didn't bother me, considering his lack of competence. I don't know if he put something on the voucher; surely not. I should have hit it fewer times. . . . I tried to go fast, but I constantly found myself lapsing into daydreaming. Difficult to control the speed, since I wasn't counting. Tired, especially when leaving for lunch at 11:45 (ate at "Prisunic"; relaxation; moments before going back inside delightful; the Fortifications, the workers. . . . Am a slave again in front of my machine).

In the entranceway I saw shunts like mine, connected in series to contact fingers on one side and to metal coils on the other.

No work from 2 to 3 P.M.—theoretically.

Stamping sockets out of bezels with Robert. C. 406426. 580 pieces at .50 per hundred; so 2.90 F. Put down 1 hr. 10 min., tempo 2.45 F per hr. Actually done from 2:30 to 4:10, that is, 1 hr. 40 min. But lost some time trying to use pliers on the first 100 and, at the end, gathering up the pieces. There again I attained an uninterrupted tempo only momentarily, and then fell back into daydreaming. Counter as a means of control; after having made 40 or 45 pieces in 5 min., I made 20 the next 5 minutes, when I started daydreaming.

No work from 4:15 to 4:30.

Total: 40 min. + ½ hr. + 4¼ hrs. + 1 hr. + 1 hr. 10 min. + ¼ hr. = exactly 8 hrs.

Back at my place (at 5:30) feeling great. Head full of ideas all evening—however, I suffered—especially at the fly-press—much more than the Monday after Montana.

Does the meal at "Prisunic" have something to do with my feeling so good in the evening?

Tuesday. No work until 8:15.

Riveting contact fingers with Léon, until late afternoon. 500 at 4.12 F per hundred, c. 414754, b. 1. For switches. Equipment for streetcars. At first very slow; Chatel had frightened me, and I dreaded making some mistake. There must not be any botched pieces, and I botched the 1st one. There were 4 parts to assemble: the contact, 2 terminal strips, and a packet of 10 pieces of foil (but some packets had only 9). You had to pay attention to the two holes of unequal size in the large terminal strip—position the smaller hole seam side up, and in the direction of the cutting. Did the first 70 in 2 hrs., I think. . . . Afterward, never stopped daydreaming. Reached an uninterrupted tempo only in the afternoon (fortified by lunch and loafing), and only by continually repeating to myself the list of operations (iron wire—large hole—seam—direction—iron wire . . .), not so much to keep myself from making a blunder as to prevent myself from thinking, which is the condition for going fast.

I profoundly feel the humiliation of this void imposed on my thought. I finally manage to go a little faster (at the end I'm making more than 3 F per hr.), but with bitterness in my heart.

Wednesday. Same until 8:30, put down 7¾ hrs., earned 20.60 F (in 8¼ hrs., that is, 2.50 F per hr.).

I don't achieve the "uninterrupted tempo" again; I ought to have finished in 8 hrs.

Polishing the same pieces until 3:45, put down 5¼ hrs., earned 13.50 F. C. 414754, b. 4. .027 per piece. It's what I did the week I was at the furnace; Mouquet took that job away from me as badly done, and in fact I was handling it badly. So I begin in a state of apprehension. I go very, very slowly at first. Catsous leaves me to myself. The 1st discovery I make has to do with the direction in which the piece must be turned: in the one in which the belt would carry it, but while pulling it in the reverse direction. In this way the piece and the belt stay in contact (at least I imagine that's

the reason). The 2nd (made a long time ago, but I apply it here) is that
a hand should do only one operation at a time. So I push with my left hand
and pull with my right; as for turning the piece, I don't have to do it, the
belt does it. As for the tempo, I start out at a comfortable pace; then, realizing I'm going extremely slowly, I strive for the "uninterrupted tempo," but
reluctantly and with a feeling of annoyance; also I feel no pleasure at all at
having mastered a trick of the trade. At noon, I eat a quick lunch at
"Prisunic," then go sit in the sun across the street from the aircraft plant.
I remain there in such a state of inertia that I arrive at the factory in a sort of
half-dream, not in the slightest hurry, at 1:13 or 1:14. . . . They were
locking the gate!

4–4:30 riveting, see next day.

Paid 125 F (4 F of which in advance). The week before, 70 F. That's
192 F for 32 + 48 = 80 hours . . . so exactly 2.40 F per hour. . . .

Conversation with Pommier—knows all the tools.

Evening: headaches and very bitter weariness in my heart. I don't eat,
except for a little bread and honey. I take a bath to help me sleep, but the
headache keeps me awake almost all night. At 4:30 in the morning a great
need for sleep comes over me. But I have to get up. I resist the temptation to
take a half-day off.

Thursday. All day: riveting armatures—had done 700 by 4:30 (in
8¾ hrs.)—in high spirits going out at noon—exhausted after the meal.
Evening: too tired to eat, lie stretched out on the bed; little by little a very
sweet lassitude—delicious sleep.

C. 421121, b. 3—.056 per piece—800 pieces. Put down 14¼ hrs.

Mind empty all day, without resorting to tricks as I did in the riveting, by
an effort of will kept up without too much difficulty. And yet I had gotten
up with a bad headache that nearly made me stay home. I'm encouraged by
the fact that this is a "good job," although it's hard. And also—especially—by a sort of sporting spirit. Work really *uninterrupted.*

Tool shop (Mouquet comes here . . .).

Italian woman and Mouquet.

"4 sous . . . an hour—that's not enough for you in this time of
unemployment?"

Ilion's reflections: "The boss will always be rich. . . . You always have
to go too fast, that's why there isn't any work. . . ."

About a "J.P." who passes by: "and to think how highly these guys are
regarded"—

Friday. Finish riveting. But some rivets are missing (to tell the truth, there were some in the grooves of the machine). 8:15 to 8:45, 50 extension pieces at .54 per hundred, c. ? (I'm sure it's 413910), put down ¼ hr. Cardboard washers, not timed, job-voucher no. 1747, ord. 1415, put down 2 hrs. (took 2¼)—covers. C. 412105, b. 1, .72 per hundred (buttons), 400 pieces. Put down 3½ hrs. (I didn't finish them by quitting time, but Chatel is finishing them). Lost 1 hr.; the day before I had picked up 3 (made up for slowness), 2 left.

Machine wrecked by Ilion (in the process of setting it up, he broke something).

The warehouse keeper: "The set-up men don't know how to use the brakes." "They don't know how to set the buttons. It's always too short, so that the valve . . .(?)."

Monday. Until 8 A.M. finished *magnetic circuits,* order 20154—only 25 left. I work with ease, without hurrying, without being slow for all that. Put down 1 hr. I have 6 hrs. in all (the voucher wasn't passed).

"*Extension pieces*" (4-sided boxes to put in a forming block). Ridiculous price (.923 per hundred), 50 pieces! C. 413910, b. 1. I put down ½ hr. Finish at 9:45. You mustn't put them in two at a time, Mimi tells me. You have to oil all of them.—Then?

Until 10:45, *foil* with Léon, next to Eugénie who is putting in rivets. C. 425537, b. 2—200 packets of 6—2.80 F per hundred. I go fast (the Wednesday after Montana, it took me 2 hrs. to do 100 packets!). So earned 5.60 F. I put down 1 hr. 50 min. (made the rate). Again I almost achieved the uninterrupted tempo.

Cutting pieces out of metal bars at the press where I spent one Wednesday with Louisette. Put the piece right at the stop, hold it exactly parallel . . . I don't go fast. That lasts until 1:50 P.M. Apparently I put down too much time by mistake: 1 hr. 40 min. C. 4009194, b. 97—346 pieces at .88 per hundred! (I think I did 360, but Friday Catsous will tell me that there were only 330!). I work without making any attempt at speed; tired and discouraged by the price, also having an excuse in the fact that the pieces are hard to get out.

Scrap from 1:45 to 3:30 (so 1¾ hrs.).

Same pieces—making them triangular, on the *same* voucher. Profound disgust, which slows me down.

Finished at 4:30—put down 3¼ hrs. in all.

Tuesday. ¼ hr. scrap.

Conversation while doing scrap; Souchal vulgar. One day Joséphine summoned him to come . . .[8] her, got Mouquet to force him to do it. Mouquet is fair, but capricious. Adjusts the vouchers you haven't made the rate on sometimes one way, sometimes another—not according to how hard the work is!

"Bimetallic strips" (pieces tricky to place against the stop: die almost flat) with Léon; C. 421227, 2,100 pieces with the buttons, so at .72. Put down 6¼ hrs. Same machine on which I made the terminal connectors the 2nd time, and that Jacquot hadn't been able to fix.

½ hr. scrap (lost 40 min. yesterday and today).

Pommera (Jacquot and the machine for the terminal connectors). Set-up men and machines.

Wednesday. ½ hr. scrap.

Piano from 7:30 to 8:15. C. 15682, b. 11, then c. 15682, b. 8, both at .495 per hundred. 180 pieces for the 1st, 460 for the 2nd. Put down 25 min., then 1¼ hrs. Lamentably slow. The woman whose friend is a painter came to . . . me[9]

Riveting, "lower support assembly." C. 24280, b. 45—200 pieces at .10 F (used to be .028!) (temporary price for the Souchal order) from 9:45 until Thursday morning. Put down 6¼ hrs. in all. Did 75 pieces in the morning, that's another 7.50 F. VERY violent headache that day, otherwise I would have gone faster. I went to bed feeling all right the night before, but woke up at 2 A.M. In the morning, wanted to stay home. At the factory, every movement hurts. Louisette, at her machine, sees that I'm not well.

A woman drill operator: her 9-year-old is in the cloakroom. Is he coming to work? "I wish he were old enough," says the mother. She tells how her husband has just been sent home from the hospital where they could do almost nothing for him (pleurisy and serious heart disease). There is also a 10-month-old girl. . . .

Thursday. ¾ hr. scrap.

C. 428195, b. 1, put down 2 hrs. C. 23273, b. 21—198 pieces (all counted) at 1.008 F per hundred (time? 2 hrs. I think). Washers: 10,000 at 7.50 F, put down 1½ hrs. for that day; lost 1¾ hrs.

8 Word unreadable in text.
9 Sentence unfinished in text.

Machine with arms. Two levers, one of which is for safety and prevents the other from coming down; I didn't understand its purpose; the warehouse keeper explains it to me [cf. Descartes and Tantalus!].

Friday. Finish washers in a hurry. Sifting through them, I notice many are botched. I pitch out as many as possible; nevertheless am very afraid. I put down 10,000, although there were already some missing in addition to the ones I pitched out, and 2½ hrs., which makes the rate on the voucher.

8–9, scrap.

9 to 10:30, pieces that are easy to do. C. 421324, voucher for 500; there are only 464; Robert makes me pass the voucher. Paid .61 per hundred. Put down 1 hr. (didn't make the rate), for I think I lost over ½ hr. watching Robert struggling with a machine. The valve no longer opened (Pommera came later; a part was missing, a locking wedge). He was there when I came; didn't stop for me. The problem happened again several times. The woman worker (for once) seemed a bit interested (I don't know her); a slightly disheveled brunette, seems nice.

10:30 to 4:30, scrap (lucky, for it's indescribably restful; in the afternoon, I even end up sitting down)—*annealing,* with only 200 pieces to do, at Léon's furnace until 2 P.M. Put down 50 min., .021 per piece; so earned 4.20 F (but was the annealing done correctly?). I don't dare put down more than 50 min., and don't take the time to work it out. It comes, alas, to 5 F per hour. Will they lower the price on the voucher because of me? I would have done better to have waited and put down at least 1 hr. In any case, lost in all 25 min.

Chatel charming—I am left in total freedom—I am treated like someone condemned to death. . . .

Nénette is suddenly serious. "You're going to look for a job? Poor Simone." She herself is laid off the following week. "You can't make it." I tell Louisette what I think of that; she replies that Mouquet refused to exempt Nénette from the lay-off. Mme Forestier had been exempted 2 years ago, but on orders from above.

Monday. Annealing plates (bobbin stops) until 9:10. 200 at .021 [421263, b. 21].

Spindles: 180 at .022 [928494, b. 48], put down 1¼ hrs. and 1 hr.

Fly-press, calibrating (like the 2nd day?) [22616, b. 17, 2 vouchers], 116 pieces at .022 per hundred—2 operations, one difficult, the other easy! Put down 50 min. (finished at 11:30).

Vouchers on which I made the rate

Scrap		Numbers	Price	Time	
1 hr.		421121 (armatures R)	44.80 F	14 hrs.	15 min.
	15 min.	24280 (support R)	20 F	6 hrs.	15 min.
1 hr.	15 min.	?	7.50 F	2 hrs.	30 min.
1 hr.	45 min.	(washers I)			
	15 min.	408294	4.20 F		50 min.
		(furnace L)	76.50 F	22 hrs.	110 min.
	30 min.				
	30 min.				
	45 min.				
1 hr.		forgot:		23 hrs.	50 min.
1 hr.	15 min.				
2 hrs.	30 min.	425537	5.60 F	1 hr.	50 min.
	240 min.		82.10 F	25 hrs.	40 min.
7 hrs. (60 × 4)					
7 hrs. + 4 hrs. = 11 hrs.					

12 hrs.

short: 20 min.

What vouchers *should I* have made the rate on? The ones for planishing (but . . .)—the sockets; the fingers (if I had adopted a good system right away . . .); the polishing, if it had not been only the 2nd time; the piano—(there it was because of headaches). The Δ pieces (demoralized by the dismissal notice).

In the future: find the *system* for safely obtaining the highest speed right away. Afterward, aim for the *uninterrupted tempo.*

But if 3 F are added for the circuits (?) and 5.50 F for the covers, and perhaps 1.50 F somewhere else, that's 10 F, I'll get 167 F for 65 hrs., that is, about 2.55 F per hour. . . .

If I get 1.70 F for these 65 hrs. and 32.50 F for the 11 hrs. of scrap and the 2 hrs. of cardboards, and 15 F for the 5 hrs. of phasing circuits, that will make 217.50 F in all, minus the deduction for Social Insurance!

Add 6 F for the foil to the 167 F; that's 173 F. Perhaps 223 F in all, of which 209 F would be for this two-week period.

On the whole, I haven't made any appreciable progress in the area of wages.

Vouchers on which I didn't make the rate

Number		Price	Time	
907405	washers L	1 F 12 [didn't make it for reason ψ !]		40 min.
Same	planishing L	.95 F		30 min.
420500	pl. shunts L	8.90 F	4 hrs.	15 min.
406426	sockets R	2.90 F	1 hr.	10 min.
414754	fingers L	20.60 F	7 hrs.	45 min.
Same	—(pol.) Q	13.50 F	5 hrs.	15 min.
413910	covers I	.27 F		15 min.
412105	covers I	2.88 F	3 hrs.	30 min.
413910	covers I	.46 F		30 min.

* * * * * *

4009194	drilling L	2.90 F	3 hrs.	15 min.
421227	bimetallic strips L	15.12 F	6 hrs.	15 min.
15682	piano B	.89 F		25 min.
Same	B	2.30 F	1 hr.	15 min.
428195	machine with arms L	2.80 F (?)	2 hrs.	
23173	—I	2.14 F	2 hrs.	(?)
421342	—R	2.83 F	1 hr.	
		80.55 F	35 hrs.	300 min.
				5 hrs.
			40 hrs.	

to be added:
1415   ?   2 hrs.

(work voucher 1747)
   80.50 F
   82.10 F

162.60 F for 65¾ hrs. of work

157	64
290	
340	2.45
20	

163	66
310	
460	2.4766
440	
24	

Small pieces: 421446, 150 pieces out of 400 at .62 per hundred, i.e., .90 F in all—put down ¼ hr.—severe cramps—infirmary.

Leave at 2:30 after having tried in vain to stick it out. Prostration until about 6 P.M, later not tired.

Tuesday. Terminals, 240 at .53 per hundred [409134, 409332].

Profound satisfaction that the work is going badly. . . . Mouquet.

Washers: 421437, b. 1—.56 per hundred, 865 per piece, put down 1¼ hrs., terminal-connector press 2.

Gear guides [12270, b. 68]: 1.42 F per hundred, 150 pieces, Robert's press (but he's on leave, it's with Biol)—they are bars that you cut by pedaling twice in succession, because the cutter isn't the proper length. They're not flat. If you put them in this way ⌣ they go in easily, but they're almost impossible to get out. This way, ⌒ very hard to put in but they can be gotten out. Biol recommends the 1st way, Pommera (very scornfully, for him) the 2nd—Mouquet comes—orders me to do it the 1st way, but gives me a wrench for getting them out (Pommera brought it; Mouquet said, "I'm going to show her"). At first I handle it clumsily. He has to remind me of the principle of the lever. . . .

Perhaps for the first time, I come back at 1:15 with a feeling of pleasure—also due to the way Mouquet spoke to me.

I enjoy doing a hard job, one that "doesn't go well." At 1:15 I tell Pommera that work that doesn't go well is much less boring. He says, "That's true." I skin my hands (one bad cut). Tempo not a problem, since the voucher doesn't matter. I notice that I effortlessly assume the "uninterrupted tempo" in front of Mouquet. But once he has left, no. . . . It's not because he's the foreman; it's because someone is watching me and waiting for me.

SCRAP: 2:30 to 3:15.

Piano: 344 sheet-metal pieces at .56 per hundred [508907, b. 10], put down 50 min.

Guides (?): 40009195, 1 hr.

Late afternoon, not tired. Go to Puteaux in beautiful sunshine, a cool breeze—(metro, collective taxi). Come by bus as far as rue d'Orléans. Delightful—go up to B.'s. But get to bed late.

THE MYSTERY OF THE FACTORY

1. The Mystery of the Machine

Guihéneuf: the machine is a mystery for the worker who hasn't studied mathematics. He doesn't see a balance of forces in it. So he has no confidence in regard to it. For instance: the turner who, by trial and error, discovered a tool for rolling both steel and nickel, instead of changing the tool to shift from one metal to another. For Guihéneuf, it's simply a cut; he just does it. The other goes about it with superstitious respect. It's the same thing with a machine that doesn't work. The worker will see that this or that needs to be done . . . but often makes a repair that, while enabling it to work, dooms it to wear out more rapidly, or to develop a new hitch. The engineer, never. Even if he never uses differential calculus, differential formulas applied to the study of the resistance of materials allow him to form a precise idea of a machine as a fixed play of forces.

The press that wasn't working and Jacquot. Clearly the press was a mystery for Jacquot, and so was the reason it stopped working. Not just as an unknown factor, but in itself in some way. It doesn't work. . . . Like the machine refuses.

What I don't understand about presses: Jacquot and the press that stamped 10 times in succession.

2. The Mystery of Manufacture

Of course, the worker does not know how each piece is used: (1) how it is combined with other pieces; (2) the successive operations carried out on it; (3) the ultimate use of the whole.

But there is more: the relationship between causes and effects in the work itself isn't understood.

Nothing is *less* instructive than a machine.

3. The Mystery of "Knack"

Circuits from which I had to remove the cardboards. In the beginning I didn't know how to separate them by tapping with the mallet. Then I did some reasoning about the principle of the lever, which was quite useless. . . . After which, I knew how to do it very well, without my ever realizing either how I learned or how I go about it.

Essential principle of manual skill in machine work (and elsewhere?) badly expressed. Each hand should do only *one* simple operation. For instance, work on metallic strips: one hand pushes, the other presses toward the stop. Sheet-metal plates: don't hold with the hand; let them rest on the hand, apply pressure in the direction of the stop with the thumb. Polishing belt: apply pressure with one hand, pull with the other, let the belt turn the piece, etc.

Changes to be Desired

Different kinds of machine-tools side by side in the same shop. The set-ups nearby. The *lay-out* of the factory aimed at giving every worker a view of the entire process (that obviously assumes the abolition of the system of set-up men).

Specializations that degrade:

Of the worker—of the machine—of parts of factories [of engineers?]

Organization of the Factory

Shortage of stools, packing cases, oil cans.

Whimsical timekeeping. And it's the worst-paid jobs that are the most fatiguing, because you exert all your strength to the extreme limit so as not to fall below the rate. (Cf. the conversation with Mimi, Tuesday, 7th week.) You exhaust yourself, you kill yourself for 2 F per hour. And not because you are doing a job that demands that you kill yourself; no, only because of the capriciousness and carelessness of the timekeeper. You kill yourself with nothing at all to show for it, either a subjective result (wages) or an objective one (work accomplished), that corresponds to the effort you've put out. In that situation you really feel you are a slave, humiliated to the very depths of your being.

Pommera respects the timekeeper (Souchal); excuses him by saying that his job is impossible, caught as he is between the management and the women. He says that when Souchal is pushing the women, they buckle down right away. There is also the issue of false timing; a voucher that makes the rate can never be corrected afterward.

For each job there is a limited—a small—number of possible mistakes, some of which can break the tool, and others botch the piece. As far as the tool is concerned, only a few possible mistakes exist for each type of job. It would be easy for the set-up men to point out these possible mistakes to the women, so that they would have a little confidence.

Notice whether or not the presses are *specialized*. Try to establish a nomenclature—planishing press—Biol's stamping press.

Foremen and bureaucrats:

G . . .

X. Comes from the corps of Maritime Engineers.

"A manager is a machine for taking responsibility," "no profession more stupid than that of manager." "A good manager must above all not be a good technician. Just know enough that he can't be made to swallow a lot of nonsense."

D . . .

X. Department of Civil Engineering.

At first manager and managing director. Has now trained a manager to spare himself work.

Became the head of the company *totally* ignorant of manufacturing technique. Felt lost for 1 year.

Mouquet (foreman).		The most interesting one is clearly Mouquet. Timekeeper an obnoxious type, vulgar, they say, with the women—always tends toward what is most base—he sets times almost at random—I never spoke to him. Pommera doesn't think badly of him.
Timekeeper (Souchal short, dark).	glass cubicle	
Mme Biay (?).		
M. Chanes.		

. . . press foreman.

Catsous   —   drilling machines.

Mouquet and the pieces I spent 5 days on at the beginning taking out cardboards.

Mouquet—sculptural, tormented head—something monastic—always tense—"I'll think about it tonight." Saw him cheerful only once.

Set-up men:

Ilion (foreman)—Léon—Catsous—Jacquot (back being a worker)—Robert—Biol.

Female workers:

Mme Forestier—Mimi—Mimi's sister—Tolstoy fan—Eugénie—Louisette, her friend (young widow with 2 kids)—Nénette—redhead (Joséphine)—Cat—blonde with 2 kids—separated from her husband—mother of the burned boy—the one who gave me a roll—the one who has chronic bronchitis—the woman who lost a child and is happy not to have any at all, and "fortunately" lost her 1st husband who had tuberculosis for

8 years (that's what Eugénie says!)—Italian woman (by far the nicest)—Alice (by far the least likable)—Dubois (Oh, Mother! if you could see me!)—the one who is ill, lives alone (who gave me the Puteaux address)—the screw-cutting machine operator who sings—screw-cutting machine operator with 2 kids and the sick husband.

Mimi—26 years old—married for 8 years to a young construction worker (knew him from Angers), who put in 2 years at Citroën and is now unemployed, although he's a good worker. At Angers she worked in a textile mill (11 F per day!). At Alsth. for 6 years. Took 6 months to acquire a fast enough tempo "to earn her living"—in the course of which she very frequently wept, thinking she would never make it. Worked another year and a half in a state of constant nervousness (fear of doing badly), although she was working quickly and well. Only at the end of 2 years did she become sure enough of herself "not to worry."

One of her early reflections: (I was telling her I was exasperated by my ignorance of what I was making); "They take us for machines . . . others are here to think for us. . . ." (Exactly what Taylor[10] says, but she says it with bitterness.)

No professional self-esteem. Cf. her response Thursday of the 6th week.

Incomparably less common than the average.

Nénette (Mme A., about 35 years old [?]). Has a 13-year-old son and a 6½-year-old daughter. Widow. Almost all her conversation consists of jokes and confidences that would make a barracksroom blush. Extraordinarily vivacious and full of vitality. Good worker; almost always makes over 4 F. In the shop for two years.

But—enormous respect for education (talks about her son "always reading").

Her rather vulgar cheerfulness disappears the week she is almost constantly without work. "You have to count every penny."

Talks about her son: "The idea of sending him to the shop—I can't tell you what that does to me" (however, a superficial observer could think she is happy at the shop).

Joséphine.

Eugénie.

---

10 Frederick Winslow Taylor (1856–1915) was an American engineer who developed a system of "scientific management" to increase efficiency and production in factory work.

Male workers:

The *warehouse keeper* (Pommera).

History: born in the country—family of 12 children—herded cows when he was 9 years old—got his certificate of studies when he was 12. Before the war never worked in a factory; worked in a few garages—never served an apprenticeship, or had any other technical or general education than what he got for himself in night courses. Served in the war (already married) as a platoon leader in the mountain light infantry (?). At the time lost the little money he had scraped together, and as a result had to work in a factory when he returned from the war. I don't know what he did the first 4 years. But afterward he was a set-up man on the presses for 6 years in another factory. And for the last 6 years, he's been keeper of the tool warehouse at Alsthom. Everywhere, he says, he's had an easy time. Nevertheless, he hopes I won't stay with the machines as long as he did.

Work:

He hands out the tools listed on the order (anybody could do that).

Sometimes he changes the order, noting down other tools that allow, for instance, 3 operations to be replaced by 2, which saves the firm money. He has done that several times. (You have to be awfully sure of yourself!) As a consequence, he has the confidence that comes from knowing that he is indispensable, and that no one would dare bother him.

Education:

Technical: knows the lathe—the milling machine—machine-setting. Explains marvelously well how something has to be done (unlike the set-up men).

General? Expresses himself extremely well. But what else?

Violinist—tall blond—boy at the furnace—one who reads *l'Auto*—nice guy at the drilling machine—little fellow who set me up at the furnace—young Italian—my "fiancé"—guy in gray at the shearing machine—young metal shearer. Bretonnet—new unskilled worker—boy from air transport—2-man team for repairing machines (. . .) [Biol's machine, Ilion's machine].

△ ET

Worker solidarity? No mass solidarity (except Louisette . . .).	Worker control over the bookkeeping?
Give them the feeling that they have something of their own to give.	Account book? Technical and organizational innovations?
Worker delegates, protection against threat of being fired.	Lectures?
Duties?	Bonuses to combat
Safety.	waste?
Organization of part-time work.	
Demands.	

Commendations

How to deal with these additional concerns? . . .

2 suggestion boxes	1 for the *benefit of the firm.*	Technical innovations.
Popularization, prepare . . .	1 for the *benefit of the workers*	Waste.

Recount the bureaucratic incident.[11] . . . Liaison.

"Capitalists' trap": modernization of machinery. One owner updates machinery that has been amortized; others *have to* do the same, even though theirs isn't amortized (because they calculate using a particular cost, not a general one). The next time, it's the first one's turn to suffer. . . .

Naiveté of a man who has never suffered. . . .

LOOKING FOR WORK

Monday. Alone. To Issy—Malakoff. Tedious—nothing to report.

Tuesday (in the rain)—with a woman (who tells me about her 13-year-old boy whom she is keeping in school. "Without it, what can he become? A martyr like the rest of us").

Wednesday—(glorious weather) with 2 metal fitters. One is 18 years old. The other, 58. *Very* interesting man, but extremely reserved. To all appearances, a real man. Living alone (his wife walked out on him). A hobby, photography. "They killed the cinema when they made it talk, instead of letting it remain what it really is, the most beautiful application of photog-

11 See above, p. 167.

raphy." Reminisced about the war in a peculiar tone of voice, as if it were a life like any other, just a harder and more dangerous job (artilleryman, it's true). "The man who says he has never been afraid is lying." But he doesn't seem to have felt fear to the point of having been inwardly humiliated by it. On work: "They have been asking more and more of the trained workers for some time; you almost have to know engineering." Tells me about the "developable surfaces." You have to find the dimensions of a flat piece of sheet metal out of which you will then make a piece full of curves and broken lines.

[*Try to find out exactly what a "developable surface" is.*]

He failed a test once, as far as I understood, because he failed to multiply the diameter by π.

At his age, he says, you are disgusted by work (work used to interest him passionately when he was young). But the problem isn't the work itself, the problem is taking orders. The jail. . . . "You would have to be able to work for yourself." "I would like to do something else." He was working (in the "Mureaux"),[12] but half-expects to be kicked out for not having made the rate (he is timed). Complains about the committees that set the times. "They can't understand." Argument with the foreman over some pieces to be made in 7 min.; he took 14; the foreman, to show him, made one in 7, but he says it was a bad piece (so it's mass-production metal-fitting?).

Speaks of his past jobs. Some cushy ones. Was a machinist in a textile mill. "That was a dream." Spent his time "doing work on the side." Obviously didn't even notice the miserable lot of the slaves. Affects a certain cynicism. However, obviously a man of feeling.

All morning, extraordinarily free and easy conversation among the three of us, on a plane above the miseries of existence that are the dominant preoccupation of slaves, especially the women. After Alsthom, what a relief!

The young one is also interesting. While we were passing Saint-Cloud, he says, "If I were up to it (he is not, alas, because he is hungry . . .) I would like to draw." "Everyone is interested in something." "For me," says the other one, "it's photography." The young one asks me, "And you, what do you like to do?" Embarrassed, I answer, "Read." And he: "Yes, I can see that. Not novels. You would rather read philosophy, wouldn't you?" Then we talked about Zola and Jack London.

12 Industrial district on the left bank of the Seine.

Both, obviously, have revolutionary tendencies ("revolutionary" very inaccurate word—rather, they are class-conscious and have the spirit of free men). But when it comes to national defense, we no longer agree. However, I don't insist.

Total comradeship. For the first time in my life, really. No barrier at all, either in the difference of class (since that has been removed) or in the difference of sex. Miraculous.

EASTER SUNDAY

On my way home from the church where I had (foolishly) hoped to hear some Gregorian chant, I come upon a small exhibition where you can see a Jacquard loom *in operation*. I—who had so passionately and vainly contemplated one at the Institute of Arts and Crafts—hasten to step in. The operator, who sees that I'm interested, explains it to me (as he finishes, he does 2 Claquesin picks . . . I intrigue him very much). He does everything: punches the card (according to *the card* pattern, not from the design of the fabric—he says he could work out the pattern of the card himself (?) and also read the pattern of the fabric from the card (?); however, when I ask him if he could read on the card *letters* to be woven into the fabric, he says—and more hesitantly—yes, but not easily). Set-up of the machine (which means arranging all the threads without making mistakes—extremely meticulous work)—and the weaving, done by throwing the shuttle and treadling; the treadle is heavy because of all the needles and raised threads, but he says he's never tired. I finally understood—more or less—the relationship of the card, the needles, and the thread. He says there is a Jacquard loom in every textile mill, for the patterns; but he thinks that practice is going to disappear. Extremely proud of his knowledge. . . .

SECOND SHOP, FROM THURSDAY APRIL 11 TO TUESDAY MAY 7,
CARNAUD, BASSE-INDRE WORKS, RUE DU VIEUX-PONT DE
SÈVRES, BOULOGNE-BILLANCOURT

1ST DAY. Gautier's shop. Oil cans [afterward, gas masks] (shops highly specialized). Some conveyer belts and a few presses. They put me at a press. Stamping pieces ⊂•⊃ to turn them into ⊂•⊃. The dot determines the position—small press, light pedal; it's the dot that gives me trouble. You have to count (not knowing how the count is supposed to be checked,

I count conscientiously; I'm wrong). I arrange them in order and count them by 50s, then do them fast. I go faster, although not as fast as I can, and do 400 per hour. In general I work harder than at Alsthom. In the afternoon, fatigue, made worse by the suffocating atmosphere, saturated with odors of paints, varnishes, etc. I wonder if I will be able to keep up the pace. But at 4 o'clock Martin, the foreman (a handsome young man with an affable manner and voice), comes to tell me quite politely, "If you don't do 800, I won't keep you. If you do 800 in the 2 hrs. that are left, I will *perhaps consent* to keep you. There are some who do 1,200." I go faster, seething with rage, and get up to 600 per hour (by cheating a little on the count and the position of the pieces). At 5:30 Martin comes to get the count and says, "That's not enough." Then he puts me to work setting out another woman's pieces; she doesn't give a welcoming word or smile. At 6 P.M., in the grip of a cold and concentrated fury, I go to the foreman's office and ask outright, "Should I come back tomorrow morning?" Quite surprised, he says, "Come in, just in case; we'll see. But you have to work faster." I answer, "I'll try," and leave. In the cloakroom, I'm surprised to hear the others gossiping, chattering, without seeming to feel the same suppressed rage that I do. However, they get out of the factory fast. Until the bell rings, they work as if they had hours to go; the bell no sooner begins to ring than they all rise up as if they were activated by a spring, run to punch out, run to the cloakroom, exchange a few words while they slip on their wraps, and run home. In spite of my fatigue, I am so in need of fresh air that I go on foot as far as the Seine; there I sit on the bank, on a stone, gloomy, exhausted, my heart gripped by impotent rage, feeling drained of all my vital substance; I wonder if, in the event that I were condemned to live this life, I would be able to cross the Seine every day without someday throwing myself in.

The next morning, at my machine again. 630 per hr., desperately straining for all I'm worth. Suddenly Martin, who comes over with Gautier behind him, says, "Stop." I stop, but remain seated in front of my machine, not understanding what is wanted of me. This gets me a bawling out, for when a foreman says "Stop" it seems you have to be immediately standing at attention, ready to pounce on the new job he is going to give you. "Nobody sleeps here." (Indeed, in this shop, not one second in a 9-hr. day is not spent in work. I have not once seen a woman raise her eyes from her work, or two women exchange a few words. No need to add that in this place the seconds of the women's lives are the only things that are economized on so carefully; in other respects, waste, waste to spare. No foreman that I've seen analogous to Mouquet. In Gautier's shop, their work seems to consist primarily in pushing the women.) They put me at a machine where all I have to do is thread in some thin, flexible metallic strips, gilded on the bottom, silvered on top, taking care not to put in 2 at once, and going "at full speed." But often they are stuck together. The 1st time I put in 2 (which stops the machine), the set-up man came to fix it. The 2nd time I tell Martin, who puts me back at my 1st machine while the 2nd one is being fixed. Nearly 620 per hour. . . . At 11 o'clock, a woman with a nice smile comes to take me to another shop; I am put in a large light room next to the shop, where one workman is showing another how to varnish with a spray gun. . . .

[I forgot to note down my impression the 1st day, at 8 A.M., when I arrived at the hiring office. In spite of my fears, I am—as an unemployed worker who has finally found a job—happy and grateful to the shop. I find 5 or 6 women whose dejected looks astonish me. I ask questions, but no one says much; finally I understand that this shop is a convict prison[13] (frantic pace, cut fingers in profusion, no scruples about laying off workers) and that most of the women have worked in it—they had either been thrown out of work last fall or had wanted to escape—and are returning with suppressed rage, chafing at their bits.]

The door opens 10 min. before the hour. But that's a manner of speaking. A small door in the gate is opened ahead of time. At the 1st bell (there are 3 at 5 min. intervals), the small door is closed and half the gate is opened. On days of pouring rain, it's quite a sight to see the herd of women who have arrived before the gate "opens" keep standing in the rain next to that small open door waiting for the bell to ring (reason: thefts; cf. dining-room). No protest, no reaction at all.

A lovely girl, strong, radiant, and healthy, says one day in the cloakroom, after a 10-hr. day: I'm fed up with working all day long. How I wish it were Bastille Day so I could dance. Me: You can think of dancing after 10 hrs. on the job? Her reply: Of course! I could dance all night, etc. (laughing). Then, seriously: it's been 5 years since I've danced. You feel like dancing, and then you dance over the washing.

Two or three melancholy women with sad smiles are not of the same common type as the others. One asks me how it's going. I tell her that I'm

13 *Bagne*, i.e., a place of confinement at forced labor.

in a quiet corner. She, with a gentle and melancholy smile: I'm glad! Let's hope it will last. And she repeats it once or twice.

In this kind of life those who suffer aren't able to complain. They would be misunderstood by others, perhaps laughed at by those who are not suffering, thought of as tiresome by those who, suffering themselves, have quite enough suffering of their own. Everywhere the same callousness, like the foremen's, with a few rare exceptions.

In the varnishing shop. Observed 5 workmen. The carpenter—my truck-driver pal—the "guy from downstairs" (tin-plating), who is co-foreman. The electrician, former seaman in the reserves (whose brief stay was like a breath of sea air for me and my pal). The mechanic (alas, barely saw him).

[Note: separation of the sexes, contempt of the men for the women, and reserve on the part of the women toward the men (in spite of the exchanges of dirty jokes) is much more pronounced in workers' circles than elsewhere.]

Women: the former metal shearer who had salpingitis 7 years ago (in '28, at the height of the boom) and couldn't get herself taken off the presses for several years—ever since then her reproductive organs completely and irrevocably destroyed. Speaks with much bitterness. But it didn't occur to her to change her job—although she could have done it easily!

LOOKING FOR A JOB FOR THE 2ND TIME

Fired Tuesday May 7. Spent Wednesday, Thursday, Friday in the dismal state of prostration caused by headaches. Friday morning, it was all I could do to get up in time to telephone Det.[14] Saturday, Sunday, rest.

Monday, 13th. In front of Renault. Overheard 3 men conversing whom I at once took to be trained workers. One, who listens with a knowing air (fine face) was hired, so not seen again. —Old workman, skilled worker on presses, tanned working-man's face—but intelligence degraded by slavery. Old-style Communist. The bosses run the confederated trade unions. They choose the leaders. In bad times, the leaders go and tell the boss, "I won't be able to hold them back unless. . . . One of them told me so himself!" And then they tell the workers, "Strikes don't succeed when

14 Auguste Detoeuf, a friend and managing director of the Alsthom Company.

there is unemployment, you're going to suffer," etc. In short, he harps on all the stupidities invented by well-protected bonzes.

The 3rd, young construction worker, trade-unionist tendencies (worked at Lyon), a good sort.

Tuesday, 14th. Morning: inertia. Afternoon, Saint-Ouen (Luchaire). The job was taken. . . .

Wednesday, 15th. Go to Porte de Saint-Cloud, but by the time I telephone Det., it's too late to go to Renault or Salmson. Go to Caudron. In front of the gate, a half-dozen trained workers, all with references in aviation: aviation carpenters, metal-fitters. . . . Again the same old story: "They won't find any trained workers like the ones they're asking for. They don't make them any more. . . ." It's still about the same thing: the developable surfaces. As far as I can understand there are two types of test: the "dovetail" ⌇⌇ ⌇⌇ (more or less), which has to fit *exactly* into a piece of sheet metal you are not allowed to file; and the developable surfaces. It seems the metal-fitters have something of the artist in them.

The one I got to know well. On the surface, all brawn and no brains. Marvelous references. A letter of recommendation from the Institute of Arts and Crafts (where he was apprenticed until age 19): "Machinist who is a credit to his trade." Lives in Bagnolet (his own little shack??), which complicates his finding a job; gives this as his reason for refusing to work more than 8 hrs., but I don't think that it's the only one. You work 10 hours at Renault. Too much for him. With the train, etc. "On Sunday you can stay in bed and rest" (so the money doesn't matter). Adds: "5 hrs., that's enough for me." Was a foreman more than once (references to prove it). "But," he says, "I'm too much of a revolutionary. I could never give the workers a bad time." The error of interpretation that he makes in regard to me, his attitude afterward. On parting: "You don't hold it against me?" Is going to come to see me at my place. But was not in front of Renault the next morning. . . . The day after, a knock. I'm in bed, don't open the door. Was it he? I'll never hear of him again. . . .

Another day, in front of Gévelot—the guy with white hair, who intended to go in for music before the war. Says he's an accountant (but makes mistakes in simple arithmetic)—looking for a job as an unskilled worker. Pitiful failure. . . . We wait from 7:15 to 7:45 in a light rain, after which "no hiring." At Renault, the hiring is over. An hour's wait in front of Salmson.

Another time at Gévelot. The women are let in. The guy doing the hiring (head of personnel?) is vulgar and callous; in another connection he also bawls out a foreman, who answers very humbly (pleasure to see that). Looks us over like horses. "That one's the strongest." His way of questioning the 20-year-old who 3 years earlier had left because she was pregnant. . . . With me, polite. Takes my address.

The one who, mother of 2 children, said she wanted to work because she was "bored at home" and whose husband worked 15 hrs. a day and didn't want her to work! Indignation of another, also mother of 2 children, very unhappy at having to work (outside Salmson).

Another time (?) met the young girl who said, "The fall of the franc will mean hard times, they say so on the radio," etc.

Another time, trip to Ivry. "No women." Headaches. . . .

Another time, outside Langlois (small shop), in Ménilmontant, at 7 A.M. (advertisement)—Wait until 8:30. Then to Saint-Denis, but it's too late.

Return to Saint-Denis. Hard to walk like this when you're not eating. . . .

Again at Luchaire in Saint-Ouen before 7:30 (it's the same day on which, in the afternoon, I will be hired at Renault).

During the final week I decide to spend only 3.50 F per day, transportation included. Hunger becomes a permanent feeling. Is this feeling more painful than working and eating, or less so? Unresolved question. . . . Yes, more painful, on the whole.

RENAULT

Milling machine operator.

Wednesday, 5th. Day I was hired, from 1:30 to 5 P.M. The faces around me; handsome young worker; the young construction worker; his wife.

Terrible emotional state, the day I was hired, and the next day setting out to confront the unknown; in the metro early in the morning (I arrive at 6:45), extremely apprehensive, to the point of being physically ill. I see people are looking at me; I must be very pale. If ever I have known fear, it is today. I imagine a shop with presses, a 10-hr. day, brutal foremen, cut fingers, heat, headaches. . . . The woman who used to work on presses whom I talked with in the hiring office didn't help to raise my spirits. When I arrive at shop 21, I feel my will grow weak. But at least there are no presses—what luck!

When, 3 months earlier, I had heard the story of the milling machine cutter that had *gone through* a woman's hand, I told myself that with such an image in my memory it would never be easy for me to work on a milling machine. However, at no time did I ever have any fear to overcome on that score.

Thursday, 6th. From 8 A.M. to noon, observed[15]—from 2:30 to 10 P.M., worked. 400 the first 2 hrs. 2,050 in all; lost 1½ hrs. or more because the set-up man made a mistake. Exhausted when I left.

The disadvantage of being in the position of a slave is that you are tempted to think that human beings who are pale shadows in the cave really exist. For instance: my set-up man, that young bastard. I need to resist that. [I got over it after a few weeks.]

Dickmann's idea. But if the workers develop other resources for themselves, and through work that is *free*, will they submit to these speeds for slaves? (If not, so much the better!)

Those who tell me not to work myself to death. One is (I learn later) the foreman of another gang, way at the back of the shop. He's very nice, has a real goodness, whereas Leclerc's (my foreman) comes more from never giving a damn. Later, on the rare occasions that I have to speak with him, he's always particularly nice to me. One day, he throws me a look while I am miserably decanting some heavy bolts into an empty packing case with my hands. . . . Never forget this man.

The foreman and the crank. He says, "Try like this," though it's obvious that it's going to come off.

Friday, 7th. Exactly 2,500, exhausted even more than the day before (especially after 7:30!). Philippe has some fun watching me. . . . By 7 o'clock have done only 1,600.

The young girl in the metro—"no heart for it." Me, either. . . .

Saturday, 8th. 2,400, cleaning. Tired, but less so than the day before (2,400 in 8 hrs., that's only 300 per hr.).

Tuesday, 11th. 2,250, 900 of them after 7 o'clock—didn't have to push myself too hard—only a bit tired when I left. Finished at 10:10.

Wednesday, 12th. Power failure (how wonderful!).

Thursday, 13th. 2,240, finished at 9:30 (*more pieces*)—1,400 of the

15 s w was then part of the shift that worked from 2:30 to 10 P.M.

above before 7 o'clock, 840 after (only 330 of them had been done by 4 p.m.). Violent headaches. Exhausted when I left. But not aching anymore. . . .

Friday, 14th. 1,350 and 300 others. Not tired.

Saturday, 15th. 2,000, finished at 8:40, cleaning; barely time to finish. Not too tired [this 1st week, packing-case problem not too great a source of anxiety thanks to the others being nice about it].

[*Sunday.* Headaches, didn't sleep Sunday night to Monday.]

Monday, 17th. 2,450 (1,950 by 8:35)—tired when I left, but not exhausted.

Tuesday, 18th. 2,300 (2,000 by 8:45)—didn't speed up—not tired when I left—headache all day.

Wednesday, 19th. 2,400 (2,000 by 8:35), very tired. The little bastard of a set-up man tells me that I have to do more than 3,000.

Thursday, 20th. Going to the shop is extremely painful; each step an effort (morally; returning, it's a physical effort). Am in that half-dazed state in which I am the victim designated for any harsh blow. . . . From 2:30 to 3:35, 400 pieces. From 3:35 to 4:15, time lost because of the set-up man in the cap—(he made me do my botched pieces over)—Large pieces—slow and *very* hard because of the new way the handle of the vise is set up. I turn to the foreman for help—Discussion—Go back to work— Mill the end of my thumb (there's the harsh blow)—Infirmary—Finish the 500 at 6:15—No more pieces for me (I am so tired I am relieved!). But they promise me some. In the end, I don't get them until 7:30 and then only 500 (to complete the 1,000). [The blond guy is afraid that I'm going to complain to the foreman.] 245 by 8 o'clock. Do the 500 large ones, in a great deal of pain, in 1½ hrs.   10 min. to set up the machine. This set-up uses another part of the cutting tool; it works! I do 240 small pieces in exactly ½ hr. Free at 9:40. But earned 16.45 F !!! (no, large pieces a little better paid). By the time I leave, I'm tired. . . .

1st meal with the women (snack).

The set-up man in the cap: "If he lays a hand on your machine, send him packing. . . . He destroys everything he touches. . . ."

He orders me to move a packing case with 2,000 pieces in it. I tell him, "I can't budge it by myself." "That's your problem. It's not my job."

Apropos of the pieces they made me—the beginner—wait for: "The foreman said that if you had to wait, you should be compensated for it out of the wages of the woman who made you wait."

Friday, 21st. Got up very late—just barely ready in time. Painful going to the shop—but, unlike the previous times, pain much more physical than moral. Still, I'm afraid of not being able to do enough. Again the feeling of "let's stick it out today anyway. . . ," as at Alsth. As of last evening, I've been at Renault 2 weeks; and I tell myself that I probably can't last more than 2 weeks. . . .

Once I'm at the shop, I have 450 pieces to finish, then 2,000; it goes all right, no counting. I begin at 2:35, do the 450 by 3:40. Then continue at the uninterrupted tempo by fixing my attention on each piece and obsessively repeating in my head, "I have to. . . ." I don't think there is enough water; lose a lot of time looking for the bucket (which was where it was supposed to be!). Then I pour in too much water; it overflows. Have to get it up, find sawdust, sweep. . . . The guy from the automatic lathes kindly helps me. At 7:20, lose a lot of time (15 to 20 min.) looking for a box. I finally find one, full of metal shavings; I go and empty it; the set-up man orders me to put it back. I obey. [The next day, one of the women drill operators tells me that it belonged to his wife, and says, "I certainly wouldn't have put it back." The drill operators are likable; a group apart.] Way at the back of the shop (21 B) I find one; a woman objects to my taking it. I give in again (wrongly!). I give up. I continue, and when I have no more than about 500 pieces to go, empty them partly onto the machine, partly into a sort of basket stuck into the machine behind me, and put the 1,500 finished pieces into the box thus emptied; time consuming and very difficult operation without help. Finally finished at 9:35. Rush to find 75 more, just to beat my record by a little. Thus: 2,525. Return to rue Auguste-Comte. Sleep on the metro. Separate act of will for each step. Once home, very cheerful. Went to bed, read until 2 A.M. Woke at 7:15 (teeth).

Saturday, 22nd. Magnificent weather. Beautiful morning. Don't think about the job except on the way there; then, painful feeling (but feeling less like a slave). The other woman hadn't come. I take the box of 2,000 (minus the 75) [heavy!]. Begin at 2:45. By 3:45, have done perhaps 425 (which would make 500). A change of machine. Easy and well-paid job (3.20 F per hundred), but more dangerous cutter. Do 350 (that's 4.20 F). Finished about 5:05. Lose 10 min. Come back to my machine; begin again at

5:15. Speed that comes automatically, without artificial obsession, effort-lessly, and merely by maintaining the "uninterrupted tempo"; did 1,850 by 8:30 (i.e., 1,350 in 3 hrs., or 450 per hr.!). 1 every 8 sec. Cheerful meal (however, the "fat woman" not there). Feeling of relaxation; Satur-day evening, no foremen, free and easy. . . . Everyone (except me) dawdles until 10:25.

On the way home—I dawdle listening to a band play. Fresh air delight-ful. Wide awake in the metro, even some energy for walking. Tired, however. But on the whole, happy. . . .

Monday, 24th. Slept badly (itching). Morning, no appetite, violent head-aches. Feeling of pain and anxiety on leaving for work.

On arrival, catastrophe: since my co-worker hadn't come in, the box the pieces drop into was stolen. I lose 1 hr. finding another (it has to have holes). I start on the job; worn cutter. A new set-up man (in gray), in the shop 1 week, replaces it for me (of his own accord!). At the time, he notices that there is a little play everywhere. In particular, the ring that holds the cutter "has been shot for at least ten years." He is surprised that "the two pals" (!) hadn't replaced it. My machine is "an old crock," he says. He seems to know something about what he is doing. But as a result, I start the job at 4:30. Discouraged, exhausted (headaches). Do 1,850 pieces in all (in 5 hrs., that's less than 400 per hr.). In the evening, I again lose time looking for a box, and then, not finding one, decanting pieces into a basket taken from the next machine. And the box into which almost 16,000 pieces have dropped is so heavy to handle that I have to empty it into another. Back home (A.-C.), tired, but not overly so. Mainly disgusted at having done so little. And dying of thirst.

Tuesday, 25th. Awoke at 7 A.M. Lengthy and tiring session at the den-tist's—toothache all morning. Almost late. Hot. Have difficulty climbing the stairs when I arrive. . . . Find my new co-worker (Alsatian woman). Again have to look for a box. . . . Take one near a machine. Its owner arrives, furious. Take instead the one that contained the pieces to be done, emptying it (200 were left). So I'm back where I started! Find another one. Go and fill it, by shovelfuls, at the lathe. Bring it back (heavy!). Then (at 2:55) go to the infirmary (I have a beginning abcess caused by a metal shaving). When I'm back, I find my 2,000 pieces emptied out near my machine (the box taken back by its 1st owner in my absence). I go looking again. Appeal to the foreman opposite the elevator. He tells me, "I'll see

that you're given one." I wait. . . . Bawls me out because I'm waiting. Go
back to my machine. My neighbor gives me a box. At that moment, my
foreman (Leclerc) turns up. Starts bawling me out. I tell him my pieces
were emptied out in my absence. He goes and has it out with my neighbor.
I gather up the pieces. Cutter change. Result: start the job at 4:05! With
a disgust that I suppress in order to go fast. In spite of everything, I would
like to do 2,500. But I have trouble keeping up the speed. The 200 left over
from the other carton go quickly (in 20 or 25 min.). Afterward, it slows
down.

Results of this system of multiple set-up men: about 6:30 the cutter
cuts badly; the set-up man in gray changes the position of the cutter—
manipulates it—changes the position again—and, I think, puts it back in
its original position. . . . By 7 o'clock, I must have made 1,300 pieces, no
more. After the break, another search for a box, juggling pieces for lack of
a box. At 9:35 or 40, finished carton (therefore 2,200). Do 50 more. . . . I
had had the cutter's position changed at 9:15 by the young set-up man
(Philippe); he had made me wait a good ¼ hr. And as it was I had called
him too late. 2,250, consequently. Mediocre. . . . Going home, have to
force myself to walk, but not, however, step by step.

Didn't maintain the "uninterrupted tempo." Hampered by my finger.
Also over confident.

Absolutely have to find a permanent solution to the box problem. And
first of all, propose to the woman who operates the lathe to give us 1 out of
every 2? She's never given any, she says. But we're never given any either.
When we were looking for boxes for 500, it was different. Now it's for
2,000. . . .

Wednesday, 26th. Tired in the morning—not much more courage than
what is needed for the day's work . . . low-grade feeling of despondency—
headaches—discouragement—fear, or rather anxiety (in the face of work,
my box, speed, etc.)—muggy thunderstorm weather.

Go to the infirmary. "They'll open it for you when it needs to be opened,
and without asking your opinion." Work. Suffer from my arm, from exhaustion, from headaches. (A slight fever? Not in the evening, in any case.)
But by going fast I manage not to suffer for a few successive intervals of
time lasting from 10 min. to ¼ hr. Pay at 5 o'clock. Afterward, I've had it.
I count my pieces, wipe my machine, and ask to leave. Go and find Leclerc
(foreman) in the office of the shop foreman, who puts me down for
insurance.

Wait ½ hr. outside this office, because no one checks. See how complicated the deliveries are. The camaraderie of the foremen.

Leaving the dentist's (Tuesday morning, I think—or rather Thursday morning), and getting on the W bus, strange reaction. How is it that I, a slave, can get on this bus and ride on it for my 12 sous just like anyone else? What an extraordinary favor! If someone brutally ordered me to get off, telling me that such comfortable forms of transportation are not for me, that I have to go on foot, I think that would seem completely natural to me. Slavery has made me entirely lose the feeling of having any rights. It appears to me to be a favor when I have a few moments in which I have nothing to bear in the way of human brutality. These moments are like smiles from heaven, a gift of chance. Let's hope that I will stay in this state of mind, which is so reasonable.

My comrades, I think, do not have this state of mind in the same degree. They haven't fully understood that they are slaves. The words "just" and "unjust" have probably retained a meaning for them, up to a certain point—in this situation in which everything is injustice.

Thursday, July 4th. Don't return to my milling machine, thank heaven! (Occupied by another woman who seems to be working *very* hard. . . .) Small machine for smoothing holes drilled in screw-threads. 2 kinds of pieces (the 2nd: nails). 1,300 of the first kind (1.50 F per hundred), 950 (?) of the 2nd (.60 F per hundred). Then 260 pieces polished on the polishing-belt (1 F per hundred).

Friday, July 5th. Tomorrow a day off; how wonderful! Slept badly (teeth). Morning, session at the dentist's. Headaches, exhaustion [also worry, which doesn't help matters . . .]. Only 3 more weeks! Yes, but 3 weeks means *n* times 1 day! But I have courage for no more than 1 day, just 1. And that's by gritting my teeth with the courage of despair. Last night the young Italian said to me, "You're losing weight (he had told me that 10 days ago); you go to the john too often (!)." That's how I feel *before* going to the job.

At the end of my strength, seeing the women nearby (machine noise ear-splitting . . .) preparing to wash their machines, and at their instigation, I go and ask Leclerc if I can leave at 7 o'clock. He answers curtly, "You're not going to come in to do 2 hrs., dammit!" In the evening Philippe orders me to wait I don't know how long, to annoy me. But I, seized by disgust. . . .

One could say that by virtue of some convention fatigue doesn't exist. . . . Like danger in war, no doubt.

Following week: Monday 8th to Friday 12th.

Monday, Tuesday. Began carton of 3,500 pieces (brass?) at 7 o'clock.

Wednesday. 8,000 pieces, or almost, in the course of the day. Finished the carton from the evening before (at 10:45). Do carton of 5,000 (began again at 11:45). Finish at 6 o'clock [dinner with A]. Exhausted. They were easy pieces (I don't know exactly what they were; brass, then steel, I think). "Uninterrupted tempo."

Thursday. Exhausted, dead tired from yesterday's effort, go very slowly.

Friday. Hairnet. Wife of the Italian.

Evening: R.P.[16] meeting—Louzon doesn't recognize me. Says my face has changed. "You look tougher."

NOTEWORTHY INCIDENTS

The set-up man in gray (Michel) and his scorn for the other two, especially the "nitwit."

The bad set-up that breaks the cutter; incidents. The nitwit setter had done a set-up that only half worked. Several times the machine stops while I am bearing down on the cutter. That had happened to me once before, and I was told, "It isn't tight enough." So I go find the setter and ask him to tighten it. At first he doesn't want to come. He says that I'm bearing down too hard. Finally he comes. Says, "It isn't there (pointing to the tightening blocks of the cutter) but there (pointing to the pulley and the belt of the milling-spindle shaft) that it's working too hard (???). Goes away. I continue. It doesn't go well. Finally a piece gets jammed in the mounting, breaks 3 teeth. . . . He goes to find Leclerc to get me bawled out. Leclerc bawls *him* out for the choice of the mounting, and says the cutter will still work. ½ (or ¼) hr. later L. comes back. I tell him, "The cutter stops sometimes." He explains (in a disagreeable tone of voice) that the machine is delicate, and that I am probably applying too much pressure. He shows me how to work—failing to notice that, at most, he is going at a tempo of 600 per hr., if that! [i.e., 2.70 F] (I have no way of timing him . . .). But

16 The journal *La Révolution prolétarienne.*

even this way, the cutter slows down the moment you apply pressure. I point this out to him. He says it doesn't matter. A time comes when the cutter stops completely, and doesn't start again. I call the set-up man, who is ready to bawl somebody out. My neighbor says, "It's too tight." It happens once more; the machine, in the process of turning, automatically tightens the shaft if a certain bolt that is supposed to keep it from tightening isn't tight enough.

You loosen by turning in the direction opposite that of the cutter.

Difficulty (for me) of conceiving how the machine works, whether I have it in front of me or not. . . .

What are the possible reasons for the cutter stopping? (Did the shaft also stop? Forgot to notice.) Some play, either in the cutter or in the piece. (That was what happened in this instance.) Too much resistance is set up if you ask the machine for more work than it can put out (was that what the nitwit meant?) [but what determines how much it can put out?].

To be studied: notion of the power of a machine.

Chartier's letter. Saw and plane. Perhaps it's different for the machine. . . .

Find out how the machines are driven by one motor. If they are arranged in order of heavy and light power needs.

Wednesday, 17th. Returned to work—weather cool—less suffering (moral) than I might have feared. I find myself again compliant under the yoke. . . .

No job. Pay a visit to the automatic lathes (Cuttat), which I had studied during the 4 days of vacation.

Until 8:30, wait for oil.

4 × 10 steel screws 7010105 | 041916 | cutter 1.

5,000 at 4.50 F, that's 23.50 F.

? little series given by Leclerc, which Michel in ¾ hr. couldn't even set up.

He comes after Michel has been laboring over the set-up for ¾ hr. "Who gave you these pieces to do?" I retort, "You!" He is nice. Orders me to change pieces; ¾ hr. lost, not paid for it! Michel says it could have been done. . . . He will set them up on another machine (that of the young girl whom I tease about him). Apropos of this, conversation with him about Leclerc. Does he know all about machines?—some yes, others no. Michel tells me he was shift foreman for 2 months, lost the job because he was too much of a nice guy!—"But Leclerc isn't mean" (I say). Michel thinks he won't stay. But he was already there when the young Spanish woman came, a year and a half ago.

C 4 × 8 steel screws (7010103) 043408 | cutter 1.
5,000 at 4.50 F, set-up 1 F, that's 23.50 F. |
I don't finish them.

Thursday, 18th. Finish the C 4 × 8s.
Brass screws (740657 *twice* || 1417 (!), large special saw: 127 | 2).
100 (!!!) at .0045, i.e., 1.45 F.
Brass fittings | 6005346 | 027947, one 1.5 cutter (?).
600 at .045, i.e., 2.25 F + .45 F = 2.70 F (cutter in backward!).

New set-up man (skilled worker? check this). He asks "what that's for," has me get the drawing, which takes a long time and doesn't help much. . . .

Earned yesterday and today (18 hrs.) 23.50 F + 23.50 F + 1.45 F + 2.70 F = 51.15 F.

Not 3 F! 2.85 F! I'll be paid that, for both the week before the 19th, and the Thursday and Friday before that (in all 7 + 7 + 9 + 10 + 9 + 10 + 9 + 18 = 79 hrs.).

The C 4 × 8 steel screws: to begin with, I do a package of 1,000. Go to Goncher's shop for the rest: not ready. He comes within an ace of bawling me out (although I'm the one who would be justified in complaining). I go back there in the afternoon for the remaining 4,000, but take them in 4 or 5 lots and have a long wait each time. That gives me the opportunity to admire the Cuttats. . . . the young set-up man, I think, finally noticed that I have no objection to this sort of waiting.

INCIDENTS

Set-up man changed. The fat incompetent guy left Tuesday afternoon. (Find out what became of him.) Replaced by one who, it seems, comes from another part of the shop. Not the don't-give-a-damn type. Nervous, with feverish, jerky gestures. His hands tremble. I feel sorry for him. He spends 1 hr. doing a set-up for me (for 600 pieces!), and still gets the cutter in backward. (It works anyway; copper, fortunately.)

Try to do the set-up myself—don't know which *side* of the rings. (They are made up of 2 hollow cylinders with different diameters.) I could easily observe which side the next time the set-up is disassembled. . . . The real difficulty is muscular weakness; I can't loosen it.

Conversation with Michel. Leclerc's technical competence? "For some machines, not for others." Not a worker. Not mean—"will be thrown out"—

He had given me some pieces that don't work well on this machine.

Friday, July 19th. Steel locking set screws, 7051634 | 054641 | cutter 1.5.

1,000 at 5 F, that's 6 F (difficult to get the set-up, and still less than satisfactory).

7 plugs (small | 7050846 | 041784 | cutter 1.5
3,000 at 5 F, i.e., 16 F | I try to change 3 set-ups, but . . .).

5 × 22 screws (?) | 7051551 | 039660 | cutter 1.2.
550 (!) at .0045, i.e., 2.25 F + .235 F + 1 F = 3.50 F (nearly).

Ring set-screws | 7050253 | 45759 | cutter 1.
500(!) at .005, set-up 1.75 F, i.e., 3.75 F.
6 F + 16 F + 3.50 F + 3.75 F = 29.25 F.

In 9 hrs., i.e., 3.25 per hr. (27 F + 2.25 F: exactly!). But in reality 8 hrs. (an hour for cleaning), which makes more than 3.50 F! exactly 3.65 F. But it's true that I had done a good portion of the steel screws the night before. . . .

Saturday. Violent headaches, distressed state, afternoon better (but weep at B's . . .).

Sunday. Italian art.

Monday, 22nd. Finished pieces from Friday (10 to 15 min.). Set up the machine myself for the 1st time (except for the centering, which I couldn't completely do, had to call and wait for set-up man [beret]). Then I change the mounting, not the cutter; but call the set-up man—the one in glasses—for the centering (which he doesn't do), but spends an infinite amount of time adjusting the depth of the cut. He finished at 10:30; I then did a carton of 1,000 pieces (earned 5.70 F in 3 hrs . . .). New carton of 1,000. The small ones with the "convex side" in red copper. Some get stuck in the mounting; I break 2 teeth. . . . By noon, have hardly made a start on a new carton of 2,000 (brass). Earned 1 F + 3.70 F + 1 F + 5 F + 1 F = 11.70 F. When I finish the carton, will have 20.70 F. *Must* still do an additional 2,000. . . .

Circular pipe-plugs—red copper, 6002400.

1,000 at 3.70 F + 1 F, i.e., 4.70 F.

Same, smaller, 1,000 at 5 F + 1 F, that's 6 F.

Afternoon.

Brass screws, 705700 | 0 | 079658 (cutter 0.8).

2,000 at 4 F + 1 F, i.e., 9 F.

Plugs (large) 6002400 | 071844.

1,000 at 3.70 F, i.e., 4.70 F.

Same, 071848.

1,000 at 3.70 F, that's 4.70 F.

Brass screws 70500 | 379652 | cutter 0.8.

Just started.

Earned: 4.70 F + 6 F + 4.70 F + 4.70 F + 1 F + 9 F = 30.10 F.

Leclerc sends for me after I finished 071841 and was just starting 848. Begins by bawling me out because I'm doing these pieces without speaking to him about them. Asks for the number. I bring him my notebook! Looks at it and becomes very kind.

Tuesday. Do the screws, 2,000 at 4 F.

C 4 × 8 steel screws | 7010103 | 043409 | cutter 1.

5,000 at 4.50 F = setting 1 F, i.e., 23.50.

23.50 F + 8 F = 31.50 F (in 2 days 61.60 F, i.e., 2 × 30.80 F, i.e., 3.08 F per hr.).

Earned in 3 days 29.25 F + 30.10 F + 31.50 F, i.e., 90.85 F, that in:

28 [29] hours

28 × 3	= 84
[29]	[87]
28 × .50	= 14
28 × .25	= 7
84 + 7	= 91.

So I made on the average 3.25 F. . . .

C. 4. 8. Began them at 11 o'clock—until 5. Cutter bad after ¾ hr. (smokes). Nevertheless, it's after 2:30 before Michel changes it. [It's my fault; why not have it changed sooner? Fear of getting bawled out. . . .] Michel says that it worked backward (?). The 2nd cutter, although installed by him, doesn't hold up (it's the new saws—too big, says my neighbor, for the number 1 cutters [1]).

—Bawled out for the broken cutter (tales of the Span. woman about how a beginner feels). Changed at 4 P.M. Afterward, I last until 6 P.M.

(broke 2 teeth). Hard, working with a bad saw. But then, gives me an excuse for not transforming myself into an automaton. . . .

Wednesday. Woes of the young Spanish woman (her pieces—her cutter—the new set-up man—Leclerc).

Last night the saw—put in at 6 P.M. by the set-up man in the beret—had worked loose by 7:15. I had told him about it in passing. I find it loose again. I call him. He keeps me waiting—bawls me out. I was applying too much pressure, it seems. I'm almost sure I wasn't (for the broken saw had given me the jitters). I tell him so. Keeps on bawling me out (figuratively speaking, since he doesn't raise his voice). This incident sends a chill into my heart for some time, since I asked only to think of him as a comrade. . . . At 10 o'clock, a new saw, also installed by him. That takes him about 20 min. Suddenly, the motor at the back stops. We wait until almost 11. [I had finished the 5,000 from the day before (and found a box for them) by 8:30.] I learn that today is payday, not tomorrow as I thought, which fills my heart with joy, for I won't have to go without eating. . . . So at noon, I don't hold back at all (pack of cigarettes—compote . . .).

At 3 o'clock, disastrous incident: I break a tooth on my saw. I know how it happened. . . . Exhausted, I'm thinking about my weariness at the M—. About Adrien—his wife—what Jeannine told me, that Michel is forcing her to work herself to death—about what Pierre ought to feel about it—about Trotsky's youth ("What a shame" . . .) and, from there, about his choice between populism and Marxism—Exactly at that moment I insert a piece that doesn't fit into the mounting (shaving or burr), I bear down on the cutter anyway . . . ὀτοτοῖ !17 I don't dare change it, naturally—The Spanish woman advises me to ask Michel for help; I speak to him, but he won't come in the late afternoon. I keep the same cutter until 7 o'clock. Luckily it holds up—but needless to say I treat it with extreme caution! About 5 o'clock it comes loose again. I don't dare call anyone, of course! I tighten it, and do 200 or 300 pieces (or a few more?) that are not centered at all. Then I finally make up my mind and succeed in centering it myself! (but with the help of a previously made piece).

Pay: 255 F (I was afraid I would hardly get 200) for 81 hrs.

Night: didn't sleep.

Thursday. Again ½ to ¾ hr. with the saw. Then Michel changes it for me,

17 "Alas" in ancient Greek.

at the same time as the one on the machine he is setting up. I do the mounting myself, but can't do the centering. In desperation, end up by asking the set-up man with the glasses for help. It's done by 9 o'clock. —Morning painful—My legs ache—I'm totally fed up. . . . (These C 4 × 8 pieces are exasperating, with the constant danger of breaking the cutter, the necessity of preserving a totally vacuous state of mind. . . .) 3 false alarms, and at 11 o'clock—a gesture, a word had attracted my attention—catastrophe: broken tooth. Fortunately, what I have to do next calls for a 1.2 cutter. If only, afterward. . . .

At noon, a piece that jumps loosens the cutter.

I again realize that I have a moral obligation to get hold of myself, if I don't want to end up with a bad conscience. And I pull myself together.

At 1:30 I tighten the cutter and center it myself [which I hadn't been able to do the day before] thanks to the decision, made at lunch, to go about it carefully [I use a previously made piece]. The set-up man in the beret watches good-naturedly and, when it's done, completes the tightening. Finished at 2 o'clock. The same one sets up the new pieces for me. Done at 2:30.

2:30–4:30, it doesn't work—Michel—his explanation, conversation with him. Set-up man in beret fixes it.

4:30–6:30, I do the rest of the 2,000 (I had done perhaps 200 of them).

Go look for a job. Leclerc as nice as can be. . . . Am especially worried about my cutter, as this job is to be done with cutter 1—some steel C 4 × 10s. At 7:30 proceed to change .8, 1.5, and the no. 1 with the broken tooth. It works. So here I am with a beautiful new cutter. . . . But I still have 5,000 of these filthy pieces to do (not completely identical, however). Beware!

Direction in which the bolts have to be turned in order to make them go toward the pulley; also direction in which the pulley and everything else turn.

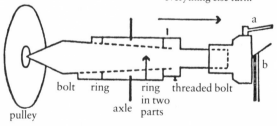

bolt ring   ring threaded bolt
              in two
pulley   axle parts

The cutter's deviation is in the direction indicated by the arrow; the result of the cutter's being mounted on a cone is that the groove not only stops being in the center, but becomes progressively less and less deep, or even stops being made at all.

Reason: not tight enough at the end—or worn cutter—or the worker is applying too much force.

Too much force: since the cutter is moving more slowly than the pulley and the shaft, everything happens as if the cutter were turning in the reverse direction (?).

Other phenomena when it's out of adjustment:

The cutter stops because the rings around it have loosened (or because they haven't been tightened enough, or because you're applying too much pressure).

The cutter stops (along with the shaft and the pulley) because the shaft is too tight at the end (*b* tightens automatically because *a* isn't tight enough) [always because the adjustment is faulty].

Today, I think one of the causes was that the mounting was not tight enough, so that the cutter had to drive down and work at the same time; hence too much force has to be applied.

At noon a joy. The NO vote, by which the workers duly and officially, etc. . . . have Saturday off.

Night: the eczema that had left me in peace for two weeks recurred with a vengeance.

Earned yesterday and today $45 \text{ F} + 2 \text{ F} + 12 \text{ F} (?) = 59 \text{ F} \ldots$ (or 58 F). Less than 3 F per hr. . . .

Friday. I have the pieces brought up to me that "Beret" was looking for last night. During this time I estimate—250 extra. Leclerc says to do them—I begin at 8:15. Did 200 by about 10:30. Have the cutter changed. Must wait . . . begin again at 11:15. Did less than 3,000 in the course of the morning (i.e., 14 F, or less—not more than 3 F per hr.!). *Very* hard work. But doesn't leave me morally crushed as on the day before. Physically, however, I'm not feeling as well. After lunch (ate for 5.50 F in the hope of fortifying myself) it's much worse. My head swims—I work mechanically. Fortunately these pieces don't jump like the C 4×8s. . . . I really think, for 2 or 2½ hrs., that I'm going to faint. Finally, I decide to slow down, and feel better. Finished after 4 o'clock (4:15 or 4:30). Leclerc tells me not to mark down the extra 250 anywhere, that I wouldn't be paid (they must be missing from another lot, he says . . .). Gives me a "cushy job" (the long brass screws at 4 F). Time to set them up, 5 o'clock. At 5:30, stop working to wash the machine (quitting time at 6:30). The hour, on the whole, relatively pleasant, except for early moments of rushing and anxiety.

Conversations with the set-up man in the beret who, it seems, is beginning to take an interest in me.

C 4 × 10 steel screws | 7010105 | 041918 | cutter 1 | 5,000 at 4.50 F. End of pay period is Monday.

Total hrs.: 8 hrs. + 10 + 10 + 10 + 10 + 9 + 10 = 67 hrs.

Earned to date 90.75 F + 47 F + 12 F + 23.50 F = 173.25 F, nevertheless, to make 3 F per hr. . . .

It would mean earning 4.50 F per hr. Monday. . . . The 4,000 at 4 F will come to 18 F (2 cartons). 27 F to go. . . . Would have to do the 4,000 in 3 hrs. *at most*. And afterward do another 5,500 . . . practically impossible!

Sunday night. Back at my place at 11:40. Go to bed. Not being able to sleep, realize about 12:30 that I forgot my apron! After that sleep even less. Get up at 5:15; at 5:45 telephone home;[18] go by metro as far as Trocadero and back (40 min. in all, in the rush hour). Also, tired and headaches.

Monday. I must get out of here this evening or tomorrow. I have a headache. Don't finish the 4,000 until noon . . . (and I even spend another ¼ hr. on them from 1:30 to 1:45).

The machine is out of adjustment again, as on Thursday. The cutter, however, is brand new. Lucien (red beret) tells me again (more gently) that I'm applying too much pressure. But I'm sure it's really because he didn't tighten it enough. Anyway, since, without my having noticed it, the cutter was already out of adjustment Friday afternoon, so much so that a number of pieces weren't even touched by it, I have to lose time sorting and doing pieces over. I also lost a good quarter hour (at least) by going with the Spanish woman to get a bucket full of lubricating soap for her new machine; it was too heavy for her to carry by herself, and the worker whose job it was to give it to her made her wait. And afterward, on top of all that, Lucien's reproaches lowered my morale and speed. I know that if it happens again things will go badly. And as always when I don't singlemindedly strain every fiber to reach the rapid cadence, I slow up. Anyway, for all that it came to 4 × 4 = 16 F + 2 F (?) for doing the set-up (2 cartons).

18 I.e., her parents' home on rue Auguste-Comte. Since she went only as far as Trocadero, her mother may have met her half way.

Brass screws (7050010 | 4,000 at 4 F |. Then 400 pieces (out of 1,000; Span. woman does the other 600). I won't get the carton for them until Wednesday.

Steel locking screws | 774815 | 000987 | 400 at .50 F per hundred | set-up 1.25 F | cutter 1.2. I do them on the Spanish woman's small machine; she has been put somewhere else. The machine setter in glasses did the set-up while I was finishing my brass screws. A little before noon, although I didn't know at the time that he was preparing that machine for me, he ordered me to change the cutter and get the pieces—this in an authoritarian tone of voice that brooked no reply, which I obeyed in silence, but which, by quitting time, was enough to have made rise in me that flood tide of rage and bitterness that when you live a life like this is constantly there deep within you, always ready to overwhelm you completely. I pulled myself together, however. He's incompetent (unskilled worker, says the Spanish woman?), that's why he needs to lord it over people.

I begin the screws at 1:45. The machine is new to me. I spend, I think, almost 1 hr. at it (the Spanish woman will do the 600 in 20 min.!). Afterward, I go ask for a box. A waste of time. (There aren't any.) A young man comes for the 400 pieces. I go tell Leclerc that there's no box. Someone I don't know (gray smock) is talking informally to him, as far as I can make out, about a bawling out that he, Leclerc, is risking. He seems displeased to see me there (that's understandable), and his displeasure makes me forget to ask him for some pieces. Later, he's strolling about in the shop; I don't want to risk getting myself snapped at, as happened the other time, so I don't approach him; and I lose more than ¾ hr. (also by going to look for the lathe set-up man who gave me the 400 pieces, to find out if there are any more, but I don't find him).

Leclerc finally gives me some C 4 × 16s.

C 4 × 16 steel screws | 7010111 | 013259 | 5,000 at 4.50 F | put down 1 hr. | cutter 1.

On the other hand I do finally have Michel set up my machine. It's 3:30, past the time for handing in the card. (There's a deadline; you can hand them in only until 3 o'clock.) So instead of catching up on my lost time (and that's the main reason I was anxious to come today) I add to it. The thought of this lowers my morale and speed. For what I make from now on counts in a two-week period that I won't complete; so what difference does my hourly average make? I'm depressed by my headaches and I'm going—without noticing it—very, very slowly. I won't get these pieces finished until noon tomorrow (and even then not completely), which comes to 15 hrs. of work (or even more). 18 F + 3.25 F + 23.50 F = 44.75 F. But in order to make 3 F per hr., I would have to have earned 45 F in these 15 hrs.

3 o'clock deadline.

Tuesday. Finished the C 4 × 16s.

M.P.R. screws, in Gorger's area (automatic lathes).

M.P.R. screws with large hexagonal heads (⬡). You have to place them so that the groove is perpendicular to the two parallel sides: (⬡). Otherwise the piece is ruined. Very hard steel. While you're placing them, you risk turning them. All afternoon (and ¾ hr. the next day) I do only one carton of 1,400 (5 F per 1,000 + 1 F for set-up, i.e., 8 F), with one interruption for 1,000 large brass screws on the machine beside me, for which I don't have the box, but which I'm sure didn't pay more than 4.50 F maximum. That is, in 6¼ hrs. (or longer?) earned 8 F + 4.50 F = 12.50 F. That's disgraceful! 2 F per hour! It's a good thing I'm telling them I'm sick Wednesday morning.

Collection taken up for a pregnant worker.[19] People give 1 F, 1.50 F (me 2 F). Discussion in the cloakroom (it had been done a year ago, for the same worker). "Well, every year! It's a great misfortune, and that's all there is to it. It can happen to anyone. —When you don't know, you shouldn't. . . ." Spanish woman: "I don't feel that this is a good reason to take up a collection, do you?" I say "Yes" with conviction, and she doesn't pursue it.

When I left Monday night intending to report sick the following morning, I was careful not to eat more than a sandwich bought at 7 o'clock, and a glass of cider. Woke up at 5:30 (on purpose). I ate a roll Tuesday morning. The same at noon. 3 rolls in the evening, and went on foot to the Porte de Saint-Cloud, plus an espresso coffee to make me sleep. But the result of this diet was to put me into a state of euphoria! . . . Only I was extremely slow on the job.

Wednesday morning. Finish the carton of 1,400 M.P.R.s. I do 200 out of the new carton—5 F or 5.80 F? I go very, very slowly, but feel, through a damned spirit of contradiction, singularly joyful and in top form.

Leclerc and Gorger [foreman of the automatic lathes], the cartons of 1,000 brass pieces. Leclerc: "If you want to stop, stop."

19 Probably to pay for an abortion.

Earned 27.50 F + 1 F + 1 F + 4 F (?) + 1 F + 7.50 F (?) = 37 F or 40.60 F | theoretically in 11½ hrs. [34.50 F . . .].

Monday-Tuesday. C 4 × 16 screws | steel | 5,000 at 4.50 F + set-up 1 F | cutter 1, 7010 III | 013252, anchoring flanges.

M.P.R. screws, steel, 4,000 at 5.80 F + set-up 2 F 1.5 | 747327 | 046–543.

Steel stop pins, 2,000 at 4.50 F + 2 F (?) | 7050129 | 099937 | cutter 1.

23.50 F + 23.20 F + 2 F + 9 F + 2 F = 59.70 F.

37 F + 59.70 F = 96.70 F in 11½ hrs. + 20½ hrs. = 32 hrs. 32 × 3 = 96.

So in terms of the 3 F minimum, I'm up to date, but barely . . . and there would be 12 F to make up from the other 2-week period! Episodes: Gorger . . .

Michel . . .

Any child can see through Juliette's little tricks . . .

Monday, in a bad way. Going back to work infinitely more painful than I would have thought. The days seem an eternity to me. Heat. . . . Headaches. . . . These C 4 × 16 screws disgust me. It's one of the "cushy jobs"; I would have to do it quickly, and I can't. Barely finished, I think, by 3:30. Prostration, bitterness at stupifying work, disgust. Fear also, all the time, of the cutter coming loose. Nevertheless, it happens. The wait to have the cutters changed. For the 1st time I succeed in changing a cutter myself, with no help at all, and Philippe says that it's right in the middle. A victory, better than speed. I also learn, after another bad experience, to adjust the tightness of the screw and handle at the end myself. Lucien sometimes completely forgets to tighten it. . . . The M.P.R. screws. Michel warns me. He doesn't set them up, but "spectacles" does it. I do the M.P.R.s a little faster than before, but still very, very slowly.

Wednesday. Steel stops, cutter 1.5.

		009182	1,000		
C 001268	{	097384	—	}	at 4.50 F (2 set-ups)
		097385	—		

Round pipe plugs in red copper 10 C.V. cutter 1.5.

$$C\ 002400 \quad \left\{ \begin{array}{cc} 071853 & 1,000 \\ 50 & - \\ 47 & - \end{array} \right\} \quad 3.70\ F$$

4.50 F × 3 + 3.70 F × 3 + 3 F . . .

13.50 F + 11.10 F + 3 F = 27.60 F, worked 10½ hrs. So am short 4 F.

Thursday. Steel lock bolts 8 C.V., cutter 1.

737887 | 084097, 3,000 at 4.50 F, set-up 1 F.

Round pipe plugs in red copper, cutter 1.5.

13.50 F + 3.70 F + 5 F + 3.80 F + 4 F = 30 F. Am short 1.50 F. So am short 5.50 F in all. Maybe it's been compensated for by the week before.

Episode of the "stops." Michel, Thursday morning.

Humid Wednesday and Thursday. Delightfully cool Thursday evening. Good. . . .

The stops had been begun the day before at 5 o'clock. On that Tuesday when I thought I was going to faint, when the weather was so humid, when my whole body felt on fire, when I had such a headache. . . . Juliette says to me, "1.5 cutter." I remove my number 1 cutter, proceed to change the 2 cutters and hand one to Philippe, saying simply, "That's a number 1."

At Renault.

Lange: foreman—former set-up man—stickler for order and neatness, apart from that. . . . Scowls, etc.; foremen treat him with respect. With me, nice enough.

Roger: (replc. Leclerc); drilling machine set-up man.

Philippe: boor; lathe set-up man.

Protruding Eyes . . . : tall blond, another lathe set-up man.

Spectacles . . .

Male workers: Armenian, milling machine operator next to 1st machine, mild-mannered worker who jokes about "women going to war." Italian who replaces him (likable).

Women: Bertrand—another neighbor (Juliette)—beginner—woman who flirts with Michel—the tall brunette with 2 kids—old woman who works on the lathes—Italian's wife—drilling machine operator. . . .

Shift foremen:

Fortin: such a nice guy . . .

Gorcher: automatic lathes, comedian, likable.

Leclerc.

Foreman across from elevator—tone of superiority in his voice intolerable.

Michel.

Lucien.

Gained from this experience? The feeling that I do not possess any right whatever, of any kind (take care not to lose this feeling). The ability to be morally self-sufficient, to live in this state of constant latent humiliation without feeling humiliated in my own eyes; to savor intensely every moment of freedom or camaraderie, as if it would last forever. A direct contact with life. . . .

I came near to being broken. I almost was—my courage, the feeling that I had value as a person were nearly broken during a period I would be humiliated to remember, were it not that strictly speaking I have retained no memory of it. I got up in the mornings with anguish. I went to the factory with dread; I worked like a slave; the noon break was a wrenching experience; I got back to my place at 5:45, preoccupied immediately with getting enough sleep (which I didn't) and with waking up early enough. Time was an intolerable burden. Dread—outright fear—of what was going to happen next only relaxed its grip on me on Saturday afternoon and Sunday morning. And what I dreaded was the *orders.*

The feeling of self-respect, such as it has been built up by society, is *destroyed.* It is necessary to forge another one for oneself (although exhaustion wipes out consciousness of one's ability to think!). Try to hold on to this other kind.

One finally gets a clear idea of one's own importance.

The class of those who *do not count*—in any situation—in anyone's eyes—and who will not count, ever, no matter what happens (notwithstanding the last line of the 1st verse of the *Internationale*).[20]

Det.'s question (working-class solidarity).

Problem: objective conditions that allow men to be 1) nice guys and 2) productive.

One always needs to have some *external* signs of one's worth for oneself.

The main fact isn't the suffering, but the humiliation.

20 "We have been naught, we shall be all."

Hitler's strength is perhaps founded on that (whereas stupid "materialism" . . .).

[If trade unionism brought about a sense of responsibility in everyday life. . . .]

Never forget this observation: in these rough beings I always found that generosity of heart and aptitude for general ideas were directly proportional to one another.

An obviously inexorable and invincible form of oppression does not engender revolt as an immediate reaction, but submission.

At Alsthom, I rebelled only on Sundays. . . .

At Renault, I had arrived at a more stoical attitude. Substitute acceptance for submission.

■ *War and Peace*

Introduction

The articles collected in the following section present the different positions on war Weil took in response to the European political situation from 1933 to 1940. She had begun the decade of the 1930s as a revolutionary, and a cursory glance at both these texts and her life during 1933–40 reveals that she went through several changes of position, first advocating pacifism, then, while still apparently holding pacifist opinions, becoming a revolutionary again and fighting briefly in the Spanish civil war, then vigorously defending a noninterventionist policy in Europe in hopes of avoiding European war, and finally advocating an armed resistance against Hitler that would be infused by actively practiced humane virtues opposing the violence, brutality, and inhumanity of the Nazis. The apparent inconsistencies in these positions and in Weil's activities in this period are not, however, signs of vacillation or inconsistency in Weil herself; she always viewed war in the larger context of oppression and was always asking the implicit question: Is war in these circumstances likely to alleviate the oppression of the masses of the people, or will it reinforce that oppression and make it even more murderous?

The first article, "Reflections on War," comes at the end of what might be described as the first period of her political life, the period of revolutionary confidence, which was being gradually eroded by what she saw happening in Germany, by her observations of what had happened to the revolution in Russia, and by her experience within the French Left. For her it was a time of increasing disillusionment with Marxist revolutionary hopes and a time of serious critical reevaluation of the Marxist belief in the inevitability of revolution; for the French Left it was a time of widespread expectation of war and confused hopes that the war might further revolution. In the midst of this atmosphere of tense expectation and confusion she set about to clarify the situation, to do what she charged that no one else on the Left had yet done, which was to apply Marxist analysis to war in order to determine what, indeed, had been the effect of war on revolutions in history and what one could logically expect that effect to be in the future.

Contrary to the Socialists' belief that revolutionary war was "one of the most glorious forms of the struggle of the working masses against their oppressors," Weil's analysis in "Reflections on War" showed that both the French and Russian revolutionary wars had actually taken political power from the people and entrenched it in the state and military apparatus, that the exigencies of war had in fact made democracy impossible, had led to the Terror and then to the military dictatorship of Napoleon in France and had given Russia "the heaviest bureaucratic, military, and police machine that has ever burdened an unfortunate people." Revolutionary war, she concluded, "is the tomb of the revolution and will remain so as long as the soldiers themselves, or rather the armed citizenry, are not given the means of making war without a controlling apparatus, without police pressure, without a special court, without punishment for desertion."

Weil extended her analysis to show that, in the modern era, war "only reproduces the social relations that constitute the structure of the regime," i.e., the structure in which managers or officers command and workers or soldiers have no choice but to obey. Because in modern war (she was thinking of course of World War I) the "controlling apparatus has no other means of defeating the enemy except to force its own soldiers to go to their deaths, the war of one state against another is immediately transformed into a war of the state and military apparatus against its own army." War, she argued, is thus the most radical form of oppression, since "soldiers do not expose themselves to death [but] are sent to the slaughter." The main enemy, she contended, borrowing Karl Liebknecht's phrase, is in our own country; she was not thinking of imperialism, as Liebknecht had, but of the structure of command and obedience in industrial production and the organization of the military; it was this structure of command, and the powerful bureaucratic apparatus that was inseparable from it, that reduced the proletariat to slavery, in peace as well as in war, but especially in war. What was crucial, she argued, was to recognize this apparatus as the enemy no matter what its name—"fascism, democracy, or dictatorship of the proletariat"—and to refuse to subordinate oneself to it and "trample underfoot, in order to serve it, all human values in oneself and others."

Thus, although Weil continued to write vigorously against war in the articles that follow, she was arguing against the type of war between nation-states that would strengthen the state apparatus and further humiliate and destroy predominantly working-class conscripts. But the civil war in Spain that broke out in July 1936 was another matter; not only was it a civil war and not an international war, but it was a civil war in which, initially at least, the Spanish workers and peasants were fighting in their own demo- cratically organized militias, a civil war in which, in the areas controlled by the Left, a genuine social revolution seemed already to have happened. Weil had great hopes that this represented the beginning of a complete so- cial transformation, and she wanted above all else to participate in it; less than a month after the war broke out she went to Barcelona, made her way to the Aragon front, and joined a militia unit. Within a week she was badly burned in a camp accident and forced to return to Barcelona, but during the month she spent recuperating in Spain she saw enough to destroy her earlier hope that a war made "by the armed citizenry, without a control- ling apparatus" could serve revolutionary ends. "The atmosphere and ne- cessities of civil war are sweeping away the aspirations that we are seeking to defend by means of civil war," she wrote shortly after her return to France in late September. In October she learned of the increasingly op- pressive regulations imposed on both industrial workers and militiamen by the regional government of Catalonia and saw her earlier predictions about the tendency of war to generate oppressive apparatuses being proved true. She saw her friends on the Left urging French intervention, a widening of the war; some even spoke of deliberately escalating the Span- ish civil war into international war. Heartsick and more than ever con- vinced that European war would be a "disaster of incomparable magni- tude," she wrote in support of French premier and Popular Front leader Léon Blum's policy of nonintervention in Spain, and then took Blum to task for the inconsistency between his position on nonintervention in re- gard to Spain and his willingness to accept the notion of collective security in regard to countries with which France had mutual defense pacts. If the Popular Front policy of mutual assistance was unreasonable with regard to Spain, Weil argued, it could not be reasonable to risk European war to defend Czechoslovakia. She was willing to take Hitler at his word that he wanted the German-speaking sections of Czechoslovakia united with the Reich and would respect the independence of the remainder of the Czech state; she was willing to accept German hegemony in Europe for as long as it might naturally last, pointing out that "in the long run, hegemony al- ways weakens the country that has achieved it"; she was willing to accept the evil consequences of Czechoslovakia's becoming a German satellite state—"the exclusion of Jews and Communists from all relatively important positions"—because she believed that the country as a whole would not have to sacrifice "its culture, its language, or its national characteristics." Her final argument on the Czechoslovakia issue was that few Frenchmen of military age, or their wives or mothers or fathers, would find it "reasonable and just that French blood should be shed for Czechoslovakia"; if war were declared, she argued, it would be in the interests of governments, not of the people.

The essay on Czechoslovakia also touches on two issues that are easy to overlook: one, the injustice of French colonialism and the moral inconsistency of France's going to war to defend the right of Czechs to self-determination when France was refusing to grant that right to its own colonies; and two, the importance of the preservation of national life and traditions. The importance of moral consistency to the success of any action and the need of the soul to be rooted in a milieu rich in historical and spiritual traditions were to become major themes in Weil's later writings. Early formulations of these ideas are found in the next essay, "Reflections on Bouché's Lecture."

Henri Bouché, a former student of Alain's, gave a lecture on national defense in which he suggested decentralization as a means of making France less vulnerable to enemy air attack; this idea greatly appealed to Weil, who had long conceived of social organization in terms of a loose federation of democratically organized collectives or small population centers. Her description of the kind of national defense that would result from this sort of organization bears a startling resemblance to the guerrilla defense of Indochina and Central America in the 1970s and 1980s. What both necessitated and made possible this kind of guerrilla defense for France, Weil argued, was France's relative loss of power in Europe—a loss that in her eyes was actually a gain, for it transformed France from a powerful modern bourgeois state regarded essentially as an oppressor and an enemy into a locus of national life, tradition, and spiritual values. Once France was no longer the strongest power in Europe Weil could begin to see in the concept of "the nation" something more than a cover for chauvinism and the will to extend the power of the state; she began to see it as associated both with a people and with a place, with "a certain spirit attached to a particular human milieu." It is this spirit infusing a country, she argued, that gives national defense its point. This kind of national defense and this concept of nation are centered in the people, not in the state; this kind of national defense can be undertaken without the danger of consolidating military and state power, can indeed, if successful, strengthen the spirit of the people. Conversely, Weil argues, when this spirit is lacking, enslavement is inevitable.

Despite this tentative awareness of a new understanding of the importance of national life expressed in "Reflections on Bouché's Lecture," in the same period Weil was also sensitive to the dangers of nationalism aroused in a country threatened with war. The real threat of war that France had experienced during the Munich Crisis in September 1938 had, quite naturally, aroused a powerful latent nationalism throughout the entire country, even among the internationalist Left. But in this case Weil feared the identification of the nation with the totalitarian state, the equation of national defense with the buildup of that state, and the indefinite setting aside, in the interests of national defense, of all other concerns. In a France transformed into an armed camp, she feared, respect for human life and liberty and concern for justice and humanity were in danger either of being forgotten or of being regarded as fairy tales.[1] Weil not only warned against this tendency but argued that, if it should happen, the democratic countries could not win the war; "in order to fight well," she wrote, "it is not enough to defend an absence of tyranny. We must be rooted in a milieu in which every activity is really oriented in the opposite direction from tyranny."

In the metaphors Weil used to describe these positive and negative concepts of "the nation" it is possible to see a parallel with an important aspect of modern feminist thought. Weil's description of the oppressive, power-oriented, centralized nation-state and the chauvinist nationalism it fosters calls to mind the oppressive structures of patriarchal society as described in the 1970s by the feminist philosopher Mary Daly. Although in the essays collected in "War and Peace" Weil did not use specifically female imagery to describe the positive aspects of the nation (in "Reflections on Bouché's Lecture" she merely argues that the nation that believes in freedom and justice must mediate those values for all of its inhabitants), in a letter written during this same period she uses clearly maternal images to describe the ideal social and political human community; she speaks of

1 In another country—Chile under the military dictatorship of General Pinochet—Weil's fear seems to have been more than realized; a political cartoon in the *Chile Newsletter* in the mid-1980s depicted a mother, dressed in rags, reading a bedtime story to her three children. "Once upon a time," she reads, "there was tea, sugar, flour, rice, potatoes, meat, coffee. . . ."

the fragility and the inestimable value of "the living warmth of a human environment, that medium which bathes and fosters the thoughts and the virtues" and praises what Mary Daly would call "biophilic societies"— forms of social life that do not kill the fragile thing that "is the medium that favours the development of the soul."[2] Like Daly, Weil identifies the patriarchal structures with slavery and death[3] and the maternal milieus with life and with the mediation of humane and transcendent values.

By 1940 Weil had come to see the war as an arena of moral as well as physical battle, success in which demanded the actual and everyday practice and strengthening of virtue; the suffering it entailed she saw as a means of purification and painful revalorization of "the precious things we allowed to be lost because we did not know how to appreciate them." In short, she thought it could and should lead not only to a social transformation of French life after the war but to a profound deepening of spiritual and moral awareness in all who participated in it or were affected by it. That she saw the war, at least metaphorically, in terms of a battle between the necrophilic values of the patriarchy and female-mediated values is suggested by her insistence on the necessity of opposing "humane" values to the inhumanity and death-oriented fanaticism of the German forces. Her much-scorned plan for a corps of front-line nurses offers a concrete image of the female as the bearer of "humane" values in the very heart of the inevitable brutality of war.

Starting as a revolutionary in 1931, Weil would have, given the chance, become a guerrilla in 1940. When the Germans brutally suppressed an uprising of students in Prague soon after the outbreak of the war, she devised a plan for parachuting arms and volunteers (including herself) into Czechoslovakia to help support popular resistance. The plan was turned down by the French political leaders to whom she presented it, and Weil then conceived of a corps of nurses who would go into battle with the soldiers to give emergency first aid to the wounded; she of course intended to be one of the nurses, and went to great lengths to try to get the project adopted by the French and later by the American government. That, too, was turned down and she tried to persuade the Free French in London to parachute her into France as a saboteur, or at least as a liaison person who

2 "Three Letters on History" in *Selected Essays* (London: Oxford University Press, 1962), pp. 79, 80.
3 Weil's often-criticized condemnation of ancient Israel and ancient Rome may be read as a condemnation of patriarchal values manifested in an almost pure form.

could communicate the feelings and the state of mind of the French under the Occupation back to Free French headquarters in London. Again, she was refused. All of these efforts, so often seen as impractical if not fatuously idealistic, purely and simply exemplify the spirit that she felt was absolutely necessary if the war was going to be a means of liberation and not simply a means of reinforcing oppressive structures of power.

■ War and Peace

Reflections on War

The present situation and the state of mind it creates once more make the problem of war the order of the day. We live now in constant expectation of war. The danger is perhaps imaginary, but the feeling of danger is real, and that in itself constitutes a not negligible factor. One cannot call the response anything but panic, less the kind of panic that undermines peoples' courage when they are threatened with massacre than one that afflicts minds faced with the problems posed by war. And in no quarter is the disarray more evident than in the working-class movement. If we do not undertake a serious effort of analysis, one day sooner or later we may well find ourselves at war and powerless not only to act but even to make judgments. And the first thing we must do is assess the traditions from which, until now, we have more or less consciously drawn sustenance.

Until the period following the last war, the revolutionary movement, in its various forms, had nothing to do with pacifism. Revolutionary ideas on war and peace have always drawn their inspiration from memories of the years 1792, 1793, and 1794, which were the cradle of all the revolutionary movements of the nineteenth century. In absolute contradiction with historical fact, the war of 1792 was seen as a triumphant outburst which, by rousing the French people against foreign tyrants, would at the same time break the domination of the court and the upper bourgeoisie and bring the representatives of the toiling masses to power. This legendary memory, perpetuated by the "Marseillaise," gave rise to the idea that revolutionary war, whether defensive or offensive, is not only a legitimate form but also one of the most glorious forms of the struggle of the working masses against their oppressors. That idea was held by all Marxists and almost all revolutionaries until fifteen years ago. However, when it comes to assessing the value of other kinds of war, the socialist tradition furnishes

This essay was published in *La Critique sociale*, no. 10, November 1933.

us with not just one but several contradictory ideas, which have never been clearly set forth and compared.

In the first half of the nineteenth century, war itself seems to have had a certain prestige in the eyes of revolutionaries; in France, for example, they sharply criticized Louis Philippe's policy of peace. Proudhon wrote an eloquent tribute in praise of war, and revolutionaries dreamed just as much of wars of liberation on behalf of oppressed nations as of insurrections. The war of 1870 forced the proletarian organizations (meaning, at that time, the International) to take a concrete position on the question of war for the first time. Through Marx's pen, the International called on the workers of the two warring countries to oppose any attempt at conquest but to resolutely join in defending their country against enemy attack.

When Engels, in 1892, eloquently evoking memories of the war that had broken out a hundred years earlier, urged the German Social Democrats to fight for all they were worth if Germany were attacked by France allied with Russia, he was speaking in behalf of another idea. Defense or attack no longer mattered; what mattered was to preserve, by offensive or defensive tactics, the country where the working-class movement was the strongest, and to crush the more reactionary country. In other words, according to this idea (which was also held by Plekanov, Mehring, and others),[1] to judge a conflict one must try to ascertain the outcome that would be most advantageous for the proletariat, and take sides accordingly.

This idea is diametrically opposed to another idea, which was held by the Bolsheviks and the Spartacists, and according to which, in every war, with the exception of wars of national defense or revolutionary wars according to Lenin, and with the exception of revolutionary wars alone according to Rosa Luxemburg, the proletariat must wish for the defeat of its own country and sabotage the war effort in it. But this idea—which is based on the notion that all wars, with the exceptions mentioned above, are imperialist in nature and thereby comparable to a quarrel of brigands wrangling over spoils—entails some serious difficulties. It seems to destroy the international proletariat's unity of action, obliging the workers in each country, who must work for their country's defeat, to thereby favor the victory of the enemy imperialism, a victory that other workers must try to prevent. Liebknecht's famous saying, "Our main enemy is in our own

---

1 Georgi Valentinovich Plekanov (1856–1918) introduced Marxism into Russian revolutionary thought in the 1880s. Franz Mehring (1846–1919) was a German Socialist.

country,"[2] clearly reveals this difficulty by assigning a different enemy to the various national fractions of the proletariat, and thus, in appearance at least, setting them in opposition to one another.

It is obvious that, as far as war is concerned, the Marxist tradition offers neither unity nor clarity. But all the theories agree on at least one point: the absolute refusal to condemn war as such. The Marxists, especially Kautsky[3] and Lenin, were fond of paraphrasing Clauswitz's formula[4] to the effect that war is only the continuation of the politics of peacetime by other means, which leads to the conclusion that a war must be judged not by the violent nature of the methods employed, but by the ends pursued through those methods.

What the postwar period introduced into the working-class movement was not another idea—for it would be impossible to accuse the working-class (or so-called working-class) organizations of our time of having ideas on any subject whatever—but another moral atmosphere. As early as 1918 the Bolshevik party, which passionately desired revolutionary war, had to resign itself to peace, not for doctrinal reasons but because of the direct pressure of the Russian soldiers, who were no more inspired to emulate the example of 1793 when the Bolsheviks invoked it than when Kerensky did. The same thing happened in other countries on the level of ordinary propaganda; the masses battered by the war forced the parties that claimed to represent the proletariat to use purely pacifist language—which did not, it must be added, prevent some of them from glorifying the Red Army, and others from voting war credits in their respective countries. Never, of course, were theoretical analyses made to justify this new way of speaking; no one even seemed to notice that it was new. But the fact is that instead of war being branded as imperialist, imperialism began to be branded as a cause of wars. The so-called Amsterdam movement, whose theoretical basis was against imperialist war, in order to make itself heard,

2 "The Main Enemy Is in Our Own Country" is the title of an important underground pamphlet written by Karl Liebknecht in 1915 while he was in prison for his antiwar politics. In it he says that the main enemy is German imperialism and urges the German people to "wage a political fight against this enemy . . . in cooperation with the proletariat of other countries whose fight must be directed against their own imperialists."

3 Karl Kautsky (1854–1938) was an important figure in the German Social Democratic movement.

4 The Prussian general Karl von Clauswitz (1780–1831) is considered to have been the foremost modern theorist on land warfare. He is best known for the idea Weil refers to above, that war is not an end in itself but a means to political ends.

had to present itself as being against war in general. Russian propaganda emphasized the pacifist inclination of the USSR even more than its proletarian (or so-called proletarian) character. The formulations of the great theoreticians of socialism on the impossibility of condemning war as such were completely forgotten.

It is as if Hitler's triumph in Germany made all the old ideas, inextricably mixed together, float to the surface. Peace appeared less precious as soon as it allowed the unspeakable horrors borne by thousands of suffering workers in the German concentration camps. The idea that Engels voiced in his article of 1892 is reappearing. Isn't the main enemy of the international proletariat German fascism, as in 1892 it was Russian czarism? This fascism, which is spreading in all directions, can only be crushed by force; and, since the German proletariat is unarmed, only the nations that have remained democratic, it seems, can do it.

It scarcely matters, moreover, whether this would involve a war of national defense or a "preventive war"; preventive war might even be better. Didn't Marx and Engels at one time urge England to attack Russia? Such a war, it is thought, would not appear to be a struggle between two rival imperialist powers but between two political regimes. And, just as the aging Engels said in 1892 when he recalled what had happened a hundred years before, it is being said that a war would force the state to make serious concessions to the proletariat; all the more so as the war that is brewing would necessarily involve conflict between the state and the capitalist class, and socialist measures would probably be pushed quite far. Who knows if the war would not thus automatically bring the representatives of the proletariat to power?

In the political circles that claim to speak for the proletariat, all these considerations have begun to create a current of opinion more or less explicitly in favor of active participation in a war against Germany. This current is still fairly weak, but it can easily grow stronger. Some stick to the distinction between aggression and national defense; others to Lenin's ideas; others, lastly—and there are still a good many of them—remain pacifist, but for the most part more out of force of habit than for any other reason. One could not imagine worse confusion.

So much uncertainty and obscurity may surprise and ought to embarrass us, if one bears in mind that it concerns a phenomenon that, given its attendant preparations, reparations, and renewed preparations, and considering all the moral and material consequences that follow from it, seems

to dominate our era and be its most characteristic feature. The real surprise, however, would be if we had arrived at anything better by starting
from the absolutely legendary and illusory tradition of 1793 and by using
the most defective method possible, one that claims to evaluate every war
in terms of the ends pursued and not by the nature of the means employed.
It is not that it would be better to condemn the use of violence in general, as
pure pacifists do; in each era war consists of a quite specific kind of violence, and we must study its mechanism before passing any judgment. The
very essence of the materialist method is that, in its examination of any
human event whatever, it attaches much less importance to the ends pursued than to the consequences necessarily implied by the working out of
the means employed. One can neither solve nor even state a problem relating to war without having first of all taken apart the mechanism of the
military struggle, that is, without having analyzed the social relations it
implies under given technical, economic, and social conditions.

One can speak of war in general only in abstract terms. Modern war is
absolutely different from everything designated by that name under earlier
regimes. On the one hand, modern war is only an extension of that other
war known as competition, which makes production itself into a simple
form of the struggle for power; on the other hand, every aspect of economic life is presently oriented toward a coming war. In this inextricable
mixture of the military and the economic, where arms are put at the service
of competition and production at the service of war, war only reproduces
the social relations that constitute the structure of the regime, although to
a considerably higher degree. Marx forcefully showed that what defines
the modern mode of production is the subordination of the workers to the
instruments of production, which are at the disposal of those who do not
work; and he showed how, since the only recognized weapon is the exploitation of the workers, competition is transformed into a struggle of
each owner against his own workers and, in the last analysis, of the aggregate of the owners against the aggregate of the workers. In the same
way, war in our time is defined by the subordination of the combatants to
the instruments of combat, and the armaments, the real heroes of modern
wars, are, just like the men dedicated to their service, controlled by those
who do not fight. Since this controlling apparatus has no other means of
defeating the enemy except by forcing its own soldiers to go to their deaths,
the war of one state against another is immediately transformed into a war
of the state and military apparatus against its own army. Ultimately, war

in our time appears to be a war conducted by the aggregate of the state apparatuses and their general staffs against the aggregate of men old enough to bear arms. But, whereas machines take away from the workers only their labor power, and owners have no other means of constraint except dismissal (which is blunted by the fact that the worker can choose among different employers), every soldier is constrained to sacrifice his very life to the demands of the military machine, and he is forced to do so by the threat of execution without trial that the power of the state constantly holds over his head. Consequently it matters very little whether a war is defensive or offensive, imperialist or nationalist; every state at war is forced to use this method, since the enemy uses it. The great error of almost every study on war—an error into which all the socialists, especially, have fallen—is to consider war as an episode in foreign policy, when above all it constitutes a fact of domestic policy, and the most atrocious one of all. What is at issue here is not a matter of sentimental considerations or superstitious respect for human life; it is a matter of a very simple observation, namely, that massacre is the most radical form of oppression, and soldiers do not expose themselves to death, they are sent to the slaughter. And since an oppressive apparatus, once established, goes on functioning until something destroys it, every war that causes an apparatus responsible for directing strategic maneuvers to be a burden on the masses forced to do the fighting must be considered, even if it is led by revolutionaries, to be a reactionary factor. And the effect on foreign countries of such a war is determined by the political relationships established domestically. Weapons wielded by a sovereign state apparatus can bring no one liberty.

That is what Robespierre[5] had realized and what the war of 1792—the same war that gave birth to the idea of revolutionary war—confirmed beyond the shadow of a doubt. At that time military technique was still far from having reached the degree of centralization it has attained in our time; nevertheless, the subordination of the soldiers charged with carrying out military operations to the high command charged with coordinating those operations had been very strict since the time of Frederick II.[6] Just as

5 In late 1791 and early 1792 Maximilien Robespierre (1758–94), the guiding spirit of the group that dominated the radical phase of the French Revolution, had opposed the more moderate Girondin group who, in hopes both of consolidating their own political power and of bringing the revolution to France's neighbors by means of "armed missionaries," had argued in favor of war with Austria and Prussia.

6 Frederick the Great (1712–86) was king of Prussia from 1740 to 1786. A military and

the revolution was getting under way, a war was about to transform all France, as Barère[7] would later say, into a vast camp, and consequently give the state apparatus that power without appeal that is characteristic of military authority. That was the calculation made in 1792 by the court and the Girondins. A legend much too easily accepted by the socialists has made the war appear to be a spontaneous outburst of the people rising up against both their oppressors and the foreign tyrants who threatened them; actually, it was a provocation of the court and the upper bourgeoisie plotting together against the liberty of the people. On the surface, it would seem that they miscalculated, since, instead of bringing about national unity as they expected, the war aggravated all clashes of interests, brought the king and then the Girondins to the scaffold, and gave the Mountain[8] dictatorial power. But that does not alter the fact that on April 20, 1792, the day war was declared, every hope of democracy sank without a trace; and the second of June[9] was followed only too closely by the ninth Thermidor,[10] the consequences of which, in their turn, soon led to the eighteenth Brumaire.[11] In addition, of what use to Robespierre and his friends was the power they exercised before the ninth Thermidor? Their goal was not to seize power but to establish a real democracy, both political and social. But by a bloody irony of history, the war forced them to leave the Constitution of 1793 on paper, forge a centralized apparatus, carry on a bloody terror that they could not even turn against the rich, abolish all liberty, and become, finally, the precursors of the military, bureaucratic, and bourgeois despotism of Napoleon. At least they kept their lucidity to the end. Two days before his death, Saint-Just[12] wrote these profound words:

---

political genius, he made Prussia into a power second only to Austria among the German states.

7 Bertrand Barère de Vieuzac (1755–1841) was a member of the National Convention and a supporter of Robespierre.

8 The Mountain was the name given a group of Jacobins led by Robespierre who sat in the highest seats in the National Convention. They supplanted the Girondins as the dominant faction.

9 On the second of June 1793, in response to a three-day-long demonstration by tens of thousands of armed Parisian workers and shopkeepers, the Girondins were expelled from the National Convention and arrested. Most of them were executed a few months later.

10 On the ninth Thermidor (July 27, 1794) Robespierre was refused a hearing in the National Convention and was arrested; he was executed the next day.

11 On the eighteenth Brumaire (November 9, 1799) Napoleon carried out a coup d'état against the first French Republic (the Directory) and established a military despotism known as the Consulate.

12 Antoine Louis de Saint-Just (1767–94), a member of the National Convention, was a close associate of Robespierre. They were executed on the same day.

"Only those who are in the battles win them, and only those who are in power profit from them." As for Robespierre, as soon as the question arose, he understood that a war could not free any foreign people ("liberty is not brought at the point of bayonets"), and that it would hand the French people over to the chains of state power—a power that one could no longer try to weaken since it was needed in the struggle against the foreign enemy. "War is good for military officers, for ambitious men, for speculators . . . for the executive arm. . . . This course relieves one of all other responsibilities. One no longer has any obligations toward the people when one gives them war." From that time onward he foresaw the coming military despotism, and continued to predict it despite the apparent successes of the revolution; he was still predicting it two days before his death, in his last speech, and left this prediction behind as a testament, but those who have since claimed him as their own have unfortunately not attached much importance to it.

The history of the Russian Revolution provides exactly the same lessons, along with a striking analogy. The Soviet Constitution suffered exactly the same fate as the Constitution of 1793; Lenin forsook its democratic doctrines in order to establish the despotism of a centralized state apparatus, just as Robespierre did, and Lenin was the precursor of Stalin, as Robespierre was the precursor of Bonaparte. The difference is that Lenin—who had, moreover, long ago paved the way for the domination of the state apparatus by forging a highly centralized party—later distorted his own doctrines in order to adapt them to the necessities of the hour; thus he was not guillotined, but has become the idol of a new state religion.

The history of the Russian Revolution is all the more striking as war was constantly its central problem. The revolution was a movement against the war started by soldiers who, feeling the governmental and military apparatus falling apart over their heads, hastened to throw off an intolerable yoke. Kerensky, invoking the memories of 1792 with an involuntary sincerity due to ignorance, called for a continuation of the war for exactly the same reasons as the Girondins had earlier. Trotsky admirably showed how the bourgeoisie, counting on the war to postpone domestic political problems and bring the people back under the yoke of state power, wanted to transform "the war of attrition against the enemy into a war of attrition against the revolution." At that time the Bolsheviks were calling for a struggle against imperialism. But it was the war itself, not imperialism, that mattered, and they saw this quite clearly when, once in power, they were forced to sign the peace of Brest-Litovsk.[13] By that time the old army had been broken up and Lenin had reiterated what Marx had said, that there was no place in a dictatorship of the proletariat for a permanent army, police force, or bureaucracy. But, almost immediately, the white armies and fear of foreign intervention put all Russia into a state of siege. The army was then reconstituted, the election of officers abolished, thirty thousand officers of the old regime reinstated in the officer corps, and the death penalty, the old disciplinary code, and military centralization re-established; the bureaucracy and the police were reconstituted along parallel lines. What this military, bureaucratic, and police apparatus did to the Russian people later on is quite well known.

Revolutionary war is the tomb of the revolution and will remain so as long as the soldiers themselves, or rather the armed citizenry, are not given the means of making war without a controlling apparatus, without police pressure, without a special court, without punishment for desertion. Only once in modern history was war conducted in this way, namely, under the Commune;[14] and everyone knows how that ended. It seems that a revolution involved in a war has only the choice of succumbing to the deadly blows of the counterrevolution or of transforming itself into a counter-revolution through the very mechanism of the military struggle. The prospects of revolution seem therefore very limited, for can a revolution avoid war? Nevertheless, we must stake everything on the slight chance that it can, or abandon all hope. The Russian example is there to instruct us. An advanced country would not encounter, in the event of a revolution, the difficulties that served as the foundation of the barbarous regime of Stalin in backward Russia; but a war of any scope would give rise to other difficulties at least as great.

All the more so, a war undertaken by a bourgeois state can only trans-

13 The Treaty of Brest-Litovsk (signed March 3, 1918) ended the war between Russia and Germany, at the cost of Russia's surrendering Poland, the Ukraine, and the Baltic provinces to German control.

14 The Paris Commune of 1871 was an insurrection of Paris Republicans who refused to accept the harsh peace terms dictated by Bismarck following the Franco-Prussian War, terms that the recently elected National Assembly was prepared to accept. Civil war broke out between the Communards in Paris and the national government seated at Versailles. The Commune lasted for two months of bloody fighting before it was finally put down by the national government. Thirty-eight thousand Communards were arrested and 20,000 were put to death.

form power into despotism and enslavement into calculated murder. If war sometimes appears to be a revolutionary factor, it is only in the sense that it is an incomparable test of the functioning of the state apparatus. At its touch a badly organized apparatus falls apart, but if the war does not end immediately and permanently, or if the breakdown of the state has not gone far enough, the result will be merely one of those revolutions that, in Marx's words, perfect the state apparatus instead of destroying it. That's what has always happened until now. In our time the difficulty that war greatly exacerbates is the one resulting from the ever-increasing opposition between the state apparatus and the capitalist system; what happened in Briey during the last war is a striking example.[15] The last war gave the various state apparatuses some authority over the economy, and this gave rise to the completely erroneous term "war socialism"; afterward the capitalist system began to function again almost normally, despite customs barriers, import quotas, and national currencies. In the next war things will probably go very much further, and it is known that quantity is capable of being changed into quality. In this sense, war in our time can be a revolutionary factor, but only if one wants to give the term "revolution" the meaning the National Socialists give it; like the economic crisis, war would arouse strong hostility to the capitalists, and this hostility would be turned, by means of the Union Sacrée,[16] to the advantage of the state apparatus and not of the workers. Furthermore, to recognize the kinship between war and fascism, all one has to do is turn to the fascist texts that conjure up "the martial spirit" and "socialism of the front." Both war and fascism essentially involve a kind of aggravated fanaticism that leads to the total effacement of the individual before the state bureaucracy. If the capitalist system is more or less damaged in the process, it can only be at the expense of human values and the proletariat, and not to their benefit, no matter what the demagogues may sometimes say.

The absurdity of adopting war as a means of antifascist struggle is thus quite apparent. Not only would it mean fighting against a barbarous oppression by crushing the peoples under the weight of an even more barbarous massacre; it would even mean extending under another form the regime we want to abolish. It is childish to suppose that a state apparatus

15 The de Wendel family, French owners of metallurgical factories in Briey (in the Lorraine, which at that time belonged to Germany), prevented the factories from being bombed by the French Air Force.

16 See no. 6, p. 104.

made powerful by a victorious war would alleviate the oppression to which the enemy state apparatus had subjected its own people; it is more childish still to believe that a victorious state would let a proletarian revolution break out in the defeated nation without immediately drowning it in blood. As for the bourgeois democracy[17] that has been destroyed by fascism, a war would not do away with, but rather reinforce and broaden, the causes that make it impossible at present.

It seems, generally speaking, that history is increasingly forcing everyone engaged in political action to choose between aggravating the intolerable oppression exercised by the state apparatuses and conducting a direct and ruthless struggle against those apparatuses in order to destroy them. To be sure, the perhaps insoluble difficulties that loom up in our time may justify abandoning the struggle purely and simply. But if we don't want to renounce action, we must understand that we can fight against a state apparatus only from the inside. And, particularly in the event of war, we must choose between impeding the functioning of the military machine in which we ourselves constitute the wheels, or helping that machine to blindly crush human lives. Liebknecht's famous words, "The main enemy is in our own country," thus take on their full meaning, and are applicable to every war in which soldiers are reduced to the state of passive matter manipulated by a military and bureaucratic apparatus, which means they are applicable to every war, absolutely speaking, as long as the existing technology lasts. And one cannot foresee the advent of another form of technology in our time. In production, as in war, the increasingly collective way in which the expenditure of forces takes place has not changed the essentially individual nature of the functions of decision making and management; it has only caused the hands and lives of the masses to be put increasingly at the disposal of the controlling apparatuses.

As long as we do not perceive how, in the very act of producing or fighting, it is possible to avoid this hold of the apparatuses on the masses, any attempt at revolution will have something desperate about it; for, even if we know what system of production and combat we wholeheartedly aspire to destroy, we do not know what system would be acceptable in place of it. And on the other hand, every attempt at reform appears childish in comparison with the blind necessities involved in the working of this monstrous machinery. Present-day society is like an immense machine that

17 I.e., the Weimar Republic.

continually snatches up and devours men and that no one knows how to control. Those who sacrifice themselves for social progress are like people who would hang on to the wheels and the transmission belts in an attempt to stop the machine, and who will be ground to bits in their turn. But the helplessness one feels at a given moment—a helplessness that must never be regarded as final—cannot exempt one from remaining faithful to oneself, nor excuse capitulation to the enemy, whatever mask he might assume. And, no matter what name it bears—fascism, democracy, or dictatorship of the proletariat—the principal enemy remains the administrative, police, and military apparatus; not the apparatus across the border from us, which is our enemy only to the degree that it is the enemy of our brothers, but the one that calls itself our defender and makes us its slaves. Whatever the circumstances, the worst possible treason is always to consent to subordinate oneself to this apparatus and trample underfoot, in order to serve it, all human values in oneself and others.

Fragment on Revolutionary War

[These questions] all come down to this: of what value to a revolution is war? On this point the legend of 1793 is the source of a dangerous misunderstanding that continues to this day in the entire working-class movement.

The war of 1792 was not a revolutionary war. It was not an armed defense of the French republic against the kings but, at least at the outset, it was a maneuver of the court and the Girondins intended to crush the revolution, a maneuver that Robespierre, in his magnificent speech against the declaration of war, tried in vain to head off. True, the war itself, through its own exigencies, then drove the Girondins from the government and brought in the members of the radical group known as the Mountain; nevertheless, the Girondins' maneuver, in the main, was a success. For even though Robespierre and his friends held responsible positions in the state, they could bring about neither the political democracy nor the social

This fragment, a variant of a part of the preceding essay, was written late in 1933.

changes that it had been their sole purpose to give to the French people. They could not even stand in the way of the corruption that finally brought about their deaths. In fact, through the ruthless centralization and senseless terror that the war made absolutely necessary, they only opened the way for the military dictatorship. Robespierre, with the astonishing lucidity that made him great, was aware of this, and said so, not without bitterness, in the famous speech just before his death. As for the effect of this war on other countries, it obviously contributed to the destruction of the old feudal order in some countries, but on the other hand, as soon as, through an inevitable development, it turned toward conquest, it singularly weakened the propagandistic force of France's revolutionary ideals, thus bearing out Robespierre's famous saying: "Armed missionaries are not loved." It is not without reason that Robespierre was accused of taking no pleasure in the French victories. This was the war that, to borrow Marx's words, replaced Liberty, Equality, and Fraternity with Infantry, Cavalry, and Artillery.

Furthermore, even the war against foreign intervention in Russia, a genuinely defensive war, whose participants deserve our admiration, was an insurmountable obstacle to the development of the Russian Revolution. This war imposed on a revolution that had a program calling for the abolition of the army, the police, and the permanent bureaucracy, a Red army whose officer corps was made up of czarist officers, a police force that lost no time coming down on Communists more harshly than counterrevolutionaries, and a bureaucratic apparatus unequaled in the rest of the world. These apparatuses were all a response to the necessities of the moment; but they were fated to outlast those necessities. Generally speaking, war always reinforces the central power at the expense of the people. As Saint-Just wrote, "Only those who are in the battles win them, and only those who are in power profit from them." The Paris Commune was an exception; however, it was defeated. War is inconceivable without an oppressive organization, without those in positions of command forming a separate apparatus that exercises absolute power over those who carry out orders. War in this sense—if one assumes, as Marx and Lenin did, that revolution in our time consists above all in immediately and permanently smashing the state apparatus—constitutes a counterrevolutionary factor, even when it is waged by revolutionaries in defense of the revolution they have made. All the more so, when war is carried on by an oppressive class, the consent of the oppressed to the war constitutes a complete surrender to the state apparatus that is crushing them. That is what happened in 1914; and we must recognize that Engels shares the responsibility for that shameful betrayal.

A Few More Words on the Boycott

The question of an economic boycott of Hitler's Germany has aroused considerable controversy among comrades who are all equally sincere. Some have a compelling desire to fight against the abominable Hitlerite terror; others are held back by fear of arousing nationalist passions. Both the socialist and the trade-union Internationals have passed resolutions (not yet implemented) in favor of the boycott; some of the leaders of the confederated trade-union organizations have taken a stand against those decisions. The one certain thing is that soon a year will have elapsed without the slightest gesture of international solidarity having been made against the unspeakable tortures being inflicted on the flower of the German working-class movement. This fact wrings the heart. It seems to me that, on both sides, the problem of antifascist action has been badly stated.

We must undertake, on behalf of our German comrades, some action that will come to the attention of the common masses of Germany. For one of the psychological bases of National Socialism is the bitter isolation felt by the German working masses, who are weighed down by the double burden of the economic crisis and the "Diktat" of Versailles. The full responsibility for this isolation lies with all of us in France who call ourselves internationalists and are so in words only. The only effective way we can fight against Hitler is to show the German workers that their French comrades are ready to make efforts and sacrifices for them. On the other hand, we must at all costs avoid stirring up nationalist passions, because if that were to happen antifascist action would not only become dangerous for France, it would also be useless as far as Germany is concerned; the German people would think the French workers were making a stand not against despotism but against the German nation, and were acting in con-

This fragment was written at the end of 1933 or the beginning of 1934.

cert with the French bourgeoisie and French imperialist interests. Perhaps this risk would be negligible had all of us who are active in the French working-class movement shown, before the coming of Hitler, that we were in solidarity with neither French imperialism nor the system of Versailles. Alas, we did not, and we will never be able to forgive ourselves. But the fact remains that now we must take into account the difficulties created by our own recent cowardice.

The solution lies in an action undertaken by the working class alone. There are some kinds of action in which the proletariat can benefit from joining with the liberal petty bourgeoisie; that was the case, for example, during the Dreyfus affair. But it is never the case when nationalism can come into play; for the petty bourgeois always show themselves to be rabid chauvinists, and there can be nothing more dangerous for the proletariat than nationalist passions, which always lead to some kind of Union Sacrée and play into the hands of the bourgeois state. The German workers must be helped by the French workers, and by them alone. The German workers can have nothing in common with the French petty bourgeoisie, which has always been the strongest pillar of the Versailles system and consequently bears a heavy share of the responsibility for the victory of National Socialism. Some will say that that is a matter of a purely sentimental order; but in exactly the same way the repercussions on the German working class of an anti-Hitler action coming from France would be mainly of a sentimental order, and would not be any less important because of that.

To tell the truth, a union of classes in an anti-Hitler action would be very much less risky today than a few months ago. . . .

Reply to One of Alain's Questions

I am going to respond only to the last of Alain's questions.[1] It seems to me to be extremely important, but I think it needs to be stated more broadly. Today "dignity" and "honor" are possibly the most deadly words in our

Alain had published "A List of Questions on Recent International Events" in *Vigilance*, no. 34, March 20, 1936, pp. 10–11. This essay, which was obviously intended for *Vigilance*, was never published.

1 Alain's last question was "Are the men who speak of honor and dignity as being more

vocabulary. It is quite difficult to know exactly how the French people really reacted to the recent events.[2] But I have too often observed that in every sort of milieu the appeal to dignity and honor in international affairs continues to move people. The words "peace with dignity" or "peace with honor"—those phrases of sinister memory which, when written by Poincaré,[3] were the immediate prelude to a slaughter—are still in current use. It is not certain that orators advocating peace by itself, without honor, would be favorably received anywhere. That is very serious.

The word "dignity" is ambiguous. It can mean the feeling of respect for oneself; no one will venture to deny that dignity in that sense should be put before life, for to prefer life would be "to live at the price of losing every reason for living." But self-respect depends exclusively on actions that one carries out oneself after having freely decided on them. A man who has been grossly insulted may need to fight in order to regain his sense of self-respect; this will be the case only if it is impossible for him to submit passively to the insult without being convicted of cowardice in his own eyes. It is clear that in such matters the individual concerned is the one and only judge. It is impossible to imagine that any man could delegate to someone else the task of judging whether or not he needs to risk his life in order to preserve his sense of self-respect. It is even more obvious that the defense of dignity, understood in this way, cannot be imposed by force; as soon as force comes into play, the question of self-respect is no longer involved. On the other hand, what rids one of dishonor is not vengeance but peril. For example, to kill someone who has injured you by cunning and without risk is never a means of preserving one's respect for oneself.

One must conclude that war is never a means to avoid holding oneself in contempt. It cannot be a means for noncombatants, because they have relatively little, if any, share in the danger; war can do nothing to change their own view of their personal courage. Nor can it be a means for the combatants, because they are under constraint. Most of them go into the army because they are forced to, and those who enlist voluntarily are

---

precious than life disposed to be the first to risk their lives? And if not, what should we think of them?"

2 Weil is referring to the German reoccupation of the demilitarized Rhineland that took place on March 7, 1936. France offered no resistance to this violation of the Versailles Treaty and the Locarno Pact, fearing that war would break out if French troops were sent into the zone.

3 Raymond Poincaré (1860–1934), president of the French Republic from 1913 to 1920.

forced to remain. The power of initiating and bringing an end to hostilities is exclusively in the hands of those who do not fight. The free decision to risk one's life is the very soul of honor; honor is not involved where some men make decisions without taking any risks, and others die in order to carry out their decisions. And if war cannot be a means of safeguarding anyone's honor, we must also conclude from that fact that no peace is dishonorable, whatever its terms may be.

In reality, the term "dignity," applied to international relations, does not refer to a feeling of respect for oneself, which cannot be involved; its opposite is humiliation, not self-contempt. These are two different things; there is a great deal of difference between losing respect for oneself and being treated with no respect by others. Epictetus treated like a plaything by his master and Jesus slapped and crowned with thorns were in no way diminished in their own eyes. To prefer to die rather than lose one's self-respect is the basis of any moral philosophy; to prefer to die rather than be humiliated is something altogether different; it is merely the feudal code of honor. One may admire the feudal code of honor; one may also, and with good reason, refuse to make it a rule of life. But that is not the issue. We must realize whom we are sending to die to defend this code of honor in international conflicts.

We send the common masses, those who, since they possess nothing at all, have as a general rule no right to any respect, or very nearly none. It is true that we are a republic; but that does not prevent humiliation from being in fact the daily bread of all the weak. And yet they live and let live. A man in a subordinate position submits to a contemptuous reprimand, with no power to argue back; a worker is given the gate with no explanation, and if he asks his boss for one, is told, "I don't owe you any explanation"; some unemployed workers gathered in front of a hiring office learn after waiting an hour that there is no work for them; the lady of the manor in a village orders a poor peasant about and condescends to pay him five sous for two hours' worth of trouble; a prison guard strikes and insults a prisoner; a judge in open court makes jokes at the expense of the accused or even of the victim; all these things happen, and yet blood does not flow. But all these people are in constant danger of having to kill and die some day because a foreign country fails to treat their country or its representatives with all desired respect. If they decided to begin washing away humiliation in blood on their own behalf as they are asked to do on behalf of their country, wholesale slaughter would take place every day in peacetime. Very few of those who possess power in any degree would be likely to survive; many military leaders would most certainly perish.

Now, the greatest paradox of modern life is not only that the personal dignity of those who one day will be sent to die for the dignity of the nation is trampled under foot in civilian life, but that also, at the very moment their lives are being sacrificed to safeguard the common honor, they are exposed to far more severe humiliations than they were subject to before. What are the insults regarded as grounds for war between countries compared to those that an officer can inflict on a soldier with impunity? He can insult him, and no response at all is permitted; he can kick him—hasn't a certain author of war reminiscences boasted of having done that? He can give him any order whatever at gunpoint, including the order to shoot a comrade. He can subject him to the meanest types of hazing as punishment. He can do almost anything, and any disobedience is punished by death, or can be. Those whom we in the rear hypocritically honor as heroes are actually treated as slaves. And of the soldiers who survive, those who are poor are freed from military slavery only to sink back into civilian slavery, where more than one is forced to submit to the insolence of men who have grown rich without running any risks.

Constant and almost methodical humiliation is an essential element in our social organization, in peacetime as well as in war, but in war to a higher degree. If the principle that obligates one to resist being humiliated even at the cost of one's life were applied inside the country, it would be subversive of all social order, especially of the discipline indispensable to the conduct of war. This being the case, that one dares to make that principle into a rule of international policy is really the height of unconsciousness. A famous saying has it that one may, if necessary, have slaves, but it is intolerable to treat them as citizens. It is even more intolerable to make soldiers of them. Certainly there have always been wars; but it is a characteristic of our era that the wars are fought by slaves. And what is more, these wars in which slaves are asked to die for a dignity that has never been granted them—these wars constitute the main wheel in the mechanism of oppression. Every time we closely and in a concrete manner examine ways of actually alleviating oppression and inequality, we always come up against war, the aftereffects of war, and the necessities imposed by preparation for war. We will never untangle this knot; we must cut it—that is, if we can.

Untitled Fragment on Spain

What's going on in Spain? Everyone has something to say about it, has stories to tell, is ready to pass judgment. Nowadays it's the fashion to take a little trip down there, see a bit of revolution and civil war, and come back with articles dripping from one's pen. You can't open a newspaper or a journal without finding accounts of the events in Spain. How could all that not be superficial? First of all, a social transformation cannot be correctly evaluated except in terms of what it brings to the everyday life of all those who make up the people. It's not easy to enter into that everyday life. Besides, each day brings something new. And then constraint and spontaneity, what is necessary and what is ideal, are so mixed together as to produce a hopeless confusion not only on the level of facts but even in the very consciousness of the actors and spectators of the drama. That very confusion is the essential characteristic and perhaps the greatest evil of civil war. It is also the first conclusion to be drawn from a rapid survey of the events in Spain, and what we know of the Russian Revolution confirms it only too well. It is not true that revolution automatically corresponds to a higher, more intense, and clearer consciousness of the social problem. The opposite is true, at least when revolution takes the form of civil war. In the agony of civil war, every common measure between principles and realities is lost, every sort of criterion by which one could judge acts and institutions disappears, and the transformation of society is given over to chance. How can one communicate something coherent, after a brief sojourn and a few fragmentary observations? At best, one can convey a few impressions, point out a few lessons.

Weil returned from Spain on September 25, 1936. This fragment was probably written shortly afterward.

Reflections That No One Is Going to Like

I know that what I am going to say will shock and scandalize many good comrades. But when one claims to believe in freedom, one must have the courage to say what one thinks, even if it's bound to give offense.

Day by day we all follow anxiously, with anguish, the struggle taking place on the other side of the Pyrenees. We try to help our friends. But that neither prevents nor excuses us from drawing lessons from an experience that so many workers and peasants in Spain are paying for in blood.

Europe has already undergone one experience of this sort, also paid for with a great deal of blood: the Russian experience. In Russia, Lenin publicly demanded a state in which there would be neither army, nor police, nor a bureaucracy distinct from the population. Once in power, he and his associates set about constructing, through a long and grievous civil war, the heaviest bureaucratic, military, and police machine that has ever burdened an unfortunate people.

Lenin was the leader of a political party, a machine for taking and exercising power. One may question his and his associates' good faith; one may at least think that there is a contradiction between the goals Lenin defined and the nature of a political party. But one cannot question the good faith of our anarchist comrades in Catalonia. Yet what do we see over there? Alas, there also we see forms of compulsion and instances of inhumanity that are directly contrary to the libertarian and humanitarian ideal of the anarchists. The necessities and the atmosphere of civil war are sweeping away the aspirations that we are seeking to defend by means of civil war.

Here we loathe military constraint, police constraint, compulsory labor, and the spreading of lies by the press, the radio, and all the means of communication. We loathe social differentiations, arbitrariness, cruelty.

Well, in Spain there is military constraint. In spite of the influx of volunteers, mobilization has been ordered. The defense council of the Generalitat,[1] in which our FAI[2] comrades hold some of the leading posts, has just decreed that the old military code is to be applied in the militias.

There is compulsory labor. The council of the Generalitat, where our

This fragment was probably written in October 1936.

1 The Generalitat was the autonomous regional government of Catalonia.

2 *Federacion Anarquista Iberica*, the revolutionary anarchosyndicalist organization.

comrades hold the economic ministries, has just decreed that workers must put in as much extra unpaid time as might be judged necessary. Another decree stipulates that workers whose rate of production is too slow will be considered seditious and treated as such. This quite clearly means the introduction of the death penalty in industrial production.

As for police constraint: the police had lost almost all its power before the nineteenth of July.[3] But to make up for that, during the first three months of civil war, committees of investigation, responsible militants, and, too often, irresponsible individuals carried out executions without the slightest semblance of a trial, and consequently without any possibility of syndical or other control. The popular tribunals established to try the seditious or those presumed seditious have been in existence for only a few days. It is too soon yet to know what effect this reform will have.

Nor did organized lying disappear after the nineteenth of July. . . .

3 The day the civil war broke out.

Do We Have to Grease Our Combat Boots?

We were beginning to get used to hearing some of our comrades sing the "Marseillaise," but since the outbreak of the war in Spain one hears on every side things being said that, alas, take us back twenty-two years. It would seem that this time we will be shouldering our packs for justice, liberty, and civilization, not to mention that this will be, of course, the last of all wars. It's also a matter of destroying German militarism, and defending democracy while allied with a Russia that is not a democratic state, to say the least. One might think that someone had invented a time machine. . . .

Only this time there is Spain, and there is a civil war. For some comrades, it is no longer a matter of turning international war into civil war, but civil war into international war. One even hears talk of "international civil war." It seems that by trying to avoid this widening of the war one displays shameful cowardice. A journal that claims to be Marxist has gone so far as to speak of the "policy of grovelling."[1]

Published in *Vigilance*, no. 44/45, October 27, 1936.
1 "La politique de la fesse tendue," literally, "the policy of extending one's buttock,"

What is at stake here? Proving to yourself that you're not a coward? Comrades, they're recruiting for Spain. You're free to go. They'll certainly find you some rifles there. . . . Or are you defending an ideal? Then, comrades, ask yourselves this question: Can any war bring more justice, more liberty, or more well-being into the world? Has the experiment been tried, or not? Is every generation going to repeat it? How many times?

But, some will say, it's not a matter of going to war. If we speak firmly, the fascist powers will retreat.

Singular lack of logic! It's said that fascism is war. What does that mean, if not that the fascist states will not shrink from the unspeakable disasters a war would bring about? Whereas we—we do shrink from them. Yes, we do and we will shrink from the prospect of war. But not because we are cowards. I repeat, all those who are afraid of looking like cowards in their own eyes are free to go and get themselves killed in Spain. If they went to, say, the Aragon front, they might meet some French pacifists, rifles in hand, who are still pacifists. It is not a matter of courage or cowardice; it is a matter of weighing one's responsibilities and not taking on responsibility for a disaster of incomparable magnitude.

We must make up our minds. Between a government that does not retreat in the face of war and one that does, the latter will ordinarily be at a disadvantage in international negotiations. One must choose between prestige and peace. And whether one claims to believe in the fatherland, democracy, or revolution, the policy of prestige means war. That being the case, it's about time we made up our minds either to deck Poincaré's tomb with flowers, or stop the swashbuckling. And if the misfortune of the time decrees that civil war today must become a war like any other, and must almost inevitably be tied to international war, we can draw only one conclusion: we must also avoid civil war.

Some of us, in any case, will never deck Poincaré's tomb with flowers.[2]

---

a vulgar pun on "la politique de la main tendue," usually translated as "the policy of making friendly overtures."

2 Former French Prime Minister and President Raymond Poincaré (who died in 1934) was largely responsible for the policies that led to French involvement in World War I.

The Policy of Neutrality and Mutual Assistance

The policy of neutrality with regard to Spain is generating such passionate controversy that no one notices what a tremendous precedent it is setting in matters of international policy.

On the whole, the French working class seems to have backed Léon Blum's efforts to safeguard peace.[1] But the least we can ask is that it back them only conditionally. We need to know if Blum's efforts will have the logical result that can be expected from them. And, frankly speaking, that logical result would be diametrically opposed to the Popular Front's program. The problem is: Neutrality or mutual assistance? In order to state it clearly, one must make a choice.

"Mutual Assistance" is the slogan that was so dinned into our ears by the Popular Front before, during, and after the election that it almost became an obsession. We were familiar with the slogan; we were used to hearing it from the politicians of the Right. At present it constitutes the entire doctrine of the parties of the Left. Blum's great speech at Geneva did nothing but develop it and set forth all its aspects. And yet Blum himself, not by his words but by his acts, is now proclaiming that it is unreasonable.

What happened on the other side of the Pyrenees in July? It was a clear-cut act of aggression, beyond the shadow of a doubt. Of course, it was not one nation that attacked another; it was a military caste that attacked a great people. But we are all the more interested in the outcome of the conflict. The liberties of the French people are closely tied to the liberties of the Spanish people. If the doctrine of mutual assistance were reasonable, if there was ever an occasion to intervene by armed force, to rush to the aid of the victims of aggression, it would have been then.

We did not do so, for fear of setting all Europe ablaze. We proclaimed neutrality. We put an embargo on weapons. We are allowing our beloved comrades to risk their lives unaided for a cause that is ours as well as theirs. We are allowing them to fall, armed only with rifles or grenades, because

---

This essay, unpublished during Weil's lifetime, was written after October 1936.

1 Léon Blum (1872–1950) was the leader of France's Popular Front government, a coalition of parties of the Left that was elected in May 1936. Spain also had a Popular Front government, and the policy of the Popular Front was mutual assistance. After the outbreak of the Spanish civil war, however, Blum reluctantly proclaimed a policy of neutrality toward Spain, fearing that French assistance might lead to European war.

they must use their living flesh as a substitute for the big guns they lack. We are doing all that to avoid a European war.

But if we have, with anguished hearts, agreed to such a situation, let no one later dare send us to war when it is a matter of a conflict between nations. What we have not done for our beloved comrades in Spain we will not do for Czechoslovakia, for Russia, or for any state. Faced with the conflict that is the most sharply painful for us, we let the government proclaim neutrality. So it should not dare speak to us about mutual assistance later on. Faced with any conflict, of whatever nature, that might erupt on the surface of the globe, it will be our turn to cry out with all our strength: Neutrality! Neutrality! We will not be able to forgive ourselves for having accepted neutrality in regard to the Spanish slaughter unless we make every effort to transform this position into a precedent that will govern all French foreign policy in the future.

Could we do otherwise? We are almost passively watching the finest blood of the Spanish people being shed, and yet we would go to war over any central European state! We are exposing a brand new revolution in the flush of youth, brimming over with vitality and possessing an unlimited future, to defeat and extermination, and we would go to war for that corpse of revolution called the USSR!

The present policy of neutrality would constitute the worst sort of treason on the part of the French working-class organizations if it were not aimed at the prevention of war in general. And it cannot effectively prevent war unless it is broadened, unless the principle of neutrality wholly replaces the murderous policy of mutual assistance. We have no business backing Léon Blum except under this condition.

Broadening the Policy of Nonintervention

Ever since the policy of nonintervention was first put into practice, one concern has weighed heavily on my heart. A great many other people must also share it.

I do not intend to join in the violent attacks, some of which are honestly

This essay, unpublished during Weil's lifetime, was written after October 1936.

meant, though the majority are treacherous, that have rained down upon our comrade Léon Blum. I recognize the necessities that make him act as he has. I admire the moral courage that enabled him to submit to them, harsh and bitter as they are, despite all the harangues. Even when I was in Aragon or Catalonia, in the middle of an atmosphere of combat and among militants who had no term harsh enough for Blum's policy, I supported that policy. As far as I personally am concerned, I refuse to deliberately sacrifice peace, even when it is a question of saving a revolutionary people threatened with destruction.

But in almost every speech our comrade Léon Blum has made since the Spanish war began, I have found, side by side with profoundly moving formulations about war and peace, other formulations that have a disquieting ring. I waited anxiously for responsible militants to react, to debate, to ask certain questions. I find that the atmosphere of confusion inside the Popular Front is reducing many comrades to silence, or to expressing their thoughts in a veiled way.

Léon Blum misses no opportunity, right in the middle of the most moving formulations, to say in substance this: We want peace; we will preserve it at any cost, unless an attack on our territory or the territories protected by us forces us to go to war.

In other words, we will not wage war to prevent Spanish workers and peasants from being wiped out by a clique of savages more or less decked out in gold braid. But if the occasion arises, we will wage war for Alsace-Lorraine, for Morocco, for Russia, for Czechoslovakia, and, if some Tardieu had signed a treaty with Honolulu, we would wage war for Honolulu.

Because of my sympathy for Léon Blum, and especially in the light of the threats that hang over our whole future, I would give a great deal to be able to interpret the formulations I have in mind differently. But no other interpretation is possible. Blum's words are only too clear.

Do the militants of the CGT[1] and the organizations on the Left accept this position? Do our country's workers and peasants accept it? I don't know. Every individual must answer for himself. As far as I am concerned, I do not accept it.

The workers and peasants on the other side of the Pyrenees who are fighting to defend their lives and their liberty, fighting to lift the weight of

---

1 *Confédération générale du Travail*, the reformist-dominated trade-union organization.

the social oppression that has crushed them for so long, fighting to take their destiny in hand, are not tied to France by any written treaty. But all of us—the CGT, the Socialist party, the working class—feel tied to them by an unwritten pact of brotherhood, by ties of flesh and blood stronger than any treaty. Compared to this unanimously felt brotherhood, of what importance are the signatures of the Poincarés, the Tardieus, the Lavals on papers that have never been submitted for our approval? If ever it were possible to justify the sum of suffering, blood, and tears that war represents, it would be when a people is struggling and dying for a cause that it wants to defend, not on account of a scrap of paper that it never had anything to do with.

No doubt Léon Blum shares the feelings of the working masses on the Spanish question. It is said that when he spoke of Spain before the leaders of the socialist federations he wept. Quite probably, if he were in the opposition he would support the slogan "Guns for Spain." What checked his natural inclination toward solidarity is a feeling tied to the possession of power: the feeling of responsibility a man has when he holds the fate of a nation in his hands, and sees himself on the verge of plunging it into a war. But if a Czechoslovakia were at stake, instead of some Spanish workers and peasants, would he be gripped by the same feeling of responsibility? Or would a certain legalistic mentality make him think that in such a case a piece of paper bears all the responsibility? This question is a matter of life and death for every one of us.

Collective security is part of the Popular Front's program. In my opinion, the Communists are right when they accuse Léon Blum of abandoning the Popular Front's program in the matter of Spain. It's true that the treaties and other documents relating to collective security do not provide for anything resembling the Spanish conflict, but that's because no one ever anticipated anything like it. But the facts are plain enough. There was an act of aggression, a clear-cut act of military aggression, although in the form of civil war. Foreign countries have supported this aggression. It would seem normal to extend the principle of collective security to such a case, to intervene militarily in order to crush the forces guilty of aggression. Instead of taking this course, Léon Blum tried to limit the conflict. Why? Because intervention, instead of restoring order in Spain, would have set all Europe ablaze. But this is how it always has been and always will be every time a local war raises the question of collective security. I defy anyone, including Léon Blum, to explain why the reasons that deter us from intervening in Spain would be less compelling if it was a question of Czechoslovakia's being invaded by the Germans.

Many people have asked Léon Blum to "reconsider" his policy in regard to Spain. There is much to be said for their position. But if one does accept nonintervention, then, in order to be consistent, one must ask both Blum and the working masses to "reconsider" the principle of collective security. If nonintervention in Spain is a reasonable policy, collective security is unreasonable, and vice versa.

The day Léon Blum decided not to intervene in Spain, he took on a heavy responsibility. On that day he decided, if it became necessary, to go as far as to abandon our Spanish comrades to mass destruction. All of us who have supported him share this responsibility. Very well then, if we are willing to sacrifice the miners of Asturias,[2] the starving peasants of Aragon and Castile, and the anarchist workers of Barcelona rather than ignite a world war, nothing else in the world should lead us to ignite the war. Nothing, neither Alsace-Lorraine, nor the colonies, nor treaties. It must not be said that anything in the world is more precious to us than the life of the Spanish people. Otherwise, if we abandon them, if we allow them to be massacred, and if afterward we waged war anyway for another cause, how could we justify ourselves?

Are we going to decide to look these problems squarely in the face, or not? Are we going to pose the problem of war and peace in its entirety? If we continue to evade the problem, deliberately shut our eyes, and repeat slogans that solve nothing, then let the global catastrophe come. We will all have deserved it for our spiritual cowardice.

2 A province in northern Spain in which the labor movement was particularly strong. Asturias was famous for a working-class revolt that took place between October 5–18, 1934. The revolt, which began in the heart of the mining district, involved 30,000 armed workers. The rebels occupied most of the towns of the province until the government brought in troops from Morocco to put down the insurrection.

A European War over Czechoslovakia?

Many people make the mistake of not squarely facing what they will be confronted with if the problem of Czechoslovakia takes the most acute form. In order not to succumb to panic, we need to draw up, as lucidly as we can, a course of action for the worst as well as for the best cases. What follows relates to the worst case: that is, if Hitler, for reasons of domestic and foreign policy, should determine to gain a striking and decisive success in central Europe.

Every international question can be considered from four points of view, which are, moreover, often related: the question of rights as such; the balance of power; France's treaty commitments; and the chances of war and peace. From none of these points of view does the preservation of the Czechoslovakian state as it presently exists seem to have the importance that is attributed to it.

FROM THE POINT of view of rights, Czechoslovakia certainly has received some pieces of German territory, and it seems incontestable that the German population in them is being persecuted to some extent. To what extent is debatable. It is difficult to make these scattered territories into a separate province enjoying full autonomy within the framework of the Czechoslovakian state; on the other hand, since they form a fringe along the edges of the German border and what used to be the Austrian border, it seems easy for a newly expanded Germany to purely and simply annex them through a process of border rectification.

One may wonder if Germany intends to seize Czech territories as well. In all likelihood, a rectification of borders would satisfy Germany, especially if France and England simultaneously approached Berlin and Prague, agreeing to such a rectification and prohibiting any more ambitious undertaking. For, in the first place, Hitler has always declared that, in Europe, he wants the German territories and nothing else. What's more, the territories with German populations contain a good part of the industrial resources of Czechoslovakia on the one hand, and the mountain ranges that protect the country on the other. The annexation of these territories by Germany would put Czechoslovakia at its mercy; Germany would have no need to attack Czechoslovakian independence in order to

Published in *Feuilles libres de la quinzaine*, no. 58, May 25, 1938.

achieve all its diplomatic, economic, and military objectives. A kind of protectorate would suit Hitler's general policy much better than annexation of the Czech territory. Further, it is probable that a simple change of diplomatic orientation on Czechoslovakia's part would suffice to eliminate the whole minority problem. To Hitler the main thing is that Czechoslovakia, regardless of whether or not it is dismembered, become a satellite state of Germany.

What disadvantages would there be in this situation? It is possible to think that making Czechoslovakia so dependent on Germany would be something of an injustice. Probably it is. But on the other hand the status quo is unjust to the Sudeten Germans, which simply proves that the right of peoples to self-determination comes up against an obstacle in the nature of things, from the fact that the three maps of Europe—geographic, economic, and ethnographic—do not coincide.

Czechoslovakia may very well become—either as a result of being weakened by the excision of its German territories, or in order to avoid such an excision—a satellite of Germany without having to sacrifice its culture, its language, or its national characteristics, and that limits the injustice. National Socialist ideology is simply racist; its only universal content is its anticommunism and antisemitism. The Czechs can ban the Communist party and exclude Jews from all relatively important positions without losing anything of their national life. In short, injustice for injustice—since there must be some form of injustice in any case—let us choose the one that has the least risk of leading to war.

Besides, even if the injustice were greater, isn't there a bitter irony in France's buckling on her armor as a redresser of wrongs? By preventing the Anschluss for twenty years, France herself, in the most flagrant manner, interfered with the famous right of peoples to self-determination. And God knows that in Africa and Asia there is no shortage of peoples for France to emancipate without running the risk of war, if it is the rights of peoples that interest her.

It is true that satisfying Germany's demands in Czechoslovakia would cause all central Europe to fall under German influence. This brings us to another point of view, that of the balance of power. Rights no longer have anything to do with it.

IT IS POSSIBLE that Hitler's efforts are directed toward one goal: the establishment of German hegemony in Europe, by war if necessary, without war if possible. Traditionally, France allows no hegemony in Europe except, when she can establish it, her own. Today a kind of unstable balance exists between the victorious France of twenty years ago and a Germany, if one may say so, in the bloom of convalescence. Is it necessary to try to maintain this balance? To reestablish French hegemony?

It is obvious, if one thinks about it, that the great principle of "the balance of power in Europe" is a principle that leads to war. Because of this principle, a country feels deprived of security and placed in an intolerable situation as soon as it is the weaker in relation to a possible adversary. Now, since no scale exists for measuring the strength of states, a country or bloc of countries has only one means of not being the weaker; it is to be the stronger. When two countries or two blocs both feel an imperative need to be the stronger, one can confidently predict war.

If one country must dominate the center of Europe, it is in the nature of things that it will be Germany. Force is on Germany's side. In 1918 Germany was just barely defeated, and by a powerful coalition. Besides, why is the possibility of German hegemony worse than French hegemony? True, Germany is "totalitarian." But political regimes are unstable; of France and Germany thirty years hence who can say which will be a dictatorship and which a democracy? Right now German hegemony would be stifling. But could it be more stifling, I'm not saying than a war, but more than the present peace, with the maddening nervous tension, the siege mentality, and the material and moral impoverishment to which we are increasingly subjected? Assuming that France still possesses a culture, traditions, a spirit that is uniquely hers, and a liberal ideal, her spiritual radiance might be much greater if she were to hand central Europe over to German influence than if she were to persist in struggling against an almost inevitable development. Besides, in the long run hegemony always weakens the country that has achieved it. But until now, both the acquisition of hegemony and the weakening that follows from it have always, if I am not mistaken, been brought about by wars. If this time the same process could take place without war, wouldn't that be real progress?

FRANCE'S TREATY OBLIGATIONS in regard to Czechoslovakia are the subject of a great deal of debate. But even a formal promise does not constitute, in international matters, sufficient grounds for action. Statesmen of all countries know this, although they don't let on that they do. Even if they didn't know it, can we allow a whole young generation to die for a treaty it did not ratify? The League of Nations treaty constitutes a formal obligation, yet virtually no action was ever taken on the basis of it, and it was tacitly recognized as nul every time special clauses were added. A little over a quarter of a century ago France violated a signed treaty when she seized Morocco, thereby risking a European war; she could certainly do just as much today in order to avoid a war. True, her prestige would then be destroyed in the eyes of the small countries, and, since the time of Talleyrand, France has traditionally depended on them for support. This policy is an application of the theory of the balance of power in Europe; France tries to use the small nations to compensate for her own inferiority. At the same time she gives herself a sort of halo of idealism—entirely un-deserved, for what atrocious woes did the carving up of central Europe twenty years ago not create! In any event, no policy ever met with more bitter failure, since it was "little Serbia" that precipitated the European slaughter whose consequences are still weighing on us. When one thinks about it, that seems to have been a necessary result, not an accident. The small countries are irresistibly tempting to the will to power, whether it takes the form of conquest or, what is preferable from all points of view, the creation of zones of influence. It is natural for small countries caught between two great nations to fall under the more or less veiled domination of the more powerful one, and if the other tries to stand in the way of this, recourse to arms is almost inevitable.

THAT IS THE central issue. Will the chances for peace be improved if France and England—assuming they agree—once more solemnly guaran-tee the territorial integrity of Czechoslovakia, or if they resign themselves, with suitable formalities, to hand it over to its fate? It is said that in the first instance, Hitler would retreat. Perhaps. But it is a terrible chance to take. He is swept along, in what he does, by a double dynamism—his own, and the dynamism he has been able to communicate to his people, which he must keep at the temperature of incandescent iron in order to preserve his power. It is true that until now he never exposed himself to the risk of war; but until now he never needed to. One can by no means conclude that he is determined to always avoid that risk. It is said that it would be madness on his part to risk a general war to attack Czechoslovakia; yes, but it would be just as much madness on the part of France and England to run the same risk to defend it. If they decide to take that risk, why shouldn't he? It seems more and more clear-cut that a firm position on the Czechoslovakian ques-tion, even if it were joined to proposals for general negotiation, would not ease present tensions in Europe. On the material level, negotiations, compromises, and economic arrangements would be highly advantageous for Germany, even necessary; but from the point of view of public opinion—and nonmaterial considerations are by far the most important for a dictatorship like Hitler's—he doesn't need any of those things. What he needs is to make periodic and brutal assertions of the existence and strength of his country. It is not very likely that he can be kept from doing this other than by force of arms.

If it were only a matter of using a bluff to make him retreat, who would not be for it? But if, as at least is possible, actual military action is going to be involved, I wonder how many mobilizable young men, how many fathers, mothers, and wives of mobilizable men one would find who consider it reasonable and just that French blood should be shed for Czechoslovakia. Few, I believe, if any at all. A war caused by events in central Europe would be a new confirmation of the sarcastic but powerful words Mussolini wrote in his preface to Machiavelli:

> Even in countries where the mechanisms (of democracy) date from a century-old tradition, there comes a solemn hour when one no longer asks the people anything, because one knows the response would be disastrous. One lifts from their head the cardboard crown of sovereignty, fit for normal times, and simply and solely orders them to accept revolution, or peace, or to march toward the unknown of war. The people are left with nothing but a monosyllable with which to consent and obey. We see that the sovereignty generously accorded the people is withdrawn from them precisely at the times that they might feel the need of it. . . . Can one imagine a war being declared by referendum?
>
> A referendum is a very good thing if it is a matter of choosing the most suitable site for the village fountain, but when the most important interests of a people are at stake, even ultrademocratic governments take great care not to entrust those interests to the judgment of the people themselves. . . .

To return to Czechoslovakia, there are only two clear and defensible choices: either France and England declare that they will go to war to maintain Czechoslovakia's integrity, or they openly agree to a transformation of the Czechoslovakian state that would satisfy the main German aims. Apart from these two choices, there can be only terrible humiliations, or war, or probably both. It's obvious to me that the second choice is infinitely preferable. One whole sector of English public opinion—and not only the Right—is ready to welcome such a solution.

Reflections on Bouché's Lecture

In order to make my own comments on Bouché's lecture, I am adopting the same position he chose, that is, taking the idea of a strengthened national defense as a hypothetical point of departure. At the present time nonviolence is perfectly defensible as an individual position, but as the policy of a government it is unthinkable.

The present system of national defense, as Bouché admirably showed, leaves room for appalling disasters in the near future, almost limitless risks, and scarcely any hope. So any less oppressive system involving less risk and more hope must be preferable. No plan for a new system can be asked to eliminate the possibility of France losing her independence; indeed, the present system, no matter how far one extends it, does not eliminate that, since a crushing defeat is always possible, and perhaps even probable.

France is a long way from being the most powerful country in Europe. So she must give up trying to shape Europe's future, even the near future, according to her views or traditions. For her, national defense must be the defense of her territory against invasion, not the defense of a system of treaties and pacts drawn up by her at a time when she could believe herself the most powerful country.

Defense against invasion seems, on reflection, to be more a matter of diplomacy than military force. Except for colonial campaigns, the wars of the past few centuries, if I am not mistaken, never had the annexation of a foreign territory as an aim or immediate pretext, although they sometimes had that result. They were always caused by disagreements over the preservation or conquest of some particular diplomatic position. France can avoid being caught in this sort of dispute by a reasonable and moderate diplomatic policy.

Such a policy must, however, be defended by a military system that would prevent an invasion of France from looking to both Frenchmen and foreigners like a colonial campaign. But since this military system would

Henri Bouché, one of Alain's former students, gave a lecture on March 28, 1938, on "The French Problem of National Defense." Weil's response remained unpublished during her lifetime.

be merely an auxiliary arm of a diplomatic policy designed to safeguard peace for France, the problem is not how to assure the defeat of the enemy in case of invasion; rather, it is how to make a potential invasion difficult enough that the idea of such an invasion does not constitute a temptation to neighboring states.

Solving this problem would not give us absolute security, but we would be more secure than under our present system, even if we were to have twice as many airplanes and tanks.

This new formulation of the problem of security would involve a complete transformation of military procedure, which henceforth, from the technical point of view, would have to constitute a sort of compromise between the methods of war and those of insurrection. As a method of civil defense against air attack, Bouché recommends decentralization; it seems to me that one could enlarge this idea and extend it to the whole conception of national defense. Political, economic, and social life in France could be decentralized, dense centers of population dispersed, and city and country life joined together. Possible armed resistance could be decentralized as well, always keeping in mind that in the natural course of things there might be no need for it. Assuming some degree of decentralization to have been achieved, it seems to me that modern technique, especially because of the speed of communications, makes a particular form of resistance possible that would more closely resemble guerrilla warfare than regular war. Don't establish fronts or besiege cities; harass the enemy, block his communications, always attack him where he least expects it, demoralize him, and stimulate resistance by a series of small but victorious actions. If, especially at the beginning, the Spanish Republicans had used such a method— they never tried it—they might not be in the deplorable state we see them in now. But, once more, the real purpose of such a system is not to force an enemy who has entered our territory to leave it; it is to give food for thought to those who could be tempted by the idea of armed invasion.

Such a conception of defense presupposes real public spiritedness and a keen awareness of the benefits of liberty in all the French people. We are not at that point yet. At present the Russian, Italian, or German dictatorships exercise an enormous amount of prestige over a considerable part of the population, beginning with workers and intellectuals, the traditional mainstays of democracy. The peasants have still not found a way of making their opinion heard in the country. The urban big and petty bourgeoisie is absorbed by narrow interests or given over to fanaticism and can scarcely be counted on for any form of civic enthusiasm. Can the idealistic and liberal spirit that is traditionally attributed to France come to life again? There is room for doubt. But if it does not, if freedom is to perish slowly in men's souls even before it is destroyed in its political form, national defense loses any real point. For it is not the defense of a word or a patch of color on the map that can be worth sacrifices, but a certain spirit attached to a particular human milieu. In the absence of such a spirit France is in danger—and we are already seeing signs of it—of falling victim to a foreign power without an invasion.

All that is in reference only to France. But as soon as the French empire is taken into consideration, the problem becomes altogether different. Bouché barely touched on this aspect of the question, probably for lack of time. It seems obvious that the French empire in its present form requires that France preserve and develop offensive armaments, and that the present military system be maintained; there are far too few French settlers for a defensive system, and the indigenous populations would rightly have little inclination for it. It seems no less obvious, given the balance of power, that if the present form of the French empire is maintained, France is almost certain to lose all or part of her colonies some day, with or without a world war. It would be infinitely preferable if it were without a war, but even without a war such a thing is not desirable from any point of view.

For the defensive method advocated by Bouché to be applied, the French empire would, as a first and essential condition, have to evolve very rapidly in the direction taken by the British empire; that is, the majority of our colonies would very quickly have to be given considerable independence, enough to satisfy them. For such a change to be carried out smoothly, preparations for it would have to be made well in advance; inasmuch as France, in her blindness, has not made preparations for it, it will not happen smoothly. But it is urgent that it be done. The French colonies are tempting spoils and a constant cause of immediate danger in the world as long as the indigenous populations have no form of national defense, and national defense presupposes a nation.

In short, the conception of national defense put forward by Bouché presupposes liberty; it is suitable only for citizens. Not only does it demand that French citizens have civic feeling and actually possess the rights of citizens, but, above all, it can be only an idle dream as long as all the territories under the authority of the French state contain more slaves than citizens. Therefore the choice now before us is to make citizens of these slaves, or to become slaves ourselves.

The Distress of Our Time

Our era is not the first in history in which the dominant feeling is distress, anxiety, a sense of waiting for one knows not what, nor the first in which men feel they have the painful privilege of being a generation destined for an exceptional fate. Since history is past and exists only on paper, it is easy to entertain the illusion that all previous periods were peaceful compared to the one in which we are now living, just as twenty-year-old adolescents always feel they are the first to have ever experienced the anxieties of youth. Nevertheless, one can say with no fear of exaggeration that the part of humanity in our little corner of Europe that has ruled the world for so long is going through a profound and serious crisis. The great hopes inherited from the three preceding centuries, especially from the last—hopes of a progressive spread of enlightenment, of general well-being, of democracy, of peace—are rapidly crumbling. That would not be so serious if it were simply a matter of a disillusionment affecting certain intellectual circles, or certain spheres particularly taken up with political and social problems. But the conditions under which we live are such that the distress touches and taints every aspect of men's lives, every source of action, hope, and happiness. Private life, in its daily course, is less and less separated from public life, and this is the case in every sphere. There have previously been times in history when great collective outbursts temporarily reduced private life to insignificance; today, however, it is the enduring conditions of our existence that prevent us from finding in daily life any moral resources that are independent of the political and social situation.

Our feeling of security is profoundly affected. That, however, is not something absolutely bad; there can be no security for man on this earth,

This short text, probably written during 1938, was not published until after Weil's death.

and the feeling of security, beyond a certain degree, is a dangerous illusion that falsifies everything, that makes' minds narrow, limited, superficial, and stupidly satisfied; we saw quite a lot of that during the so-called period of prosperity, and we still see it in a few—increasingly rare—sectors of society in which people feel protected. But the total absence of security, especially when the catastrophes to be feared are incommensurable with the resources that intelligence, action, and courage might be able to provide, is no more favorable to the health of the soul. We saw an economic crisis in several large countries deprive a whole young generation of any hope of ever being able to enter into the social structure, earn a living, and maintain a family. We have a good chance of shortly seeing a new generation in the same impasse. We saw and we continue to see conditions of production that bring on old age—and an old age with no means of support—at forty for people in some social categories. The fear of war—a war in which nothing would be left intact—has stopped being a subject of lectures or pamphlets and has become a general preoccupation; it is increasingly becoming a daily preoccupation as civilian life is everywhere subordinated to military preparation. Modern means of communication—the press, the radio, the cinema—are powerful enough today to rattle the nerves of an entire nation. Of course, life always defends itself, protected by instinct and a certain layer of unconsciousness; nevertheless, the fear of great collective catastrophes, awaited as passively as tidal waves or earthquakes, increasingly colors the way each man sees his personal future.

Fragment Written after September 1938

These last few months in France have seen signs of a profound change in the way people are thinking. Its consequences cannot as yet be foreseen, but the process itself is well worth our attention. Men who only a short while ago were democrats, socialists, syndicalists—some well known and in positions of authority, others obscure and powerless—are fairly clearly showing that they are not far from wishing that France had a totalitarian dictatorship like the one that is enabling Germany to triumph in Europe. Perhaps some of them do more than wish it; perhaps they are already thinking of paving the way for it. And if Russia were a stronger ally, we would probably see everyone that we call bourgeois make a corresponding shift from horror to love of Russia, as we know some of them have already done. Italy suddenly lost the esteem of those who not so very long ago were praising the regime almost to the point of adoration. It seems incredible that barely two years ago it was hard to imagine a war in which France would not be split into two camps, both of which would put doctrine ahead of country. So intense were the passions that some people harbored for Russia and Republican Spain, and others for Italy and even Germany, that one could think, in a mobilized country, they would blot out the concern for defending the country. In two years what changes have taken place! Today almost the only thought in anyone's mind is "the Nation." Those who are still attached to other ideas are forcing themselves to hold on to them, and even so, their attachment to them is less firm than they think.

Thus, among those who don't resist, all other ideas—whether of preserving and increasing the leisure, well-being, and liberty of the people at the expense of privilege, or of preserving privileges and the pride that goes with them—vanish in the face of the desire to aggrandize the nation. Which is not to say that the slightest degree of public spiritedness enters into it. It goes without saying that people are still making money in the aircraft industries, to the detriment of the state, just as they did before; some make millions; others, modestly, hundreds or tens of thousands of francs. But that's not a way of thinking; it's a practice. Likewise, the aircraft workers, on their necessarily much lower level, do not, however much they hate the Munich policy, want to work sixty hours a week or be paid meager wages. It is not interests that one sacrifices to the nation; it is rare to sacrifice any interests unless some kind of force helps one to do so. What one sacrifices are the ideas in the name of which one defended one's interests and which ennobled them by giving them a universal significance. However, the sacrifice of ideas after a while leads to the sacrifice of interests, for it involves submission to the force that will wipe them out.

Those who approve of the Munich policy[1] usually scoff when their opponents speak of humiliation. They are wrong to do this. There really was,

---

1 The Munich agreement, signed by France, England, Germany, and Italy on September 30, 1938, ceded the Sudetenland (the western areas of Czechoslovakia in which the majority of the population was German-speaking) to Germany.

in September, a widespread feeling of humiliation in France; what can be better proof of it than the kind of stupor—the normal response to a recent humiliation—into which we have all been plunged since then? But it is quite correct to say that it is not a matter of national humiliation. We were humiliated much more deeply than in our attachment to national prestige; we all suffered in our innermost selves what is, in truth, the essence of any kind of humiliation: the abasement of thought before the power of a fact. To try to find the person that one still was yesterday and not be able to, not because one has been renewed through some mental or physical effort, but because between yesterday and today, without one's having willed it, some external event happened—that is what it means to be humiliated. When the event in question is due solely to the action of inert matter—a flood, an earthquake, an illness—one finds in oneself the means to pull oneself together. When what happens is due to a human action, one cannot get over it. One realizes that men have the power, if they so desire, to tear our thoughts away from the objects to which we used to apply them, and force on us, totally and unremittingly, some obsession that is not of our own choosing. Such and nothing less is the power of a fact. It dominates all our thoughts, and when it does not change their content, it changes their coloration.

So what happened to us in September?[2] It's very simple; we saw the war as a fact, although it has not yet happened. And at the same time, though we still had peace, it no longer seemed to be a fact. During those few weeks some people expected one outcome, others another, and within the same person expectations changed several times a day. But I do not believe there

2 The Munich crisis began on September 15, when Hitler demanded self-determination for the Sudeten Germans and threatened to attack Czechoslovakia if Britain, France, and Czechoslovakia did not accept his demand. Under pressure from Britain and France, who feared that a Czech refusal would result in war, the Czechs agreed. Informed of this on September 22, Hitler then demanded that the Czechs evacuate the Sudeten areas so that a German military occupation could begin on October 1, and threatened to attack Czechoslovakia if his ultimatum were not accepted by 2 P.M. September 28. Czechoslovakia mobilized on the twenty-third, and France began a partial mobilization on the twenty-fourth. On September 25 Czechoslovakia refused the ultimatum, and both Britain and France said they would support their treaty obligations if Czechoslovakia were attacked. War seemed inevitable. On the morning of September 28, only a few hours before the ultimatum was due to expire, Hitler accepted Mussolini's proposal to invite the Four Powers to meet at Munich the next day to try to resolve the Czechoslovakian problem. Britain and France accepted Hitler's demands and forced Czechoslovakia, which was not represented at the meeting, to accept by saying that if she persisted in her refusal she would have to face Hitler's attack alone.

is anyone who did not at some time feel the presence of war. And now, although peace still exists, and perhaps, if fate wills, may still last for a long time, we scarcely feel the presence of peace. So, even though we still talk about war and peace as we did before, and some people endeavor to say the same things about them as they said before, it is no longer the same war or the same peace. The idea of war that we once had, which seemed preposterous even when we said it was inevitable, more closely resembles peace than what we think of when we speak of peace today, now that we have had a real brush with war. Is it any wonder that the word "nation," so long relegated to the cold and indifferent terminology of official vocabulary, today contains an inexhaustible wealth of unanswerable arguments, and that the name of France constantly recurs beneath one's pen and on one's lips? A country becomes a nation when it takes up arms against another or prepares to do so. Is it any wonder that we tend to imagine our country's future as an entrenched camp, with no leisure or liberty, and with death or torture as punishment for deserters? All of us, either before or after 1914, have read in history books or old chronicles frightful accounts that we knew were true, but that even so we could not take for anything but stories. We were wrong, of course, because those atrocities had in fact occurred. Without having yet reached it, today we are moving toward a condition in which respect for human life and liberty, concern for justice and humanity, and the desire to increase leisure, well-being, enlightenment, and every kind of enjoyment among the mass of the people will, in their turn, seem like fairy tales to us. We will be just as wrong, and we will be wrong in the same way.

Is it any wonder that a syndicalist, for example, does not give up calling himself one, but abandons the ideal that syndicalism stood for and that he once professed, in order to apply his thoughts exclusively to defending the nation and building up the totalitarian state? It's as if one were amazed to find that a man, after having suffered an injury, hates the person who injured him, although he did not hate him before; or becomes frightened in the face of a danger that he defied when he was only anticipating it. Certainly, virtue consists in feeling no more hatred after an injury than before, and no more anxiety prior to a danger than when facing it. But virtue is difficult and rare. Today, in regard to affairs of state, virtue requires not that one think about the same things as before, but that one keep in mind everything that one thought about before. Reason, which is the same thing as virtue, consists in keeping alive in one's mind, in addition to the present, a past and a future that bear no resemblance to it.

Fragment Written after September 1939

In order to hold out through all the forms that time may give to this struggle in which the only two major European countries that have remained democratic are matched against a totalitarian regime, we need first of all to have a clear conscience. Let us not think that because we are less brutal, less violent, less inhuman than our opponents we will carry the day. Brutality, violence, and inhumanity have an immense prestige that schoolbooks hide from children, that grown men do not admit, but that everyone bows before. For the opposite virtues to have as much prestige, they must be actively and constantly put into practice. Anyone who is merely incapable of being as brutal, as violent, and as inhuman as someone else, but who does not practice the opposite virtues, is inferior to that person in both inner strength and prestige, and he will not hold out in a confrontation.

Certainly, from a national standpoint, almost all Frenchmen have clear consciences. But there are several ways of having a clear conscience. A contented bourgeois who is ignorant of the realities of life has a very clear conscience; a just man has a clear conscience in a quite different way. Generally, his conscience is less clear, but he has a radiance and a power of attraction that the former lacks. Almost all Frenchmen are convinced that, in a general way, what France has done, is doing, and will do, apart from a few rare and unimportant exceptions, is just and good. But this conviction is theoretical, for it is almost always accompanied by a great deal of ignorance; it does not constitute an inner source of energy. Likewise, foreigners associate France's name with the great humanitarian ideals and the principle of justice so often invoked by her, but this association is hardly more than a habit, a commonplace, and it does not generate an irresistible power of attraction, as we need it to. Anyone who in recent years stepped from the territory of a totalitarian country onto French soil found himself suddenly able to breathe, whereas before he had been suffocating.

But one could still not say that the atmosphere in our country is really impregnated and charged with the ideal in whose name we are fighting. In order to fight well it is not enough to defend an absence of tyranny. We must be rooted in a milieu in which every activity is really oriented in the opposite direction from tyranny. Our domestic propaganda cannot be made of words; to be effective, it must consist of dazzling realities.

Fragment Written after June 1940

You don't need a tank or an airplane to kill a man. A kitchen knife is enough. If those who have had their fill of the Nazi executioners all rise up together, at the same time that the armed forces strike the decisive blow, deliverance will be swift. But in the meantime we must both refrain from squandering human lives needlessly and keep from falling into inertia, believing that the liberation will be carried out by others. Each of us must know that one day it will be his duty to take part in it, and hold himself in readiness.

This period of painful waiting is of the utmost importance for the destiny of France. France's future will have been forged by these years of apparent passivity.

We must focus our thoughts, beyond each day's personal sorrows, on the immense drama that is being played out in the world; we must prevent suffering from causing disunity among Frenchmen through ill humor, jealousy, or shabby efforts to have a little more than one's neighbor. On the contrary, we must turn suffering into an indissoluble bond through generosity and mutual aid. We must think of the precious things we allowed to be lost because we did not know how to appreciate them, things that we have to regain and that we will have to preserve, things whose value we now know. . . .

■ *Philosophy*

Introduction

Following the German occupation of Paris in June 1940, Weil and her parents fled to the south of France, finally settling in Marseilles, where they remained until May 1942. As is reflected in the notebooks she kept during the approximately twenty months of her sojourn in Marseilles, she spent this time musing deeply on a wide variety of subjects, among them science, art, folklore, and religion. In the spring of 1941 she devoted considerable thought to science, returning to terrain she had worked in "Science and Perception in Descartes," but seeing it from a considerably different perspective. In 1929–30 she had criticized modern science for its elitism, its devaluation of ordinary perception and ordinary thinking, its tendency to separate itself from the world and to pursue purely abstract systems of relationships; she had proposed a conception of science that would make it an instrument by means of which all human beings could discover for themselves indubitable knowledge of the world and thereby come to "possess"—master, be able to act on—the material world. By 1941, however, she was no longer satisfied with the conception of the world as mechanical necessity that underlay both the view of science she had criticized and the one she had proposed. "It is true," she wrote in "Classical Science and After," a long essay composed in the spring of 1941, "that the matter which constitutes the world is a tissue of blind necessities . . . ; it is true, too, in a sense, that they are absolutely indifferent to spiritual aspirations, indifferent to the good; but also, in another sense, it is not true. . . . We are ruled by a double law: an obvious indifference and a mysterious complicity, as regards the good, on the part of the matter which composes the world; it is because it reminds us of this double law that the spectacle of beauty pierces the heart."[1]

Weil found in the science of ancient Greece the combination of mathematical rigor and metaphor that corresponded to this "double law." In the

1 *On Science, Necessity, and the Love of God* (London: Oxford University Press, 1968), p. 12.

large place given to the study of proportion in Greek geometry she saw both the desire to arrive at an exact mathematical expression of the relationships that constitute the fabric of necessity and the desire to contemplate those relationships as metaphors revealing the nature and the activity of the mind of God. The blind necessity revealed in geometry, she wrote, "appears to us as a thing to be overcome; for the Greeks it was a thing to love, because it is God himself who is the perpetual geometer."[2] She turned to Greek science, then, as a corrective model for modern science's partial and even inhuman representation of the universe—inhuman in that it deliberately excluded the aspiration of the human heart toward the good, an aspiration that Weil considered to be as real and as factual as "the trajectory of a planet."[3]

Weil's mature critique of the problems of modern science can be found both in "Classical Science and After" and in the last section of *The Need for Roots,* written in London only a few months before her death. The informal essay that is translated here—a review of two lectures and the defense of a philosophy dissertation she attended in the spring of 1941—contains a brief summary of her thought on the relationship between modern and Greek science and points out the latter's usefulness as a model. The other two sections of the essay—on the art and philosophy of China and on the philosophy dissertation defense respectively—offer a glimpse of Weil's aesthetic thought and a confirmation of the direction of her late philosophical movement: back toward Plato, and outward toward "what is called the transcendent."

2 Ibid., p. 21.
3 *The Need for Roots* (New York: Harper Colophon Books, 1971), p. 243.

■ *Philosophy*

In the last few weeks philosophy lovers in Marseilles have had three agreeable occasions on which to meet. The Society for Philosophical Studies brought its lecture series to a close by evoking the Orient and Greece, two wellsprings of wisdom and serenity toward which, fortunately, many minds are now being driven because of the distress of the present time. And the society's president, M. Gaston Berger, defended his philosophy thesis at Aix.

M. Marcel Brion, who is well known for his studies of aesthetics, among other works, took as his subject an extremely interesting parallel between the painting and philosophy of China. It has to do, of course, with Taoism. Quite appropriately, he mentioned Confucius only in passing; the marvelous passages he cited were all taken from Taoist writings or Buddhist writings closely related to Taoism. One immediately felt, on hearing them, that the parallel between philosophy and painting was not at all forced, for these texts have an obvious relation to artistic thought. Unfortunately, one lecture is too short a time to draw such a parallel with sufficient precision, and M. Brion stopped at a point at which his audience would have very much liked him to continue, for he was just getting to the heart of the matter. At least, he left his hearers with the desire to spend a few hours in contemplation of Chinese paintings; if that is not possible, they may meditate on Taoist sayings.

M. Brion spoke in such a way as to arouse in the audience feelings of interest in and attraction for the Orient, which he constantly contrasted to the West to the latter's disadvantage. Certainly, when one's subject is the Orient, there is nothing wrong with contrasting it to the West only in order to show its superiority, but this contrast is perhaps emphasized too much. Is there really anything that is foreign to us in Oriental thought? If we could but realize it, we would recognize that there is in Oriental thought

Published in *Cahiers du Sud*, no. 235, May 1941, under the pseudonym "Emile Novis," an anagram for "Simone Weil."

that which is most intimate to every one of us. Every Taoist saying awakens a resonance in us, and the Taoist texts evoke by turns Heraclitus, Protagoras, Plato, the Cynics, the Stoics, Christianity, and Jean-Jacques Rousseau. Not that Taoist thought is not original, profound, and new for a European, but like everything truly great, it is both new and familiar; we remember, as Plato used to say, having known it on the other side of the sky. Isn't this country beyond the sky that Plato remembered the same as the one where, according to the texts cited by M. Brion, the wise man frolics, beyond the Four Seas, beyond space?

The same can be said of art. The idea of painting having a connection with philosophy is not a new idea for us if we have read Leonardo da Vinci. Leonardo may have been the only one in our tradition to say that painting is a philosophy that uses lines and colors, but possibly he was not the only one to think so. Can real art be anything but a method of establishing a certain relationship between the world and the self, between oneself and the self, that is, the equivalent of a philosophy? To be sure, many Western artists have thought otherwise, but they are undoubtedly not the greatest. Undoubtedly the greatest artists conceived of art as did the painter in the marvelous anecdote quoted by M. Brion; having vainly asked the emperor to go with him into a painted grotto at the bottom of his picture, he went into it alone and never reappeared. One might very well imagine Giotto entering into one of his Paduan frescoes in that way. When M. Brion speaks of the importance of the void in Chinese painting—"Thirty spokes unite in the hub, but it is the empty space at the center that enables the wheel to be used," says Lao-Tsu—one also thinks of Giotto, in whose work a void in the middle of a fresco often has such a powerful effect. The Chinese reject symmetry, whereas we take delight in it, because, according to M. Brion, they chose the tree as the model of equilibrium and we, following the Greeks, chose the human body; but the quest for equilibrium is common to both kinds of art, and that makes them more related than they are different. Chinese painters, according to M. Brion, have such a need for the infinite that it compels them to handle perspective in a peculiar way and to almost dissolve forms; the Greeks, on the other hand, looked for the definite, the limited, everywhere; nevertheless, the same human need is involved. Man cannot get over regretting that he has not been given the infinite, and he has more than one way of fabricating, with the finite, an equivalent of the infinite for himself—which is perhaps the definition of art. But the highest praise that can be given M. Brion's talk is that, while presenting Chinese art as foreign, he makes it seem so closely akin to us.

M. CORNIL, Dean of the Faculty of Medicine, carried us back to the Golden Age of Greece when he spoke to us about Hippocrates. He is well qualified to do so, being a doctor who reflects on his art and on matters beyond his art; and a doctor of today deserves more credit for acquiring a broad culture than a Greek doctor, now that the age itself locks everyone, almost by force, into a specialty. M. Cornil made Hippocrates seem not remote from us, but close at hand, an easy thing to do when one knows and understands him, for what is closer to us than Greece? It is closer to us than we ourselves. It is doubtful that we have a single important idea that the Greeks did not have a clear conception of; M. Cornil reminded us, for example, that they had a clear conception of evolution.

Hippocrates had the idea of the experimental method as clearly as any man in the succeeding centuries, if not more so, as is shown by the splendid quotation judiciously chosen by M. Cornil.

> I commend reasoning when it is based on experience and methodically orders the sequence of phenomena. If it starts with the facts as they have obviously taken place, it discovers the truth through the power of the meditation that lays stress on each particular object and then classifies each of them according to the way they naturally follow one another. . . . I believe that every art is based on the method of observing all the facts individually and then grouping them according to their similarities.

M. Cornil made it quite evident that Hippocrates' greatness consists not in his fondness for experiment, for there were a number of excellent empiricists in his time, nor in his liking for philosophy, for a number of philosophers talked at length about medicine, but in his methodical use of philosophical thought, and especially Pythagorean thought, for an ongoing investigation of experience.

The Pythagorean method, as set forth in the *Philebus*,[1] requires that in every instance one try to find definite objects, if possible defined by ratios, countable, if need be merely theoretical, in order to classify the innumer-

---

1 For Socrates' description of the Pythagorean method, see Plato's *Philebus* 16c–e, 18b–d, 23c–25c.

able varieties of particular cases. This method still dominates science today. The Hippocratic theory of the four humors and the theory of the critical days in illnesses are among its applications. Also supremely Pythagorean is Hippocrates' principal idea, namely, that health and illness are defined by relationships—relationships between the soul and the body, between the parts of the body, humors, organs, and functions, and between man and his environment—and that, when these relationships are in balance, in harmony, there is health. That is an insight that we are far from having exhausted. We are able to understand it better now than we could fifty years ago, for today the idea of totality is reappearing everywhere in science: in biology and medicine, where Hippocrates has been restored to a place of honor; in physics, where they are beginning to conceive of studying a phenomenon as a whole, including the instruments used in measuring it; and in mathematics, where they are starting to base everything on the theory of aggregates and the theory of groups. But so far this development in science is producing mostly trouble and confusion. We lack the virtue and the intelligence needed to raise us to the level of Greece, where all forms of thought were united.

In one sense, Greek science is much closer to our own than we think, and it is anything but a rough outline. The *Epinomis*[2] defines geometry as the science of generalized number; some Greek astronomers hypothesized that the earth was a sphere and that the earth and the planets moved around the sun; Eudoxus, the inventor of the integral calculus, had conceived of combining several movements in a single trajectory; Archimedes founded mechanics with the theory of the lever and physics by searching for something analogous to the lever in natural phenomena. But in another sense we are a long way from Greek science, which is far above us; for its branches are interrelated, and in its entirety it is related to every form of thought.

Among the Greeks, epic poetry, drama, architecture, sculpture, the conception of the universe and the laws of nature, astronomy, mechanics, physics, politics, medicine, and the idea of virtue all have at their center the idea of balance that goes with proportion, the soul of geometry. With this idea of balance, which we have lost, the Greeks created science, our science. Imbalance was inconceivable to them except as something that

2 Geometry is defined as an "assimilation to one another of numbers which are naturally dissimilar, effected by reference to areas" (*Epinomis* 990d).

comes after equilibrium, in relation to it, as a breaking of the equilibrium; illness, for example, as a disturbance of health. We, on the contrary, tend to consider health as a special case of illness, a borderline case that marks the limits of illness. This way of looking at things, extended to psychology, accounts for a great deal of the baseness of soul that is so widespread in our era. In Greece, the idea of balance gave every type of scientific research an orientation toward the good,[3] and medicine, of course, more than any other. M. Cornil showed by numerous quotations that for Hippocrates, virtue and something approaching sanctity were part of the definition of the real doctor.

There can be no question of our returning to Greece, for France has never been in contact with Greek civilization, except perhaps at the time of Vercingetorix. Vercingetorix was conquered, and the Druids, who may have taught doctrines similar to those of Pythagoras, were massacred by the Emperor Claudius. But if we were worthy of it, it might be possible for us to go toward Greece. A lecture like the one given by M. Cornil may help to plant a desire to do so.

M. BERGER's defense of his thesis also carried us back to Greece. Not that the subject particularly had to do with Greece; the minor thesis was on the great contemporary German philosopher Husserl, and the main thesis was an original work by M. Berger on the conditions of knowledge. But in following the discussion—which M. Berger's exceptional clarity of mind made easy to do, despite one's not having read the book under discussion—one could not help thinking of Plato. M. Berger's method is not to ask himself whether an idea or an assertion he has encountered is true, but to ask what it means; this is the same method that Socrates used. "If we were clever . . . , we would contend like the sophists do, opposing assertions with assertions; but we, simple people that we are, first want to consider what these things that we think, in themselves and by themselves, can really be." This is also the method of all the philosophers descended from Platonism, such as Descartes or Kant, but they did not state it formally, and did not realize it clearly enough, and that worked against them.

---

3 Weil seems to be referring to the Platonic-Pythagorean teaching that "any compound, whatever it be, that does not by some means or other exhibit measure and proportion" has no value at all, and is not even a real mixture, but "a miserable mass of unmixed messiness." The presence of measure and proportion are thus characteristics of the good. See *Philebus* 64d–65b.

To tell the truth, there can be only two kinds of philosophers, those who use this method and those who construct a representation of the universe to their liking; the latter alone can be said, strictly speaking, to have systems, whose value consists only in a certain poetic beauty, and especially in the marvelously penetrating formulas scattered through some of them, as is the case with Aristotle and Hegel. But the former are the true masters of thought, and one does well to follow in their footsteps, as M. Berger does. His method enables him to eliminate meaningless problems; he refuses to pose the problem of whether or not knowledge has any value because knowledge is given, is intermingled with thought, and the thinking being cannot escape from it; he refuses to pose the problem of the existence of objective reality, because a reality outside ourselves is given at the same time as our own; it is just as impossible to reject, and we continually experience it. That is an excellent starting point.

The extraordinary thing is that the philosophies that follow this method are all oriented toward salvation; M. Berger is no exception to this rule. Thinking it was original, someone drew attention to M. Berger's view that philosophic reflection depends on an effort of detachment that goes beyond the intelligence and involves the whole man; but this is pure Plato. "One must turn toward the truth with one's whole soul." Besides, to be original on that point is not to think differently from Plato; it is to do on one's own account what Plato did twenty-five centuries ago, and indeed turn toward the truth with one's whole soul.

Of course, without having read and examined M. Berger's book closely, one cannot ascertain whether or not the ideas it contains are really presented, each in its turn, in such a way as to reveal their meaning, or whether it carries the imprint of a soul entirely turned toward truth. In any case, M. Berger defended himself quite well, without being afraid to say what he thought about objections that did not always seem very pertinent. For example, someone thought he detected a tendency to mysticism and an attraction to Hindu thought in M. Berger's book; this was pointed out with a shade of reproach, as if there were heresies in philosophy. No doubt, with us mysticism and the Orient are often a cover for shoddy merchandise, but that is through no fault of their own. If one wanted to rule out attempts to conceive of what is called the transcendental, one would have to admit only those whom Plato called the uninitiated. Fortunately, things haven't come to that at the university, since M. Berger was granted the title of doctor cum laude. And, what is heartening, the discussion was attentively followed by a large number of students in this city of Aix where the yellow stones, the lovely little squares, and the young people who fill the streets make one think of some Italian university of the Renaissance.